TAKEN BY THE ALIEN NEXT DOOR

ALIENS AMONG US #1

TIFFANY ROBERTS

BLURB

An undercover alien. A curvy human female he's desperate to claim. One month to make her his.

Tabitha Mathews has never had much luck with men. Her past relationships only left her heart aching and her self-esteem beaten down. But who needs them? She's doing just fine on her own. She has a booming home business, an adorable, mischievous dog, and she just became a first-time homeowner...right next door to the hottest man she's ever seen.

Oh, did she mention that he happens to be an alien? An alien with dreamy, glowing eyes, wicked fangs and claws, and a tail.

But she's not supposed to know that, and only finds out after her wonderfully considerate dog leaves a big, odorous gift in her neighbor's back yard—which promptly results in her being kidnapped.

Now she's tied to the alien's bed, because of course he's come to Earth in search of a mate—and he wants Tabitha to fill that role. More specifically, he wants her to carry his baby.

Saying he's moving fast seems like a bit of an understatement. Is Tabitha willing to accept her alien abductor as a mate? Is she ready to be a mother?

And he's generous enough to give her four whole weeks to decide.

It's not like it's the biggest decision of her life or anything...right?

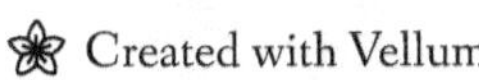 Created with Vellum

To everyone who needs a hug right now.

And to you, my other half, through thick (literally—wait, did I just burn us both?) and thin, good and bad, I love you.

ONE

Zevris's phone chimed from the passenger seat, indicating another received message.

He gritted his teeth and tightened his grip on the steering wheel, making the leather covering creak. The vehicle's speed crept higher—sixty-one, sixty-two, sixty-three. Eight miles per hour over the speed limit, then ten. A small, tight, sinking feeling settled low in his gut as his body was pressed back against the pilot's chair.

Driver's seat, he corrected.

He'd never encountered a language with so many words that had similar but nuanced meanings, and that wasn't even taking into account that there were differing dialects of English spoken in different parts of this world that complicated things even further.

His phone chimed again. He wound his tail, which was currently hidden in his pants, tight around his calf. For an instant, he had the impulse to snatch the phone off the seat, crush it in his fist, and throw the damned thing out the window.

He'd been tempted to do so to Kindra's phone more than once during dinner this evening.

With a growl, he eased off the accelerator. His frustrations were valid, but he could not—would not—allow them to cloud his judgment. Speeding in these rolling deathtraps humans called automobiles was a crime. His mission parameters specified that he was to avoid undue attention, and though the local human authorities were the least of his concerns on that front, he could not ignore their existence.

A faloran *althicar* was not meant to be on Earth.

Keeping his eyes forward, he reached aside, plucked up the phone, and fumbled with it for a moment before finally flicking the mute switch on the side. He'd had more than enough of such devices for one lifetime.

I need only complete this mission, and I am free. My service will be over, and I may find peace...

Zevris forced a heavy breath out through his nostrils and tossed the phone down. Somehow, he managed to still his mind and simply drive for a few minutes. The freeway was flanked on either side by lush trees and shrubs in brilliant greens that were contrasted by tufts of dry, pale brown grass beneath them. The dichotomy seemed a fitting one for humans; Earth's dominant species was an indecipherable bundle of contradictions and conflicting natures.

Kindra had been one in a long line of failed connections for Zevris. He'd *dated* numerous human females since he'd arrived on Earth nearly a year before, and each of those would-be relationships had quickly crumbled for various reasons.

Some of the females, especially early on, had seemed attracted to him physically but were made uncertain by his mannerisms and speech patterns. It had taken time to understand a frustrating truth about the English language—using a word exactly according to its definition did not necessarily mean it was the *right* word. He still made those mistakes, despite his self-awareness.

He'd also learned another early lesson—females were not keen on discussing the matter of procreation on first dates. His attempts to be honest and up front, at least as much as he was able, had not produced the intended results.

The phrase *I want you to carry my offspring* was not one that human females found endearing.

A few relationships had fizzled because of what the humans called *chemistry*. He was fairly certain by now that those females had not been referring to the scientific discipline concerning the composition of matter. As time had gone by, more and more relationships had ended because he'd learned to recognize that they simply would not work. There'd been some deep disconnect between himself and those females that made the forging of a mating bond impossible.

Despite the urgency, despite their race's desperation, a faloran could not *entirely* force the mating bond. There needed to be some sort of connection there, some sort of spark.

Zevris had yet to find such a connection.

His freeway exit loomed ahead, and he guided his pickup truck into the appropriate lane to take the offramp. He knew the area well enough that the route to his dwelling was second nature. As he guided his vehicle along the roads and through the turns with practiced ease, his mind took to wandering— something it had rarely done before he'd been sent to Earth.

He'd not performed any exerting physical activity today, but found himself drained regardless, as though a little of his life force had been stolen away.

The first minutes of his initial face-to-face meeting with Kindra had consisted of her pressing her body against his, as though they were already a mated couple, while she held her phone high to capture a maddening number of still images of the two of them, repeatedly checking the results and trying new angles until she'd found one she was apparently satisfied with.

There'd been no formal introduction, no discussion, no request for his permission. The only thing she'd said to him by the time they'd been seated at their table was, "You're even hotter than in your pictures."

Immediately after they'd sat down, she'd posted her chosen image to some social media outlet, and had spent the next fifteen minutes—to the annoyance of both Zevris and the food server—replying to comments on the image.

He'd kept count during their meal; she had looked at him directly a total of five times over the hour and twenty minutes they were at the table, and had not once set her phone down, even when she'd begun eating her food. In fact, she'd taken a picture of said food right after it had been placed down before her. Zevris had deliberately spoken to her in a manner that local humans seemed to find strange just to see her reaction.

If Kindra had noticed, she'd made no indication. She'd chatted incessantly throughout the meal, rarely leaving him any room for input. She talked about her ex-boyfriend, about drama within her friend group, about how much she hated her boss, and mentioned many, many times that she was on her way to becoming an *influencer*. Even after nearly a year on Earth, attempting to absorb the culture and the way these people used their language, Zevris had understood little of what Kindra had spoken about.

Zevris turned his vehicle onto his street, and he was stricken by an unexpected wave of familiarity and comfort.

This place is not my home, he reminded himself. *This is just another theater of operation during another mission. My final mission. Soon enough, I will return to my true home...*

His lips fell in a deep frown as he turned into his driveway and shifted the truck into park. A press of a button powered off the growling combustion engine. Normally, this routine activity spawned a very specific thought in his mind—why did the humans call the place they parked their automobiles *driveways*?

That thought did not come now; another dilemma was consuming his thoughts.

Was the world of his birth, Strion, truly his home anymore? He'd spent his entire adult life away from it, jumping from world to world as the assignments from *Exthurizen* Command were passed down, his neural transceiver constantly loaded with new languages, new cultures, new maps and documents and information. His homeworld was little more than a distant memory.

He spat a curse, grabbed his phone, and dropped his hand to the door handle.

The phone vibrated, and Zevris paused.

He knew without looking that every one of those chiming alerts had signaled a message from Kindra. He could almost hear her voice, as though the echoes of her relentless prattling were still resonating in his ear canals, and barely suppressed the shudder threatening to course along his spine.

His fingers flexed and his tail twitched as the urge to destroy his phone intensified. Zevris understood that the impulse was in some way born from repression; he'd not had a decent fight since arriving on this planet. Violence, though glorified in human media, was frowned upon in reality. It was, in fact, illegal here.

At least it was illegal as far as Zevris could tell. Human laws, like humans themselves, were unnecessarily complicated.

With a huff, he removed his hand from the door handle, unlocked his phone, and selected the message application without allowing himself to register the number of alerts noted on the display. He tapped on the entry labeled *Kindra*. The cascade of messages on the screen nearly made his head ache.

Where r u

Did u leave?

Not 2 sound mean or anything but thats a dick move. U couldve said something

Its kinda bs that u didnt tell me you were going

Especially cuz I was going 2 ask u for a ride home

I mean we had like a good time right? And u r rlly rlly hot. So maybe...

U wanna swing by my place 2nite?

My roommate is home but she is down for w/e and she thinks ur hot 2

Dont play hard 2 get I no u want me

U better not b ghosting me. Do u even know who I am?

WTF

Like who do u even think u r?

U better get over urself b4 u lose out on ur chance at this

Kindra had included an image of herself taken from a high angle, her lips in an exaggerated pout, her chest thrust out to display her ample cleavage.

Zevris tilted the phone, narrowing his eyes. In the picture, Kindra had one arm tucked under her breasts, propping them up and making them look fuller. Was that normal behavior for females in general, or was it simply a mannerism of the females of Earth?

The phone vibrated again, and yet another message appeared.

I did u a favor goin out with u

U selfish prick

Hand trembling, Zevris tipped his head back, closed his eyes, and forced himself to breathe. Were these the sorts of struggles his forefathers had gone through in finding their mates generations ago, before the plague had decimated the population of faloran females? He couldn't imagine any civilization, any species, that could survive long like this if his experiences were indicative of the wider human courtship experience.

He refused to give in to frustration. A broken phone was an unnecessary hassle—one that would have a direct effect on his mission. Humans relied upon their handheld devices for a startling amount of their everyday activities, including the courtship rituals they called *dating*. Without a working phone, Zevris would be effectively cut off from human society.

Not that it would actually hurt his chances. One could not do much worse than absolute failure.

He exhaled, opened his eyes, and looked down at his phone. Even this—one of the larger models available —was a bit small in his hands, and he had to move his thumbs with care to properly enter his response to Kindra.

I paid for your meal. Shouldn't that be considered a favor to you?

Kindra's reply came within a couple seconds.

I didnt ask u 2 do that so i dunno wtf ur point is?

Clenching his jaw and barely keeping himself from growling, Zevris typed, *According to your FindMeAMatch profile, Kindra, you are 24 years old. Well into your adulthood. How have you failed to grasp the basics of the English language? It astonishes me that anyone as self-absorbed and*

Zevris grunted, halting his thumbs. He shook his head as he deleted the message he'd just written. Better to finish this quickly. As unpleasant as the dinner had been, he would not take out all his anger on this human. Perhaps she deserved some small portion of it, but he knew it would be all his rage released or none at the moment.

I have no further interest in you, female. He pressed the send arrow.

There. It was done.

The phone buzzed.

FEMALE?????

The message was followed by a small bubble with three dots flashing one at a time.

Zevris sighed and ran a hand through his short hair before opening the truck door and climbing out. He drew in a deep breath, appreciating the fresh air, and eased the grip of his tail on his leg. A gentle breeze was flowing through the trees and bushes planted in the neighborhood's neatly manicured front yards.

Flicking the lock button near the handle, he closed the door. He walked to the mailbox at the end of the driveway, opened it, and removed the envelopes from within, glancing through them. Bills and junk—the two forms of mail that seemed to bind all humans together in a common experience.

Zevris could not understand why humans so often insisted upon utilizing such outdated and wasteful means of communication. Given their current level of technology, they were more than capable of conducting all such communications electronically.

Of course, he'd seen a great many other issues here on Earth that humans were more than capable of overcoming with their technology and ingenuity yet seemed unwilling to fix, so he wasn't surprised.

He glanced down at the phone.

The dots continued blinking.

A chorus of laughter from children playing down the street drew his attention momentarily aside, but it was not the young ones that his eyes settled upon.

There'd been a *FOR SALE* sign posted at the neighboring property for the last couple months. Zevris had seen strangers come and go, often led by well-dressed humans with friendly, sometimes overeager smiles. *Realtors.* That was the word.

A smaller sign had been attached to the post above the original one.

SOLD.

That meant he would have a new neighbor. Perhaps he could befriend that neighbor, and through that friendship pick up the understanding he required to move his mission forward. He'd attempted to be friendly with several of the other neighbors, and many had reciprocated at first. Over time, it became clear that most of the people in the nearby dwellings simply preferred to keep to themselves. One man from across the street, however, had grown cold when he realized Zevris's garage was being used as a woodworking shop.

Even though Zevris utilized his power tools only during normal daytime hours, in accordance with the town's noise ordinances, he'd had a few complaints filed against him.

The local authorities had been understanding the few times they'd come to investigate, and Zevris's dealings with them had been surprisingly easy. It had likely helped that, when asked to demonstrate the level of noise produced in his shop, he'd activated and adjusted the sound-dampening devices he'd installed throughout the home. The officers had barely been able to hear the table saw running from a few feet down the driveway, much less from the opposite side of the street.

Though he knew it was petty, Zevris had been sure to deactivate the dampeners after the police departed.

Those noise complaints had been rejected time and again, and eventually the neighbor had seemed to relent. Now, Zevris was merely subjected to the man's glares and passive aggressiveness. He took some pleasure in responding to them with what he hoped were warm, friendly smiles.

On his way to the front door, he paused and crouched beside the flowerbed under the front window. His chrysanthemums were in full bloom. They were arranged in alternating colors—orange, white, yellow—and added a splash of vibrancy that broke up the greenery so common everywhere.

Zevris would never have imagined himself as a gardener, but the homeowner's association required ornamental plants in every front yard, and he'd needed to learn in order to comply and avoid complications. He didn't understand why anyone had the right to tell him what to plant on a piece of land that was supposedly *his*, but it was not his responsibility to unravel the reasons behind strange human behaviors. He just needed to learn enough about them to obtain a human mate.

He lowered his hand, touching a finger to the dirt beneath the plants. It was starting to dry out; he'd need to water them in the morning.

Rising, he continued to the door. A glance at his phone showed the dots still blinking. Apparently, Kindra had a great deal to communicate.

Zevris deactivated the internal defense system he'd installed—simple forcefields to seal the doors and windows—unlocked the door, and stepped into his dwelling. Even with the door closed behind him and the blinds shut, there was enough light for him to see clearly, but he flipped on the overhead lights regardless. It had taken some time to gauge how poorly most humans saw in low lighting, but it was knowledge of which he regularly made use.

Small details were what held fronts like this together. As oblivious as many humans often seemed, they were surprisingly observant at their cores. They had an almost instinctual talent for detecting minute oddities that many other species might never have noticed.

The phone vibrated. He lifted it to discover a massive block of text on the screen.

Without reading a word of the text, Zevris blocked Kindra's number.

He kicked off his boots, tossed his phone onto the counter, and sent a mental command to deactivate the holoshroud connected to his neural transceiver.

For an instant, the air around him rippled and shimmered as the hologram that disguised his true appearance broke down into a wire-like mesh of light and faded completely. A brief thrumming sensation rippled across his skin; he'd felt it every time he'd deactivated the holoshroud, and it was always so faint that he'd long wondered whether it was real or imagined.

Though the holoshroud's projection didn't physically alter Zevris in any way, he always felt more himself while it was deactivated. Perhaps there was some wisdom to be found in human sayings about the power of the mind.

Or, perhaps, Zevris was simply tired of never being...himself.

Outside this dwelling, he had to be Logan Ellis, a thirty-two-year-old human male who had moved to the area last year after relocating from a small town in a place called Montana. Logan made his living as a woodworker and had just learned to sell his creations online. He was a simple man, a lonely man, and he wanted nothing more than to find a woman for lasting companionship.

Inside this dwelling, he was Zevris Akkaran, an *althicar* serving in the *Exthurizen*—a secretive branch of the Azmus Protectorate's military—who had performed covert operations on more than a dozen alien planets. He had fought open battles, he had conducted ambushes, he had sabotaged enemy operations and stolen intelligence, had assassinated key targets. He'd spent most of his adult life embedded in hostile areas without direct contact with or support from his commanders. He was a simple male, a lonely male...and he wanted nothing more than to find a female for lasting companionship.

He ran a hand over his face, muttered his favorite human

curse—*fuck*—and headed upstairs to undress and shower. His weariness only strengthened as he stood under the steaming water, and he knew it was not merely a matter of this evening's events. He'd been tired for a long while. That was why he'd requested his release from service.

This was his final mission. This was the last operation he would conduct as *Althicar* Akkaran. After this, he wouldn't have to bounce from planet to planet, constantly adapting to new places and cultures, constantly living in immediate danger. He just needed to make it through this assignment, and it would all be over. He could find a new purpose. He could rest.

All he needed to do was find a human female who he was drawn to enough to form a mating bond—and who was willing to enter that undying bond with him. A simple, straightforward objective.

On a planet filled with people who were anything but simple and straightforward.

Zevris had a feeling he was going to be on Earth for a long, long time.

TWO

ZEVRIS GRUNTED as he shifted his gaze back and forth between the two boxes of cereal. They bore different images on their faces, had different names and color schemes, and displayed the logos of two separate—presumably competing—manufacturers. Each called itself *part of a balanced breakfast,* and both proclaimed *America's favorite cereal!*

His understanding of the word *favorite* made those proclamations confusing. In that context, the word was being used as a singular modifier. If there were two cereals that were America's favorite, would it not have been written as *One of America's favorite cereals?*

Placing a hand atop either box, he turned them simultaneously so the nutritional information on each was facing him. He scanned the words, many of which were meaningless to him without a search through the data in his neural transceiver, and the correlating numbers. The numerical values were quite similar between the two cereals, and the ingredients listed were nearly identical—and even more meaningless than the nutritional terms.

With another grunt, he opened both boxes and dumped the cereals into the large bowl between them. He poured in cold milk next, put the milk jug and cereal boxes away, and carried his breakfast to the kitchen table. He would not speculate as to why humans drank milk—the nourishment some creatures provided to their young from their own bodies—throughout their adult lives. He'd already lost himself in that contemplation a few times before, and it had brought nothing but further confusion.

It was enough that the taste was enjoyable.

As he ate his cereal, he unlocked his phone and opened FindMeAMatch. Checking through his matches on this application and the various websites he'd registered for had been a daily ritual for most of his time on Earth. He'd made use of as many modern dating services as he could in the hopes of his wide search turning up the right female with whom to advance his mission.

For a long while, these daily searches had even been exciting. He'd never seen so many females. Even knowing the male to female ratio amongst his own people had been closer to one-to-one in the days of his forefathers hadn't prepared him for the abundance of women on Earth. And there was something inexplicably appealing about human females.

But none had truly called to him, none had really sparked his interest, none had been the *perfect, lifelong match* that Find-MeAMatch had promised. And his enthusiasm for these searches had waned greatly in the week since his date with Kindra.

His cereal crunched between his teeth as he flicked through the FindMeAMatch profiles. All he could see now were the subtle warnings hidden in each one, the hints that the experience would be somehow unpleasant should he meet with these females, that it would be a waste of his time. He was more attuned now than ever to the little lies humans so casually—and so often—told. The games they played in pursuit of mates—or, more accurately, in pursuit of sexual partners.

Preening to flaunt one's accomplishments and strengths was one thing, but pretending to be something one was not in order to attract a mate was another matter entirely.

Zevris snickered and shook his head. With half his mouth still full of cereal, he said, "Because that's not what I'm doing at all."

Greetings, female. My name is Zevris Akkaran, a faloran military operative from a neighboring galaxy. I am in search of a mate. Are you receptive to the planting of my seed that we may form a mating bond?

This entire situation would be comical were it not for the simple fact that the survival of his species depended upon locating females who were receptive to mating bonds—and therefore reproduction. The faloran species had survived two generations after a devastating virus had claimed most of their females.

They would not survive two more.

A metallic crash from outside jarred Zevris from his thoughts. His first instinct was to reach for a weapon, but he quickly cast that instinct aside. Stepping out of his dwelling with a faloran plasma pistol in hand would undoubtedly raise questions he was not prepared to answer.

Someone shouted something outside; the voice was masculine, but the words were too muffled to understand.

Zevris shoved himself up from the table and strode toward the front door. He deactivated the security field, unlocked the deadbolt, and took the knob in hand.

He froze. The dark claw on the end of his thumb, though mostly retracted, was fully visible—and it was clearly nothing like a human fingernail. He'd forgotten to reactivate his holoshroud.

"You damned fool," he snarled to himself as he activated the hologram. That barely perceptible shimmer warped the air briefly, affording him a glimpse of the assembling light-hexes that vanished as they formed the illusion to mask his true appearance.

It did not matter that this was a noncombat mission, it did not matter that its nature was different from any he'd undertaken. He could not afford complacency. He could not allow himself to be...comfortable here.

Zevris opened the door and stepped outside.

A huge truck was on the street just beyond his driveway, its tail end hanging over his lawn and its rear wheel inches from his grass. The misshapen remains of his mailbox lay on the ground beneath the truck, though the metal post upon which it had been perched remained in the ground. Of course, it was also bent, leaning at a harsh angle.

He curled his hands into fists and clenched his jaw. How could anyone live on this planet without going mad? Earth itself seemed eager to assail each of its inhabitants with an endless chain of hardships, whittling away at patience and willpower, crushing them beneath a gradually increasing weight that—

It is a mailbox. What difference will it make if I receive paper mail or not? This is not worth my anger.

The truck pulled forward, drawing Zevris's attention back to it. There were large words printed on the side. *Grayson Brothers Movers—If our prices don't move you, our professionalism will!*

Zevris walked along his driveway, watching as the moving truck readjusted and, after several tight turns, backed into the driveway of the neighboring dwelling—the house that had recently been sold. The realtor's sign was gone now; had it been removed early this morning, or had he simply missed the detail sometime over the last few days?

Two burly human males climbed down from the cab of the moving truck. The driver walked to the truck's rear and opened the roll-up door while the passenger, tugging up the waist of his jeans, moved toward Zevris. The name printed on the chest of his shirt was *Frank*.

"Didn't even see it there. Narrow street and all, you know?" Frank shrugged, palms skyward, and turned as though to join his companion.

"I expect compensation for the damages," Zevris said.

Frank glanced over his shoulder. "Oh, yeah, yeah. Absolutely. I'll be sure to pass it on to the office."

Zevris squeezed his fists a little tighter. He could almost feel the tendons creaking in his hand. "Is it not customary to exchange information in such cases?"

"We'll just note it on our work order," Frank replied, raising his voice over the clanging sound of the truck's ramp being pulled out and dropped down.

A low growl rumbled in Zevris's chest, but he silenced it before it became audible. He was more than a little annoyed about the damage to his mailbox, and Frank's dismissive tone certainly wasn't helping that, but what recourse did he have? Attacking these men in a fit of rage wouldn't solve his problems —it would only create new ones.

He huffed through his nostrils, turned away from the men and their truck, and strode to his fallen mailbox. The deep frown that curled his lips was not half as severe as the angle to which the mailbox's metal post had been bent. Crouching, he grasped the misshapen box in both hands and lifted it from the ground.

The mailbox door fell open, snapped off its hinge, and clattered on the driveway. The red plastic flag on the side dangled limply. Zevris's frown deepened.

The door of the neighboring home creaked open, the sound followed by a dog barking.

"Where ya want this stuff, lady?" the moving truck driver asked.

"Most of the boxes are marked. If they're living room, kitchen, or work stuff, they'll be downstairs. The rest will go upstairs."

That voice was sweet, soft, feminine, and it coaxed Zevris's attention away from his mangled mailbox. He turned his head toward the source just as one of the movers dropped a box, which landed on the truck's ramp with a dull, rattling clang.

"*Please* be careful with those!" the female said, raising her hands and spreading her fingers wide.

There was a dog standing beside the female's legs, a big beast with brown and black fur. The dog had its head down, sniffing at the ground as though it were the most fascinating thing in all the world. But that could not be right—because as Zevris lifted his gaze, his eyes settled on the *real* most fascinating thing in this world.

The female was beautiful, and the fullness of her beauty grew more apparent as she turned toward Zevris. She had long, flowing blonde hair which fell in waves down her back, though some of it was pulled back from her face and twisted atop her head in a haphazard knot. Dark, gently arched brows rested above wide, bright eyes that were framed with thick lashes. She had a straight nose, plump, pink lips, and a small cleft in her chin.

His gaze dipped to take in her body. She wore a long-sleeved fitted T-shirt that showcased her ample bosom and hugged her waist. The writing across her chest said, *I cannot lye, I love making soap.* Her jeans clung to her flaring hips, rounded ass, and legs, accentuating her every tantalizing curve —and those curves were quite generous. Generous, and *delicious.*

Zevris's fingers flexed, and his claws extended unbidden. He had the sudden urge to grab hold of this female, to feel her yielding flesh beneath his fingertips, to draw her body flush against his. Something in his lower abdomen drew taut. Heat stirred in his chest and pumped through his veins. It spread into his groin and pooled in his balls, making them heavy, before permeating his hardening cock.

He swallowed. His mouth and throat were suddenly dry, and he could feel his pulse throughout his body—especially in his shaft.

Zevris ached with a hunger that had nothing to do with his unfinished breakfast.

The female's eyes fell upon him. They widened infinitesimally, and Zevris swore he saw that same attraction he felt, that same *spark*, in her. Her cheeks pinkened. Then her gaze shifted to the mailbox in his hands, and her eyes rounded.

"Oh my gosh, what happened?" she asked as she hurried toward him.

The dog lifted its head and followed her with a bark.

Now that she was so close, her scent drifted to Zevris. He inhaled it deeply. It was reminiscent of lavender and warm vanilla, with hints of exotic spice and a dash of something decidedly and indefinably feminine. The combination was unlike anything he'd smelled on this world or any other; it was completely unique to her. How could any fragrance be so sweet, so alluring, so...comforting?

Humans consider staring rude.

But Zevris could not bring himself to pry his eyes from this female. He rose from his crouch, still holding the battered mailbox, and his new perspective only offered him new appreciation of her.

Despite the height afforded by her brown, heeled boots, Zevris towered over her. His urge to take hold of her intensified. He wanted to take her in his arms and shield her with his body, wanted to be the only shelter she would ever need, wanted to protect her from anything the universe decided to throw her way.

He wanted to press her to the ground and cover her with his body. And he wanted those shapely thighs around his waist as he—

"Mailbox. Truck hurt...uh..." Zevris shook his head, clearing away those primal thoughts—or at least forcing them out of the forefront. It was no easy feat with her heady scent fresh in his nostrils. "The movers ran over my mailbox. I can't imagine how fast they must've been driving to accomplish this."

He lifted the mailbox in demonstration. The dangling red flag swung back and forth slowly, producing a series of sad little squeaks.

The female looked back at the truck. "They did that?" Shaking her head, she turned that exquisite face back toward him. "I am so, so sorry. I've never worked with them before. I only found them from a quick internet search, and their ratings seemed okay for the price. Are they at least going to pay to have it replaced?"

Eyeing Zevris, the dog approached cautiously, growled, and barked.

The female frowned at the dog and scratched him behind his ear. "Dexter, hush."

Tilting its head, the dog—Dexter—regarded the female. Zevris could not determine whether the animal's questioning expression was merely an effect of his own imagination. Nonetheless, Dexter seemed to comply with the female's order.

Zevris's gaze lingered on the dog for a moment longer before he returned it to the female.

Her eyes were green—a vibrant shade of it that humans likened to the gemstone called emerald. They complemented her golden hair and pink lips perfectly.

"Supposedly," he replied, "though I'm not overly confident that they'll follow through."

"If they don't, I'll gladly pay to make it right." She chuckled a bit nervously. "Tabitha, Destroyer of Mailboxes, is not the first impression I wanted to make with my new neighbors."

"Tabitha," he purred, one corner of his mouth curling upward. "Is that your name?"

A blush stained her pale cheeks. "Oh! Yeah. I mean, not the Destroyer of Mailboxes part, but yes, my name is Tabitha Mathews." She stuck her hand out. Her nails were short and blunt, but they were painted a vivid pink.

Zevris tucked the mailbox under his arm and extended his own hand.

When he took her hand in his, electricity crackled along his arm, and the heat in his chest flared. All his urges—to hold her, to protect her, to mate with her—increased tenfold, and now he found himself also battling the impulse to lift her hand to his lips.

Tabitha's breath hitched. The pink on her cheeks darkened. Her skin was soft and smooth but for the hints of calluses on her forefinger and thumb, and her touch was warm and delicate. What would her fingers feel like elsewhere on his body?

"I'm Ze—" He caught his lower lip between his teeth, nearly puncturing it with a fang, and cleared his throat. "Logan. Logan Ellis."

Damned fool is far too weak a term to describe me. Nearly destroying my cover twice in a single morning?

He'd never been so careless.

Tabitha smiled wide. "Nice to meet you, Logan."

Dexter barked again.

Tabitha rolled her eyes and sighed, though she was smiling playfully. "And that annoying but adorable mongrel is Dexter."

"I am happy to meet you, Tabitha. And to meet Dexter, too." Zevris still could not bring himself to look away from her, and it took all his willpower to finally, albeit reluctantly, release her hand. Silence stretched between them; it was mere seconds, barely long enough to draw a full breath, but it felt like an eternity as his mind raced.

What were the things humans usually chatted about idly? Which topics were suitable for *small talk*?

Why had her scent and its effects not faded?

The human social skills he'd slowly built during his time on Earth seemed to have vanished in those moments, leaving Zevris with nothing but instinct—and his instinct was to be direct. The games humans played in their courtship rituals did not come naturally to him...and he suspected they didn't come naturally to most humans, either.

"Tabitha, you are the—"

Zevris wasn't sure what he'd meant to say. *You are the one,* perhaps, or *You are the most beautiful female I have ever seen.* Unfortunately, neither he nor Tabitha would ever know how his sentence was meant to end, as his words were cut off by the sound—and feel—of liquid splattering on his boot.

An instant later, he felt the warm liquid seep through the lacings and tongue to reach his foot, where it ran down to soak the insole. A strong, acrid scent struck Zevris's nostrils.

Zevris glanced down to see Dexter at his feet. The dog had one of his hind legs raised in the air as he unleashed a stream of urine onto Zevris's boot.

"Oh my God! Dexter, no!" Tabitha reached down, grabbed

the dog by the collar, and pulled him away, leaving a trail of urine on the driveway. "Bad! Bad, bad, *bad* dog!"

Dexter ducked his head and glanced at Zevris, tongue hanging out as though in mockery.

What had that slobbering beast just done? *Why* had it done it?

"I...I don't know what to say." Tabitha looked up at Zevris but seemed unable to meet his gaze. Her face was bright red. "Sorry doesn't seem good enough, but...that's all I can do. I am *so* sorry."

Zevris released a slow breath and glanced down at his soaked boot. It had served him well through rainy Oregon weather, but apparently its water resistance was easily overcome by animals that didn't know how to keep their tongues in their mouths.

And damn those beasts for making that...*cute.*

"It's...fine," he said, tensing the muscles in his leg to keep himself from shifting his foot. He knew that it would feel infinitely worse once he moved it.

"No, it's not. It's horrible. Oh my gosh, I'm mortified." She pressed a hand to her face, covering her eyes. "I'll pay for those, too. It...it was nice meeting you. I'm sure you can't say the same to me, and I totally understand that. So I'll just... Goodbye."

Zevris was more stunned watching her hurry back to her home—muttering to the dog in admonishment the whole way— than he'd been by Dexter's actions. If there were a right thing to have said in that situation, he could not have guessed it on his own, and his mind didn't produce any options until she was already in her own driveway.

It's fine, really. Don't worry about it, Tabitha.
It's worth it just to have met you.
I'll forget the boots if you have dinner with me.
Don't go.

And then she was out of sight, having rushed into her garage with Dexter in tow.

The two movers had halted on the truck ramp with a long dining table between them to stare at Zevris, smirking.

"Tough break there, buddy," said Frank.

"That sucks," said the other.

Zevris's brows slanted down, and another growl brewed in his chest. "You will see a tough break if you don't take care of my fucking mailbox, *buddy*."

"I dunno. Might forget about it," Frank said. "Not even a dent on our truck, so how would you prove anything?"

Zevris glared at the man, who maintained his smirk. Frank's expression said, *What will you do about it?*

There were no conscious thoughts in Zevris's mind when he took his first step toward the movers. His foot came down on the driveway, his boot made a squelching sound, and he felt moisture gush from the insole and bubble around his foot and toes.

He did not let that stop him.

The movers set down their table, the driver giving Frank a questioning look.

"So what, you hit the gym a few times a week and think you're a tough guy?" asked Frank.

Zevris halted at the back end of the truck. He curled his hands into fists, felt his claws digging into his palms, and his muscles tensed. The mailbox tucked under his arm groaned slightly as he inadvertently crushed it a little more. He knew he should have stopped himself well before this point—and knew, also, that he could not stop.

He turned and kicked the truck's rear bumper.

With his soiled boot.

The metal bumper clanged and groaned, bending beneath the force of the blow, and the impact that jolted up Zevris's leg was oddly satisfying—satisfying enough for him to pull back before he could put his full force into it. When Zevris lowered his foot, there was a boot-sized dent on the moving truck's bumper.

Zevris settled his gaze on the stunned movers. "Looks like you have quite a dent to me, *buddy*. You ought to get that taken care of. I am sure your insurance will cover it—along with the mailbox you destroyed when you got it."

He turned and walked back to his house without a backward glance, gritting his teeth and refusing to let the squelching of his boot affect his gait.

There was no telling whether this was the worst day he'd had on Earth or the best, but either way...it was the most memorable.

"Tabitha," he said to himself as he tugged his boot off at the front door.

He smiled despite everything.

THREE

TABITHA GRITTED her teeth and grunted as she heaved the big, heavy box—clearly marked *KITCHEN*—onto the kitchen counter, having just hauled it in from the living room. It clanged loudly, and she winced at the sound.

"Stupid moving company. I am soooo going to one-star their asses," she muttered as she folded her arms over the top of the box to take a breather. Her face was flushed, and she was sore, exhausted, hungry, hot, and sticky with sweat. The underside of her bra was soaked, uncomfortably rubbing against her skin.

Because under-boob chafing was the *perfect* way to end a day of hard work.

What in the world possessed me to wear an underwire for this? I should've gone with a sports bra.

Unpacking was taking far longer than it should have thanks to the movers. Why had none of the reviews mentioned how slow and incompetent they were? Not only had the movers taken their time, often standing around, talking, and checking their phones, but they hadn't even bothered to pay attention to the labels on the boxes. She'd spent a big chunk of her day just moving boxes to the correct locations before she could even begin unpacking.

Boxes marked *LIVING ROOM* had ended up upstairs, and the ones marked *KITCHEN* had been stacked both in the living room and buried under other boxes in the master bedroom. And the most ridiculous part of that was the movers had literally walked through her kitchen to get to the living room!

She could have sworn they had done it on purpose.

"The jerks."

Tabitha glanced out the kitchen window.

Night had fallen a while ago. With fall fast approaching, it was getting dark earlier, making it feel later than it actually was. She'd just unpack a few more boxes and eat one of the sandwiches from the cooler for dinner before rewarding herself with a nice, hot soak in her new bathtub. It'd been a long day—a long week, really, as she'd packed and prepared for the move— and she felt like she more than deserved it.

Drawing back, she pulled her cellphone out, unlocked it, and navigated to her current playlist. Once a Lady Gaga song was playing, Tabitha set the phone down and got back to work, singing and dancing along to the tune. She ripped open the box and transferred the pots and pans inside it to the wide drawer under the double oven.

Despite the day's many frustrations, she was excited to set up her workspace and begin this new chapter in her life. She was a little anxious, but wasn't anyone who'd quit their fulltime job so they could follow their dream? Tabitha wasn't too worried. She had a great following on her YouTube channel, Lush Lathers, which had started blowing up over the past two years. And it was all thanks to Nan, her grandmother. The woman who had adopted and raised Tabitha.

Some of Tabitha's earliest memories were of watching Nan

make soap and candles. It had been so fascinating to see Nan with those big rubber gloves on as she mixed ingredients, or to see her deftly carving wax into all sorts of fanciful shapes. When Tabitha had turned seven, she'd started helping a little, though it had been years before she was allowed to deal with any of the chemicals.

Still, it hadn't been until middle school—when other kids got particularly mean to a chubby girl with no mom and dad—that Nan really pushed Tabitha to get involved. They'd spent so many days trying new combinations of colors and scents, laughing together.

Nan had always said there were no mistakes. She'd especially liked saying that when their experimental combinations produced smells that were particularly overwhelming, which always resulted in hysterical laughter from both of them as they ran around the house opening windows.

Now that she was older, Tabitha knew all that time making soap and candles with Nan had been more than important bonding. Nan had done it, at least in part, to give Tabitha an escape. To give her something she could control while the world outside just seemed increasingly bigger and scarier.

Tabitha paused as she placed a glass in the cupboard, frowning. Her eyes burned with the threat of tears. Had Nan really been gone for two years already? Tabitha missed her more and more every day.

She resumed her work, unwrapping the drinking glasses from the thick paper protecting them and storing them in the cupboard.

Nan had made sure Tabitha could follow her dreams by leaving everything to Tabitha in her will. She hadn't been wealthy by most measures, but it had been enough to give Tabitha the ability to put more time and focus into her blossoming business, and that focus had provided just enough of a distraction from the pain of loss to keep Tabitha going.

Selling Nan's house, which had been the only real home Tabitha had ever known, had been a bittersweet process, but it had also been one of Nan's last wishes. She wanted Tabitha to move on—to make her own life and new memories.

A light scratching at the sliding patio door called Tabitha's attention away. She walked over to the door to find Dexter, Nan's seven-year-old German Shepherd, staring up at her from out back with his big brown eyes, tongue hanging out.

She slid the door open to let him in. "I'm still mad at you. I can't believe what you did today. What would Nan think?"

Dexter closed his mouth, and, somehow, his eyes got bigger, softer, and more pitiful.

"Don't you give me that look. Stop it..." She fought to hold back a grin, shaking her head at herself when she failed to do so. Crouching, she held her arms out, and Dexter came forward to lick her face. Tabitha laughed and turned her face away as she took his head between her hands, giving him a good scratch behind his ears. "I can't stay mad at you. But you're still in the doghouse. No treats for you tonight."

He whined.

"Nope, I don't want to hear it. Are you hungry?"

Dexter's ears perked, and he wagged his tail.

"Yeah, boy? You want food?" she asked playfully, pitching her voice higher.

He barked his agreement, tail swinging so quickly now that his rear end was shaking along with it.

She chuckled and stood, walking to the counter. She set the already unpacked dog dishes on the floor, filled one with cold water, and poured a cupful of dog food into the other. Dexter bumped her hand away before she'd even finish dumping the food in, eagerly chowing down.

As she washed her hands in the sink, Tabitha looked out the window that faced the house of her out-of-this-world, unbelievably sexy neighbor. She cringed. First the movers ran over his mailbox, then her dog peed on his foot. She'd made herself out to be the worst neighbor in history—and on the first day!

"Great way to make a first impression, Tabby." She crossed her arms atop the counter and leaned on them, propping her chin on her palm. "He's not likely to forget you."

It wasn't like she'd had a chance in hell with him to begin with. Logan was the most attractive man she'd ever seen. He was tall, tan, and clearly well-built beneath his clothes. His dark hair was shaved on the sides and longer on top with a couple rogue strands dangling over his bright, piercing blue eyes to give him a rakish appeal. He had thick, arched brows, a long, narrow nose, and some dark stubble along his strong, square jaw. And those lips... Those full, sinfully sculpted lips were made for kissing. Or biting.

She wanted to do both. Definitely both.

But guys like him didn't go for girls like her. They preferred women who'd choose a salad and the gym over those who'd grab a pint of ice cream and plop down on the couch with a blanket to binge watch a TV show.

Tabitha sighed morosely. Pushing herself away from the counter, she dug her cooler out from beneath a stack of empty boxes, grabbed a turkey and swiss sandwich and a bottle of water, and sat at her dining table to eat.

At least the movers had put *that* in the right place.

Even with the music playing on her phone, the house felt so quiet, so empty. Tabitha had always lived with someone. It had been her grandmother for most of her life, who'd always had the radio on in the background playing anything from Golden Oldies to classical to contemporary pop. Nan's appreciation for music had known no bounds.

When Tabitha had graduated from high school and taken a job at a local department store, she'd met Mia—and the two had immediately become best friends. It hadn't been long before they'd decided to rent an apartment together. Nan had been encouraging, and when Tabitha had voiced her hesitation in moving out, the older woman had given her a literal kick in the ass—though it had been the most loving kick imaginable.

That apartment had always been filled with sound, whether it was Mia's constant chatter, the television playing an endless succession of horror movies and angsty teen dramas, or the playful banter when Mia's boyfriend, Josh, was over and they'd all play video games on the couch together. Tabitha had never been big on games—she preferred having her nose stuck in a book—but they were sure as hell fun with some friends.

Now there was none of that. Just the music from her phone, which seemed somehow too small to fill the emptiness here, and the sound of Tabitha chewing her white bread, turkey, and swiss.

And that of Dexter licking himself on the floor.

Tabitha wrinkled her nose. "Ugh, Dex, do that someplace private, will ya? Some of us are eating."

The dog ignored her. Typical.

She picked up her phone and checked her social media apps. There were multiple notifications and messages, none of which she had the energy to respond to currently. She'd put that on the list of to-dos for tomorrow.

She skimmed through the most recent posts as she ate, smiling when she saw a picture of Mia kissing Josh's cheek while he grinned at the camera. Tabitha turned off her music and watched a clip of today's news. After only a minute, she decided that was too depressing, so she scrolled on until she found a compilation of cute cat videos, laughing at all their cute, crazy antics.

Tabitha glanced at Dexter, who was lying on the floor at her feet. She gave him a gentle nudge with her toe. "How about it, Dex? should we get a cat?"

He looked up at her with disinterest and huffed. She chuckled.

Once she was done with her sandwich, she stopped the cat video and closed all the apps on her phone, plunging the room into silence. She knew Portland wasn't the noisiest city in the world, but she hadn't realized until now just how much background sound there'd been while she lived there. In comparison, this suburb was as quiet as a tomb.

Living alone was going to take a lot of getting used to.

Could always invite the neighbor over...

She recalled Logan's eyes; they were so intensely, impossibly blue. They'd been focused on her so solidly that for an instant she'd almost made the mistake of thinking he couldn't see anything else. It had been a moment out of one of the many romance books she loved to read.

And it couldn't have been anything but her imagination.

"Yeah, because I'm sure he'd love the chance to get peed on again," she muttered, pushing herself to her feet.

She tossed the empty sandwich bag into the trashcan before walking toward the front door. Her muscles were stiff and sore, and her feet ached, crying out in protest of her every little movement. Apparently, her body had simply waited for her to sit for a few minutes to decide it had been utterly wrecked over the last few days.

Tabitha made sure the door was locked and set about turning off the downstairs lights. "I am so ready for that bath."

Just as she'd flicked off the kitchen light, motion from outside caught her attention. Brows furrowing, Tabitha walked to the window behind the sink and leaned toward it to get a better look.

A tall, dark figure was walking down Logan's driveway in long strides. Tabitha's heart fluttered in panic, but she quickly realized that it was Logan himself. The exterior lights of his home were off, leaving his property blanketed in shadow save for the tiny points of reflected light on his windows and truck that only seemed to deepen the surrounding darkness.

She shifted along the window to keep him in view as he reached the end of his driveway. He turned his head from side to side, and half his face was briefly illuminated by light from the lamppost in a neighboring yard. His eyes looked just as dark as the night sky now.

He had something tucked under his arm like he was a linebacker carrying a football, but the object was too large to be a ball, and he held a gun-like item in his other hand.

Tabitha found herself holding her breath as Logan crouched. Between the lighting, the angle, and his back being toward her, she had difficulty telling what he was doing, but he was definitely putting out a weird vibe. If he were behaving this way in his back yard, it totally would have screamed, *I'm about to bury a dead body.*

He placed the larger of the two objects on the ground, and only then did she realize what it was—his dented, deformed mailbox. He seemed to be examining something around the bent post upon which his mailbox had been seated until Grayson Brothers Movers had introduced themselves to it.

Those movers had really done a number on it. Logan had every right to be furious; based on Tabitha's experience with the movers, she wouldn't doubt that they'd been *trying* to destroy his mailbox just for kicks.

Logan shifted, taking the gun-like object—some sort of power drill, maybe—to the base of the post. She couldn't tell what he was doing, but there were a few sparks that cast brief, bright flashes and made after images creep across her vision. He stood upright and moved around to the other side of the post, putting his back to the street. The post looked to be bolted into the ground again, but it was still bent out of shape.

His mailbox would've looked like it was tilting its head in disbelief if he put it on like that.

Placing one hand on the post below the bend and the other above it on the opposite side, Logan braced his feet around the base of the post. He raised his head and scanned his surroundings as though searching for onlookers.

Tabitha's heart leapt into her throat, and her cheeks blazed as she shied back from the window—but she kept him in sight.

Logan looked down again. Tabitha heard a faint groan of metal as he bent the post back into shape. He paused once, readjusting the position of his hands, before completing his work. As far as she could tell in the dark, the post was straight now.

Leaning forward, he snatched the mailbox off the ground. His hands and arms moved, and the mailbox seemed to change shape as they did. An image flashed through Tabitha's mind—Superman, with muscles bulging, bending a steel beam. After a few moments, Logan picked up the drill, set the mailbox atop the post, and apparently reattached it with a few more bright sparks.

Though it was impossible to tell from her viewing angle, especially in such poor lighting, his mailbox looked decidedly less battered than it had before. In fact, the whole thing looked as straight as it must've been before its run-in with the moving truck.

That...that was impossible. Wasn't it? Tabitha could've sworn both the mailbox and its post were made of metal. Logan looked strong, but it had to take an awful lot of strength to bend steel...

The sort of strength usually boasted by alien superheroes, right? Are you kidding, Tabby?

He stood up and stepped back, tilting his head as though surveying his work. A moment later, he was walking to his front door in those long, smooth strides. He slowed to a stop as he neared his truck. Logan's head turned to the side—not just toward Tabitha's house, but directly to the very window through which she was watching him.

Her eyes widened, and with a gasp, she ducked behind the counter, her heart hammering against her ribs.

Nope. No way had that happened. A person couldn't just bend metal like it was made of clay. It was late, it was dark outside, and Tabitha was tired. Her mind was simply playing tricks on her. She looked at Dexter, who stared at her with his head cocked, likely wondering what she was doing on the floor.

Blowing the loose strands of hair from her face, she grasped the edge of the counter and slowly pulled herself up, peeking cautiously out the window again.

Logan was gone.

What was she *doing*? She was spying on the hot guy next door like she was some nosey busybody. What if he had seen her? Shame filled her.

Great. Now she was one of *those* neighbors.

Tomorrow, she would make it right.

FOUR

Tabitha chugged the rest of her morning coffee—if she could even rightly call this diabetic's-worst-nightmare concoction of sugar and cream *coffee*—and set her mug on the counter. There was so much to do today, and she was already running behind after having slept later than she'd intended. But first...

"Come on, Dex!" she called. "Walk time."

Dexter raced over to her from the living room, his paws pounding the floor, tongue hanging out, and tail wagging in excitement. He circled her impatiently as she tried to grasp his collar and connect the leash.

"Calm down," she laughed. "You ready?"

Dexter barked. He ran to the front door, tugging her along, looking at it and back to her again and again as though to say, *hurry up already.*

She snatched her keys, the envelope beneath them, and a doggy poop bag off the stand beside the door, stuffed them all into her hoodie pocket, and opened the door. Dexter practically dragged her outside, forcing her to plant her feet firmly and brace her legs so she could stop long enough to lock the door. Once it was secure, she allowed the dog to lead her down the driveway and toward the sidewalk.

It was a crisp morning, and the cool, damp air teased her face and bit just a touch through her leggings and hoody. Tabitha took in a deep, appreciative breath.

The sky was gray and overcast, with only a hint of sunlight breaking through the clouds in the distance. Her shrubs and grass were thick and green, though her yard lacked the colorful array of flowers that brightened Logan's yard. She was eager to plant her own in the spring. But right now, her favorite season was preparing to settle in, and there were already a few leaves turning colors.

As they neared Logan's mailbox, Tabitha pulled Dexter to a stop. At a glance, there was nothing wrong with the mailbox— or the post upon which it was set. The post was straight, the box itself undented, the door was attached, and the little flag was firmly in place, a far cry from the condition the mailbox had been in the day before.

She tapped on the post with her knuckles, producing a dull, metallic clang, and frowned.

Maybe...maybe he hadn't fixed it. Maybe he'd replaced it with a new one. Maybe everything she thought she'd seen last night had been a trick of the poor lighting and her own mental and physical exhaustion.

But the black paint on the side of the mailbox was cracked and flaked off in places, revealing dull metal beneath, and when she ran her fingers along the post, they brushed over a few spots where the metal was rougher, as though it had been scratched.

Could she have seen what she thought she'd seen?

A super strong, super sexy man with superpowers. Sure, Tabitha.

She rolled her eyes at herself as she opened the mailbox.

Dexter tugged on his leash.

"Just a sec, Dexter," she said as she removed the envelope from her pocket, slipped it inside the mailbox, and closed the door.

"Does it meet your standards?" someone asked in a deep voice that was spiced with just a hint of an exotic, unplaceable accent.

Tabitha started, eyes snapping up to Logan, who was standing in his driveway less than ten feet away with his hands tucked in the pockets of his snug blue jeans. She hadn't heard his door open or close, hadn't heard him approach.

He was just as devastatingly beautiful in his red and black button-up flannel shirt as he'd been in his faded T-shirt yesterday.

Cheeks warming at being caught, Tabitha glanced back at the mailbox and flashed Logan a wide smile. "Uh...yes! I was just...admiring your new mailbox. You work fast. You must be really good with your hands."

What the frick, Tabitha? Really?!

Logan's brows rose slightly as he stepped toward Tabitha. She found herself tipping her head back slowly to hold his gaze; he was so big, so tall, that for once she felt...small. She took a subconscious step backward when he withdrew his hands from his pockets.

Without looking away from her, Logan set one of his large hands atop the mailbox. "It's the same mailbox. And I am really good with my hands."

Had she thought it was cold out here? Because right now, she was sweltering.

She stared at his hand, with its long, defined fingers, and clean, trim nails. It was a working man's hand, and possibly the sexiest hand she'd ever seen.

"I...bet you are." Her eyes flared, and she turned them back up to his, but he didn't meet her gaze. He was looking at her chest.

Is he staring at my boobs?

She cleared her throat, face burning as she self-consciously raised her arm to cover herself. "Anyway, um, I just want to say again that I am *so* sorry about yesterday. Great way to make a first impression, huh?"

"The incident with my mailbox was not my first impression of you, Tabitha," he said as he finally made eye contact again. "I feel as though I'm missing something. Are you the compulsive liar?"

Tabitha flinched, tightening her grip on the leash as Dexter pulled it taut. "What?"

"Yesterday you could not lie, but today you are a liar." Logan dipped his chin, and his eyes flicked to her chest again for an instant.

She followed his gaze to her hoodie. "Oh! *Ohhh.*" It hadn't clicked until he'd pointed it out. He hadn't been looking at her breasts, he'd been reading her hoodie.

See? Not his type, Tabby.

She pinched the side of the hoodie near the end of the text, which read, *Compulsive Lyer.* "It's just a pun. Lye is an ingredient in soap. I...guess you might call me a little obsessed when it comes to making soap and candles. I had a bunch of shirts and hoodies custom made to wear for my videos, and they seem to be pretty good conversation starters when I'm out and about."

Releasing her hoodie, she looked back up at him; he was staring at her with the same intensity she'd seen in his eyes yesterday. The kind of intensity that sparked heat in her core.

Logan eased closer to her. The movement was small and subtle, but she couldn't ignore it, couldn't slow her quickening heart. He was near enough now that she could smell him—sandalwood and musk with hints of amber and cedar.

Tabitha had the sudden, horrifying, tantalizing urge to bury her face against his chest and breathe him in.

"Are your videos about making soap?" he asked.

"Um, yes. And candles, but mostly soap."

Why did he have to smell so damn good?

He moved infinitesimally closer. "And you are in them?"

"Well...yeah."

"Perhaps I should watch them."

Is he...is he flirting?

No. No way. He...he's just playing with me.

If her cheeks weren't already red, they certainly became so in that moment. Tabitha lowered her gaze. "Oh, you don't have to. It's just mostly about the process of making them, and how I come to my decisions on scents and colors, and, um... I don't think you'd find them very entertaining."

The last thing she wanted was for this too-sexy-to-be-real man to see her at her dorkiest and most awkward. Her videos had become an outlet for her to chat with her audience and tell stories, to make corny jokes, to be...herself.

She felt his gaze upon her, raking over her slowly, and a delightful shiver nearly coursed up her spine. No one had ever looked at her the way he was.

"I may not learn much about soapmaking in the process"—he raised a hand and hooked the pocket of her hoodie with one of his long fingers, pulling it toward him slightly—"but I would be *lying* if I said I would not enjoy watching you."

Tabitha's breath hitched. Her eyes were wide as she again met his gaze.

Was it possible to come from words alone? Because she was pretty sure she just had. Logan's deep, baritone voice resonated through her, flooding her with heat, making her nipples hard and causing her pussy to ache and clench with desire.

She would never have imagined that so terrible a pun could be such a damned turn on.

Something bumped against her leg, providing just enough of a distraction for Tabitha to force her gaze away from Logan and look down.

Dexter had positioned himself next to Logan and was sniffing the man's boot. He raised a hind leg.

Tabitha gasped and jerked away from Logan, giving the leash a tug. "Dexter!"

"No," Logan said to Dexter, his voice thrumming with authority—but, surprisingly, not bristling with the anger he had every right to express in that moment.

Dexter whimpered, lowered his leg, and backed away, looking up at Logan with those big, sad, puppy dog eyes. Logan held the dog's gaze.

"Don't you give us those eyes, Dexter," Tabitha said, hand on her hip. "I just... Seriously? Again? I can't believe you." With a nervous laugh, she looked back at Logan. "I, uh...guess he likes you."

Logan chuckled. "I would hate to see how he'd behave if he didn't."

Why, oh why, did he have to look even better when he laughed? His amusement made his eyes a little brighter, almost like they were glowing, and turned his smile into something that could make her melt right here in the street.

"Yeah, me too." She took a couple steps away, tugging on the leash again to let Dexter know she was ready to walk. "I, uh, should go. Just so he doesn't get any more ideas."

Dexter didn't need any more coaxing. He was already taking off down the sidewalk.

Logan took a step toward her. "Would you be averse to me accompanying y—"

"No, no. It's all right. Have a great day!"

Tabitha turned around and fled; she'd never walked faster than she did in that moment.

Why was it every time she was near him, she always ended up running?

Because he makes me feel things way too strongly, and I...I can't get hurt again.

Logan had been flirting with her. It hadn't felt contrived or artificial, hadn't felt malicious, it had felt...real. Well, at least until Dexter had ruined it.

She glared down at Dexter. "Not cool. You're *so* not getting any treats today."

Zevris watched Tabitha walking away with his brow furrowed and a strange ache in his chest. Heat thrummed just beneath the surface of his skin. Part of him was eager to give chase, and he knew, despite how fast she was walking, that he could easily catch up to her if he wanted to.

In his mind's eye, he saw himself stalking after her, saw his strides devouring the distance between them, saw himself grab her by the arm and spin her to face him. In his imagining, her skin was pinkened, her eyes glossy with desire, and he—

He grunted, shattering his own reverie.

Zevris wanted this odd little human, wanted her more than he'd even dreamed possible, but it would do him no good to stand here in the street fantasizing about her. All that would come of that was an erection—or a full-on erection, anyway, considering his shaft was already partway there. And that would be both uncomfortable and quite visible to anyone looking thanks to his snug jeans.

Unbidden, his gaze dipped to Tabitha's backside. Her hooded sweater had ridden up in her haste, granting him a perfect view of her rounded ass, which her black leggings hugged closely. The tightness and heat in his gut intensified, and his cock, caught between his pants and his thigh, hardened further.

After almost a year of wondering what it meant, he finally understood one of the human phrases he'd heard so often.

That ass, though.

As his eyes trailed down her legs and back up again, a firestorm ignited within him. He very nearly dropped a hand to his groin to squeeze his shaft, desperate to alleviate the pressure, to address his growing discomfort. Only his military discipline stopped him; he was on the street in daylight, and humans frowned upon such public displays.

I've many things to do today, regardless.

Zevris willed himself to turn away from her, but found himself staring until Tabitha, his alluring little human, had walked around a corner and vanished from his view.

Though she was gone, her scent lingered in the air, easily discernable from all the rest. Today, its vanilla note was more pronounced. Zevris breathed it in, closing his eyes for a moment as he let her fragrance flow through him and overwhelm his senses. Some part of him might've been content merely with his every inhalation being perfumed by her scent.

Yet there was more to her scent than its allure or the hunger it roused within him—there was information in it. Or rather there was information in what was absent from it.

Both times he'd scented her, Zevris had picked up on a hint of the beast—Dexter. Dogs and cats, the most popular human pets, were species driven by scent in many ways, and they left traces of their own smells on everything. Tabitha had not escaped when it came to Dexter, though it was faint enough to easily ignore.

But there had been no trace of another male's scent on Tabitha. Even when Zevris had been so close to her that he had heard her heart beating, he hadn't smelled anything that suggested she'd been near another male—not yesterday and not this morning.

He knew it was a leap in logic, but that lack of male scent could very well have meant Tabitha was without a mate, that she was unclaimed...that she was *single*.

I will mark her.

Zevris lifted a hand and combed his fingers through his hair, extending his claws just enough for their tips to graze his scalp.

What am I doing?

He caught a fistful of his hair and squeezed. His experiences in covert operations had taught him how powerful emotions like hope could be—and how dangerous. It was wholly exploitable, used as a weapon as easily as it could be used as a source of inspiration, and he knew better than to base plans around it. He needed intelligence, information, insight. Evidence. He couldn't risk his mission—his entire species—based on the small chance that Tabitha was single, that she was interested in him, that she was...that she *could be*, his mate.

He needed to be certain that she was unclaimed by another, that she was seeking a mate and not a *fling* like so many of the Earth females he'd met.

Zevris swore he'd seen that gleam in her eyes again this morning, that reflection of his yearning, that flame of desire. He also swore he'd smelled a hint of her arousal—just enough to set his blood ablaze but not enough to make him lose control.

What would his name—his true name—sound like from her lips, spoken in her soft, lyrical voice?

Clenching his jaw, he turned toward the mailbox. Even if this was not a combat mission, it was a military mission, and he would conduct it with the same precision and attention to detail he'd maintained through all his deployments.

Because that approach has been so successful thus far, right?

He was about to walk back to his dwelling when something caught his eye—the mailbox door was ajar. As he reached forward to close it, he paused, glancing down the street in the direction Tabitha had gone. Were there any humans truly so interested in mailboxes as to warrant the vigorous inspection she'd given his?

Zevris turned his head again, this time looking toward Tabitha's house. One of her windows—the kitchen window—was visible from where he stood, albeit at an angle. He could make out what looked like a curved sink faucet at the forefront, with the top of a chair and her table visible beyond it.

Last night, he'd seen only darkness in that window. The reflections on the glass had been just strong enough to disrupt his vision. But he swore he'd felt eyes upon him. Her eyes...

Had she seen him? If so, how much had she seen?

Zevris gritted his teeth and coiled his tail tighter around his leg. It was almost like he *wanted* to be discovered lately. What was the human phrase? Blowing his load, or something along those lines?

No...not load, *cover*. He wasn't fully certain, but he suspected that first phrase had a very, very different meaning. Regardless, he could not allow his true nature to be exposed. His people were relying upon him.

Althicar Zevris Akkaran had conducted countless dangerous missions during which the slightest mistake would've meant his death, and he'd never suffered a single moment of doubt or hesitation. Why should he suddenly doubt now?

He dropped his gaze to the mailbox again and tilted his head when he caught a glimpse of white through the gap. It had been empty when he'd reattached it to the post last night, and the mail carrier usually didn't come around until early afternoon.

Zevris opened the mailbox and removed the envelope lying within. It had no postage, no postmark, no addresses. There was only a name printed in large, flowing letters. *Logan.*

Turning the envelope around, he opened it and removed the contents—a check with a bright pink sticky note attached to it.

So, <u>SO</u> sorry about yesterday.
Please use this for boots and mailbox.

It was written in the same big, bubbly letters as the name on the front of the envelope, signed by Tabitha and marked with two dots and a curved line. A smiley face. The little face was slightly crooked, and the dots were larger than usual, granting it an unexpected charm.

Logan removed the sticky note. The two-hundred-dollar check beneath it was made out to Logan E. The note line simply said, *Sorry!*

His understanding of the way humans assigned value to their belongings, time, and money was still vague, complicated in large part by the fluidity of their economy and the way those values constantly shifted and changed, often based on seemingly arbitrary factors. But he had dealt with humans on a more personal level often enough to know that for most of them, two hundred dollars was not an insignificant sum.

Zevris chuckled and shook his head. Perhaps he should have been clearer in communicating that he'd expected no compensation from her, but he had a feeling that she would've done something out of guilt regardless.

Not purely guilt. She has integrity. That's what drove her to this.

His dispute with the movers hadn't been about money—it had been about them accepting responsibility for what they had done. A genuine apology would likely have been enough to appease Zevris, but that had apparently been too much to ask of Frank and his coworker. But Tabitha, who hadn't even caused the accident, had taken personal responsibility for it.

Perhaps the matter of her dog urinating on Zevris's boot could be looked at differently. The beast was her responsibility, and it did not seem to respect her commands. But Zevris couldn't see it that way. Dexter had a mind of his own. Even falorans, for all their advanced technology and millennia of spacefaring history, were sometimes subject to their instincts.

He could not consider the Dexter incident to be Tabitha's fault—and she'd already taken responsibility and apologized, regardless.

He walked back toward his dwelling, his attention divided between his destination and the handwritten note. He still couldn't understand the human insistence on using paper for communication when their digital means of connecting were so much faster and less wasteful, but there was something about Tabitha's gesture, about the thought she'd put into it, that was... endearing. Writing something out by hand, in ink, just seemed more intimate than tapping some virtual keys on a touchscreen.

As he reached his front door, he paused and succumbed to the sudden impulse to lift the note to his nose. He inhaled deeply and groaned as his cock stirred anew.

The paper smelled of vanilla and lavender. It smelled like Tabitha.

"*Karak'duun*, I'm in trouble," he muttered as he tucked the check into the envelope and stepped into his dwelling.

FIVE

ZEVRIS PULLED his vehicle into a parking place in front of the Hardware Emporium and turned off the engine. Though the lack of consistency could become worrisome if he dwelled upon it too long, he was glad that, unlike *driveway*, the term *parking lot* made sense.

Of course, if he allowed his mind to wander regarding the different meanings of the word *park*, he was bound to end up with a headache. He was convinced that the ancient humans who'd developed the English language must either have been very cruel or fancied themselves amusing. It had likely been both.

He climbed out of the truck, closed the door, and walked toward the building. The Hardware Emporium was considered a home improvement retailer, specializing in the materials and tools necessary for construction, maintenance, and renovation. Zevris had come here often to supply his woodworking and purchase parts for minor repairs in his home. Normally, he'd have deferred to experts for such repairs, but he preferred having as few humans enter his dwelling as possible. Though he'd tried to furnish the house in a way that would resemble an average human residence, there was no telling what small details could rouse suspicion.

All he knew was that it didn't have to be anything as blatant as a plasma pistol accidentally left on the coffee table or a holographic display projecting on the kitchen counter.

As he stepped into the store, his nose was struck by the mingling scents of the plants on display to the side—earthy, floral, and *alive*. For all the frustrations Earth had caused him, Zevris was glad that he'd been sent to a verdant region. It had been a long while since he'd been able to enjoy greenery like he'd found here in western Oregon.

He continued deeper into the store, walking along aisles that had become familiar to him. Though he had a list in mind of exactly what he needed to purchase and knew where each of those items was located, he found himself wandering. More than once, his fingers twitched, and he had to battle the urge to take the folded envelope out of his back pocket, to inhale Tabitha's scent from it, to grin at the crooked little smiley face she'd drawn.

The warrior in Zevris told him she was his to claim, told him to take her. To stride up to her, pull that luscious body against his while staring fire into her lovely green eyes, and slam his mouth over hers in a kiss. To tell her that she was his mate—that she was *his*.

Yet even though he did not fully understand human courtship rituals, he knew that was certainly not their way. Tabitha was not a female to be forced into submission, but a female to be wooed.

If only the instructional videos humans called *pornography* weren't so sorely lacking in terms of courtship. Every one he'd watched skipped almost immediately to mating and had no information on building a relationship.

His successes in the field of wooing were minimal thus far. If songs were ever written about his ability to court human females, they'd undoubtedly be the sort sung in jest by soldiers who were far too deep into their cups.

Zevris strode along the paint aisle, his eyes darting from side to side to take in the myriad of colors. Which was Tabitha's favorite? He was hesitant to assume anything, knowing how unpredictable and contradictory humans could be, but he somehow doubted that she had a single color she liked more than the rest. She seemed the sort to enjoy an array of colors, all as bright and vivid as her.

Though when he thought about it further, perhaps she did prefer one color. Her fingernails had been the same pink as the note. Was that merely coincidence, or was it a sign?

Why do I continue with these thoughts as though she hasn't already fled from me twice?

And yet she'd also shown signs of interest in him. She'd looked at him with heat in her eyes, with desire, and he'd scented her arousal when she was near. Even when she'd run, some primal aspect of Zevris had taken it as a challenge, as an invitation, to give chase. His instincts seemed to recognize some unspoken message—she *wanted* him to claim her. All of it was enough to drive him mad. It was a wonder he'd not taken her there on the street.

Releasing a huff through his nostrils, Zevris altered his course to head directly to the lumber section of the store, increasing his pace.

This Earth assignment was not the first time he'd had to assume a different identity and conform to the standards of an alien race, but it was the first time he felt like he was...losing himself during the process.

I am but weary. This final mission was simply one too many to undertake.

But he knew before that thought was even complete that things were not so simple—nothing ever was. He couldn't deny what had flashed through his mind when the *ultricar* had offered this assignment.

This was Zevris's chance to find a lifemate. To finally settle in one place, to have a family. He'd never considered any of it before; it would've been foolish to do so, given his people's situation. Faloran females were so rare now that the Azmus Protectorate, the falorans' governing body, usually acted as matchmaker. They choose males to match to females based on ancestral medical history and genetic compatibility, hoping to produce offspring that would overcome the plague's crippling legacy.

Of course, Protectorate matchmaking never guaranteed there'd be enough of a connection between the couple for a mating bond to be formed, and the chances of any one male being chosen were next to zero.

Courtship rituals, spontaneous couplings, and families were a relic of the past, something that had died out with Zevris's grandfather's generation. Zevris hadn't known what he would do with himself after being released from service, only that he had tired of fighting...but this mission had given him potential direction.

It had given him something to hope for. More than ever, finding a mate and having children was deeply meaningful and important to the faloran people. But this mission marked the first time it had become a real possibility for Zevris.

Tempering that spark of hope was difficult, though he'd known from the beginning that falorans and humans being able to procreate was purely theoretical. The two species were close enough on a genetic level—and faloran genes were extremely adaptable regardless—but there'd yet to be a confirmed case of a mating bond being formed between a faloran and a member of any other species.

The difficulty of this assignment had only exasperated Zevris's weariness. He'd never expected it to be over in days, but he'd underestimated how hard it would be to find the right female on a planet with billions of them to choose from.

Zevris had weathered countless battles, had spent long, cold nights hiding in muddy holes to evade capture, had seen death aplenty—and had delivered it with his own hands. But dating on Earth had presented a sort of mental and emotional strain for which he never could have prepared.

He growled low in his chest and shook off those thoughts. He was in this store for a simple and specific reason, and it was best that he completed that task and returned to his dwelling without delay.

Still, he took his time in selecting the wood he required. He ran his fingertips along each prospective piece, feeling out the grain, seeking the little imperfections that might have spoiled his work—and those that might have complemented it. He'd taken up woodworking as part of his cover, never having expected it to be so challenging. He'd also never expected it to be so fulfilling.

Before long, he found himself selecting several more pieces beyond what he'd planned not because he needed them, but because they felt right, stacking them all on a flatbed cart. He wasn't sure what they were right for...but for some reason, they brought Tabitha to mind.

He'd have to make something for her eventually.

But *what*?

Though he'd shown unexpected aptitude for woodworking, his relatively limited experience had thus far kept his repertoire somewhat sparse. He doubted she would think a birdhouse was an endearing courtship gift. No matter how elegant and level a shelf he could shape and hang, he did not see how it would say, *I am your male, become my mate.*

Zevris's mind raced as he pushed the flatbed to the front of the store.

What did Tabitha like? What would she find thoughtful, and what would she most appreciate? He knew so little about her. Well, apart from her self-proclaimed obsession with making soap and candles, both of which he was equally uninformed about.

Research and preparation, just like any other mission.

His neural transceiver was crammed with information about Earth; there was bound to be something in its data about soap and candle making. And if not...there was a vast amount of knowledge to be accessed on the internet, so long as one was able to sort through the false or misleading entries.

Considering the staggering number of invasive advertisements and viruses that pervaded the internet, Zevris was grateful that his superiors had decided not to link his neural transceiver directly to human information networks.

He took a place at the end of one of the check lane lines and leaned his forearms on the flatbed's handle. The soft chatter of cashiers and customers become a meaningless drone to Zevris, run through by the erratic beeps of items being scanned into the computers to tally prices and track sales.

For his first several months on Earth, Zevris had paid close attention to every conversation between humans of which he'd been within earshot, hoping to extract any information he could from them, paying special mind to the cadences with which they spoke and the words they used.

He'd fallen out of that habit as he'd slowly realized the truth about the majority of those overheard exchanges—that they were ultimately meaningless. Most humans treated interactions with one another as formalities, as exchanges of pleasantries that were demanded by societal pressure. But that wasn't always the case. People who were close friends, family, and mates seemed to have far more meaningful interactions.

Zevris's encounters with Tabitha certainly hadn't felt meaningless.

The line moved up, and Zevris stepped forward, sure to leave ample space between the front end of his flatbed and the ankles of the human in front of him. For creatures that so often complained about their personal space, many humans seemed to invade one another's constantly.

He let his eyes wander, and they soon fell upon a display rack in front of him. Atop its uppermost shelf was a collection of little plants in little pots, perhaps half a dozen in all. Each plant was covered in thin white spines that jutted outward from the thick stems.

Cactuses.

Zevris remembered them from the studies he'd undertaken before arriving on Earth; they had been marked as a plant he was unlikely to encounter in person, but which was part of humankind's wider awareness and culture. He'd taken note because they were reminiscent of vegetation he'd seen on his home planet long, long ago. They weren't an exact match, but the similarities were enough to trigger a burst of nostalgia for a place he hadn't visited for more than half his life.

Each cactus had a small flower growing atop it. Three were red, two were yellow, and one—the most vibrant of all—was pink.

Zevris smiled. Nostalgia had sparked warmth in his chest, but it was nothing compared to the feeling instilled in him by that shade of pink, which immediately returned his mind to Tabitha. Perhaps he would do best to look at the cactuses not as signs of the home he'd left behind, but the home he might have found. The home he hoped to make.

Beside the other blossoms, that pink flower was uniquely lovely. Just like the human females he'd encountered—each had been attractive in her own way, but Tabitha was lovely beyond compare. She stood out to Zevris like none of the others had. His two brief conversations with her had been refreshing and enticing, having gifted him tantalizing glimpses of her personality. That was something a few of his past dates had failed to achieve even during hours-long dinner dates.

As he neared the rack, he reached forward and picked up the pink-flowered cactus by its tiny terra cotta pot. Was it not a human courtship custom to give flowers to the female one meant to woo? Perhaps this was a way to signal his intentions without seeming overbearing.

Without making her run away again.

Had he pushed her too far, or was there something else wrong? Perhaps he'd failed to find the balance between being forward and reserved. Perhaps she was attracted to him physically, but he'd failed to intrigue her enough during their conversations. Or had he simply failed to show the *proper* signs of interest?

Being rejected by human females was nothing new to him, but he really wanted to get this right with Tabitha. He wanted her.

When it was his turn to be checked out, he placed the cactus on the counter, purchasing it along with his other selections.

The pot fit perfectly in one of the cupholders in the cab of his vehicle; he placed it there carefully before loading his wood into the vehicle's open bed.

Truck, not vehicle, he reminded himself as he secured the tailgate. Both terms were technically correct, but humans did not use the latter as often or as casually as the former. Car, truck, van; those were the words they preferred for their auto-mobiles.

He climbed into the truck's cab and began his journey home.

Though the drive was smooth, and the traffic was relatively light, Zevris drummed his fingers impatiently upon the steering wheel whenever he was behind a slower vehicle, and more than once had to bite back the urge to press the accelerator to the floor. There was a strange blend of tightness and hollowness in his belly that reminded him of the pre-drop anxiousness he'd so often experienced even after going through numerous drops onto hostile planets.

His eyes repeatedly flicked toward the cactus sitting in the cupholder. Each time he looked at the plant, he wondered how Tabitha would react to it. Would she like it? Would she be grateful? Did she like him?

Karak'duun, I'm acting like a human adolescent pumped full of hormones and self-doubt.

At least that was what he'd been led to believe; his knowl-edge pertaining to that age group had been gained primarily through human entertainment. He'd not had any interactions with teenage humans apart from a few cashiers in various stores.

"The cactus is fine," he said, forcing his eyes back onto the road. "It is a hardy plant. It has weathered far worse than this drive."

He managed to complete his journey without unsafely passing other vehicles or exceeding the speed limit—or at least not exceeding it more than the cars that made up the bulk of the traffic. But when the entrance to his neighborhood came into view, he had to squeeze the steering wheel and clench his jaw to keep from accelerating. Getting to his dwelling a few seconds sooner wouldn't help anything.

And there were children who often played on these streets. Even if he was of a different species, from a different world, Zevris refused to endanger the lives of children, whether by reckless driving or any other actions.

He backed into his driveway, turned off the truck, and again engaged in a battle of will versus impulse, just barely stopping himself from leaping out of the cab and sprinting to Tabitha's door. Zevris could not recall a single moment in his life during which he'd been so excited and nervous at once.

And all over a little plant that would stab him if he touched it.

He frowned as he reached down to collect the cactus. The pot fit perhaps a little *too* well in the cupholder; its rim was below that of the cupholder, leaving only the cactus's spiky body protruding.

I suppose being a member of a highly advanced species is no guarantee of intelligence.

Zevris fumbled to work the tip of a claw between the cupholder and the pot so he could coax it up. But his fingers were big, the gap was small, and the angle to which he had to bend to make the attempt was uncomfortable.

"This is why you have not found a mate here, *Logan*," he muttered. "Who wants any male foolish enough to get a cactus stuck in a cupholder?"

After another minute of struggling—and a few frustrated grunts and growls—he finally wedged his claw between the pot and the cupholder. Using that claw like a prybar, he carefully raised the pot until he could press a finger to the other side. He lifted the plant free, keeping his hands angled away from those small, wicked spines.

Now that he had the plant in hand, his frown deepened. Rather than a small sense of accomplishment, he had a moment of doubt; why was he gifting the female he desired a plant that could make her bleed?

He cast that doubt aside. It was because of the cactus's beauty—because of Tabitha's beauty.

Zevris exited the truck, holding the pot delicately in his fingers, and walked to Tabitha's residence.

As he approached the front door, a sound gradually took shape—music. It was a deep, thumping but muffled bass, and it was coming from inside Tabitha's home. Even when he was standing on the front step, only the bassline and the words 'What is Love?' were clear.

He pressed the doorbell. Its ring rose over the music, a high contrast to that low bass. Before the bell had even finished ringing, Dexter was barking. Someone cursed—a curt *damn it*—followed by the sound of something falling. A moment later, the music stopped.

The barking grew in volume as Dexter neared the door, and his claws were soon scraping the other side.

"Just a minute!" Tabitha called, and then lowered her voice. "Dexter, hush. What has gotten into you? You've never acted like this before." She grunted, and claws clicked against the floor. "Come on. You're going out back."

It was difficult not to imagine the scene behind the door. Did she have a hand on Dexter's collar as she tried to guide the animal to back yard? Was she bent over, her pants sculpted to her delicious legs and backside? Was her hair hanging about her shoulders freely, begging for Zevris's hands to run through it?

He glanced at the cactus. Its bright pink petals—so close to the shade of her fingernails—bolstered his resolve.

Zevris inhaled deeply. There was a faint scent on the air, a new scent, with vaguely floral notes. He knew some of the common ones, like lavender and roses, or the chrysanthemums in his front yard, but this was different from those. There was something to this scent...

It produced gentle warmth in his nostrils. The sensation spread to his chest and blossomed low in his abdomen, tingling across his skin and through his limbs. He curled his free hand into a fist, holding it firm at his side to resist the wild urge to reach for the door handle.

Tabitha's lips were pink, too. Perhaps not as vibrant as her nails, but their pink was softer and infinitely more enticing. What other parts of her were that color? Her nipples, her—

The door swung open, and there she was, his female, with her hair piled and knotted messily upon her head, stray wisps of it framing her beautiful face. She was wearing a pair of clear protective glasses, similar to those he wore in his workshop, large yellow rubber gloves, and a black apron with white ruffles and words printed across the front. *I used to be addicted to soap, but I'm clean now.* There was a big, dark spot on the apron, just below her breasts, as though she'd spilled something on herself.

Her scent teased his nose for an instant before that mysterious floral fragrance assailed him in full force, overpowering all other smells.

Zevris's blood turned to magma, boiling in his veins, and his heart sped to pump that liquid fire faster and faster. Heat rushed to his groin and suffused his cock, which was instantly hard and throbbing within the confines of his jeans. His claws extended involuntarily; those on his free hand dug into his palm, somehow intensifying the heat within him. His tail, just as trapped in his pants as his shaft, coiled around his calf and squeezed.

Despite those intense sensations, all his focus was upon Tabitha, who stared at him in wide-eyed surprise. His mouth watered as he took her in. He wanted to tear off everything she was wearing, wanted to reveal her soft, pale skin and large breasts, wanted to shove her to the floor so he could thrust between her legs and rut—

He grunted, clenching his teeth. That strange scent dominated his every inhalation; there was no escaping it.

Zevris closed his fist a little tighter. His claws produced growing points of pain on his palm, offering him a tiny distraction. He rasped, "Tabitha."

She smiled wide. "Hi! I...wasn't expecting you."

Had he violated some cultural norm? Was there some rule about needing an invitation to go to someone's home? Zevris couldn't recall, couldn't form a clear thought through the haze in his mind. The pain on his hand had only deterred his flaring desire for a few seconds; that inner heat was still intensifying, threatening to consume him.

Tabitha's smile faded slightly. "Are you okay?"

Don't just stare, Zevris. Speak, damn you.

"I...didn't mean to..." He struggled to find the word. It was somewhere in his head, currently buried beneath a thousand half-imagined images of Tabitha in various states of undress, many of which had her positioned tantalizingly as he rutted her. His cock pulsed with a deep ache.

Intrude. That was the word, but it refused to come out as he fought to stop himself from stepping into her home and grabbing hold of her—and from spilling his seed where he stood.

Tabitha arched a brow. "Look, if it's about the money, I do *not* want it back. Just saying that right now. So if that's why you're here"—she lifted her arm and pointed at him—"you just can turn around and—" Her eyes fell on her hand and rounded.

She laughed nervously as she glanced up at him and yanked off her gloves, tossing them behind her without looking. She plucked her safety glasses off her face, folded the arms in, and tucked them into the pocket of her apron before idly wiping at the large wet spot.

The mystery smell strengthened, but now it was mingling with Tabitha's scent, creating something irresistibly arousing. Zevris's muscles tensed, and his shaft twitched as though trying to force its way toward her.

"Sorry," she said. "You caught me in the middle of something, and I kind of had a spill. I know what this must look like, but I was definitely *not* making drugs." Her lips quirked in an uncertain smile.

He had the vague sense that he should have apologized for causing her distress, that he should have offered some sympathy, but his body seemed to want nothing more than to bury his cock in her heat.

Abort mission. Now. Get the fuck out of there.

Before you do something you regret.

"Are you spoken for?" he blurted.

Her brows creased. "What?"

"Are you spoken for? Do you have a male?"

"A male? Do you mean...a boyfriend?"

Was he truly being that unclear? "Yes. A boyfriend. Husband. Mate."

"Oh!" her cheeks flushed. "No, no I...I don't have anyone." She caught her bottom lip with her teeth, narrowed her eyes, and leaned closer to him. "Are you okay, Logan? Your eyes look—"

Zevris lifted the cactus, inserting it into the space between himself and Tabitha as though it could act as some deterrent to the wild desires roiling within him. He wanted to lick that mysterious, maddening scent from her skin, wanted to fill the air with her soft cries as he pounded into her, wanted to fill her with his seed and forge that mating bond right now, right in her foyer, marking her as his forever.

Instead of doing any of that, he said, "This is for you."

Her gaze fell on the cactus, and her brows rose. "For me?"

She reached for it, her fingers brushing against his as she took the little plant from his grasp, sending thrilling sparks across Zevris's skin that made him shudder. "You didn't have to do that. Thank—"

"Goodnight," he said hurriedly, turning away and forcing himself to walk before she could utter a response. He'd climbed cliff faces hundreds of feet tall that were easier to traverse than the sixty feet between her front door and his, but he did not allow himself to slow, did not allow himself to look back. He did not allow himself to succumb to those fiery urges.

Even a moment's hesitation would have had him turning and racing toward her, ripping off his clothing as he moved without a care of what the neighbors would see. Her clothes would have met their end the instant he reached her.

Somehow, he managed to get his housekey into the lock on the first try after deactivating the door's forcefield, though his hands were stiff and trembling. He opened the door, darted through, and slammed it shut all within a fraction of a second, pressing his back against it as he fumblingly locked the deadbolt.

He hoped the combination of that barrier and the distance between him and Tabitha would be enough.

Heat sizzled beneath his skin in waves, coalescing in his loins. His entire body buzzed with an itch he wasn't sure he could scratch—and there was little space in his mind for anything but the need to fulfill his desires. To find release.

Zevris was only vaguely aware that he'd deactivated his holoshroud as he unfastened his belt and opened his jeans. In his desperation, he nearly tore off the button and broke the zipper, and he was only able to force the jeans slightly down his hips before he wrapped his hand around his cock and pulled it free.

It ached and throbbed so hard it hurt, and it was so sensitive that even the feel of the air against its skin was almost more than he could bear. His balls were tight and heavy, his breaths already short.

Hissing a curse, he slid his hand down his shaft.

He slapped his free hand against the door, raking his nails across the painted surface. The feel of his hand on his cock was a blend of pleasure and agony unlike anything he'd experienced. Baring his fangs, he tipped his head back, closed his eyes, and pumped his fist. It was Tabitha he saw behind his eyelids as he worked—her eyes, that vibrant green; her lips, so soft and full and pink; her lush breasts and flaring hips; her tantalizing thighs and backside.

Within moments, his ragged breaths were coming out in snarls. He offered himself no mercy, moving his hand up and down his shaft at a relentless pace, imagining it was her hand there instead—or her plump lips wrapped around him as she sucked him deep.

He tightened his grip with another snarl. The pressure in him built rapidly until his hips were bucking and he couldn't think, couldn't separate himself from the sensations, from his desire.

His muscles seized, and his balls tightened impossibly further.

"Tabitha," he growled as that pressure finally burst. Seed erupted from his cock in a powerful jet, running hot over his fist and easing the slide of his hand.

Shuddering, he milked himself for whatever was left, spilling more and more seed onto the floor. When he finally stopped and opened his hand, his fingers were stiff and sticky. He forced his eyes open and glanced down at the mess he'd made.

It looked like a gallon of his seed had splattered across the laminate flooring, its pale color in stark contrast to the carbon gray planks beneath. For as much as he'd spilled, for as much pleasure as he'd felt, he remained...unfulfilled.

Release was not what he craved...*Tabitha* was.

"*Svesh*," he rasped between labored breaths. His skin was still taut, his blood still aflame, his mind still hazed with insatiable lust.

Zevris had taken himself in hand many times over the course of his life. For most male falorans, it was the only means available to relieve any sort of sexual tension without taking another male as a lover, the only way to ease the instinctual cravings. Orgasms did not necessarily involve ejaculation— because ejaculation was the means of forming a mating bond with a female. He'd spilled a little from time to time, as was only natural, but never like this.

"Tabitha," he repeated, letting his head fall back against the door again.

Some foggy part of his mind suggested that the mystery scent she'd spilled on herself was responsible for this, but he ignored it. Now was not the time to speculate. Just the sound of her name on his lips—just the thought of her—had his hand moving back to his still-hard shaft.

He wrapped his fingers around his cock and squeezed, growling again.

This was going to be a long night.

SIX

Zevris lowered himself slowly, bending his arms and refusing to let his elbows buckle against the immense force of the grav generator he'd placed on his back. He halted when his chest was within an inch of the concrete floor.

Though his muscles burned and teetered on the verge of being overcome by tremors, he held the position, staring down at the smooth but imperfect concrete and the wet spots upon it that had been left by his sweat. As though in mockery of the burden placed upon the rest of his body by the grav generator, his tail swished from side to side freely, its tufted tip occasionally brushing over his calves.

Usually, exercise offered a brief respite from the stresses of Zevris's everyday life—which had, for many years, involved the very real chance of death at the hands of enemies who were actively hunting him. The physical exertion required a significant portion of his willpower to overcome, required him to focus on every fiber of his body to keep them working in unison, to push past whatever limits by which he'd thought himself restrained.

But his mind kept twisting back to Tabitha.

With a heavy exhalation, he pushed himself up, straightening his arms and locking his elbows. A bead of sweat ran down his face, slowing as it reached the tip of his nose. It dangled there, creating a faint tickling sensation that should've been unnoticeable given the almost unbearable artificially generated weight pressing down on his back. His arms trembled slightly, and his toes, bent harshly against the hard floor, seemed ready to snap off entirely.

He closed his eyes and focused on taking slow, measured breaths, focused on the agony pulsing through his arms, thighs, and abdominal muscles, focused on the phantom ache in his groin.

Tabitha emerged in his imagination, looking up at him with her big emerald eyes gleaming lustfully.

Zevris's shaft twitched. He bared his fangs and growled, willing the mental image away. The last thing he needed while the grav generator was active was to lower his body and have his throbbing cock suddenly take the fullness of his amplified weight on its head.

Even if it contained no bones, it could still be broken.

I'm amazed it's still attached after the treatment I've had to give it.

The droplet fell from his nose, hitting the floor with a dull splat. Zevris released another heavy breath and sent a mental command through his neural transceiver, deactivating the grav generator. The extra weight vanished suddenly enough that his balance nearly faltered; he'd not realized how hard he'd been pushing against it.

He reached back and plucked the tiny grav generator off his back before standing up. He dropped the generator into the pocket of his sweatpants, snatched the towel off the workbench, and mopped the perspiration from his forehead. As he combed his fingers through his hair, pulling the loose strands out of his face, he drew in a deep breath through his nostrils. The air was redolent of wood, varnish, and paint, of machine oil and the metallic tang of tools and hardware, mixed with a hint of his sweat that had settled atop the mixture.

All those smells were familiar to Zevris, and they were oddly comforting. This garage—his workshop—had become a sanctuary for him. While he was in here practicing his adopted craft, the universe's problems were far away. The pressure of having to save his entire species did not follow him into this space. All those years of training, dangerous operations, and combat fell away, leaving nothing but a lone male trying to shape wood into something new.

He'd spent his whole day yesterday—from just before sunrise to well after sunset—in here trying to work, drifting from project to project with no sense of direction. That was not normal for him. It also wasn't normal that he'd stopped so many times between those projects to take his cock in hand and pump himself to climax, or that he'd spent the night before yesterday unable to remove his hand from his shaft.

Though that unknown floral scent from Tabitha's house had faded from his nostrils not long after he'd first smelled it, its effects had proven devastatingly tenacious. He'd only begun to regain control of himself last night—a good twenty-four hours after it had first hit him. Whether that smell had acted as some sort of aphrodisiac or his body had confused it for a potent pheromone, it had haunted him.

Tabitha had haunted him.

His tail curled, its tuft briefly trailing over the floor. Tilting his head back, Zevris clenched his hair in his fist and dropped his other hand, which still held the towel, to his groin. He pressed down on his dully throbbing cock.

In the hours following his disastrous cactus delivery, Zevris had stroked himself to climax at least half a dozen times. Each peak had been less fulfilling than the last. Only exhaustion had eventually broken the cycle.

That cycle had commenced the second he'd awoken yesterday. By the time he'd fallen asleep last night, he'd been far, far past being able to count the number of times he'd stroked himself. Even now, he still felt the echoes of those impulses. And over the last day and a half, he swore he'd detected random, phantom traces of that maddening floral scent, even over the odors of hot metal and sawdust.

He swore he'd smelled *her*.

Zevris's fingers curled reflexively. He refused to let them close around his shaft. He'd resisted today, had made it all the way to this afternoon without giving in to the insistent ache in his balls. He'd by no means been free of temptation, but it was a vast improvement in self-control over the day prior.

The fragrance that had filled him with consuming lust and arousal had only magnified what he'd already felt. Zevris *wanted* Tabitha. He wanted to do all the things he'd imagined doing with her while he'd been in that druglike daze. He wanted to put everything he'd learned from the instructional videos to use, wanted to bring her great pleasure, wanted to show her that he was worthy, virile mate.

He groaned, huffed through his nostrils, and forced himself to move.

At least he'd maintained just enough control to recognize that throwing himself atop her wouldn't have been the right choice. It didn't matter how much lust he thought he'd seen in her eyes...he could not do any of those things without her say.

Slinging the towel over his shoulder, he opened the interior door and entered the laundry room. The garage door slammed shut behind him; it always did unless he kept hold of it and closed it with deliberate gentleness.

He continued into the kitchen, where he poured himself a glass of orange juice. It was one of the many sweet, flavorful Earth beverages he'd come to enjoy, and it was always particularly refreshing after a brutal round of exercise with the grav generator.

Heat coursed just beneath his skin, sparking a series of mild itches throughout his body. Despite the physical exertion and the burn in his muscles, he still felt unfulfilled, still felt as though he were missing something. His heart had not yet slowed since completing his workout.

It is merely the aftermath of my exercise. It has nothing to do with my thoughts of her.

Zevris lifted the glass to his lips and drank as he walked to the sliding glass doors near the dining area. Perhaps it was merely warm in his dwelling. There was a breeze outside today that bore a taste of autumn crispness; allowing some of that air into the house couldn't hurt.

He opened the sliding door a few inches and leaned a shoulder against the doorframe as he sipped at his drink. The breeze flowed in through the screen door, carrying the mingled scents of the grass and flowers in his back yard and those of the lush trees beyond his rear fence. A bit more muted but impossible to miss were the smells of someone roasting meat on a grill...and Dexter.

Before his thoughts could leap back to Tabitha, Zevris dumped the remaining orange juice into his mouth, gulped it down, and hurried to the sink to rinse the glass. His tail swished behind him impatiently.

Did she like the gift? Did she understand my intent?

Another pulse in Zevris's groin made his fingers tighten around the glass. He froze, jaw clenched and arm trembling. Perhaps he'd been mistaken in assuming he had overcome the effects of that scent.

Or, perhaps, he'd been mistaken about the true intensity of his desire for Tabitha.

Zevris placed the glass in the dishwasher as delicately as he could before hurrying upstairs. He didn't allow himself any hesitation in placing the grav generator on the bathroom counter, undressing, and getting into the shower.

As he washed himself, he steered his thoughts toward mundane subjects—the items he would need to purchase during his next trip to the grocery store; which of his numerous unfinished projects seemed to be the most inspired; whether he'd received this month's bill from his internet provider. But his mind repeatedly found its way back to Tabitha.

What would it be like to have her hands running over his skin like this? How would it feel to have her soft, voluptuous body tucked against him with this hot water cascading over them? To have her arms and legs wrapped around him as he pounded into her?

"*Karak'duun,*" he spat, halting his hand, which had been sliding down toward his hardening shaft. He forced that hand forward instead, grasped the shower control handle, and cranked it all the way to cold.

Zevris slapped his hands on the wall and leaned into the frigid water, ignoring the icy burn as it battled the heat roiling inside him.

I am on a mission that may save my people.

I am an althicar, *one of the most disciplined, effective, and feared special operatives in the known universe.*

I am in control of myself—body and mind.

He wasn't sure how long he stood there before his blood finally cooled and his arousal faded, but he fell into a sense of clarity that was welcome after the lust-addled fog of the last forty-or-so hours.

His desire for Tabitha was undiminished; he was determined to make her his. But he could approach that matter from a rational position and figure out the best way to woo her without losing control, without going mad with lust, without taking rash action or acting on impulse. The unexpected effects of that scent had ruined his first attempt at traditional human courtship, but that did not mean all was lost.

He finished his shower, and as he dried off and combed his hair, he formulated a strategy. Would the droves of books, articles, and videos on the internet related to *picking up* females offer any help? He'd found no success with such techniques thus far, but could that simply have been a matter of unpracticed or improper application? Which information was genuine, effective, and honest?

No. He knew that his lack of success had little to do with those techniques. None of the females he'd attempted to form a relationship with had ignited a spark in him like Tabitha had. He'd never looked into a female's eyes and *known* that she would be his lifemate. Not until Tabitha.

After running the towel over his head again to wipe away any excess moisture, Zevris tossed it into the hamper and pulled on a clean pair of sweatpants.

Not for the first time, he wished this mission could've been easier, more straightforward, more...impersonal? The idea of forging a lasting relationship with an alien female was, in many ways, more intimidating than standing face-to-face with a hostile military force. At least he knew what to expect with the latter.

How much simpler this would have been were he authorized to simply take Tabitha, declare her his mate, and carry on.

He plucked the grav generator off the counter and walked into his bedroom. Now, the air in his dwelling felt pleasantly cool, a welcome balm to his formerly heated skin. He stopped in front of the wall-mounted television, pulled it away from the wall, and turned it to a sharp angle. A wave of his hand—and an invisible scan of his genetic code—deactivated the lock on the hidden wall compartment, which in turn deactivated the hologram masking its existence.

The panel—two feet wide and half as tall—slid open silently. Inside was all the equipment he'd been issued for this mission. A compact navigation device that could interface with his neural transceiver, a handful of leftover forcefield generators and sound dampeners, a long range listening and scanning device, a bundle of compact rations, a few sets of fully adjustable restraints, a communications disc, and a plasma pistol. All the items were compact and easily transported, most barely the size of his fingertip. Even the pistol could be easily disassembled into two pieces that could fit into the pockets of his jeans without rousing suspicions.

He returned the grav generator to its case and was about to close the compartment when he noticed the faint blue light within. It was emanating from the comm disc, which he'd haphazardly tossed into the compartment after his last communication with the *ultricar*.

That light meant his commanding officer needed to speak with him, likely to request another status update on the operation.

"I guess they don't want to wait until I have something important to report," he muttered as he removed the disc, clutching it loosely in his hand.

He'd made countless such reports over the years, had provided his *ultricar* with countless bits of information, had treated such communications with respect and solemnity. But he couldn't help feeling like this one would be a waste of the *ultricar's* time.

Zevris brought the comm disc downstairs, his tail still flicking restlessly as he walked. He placed the device on the coffee table—which he'd not once used for coffee—and walked into the kitchen, where he perused the various beverages in his refrigerator. Something sweet once again sounded appetizing.

Somewhere outside, a dog barked. It was strange how quickly that had become a normal sound to Zevris. It had set him on edge for days upon his arrival on Earth, stirring memories of being hunted by trained beasts on far-off worlds, memories of gnashing teeth, tearing flesh, flowing blood...

When he'd realized that most dogs were primarily interested in running through grass, chewing on toys, drooling on every object they could find, and locating the perfect place to urinate, his concerns had eased.

Stranger still, however, was that he somehow knew these particular barks were from Dexter. That only pushed his thoughts back toward the dog's owner.

I bet Tabitha is sweet...

Frowning, he selected a can of cola, closed the fridge, and popped open the tab. He sipped the drink as he walked to the couch.

He'd always firmly believed in reporting every detail, well aware that the *Exthurizen* intelligence analysts could glean some value from it that he may never have realized himself. But something about this situation... His instinct was to leave Tabitha out of his report.

Perhaps that was the human influence on him—he didn't want to *jinx* anything. He recognized it as a foolish superstition, but all the same, it was a strong acknowledgement of the fickleness of chance.

Tabitha was not yet his mate. He'd inform command of her when his relationship with her had moved a little further along.

Zevris sat down, took another sip of his drink, and set the

can down on the coffee table—with a coaster beneath it. He'd come to appreciate the table's craftsmanship and finish and wanted to preserve both as best he could. After a moment's consideration, he placed a second coaster down, moving the comm disc to rest atop it.

He pressed the button on the side of the disc. The blue light brightened as the device scanned him, confirming his identity. A moment later, a holographic projection materialized over the disc—*Ultricar* Khelvar Bathiras, Zevris's commanding officer, depicted in three dimensions from the chest up.

Zevris rested his elbows on his thighs and leaned forward. "*Ultricar*."

"*Althicar*," the *ultricar* replied. His normally stoic expression hardened around his mouth and brows, but something in his eyes softened. He continued in the Faloran tongue. "Tell me you have good news, Zevris."

It had been over a month since Zevris's last communication with his commander—over a month since he'd last heard his native language spoken aloud—but he could derive no comfort from it now. He frowned. "Little has changed, Khelvar. My continued efforts have yielded no results."

Though those Faloran words came as easily for Zevris as ever, they felt oddly alien on his tongue. That sense, though small, was jarring.

"Everything depends on this, Zevris. It is no secret. Our people are fast running out of options."

"I understand. It is why I accepted this assignment."

Khelvar lifted a hand, scratching at his cheek with his claws. It was a nervous tick the *ultricar* only displayed when circumstances were dire.

Zevris's heart quickened, and his brow furrowed. He suddenly felt as though a molten hot spike had been plunged into his chest. "Has something happened?"

"No," Khelvar replied with a dismissive flick of his fingers. "No new disasters. Just the old, slowly creeping doom."

For a few seconds, Zevris studied the *ultricar's* face. Khelvar had been an *althicar* operating in the field, already several years into his service, when Zevris's service had begun, and Zevris's first operation had been as a member of Khelvar's team. They'd known each other for a long while, but only now was Zevris beginning to notice—and understand—the subtle changes to Khelvar's face. Those changes went beyond normal aging.

The *ultricar* was tired. Perhaps not for the same reasons as Zevris, but his weariness looked just as thorough, just as heavy. It was the sort of weariness that had nothing to do with the physical; it was embedded deep in what humans called the *soul*.

"What is wrong, Khelvar?"

"Orders have been passed down. I am to extract you and embed a new *althicar* in your place."

Zevris's heart stilled. The tightness in his chest strengthened, coiling around his insides like one of Earth's constricting serpents. Of all the things he might have expected to hear, of all the bad news he might have imagined, he could never have anticipated this.

"This is not meant to stain you with dishonor, Zevris," Khelvar continued. "You are the best *althicar* with whom I have ever served. But your release from service was meant to go into effect after this final mission, and with no progress to show... Command has decided we will not keep you there indefinitely. You've done your part a dozen times over. You've more than earned your trip home."

A few days ago, Zevris might have been concerned with the potential dishonor. Failure was no source of shame for an *althicar*—so long as it was failure suffered while fighting with one's all. *Althicars'* duties placed them in immense danger, forced them to face staggering odds, all the time. But so much of the respect and fear the *Exthurizen* had built over the last two generations had been due to the tenacity displayed by its field operatives.

An *althicar* saw his mission to the end no matter what. Leaving an operation incomplete...that was not the way *althicars* conducted themselves.

But Zevris couldn't have cared less about all that now. His thoughts, his shock and concern, were turned toward Tabitha. Would he be separated from her before ever truly having a chance to win her? Would he be left with nothing more than a few memories of her?

"We have other *althicars* on Earth, do we not?" Zevris asked numbly.

Khelvar huffed and briefly bared his fangs. "You know I am not authorized to share that information."

Because of Earth's status as a developing world, races like the falorans were bound by intergalactic agreements to refrain from making contact with the planet's native species. Zevris was not supposed to be here. None of the alien beings hiding on Earth—many of whom were suspected to be fugitives and criminals—were meant to be here. To keep this operation secure, the individual *althicars* sent had not been informed of the whereabouts or identities of their comrades. The lack of knowledge would make it impossible for any *althicar* to betray the other operatives.

It was also much easier for the Azmus Protectorate to claim a single compromised *althicar* had been a rogue operative and deny responsibility.

"Has anyone made progress?"

Khelvar was silent for several seconds before replying in a

gravelly voice, "I believe you already know the answer to that question."

Zevris did, at heart. They'd all managed as much—or as little—progress as he had. He wasn't sure whether to take comfort in that shared failure or be disheartened by it.

He leaned back on the couch, tipping his head back to stare up at the ceiling. He'd made a grave mistake—he'd allowed himself to hope. He'd allowed himself to plan, if only a little, based on desires that had not yet taken root in reality.

"How long?" Zevris asked.

"Thirty days. Earth time."

"If I were to advance the mission during that time? If I were to form a mating bond?"

"Then you would effectively extend your service period." There was a moment's pause before Khelvar spoke again. "When you came to me and requested release, Zevris, you were ready to be done. I offered you this mission because you're my best, and this is important. More important than anything else. But I never meant for it to be a punishment. I hoped it would be a chance for you to find something... *more*. Something beyond what you've always known."

Zevris lifted his head to look at Khelvar.

The *ultricar* was frowning, his brow heavy and eyes concerned. "You don't need to push. This is not going to mar your record with a failure. Just...prepare to come home."

But Strion—the planet he should have called home—was the farthest thing from Zevris's mind in that moment. After eleven months of failure, he now had a mere thirty days to woo the female who had captivated him. The sudden imposition of a deadline was terrifying.

And yet...it was also another flicker of hope. He would have to work harder than ever to solve this problem—to properly court his female. It would be the final, most complex, most important undertaking of his career as an *althicar*—the most important undertaking of his life.

It really was too bad he couldn't just take Tabitha and figure out the rest later.

SEVEN

"I LOVE IT! Your new house is freaking adorable," Mia squealed through the speaker as Tabitha aimed the phone's camera at the front of the house. "They're like perfect little dollhouses all lined up."

Tabitha raised a hand and shielded her eyes from the sun as she scanned the row of houses along the street. Each home differed slightly in color and layout. They all stood two stories tall, they each had a single car garage and one tree in the front yard, though the species of tree and the shrubs and bushes around them varied from place to place. A few had iron-railed balconies on the second floor—which Tabitha was mighty jealous of.

There was just enough variety to keep the neighborhood from looking boring and uninspired, but the many similarities between properties made them all seem like pieces in a puzzle fitted neatly together.

"Huh. You're right," Tabitha said. "They do look like dollhouses."

And she absolutely loved them.

She lowered her phone and switched back to the self-facing camera as she walked toward her front door. Mia's face appeared on the screen. Her brown hair was pulled back into a ponytail, her dark brown eyes gleamed with excitement, and she wore a huge grin. Her red lipstick was a stunning contrast to her dark complexion.

"I can't wait to visit once you're all moved in," Mia said, picking up a slice of pizza off her plate and taking a bite. She chewed for a moment before moving the food to the side of her mouth to talk. "How'd the move go?"

Tabitha wrinkled her nose as she opened the door and carefully let herself into the house. Dexter jumped down from the sofa and rushed toward her, his nails tapping on the floor. She quickly shut the door before he could make a break for it.

"The movers were horrible." Tabitha scratched Dexter behind his ears and made her way into the kitchen. "They took forever unloading the truck, and they didn't pay any attention to the labels on the boxes so everything wound up scattered all over the house. *And* they weren't careful with anything." She set her cell on the phone stand atop the dining table.

"Did they break anything?" Mia asked.

Dexter walked to the patio doors. He pressed his wet nose against the glass and stared outside. His breath fogged the glass around his snout, prompting him to shift his nose aside for a clearer view. He repeated this process several times.

"A few things. I'm glad I was paranoid enough to wrap everything in an extra layer of paper and bubble wrap when I packed, or I would've lost a lot more than a couple glasses and a soap mold. Though I still have more unpacking to do, so who knows the extent of the damage." She opened the fridge, taking out a water bottle. "Oh, and they also ran over my neighbor's mailbox."

"You're kidding!"

Tabitha shook her head as she sat down at the dining table and unscrewed the cap of her water bottle. "They were horrible about it, and I don't think they even plan make it right. But that wasn't the worst of it."

"It's not? What'd they do?"

"It wasn't them, it was Dexter."

Dexter's ears perked, his tail wagged, and he turned his head toward her with his tongue dangling. He looked so sweet and innocent, but Tabitha wasn't fooled. He was mischievous to his core.

Mia's brow furrowed. "What'd that precious pup do?"

Tabitha rolled her eyes and snorted. "Precious? He peed on my neighbor's foot!"

"He did not!"

"He did."

Mia cringed. "Wow. You totally know how to make an entrance, Tabby. I hope she's not too angry?"

Tabitha tucked her loose hair behind her ear. "It's...actually a he."

She shifted her eyes to the cute little cactus with the pink flower sitting on the windowsill by the sink and smiled.

Her thoughts immediately turned to Logan. It'd been so nice of him to bring her a housewarming gift, especially considering everything that had happened, but she wasn't quite sure what to make of him and his behavior that day. There'd been moments during her conversations with him when she could have sworn he was looking at her like he wanted to, well...*devour* her. But he'd run away last time like his hair was on fire or something.

She was pretty sure that anything she'd seen on his face had just been a projection of her own wants, her own desires, that she'd only seen what she wanted to see. And Tabitha wanted Logan—badly. He was her perfect fantasy.

The only problem was...*she* wasn't any guy's perfect fantasy.

"Wait... What's this? Are you averting your eyes? Is that longing I see?" Mia asked.

Tabitha glanced at the phone, saw Mia's knowing grin, and dropped her gaze to her water bottle as her cheeks warmed. "No."

Mia leaned closer to the screen. "You liar! Oh my, God, and you're blushing! Is he cute?"

Laughter spilled from Tabitha, and she shook her head. "My dog peed on his boot, Mia!"

"Was he angry?"

"Actually...no, he wasn't."

"Then who cares! Now tell me, is he hot?"

Dexter scratched at the patio door and whined.

"Just a minute." Tabitha took a drink before setting the bottle on the table. She stood, walked to the door, and slid it open. Dexter darted outside. A gentle breeze whisked into the house, fluttering Tabitha's hair and carrying the scent of someone barbequing.

Dexter wandered toward the fence, head down as he sniffed the grass. Tabitha closed the screen door, turned around, and went back to her chair.

"He's gorgeous," Tabitha said. "I don't think I've ever seen a man so damn beautiful."

"Beautiful? Can guys be described as beautiful?" Mia took another big bite of pizza.

Tabitha chuckled and took another quick drink from her water bottle. "Yes, Mia, men can be beautiful, too. They don't all have to be hairy lumberjacks like Josh."

"Hey, I love my hairy lumberjack," Mia said with a laugh. "Okay, so describe this guy to me. Unless...you snapped a picture of him?"

"Of course not! I'm not some pervy stalker."

Mia sighed. "Alas, then you will just have to use your words, and I will have to use my imagination."

Tabitha ran the tip of her finger through the condensation on the side of the water bottle. "Well, he has black hair in a gentleman's haircut. It's a little on the longer side on top, so he usually has these strands dangling in front of his F-me blue eyes..."

"Reeeeeally? And was he giving you that fuck-me look?"

Tabitha laughed, but the fire Logan's stare had ignited in her core was still burning. He'd been standing so close to her the other day when he'd hooked her hoodie with his finger that she'd actually felt his body heat. "Stop. He's a total stranger."

"So? There's always lust at first sight." Mia snickered. "You've obviously been struck."

Tabitha grinned. "Yeah, cupid hit me with an arrow right in my lady bits. This guy's like a total fantasy come to life. He has golden skin I'd like to run my hands all over, and he's really tall, like we're talking at *least* six and a half feet."

"Shh," Mia said, putting a finger to her lips. "Don't let Josh hear you. You know how he is about his height."

"Josh isn't short."

"No, but since I'm an inch taller than him, he gets all self-conscious. Anyway, continue! I want to hear more about this sexy mystery neighbor or yours."

Warmth flooded Tabitha's cheeks. Why was she doing this? What could ever come of it? She wasn't looking for a one-night stand. She'd been someone's one-night stand once, and she'd hated it. Afterwards, she'd had this icky feeling, like she'd been used—because she had been. Worse, she'd been used as joke.

No, she'd had it with men that didn't love her for who she was, no matter her size. She wanted someone who would be her *forever*. Someone who didn't want to rush things, someone who wanted to take the time to get to know each other before jumping into bed. Someone who wanted a relationship, not just a quick lay.

Yet still...

"He's built, too. Not like a bodybuilder, but like...a sword-swinging warrior from a romance cover. And his eyes!" Tabitha propped her elbow on the table, settled her chin in her palm, and looked toward the cactus with a smile. "Oh Mia, his eyes are breathtaking. They're so blue they nearly glow."

Mia laughed. "I take it you really like Mr. Fuck-Me-Eyes. What's he like?"

Tabitha turned her gaze back to Mia and arched a brow. "I just met the guy."

"Yeah, but from your expression, you've had more than just the my-dog-pissed-on-your-foot encounter with him."

Dexter barked outside, but Tabitha ignored him as she ran her fingers through her hair and leaned back in her chair. "Logan is...strange, but in an endearing way."

"Strange how?"

"I'm not sure." She caught her bottom lip between her teeth.

Are you spoken for? Do you have a male?

"He says things differently," Tabitha said. "He has an accent, too, though it's not anything I can place. He probably just words things a little oddly sometimes because English isn't his first language."

Mia laughed. "Okay, you just made him one-hundred times hotter now that you said he has an accent. Accents *always* make men hotter."

So true.

"Anyway, enough about my neighbor. It's not like anything is going to happen." Before Mia could refute that, Tabitha hurried to asked, "How's things with Josh? He moved in, right?"

"Yeeeeeees."

"Why are you saying it like that?"

Mia grinned, lifted her hand, and brought it closer to the camera, allowing Tabitha to see the sparkling diamond ring on her ring finger.

Tabitha gasped. "He proposed?

Dexter barked again.

"He did, just last night actually," Mia said, lowering her hand.

"And you're just now telling me?" Tabitha clasped her hands to her chest, feeling both a terrible ache of longing and a warm flare of excitement. "I'm so happy for you!"

Mia looked down at her ring and smiled. Her eyes softened before she looked back at Tabitha. "You're going to be my maid of honor, right?"

Dexter's barking continued.

"It would be my honor...as long as you don't stick me in some ugly dress."

Mia laughed. "I wouldn't do that to you."

"As if I'd believe you," Tabitha said with a chuckle. "Your favorite color is orange."

"Orange is a perfectly good color!"

"I refuse to look like a pumpkin."

"But pumpkins are adorable, and so are you."

Tabitha laughed, shaking her head. "I hate you. One second, let me check on Dexter."

Capping her water, Tabitha stood up and walked to the door. She frowned as she scanned the yard for Dexter. Where was he? Sliding open the screen door, she leaned outside and called his name.

Motion caught her eye; Dexter poked his head up out of a hole in the ground next to the fence before disappearing again.

"Are you for real?" she asked, aghast. Hurrying back into the house, she moved to her phone. "Mia, I'll have to call you back another time. I swear this dog is going to be the death of me."

Mia laughed. "Okay. Enjoy your new home and talk to you soon!"

"Thanks. And congrats on your engagement! Love you. Bye!"

Tabitha ended the call and rushed back to the door. "Dexter, come!"

The dang dog ignored her.

Growling, she stepped outside, closed the screen behind her, and made her way toward Dexter. Though the cement patio was warm and dry, the grass was cool, soft, and still slightly damp from watering.

"Nan, I don't know how you put up with his antics," she muttered. "Though he does give some good cuddles and loves. Guess that makes up for *some* of this..."

Tabitha reached the hole the dog had dug, and her heart jumped. There was no Dexter.

There was no Dexter because he'd tunneled under the freaking fence and was now in her hot neighbor's yard!

"No. Nope. Cuddles and loves definitely don't make up for this."

The fence was too high for her to see over, so she leaned forward and peered between two of the wooden slats. She spotted Dexter roaming the lawn—a very nice lawn—with his tail wagging as though he didn't have a care in the world.

"Dexter! Get back here," she said, trying to instill her voice with as much authority as possible.

Dexter paused, glanced back at her, ears perked, and

continued wandering. He stopped when he reached a cluster of yellow daisies.

"Dexter. Come. Here. Now."

The dog sniffed around the daisies before pawing the ground, digging up a few of the flowers. The daisies flew behind him and fell on the grass, crumpled and limp, looking like shadows of their former selves. Dexter turned and squatted.

Tabitha's eyes widened in horror. "No! Don't you dare take a—Dexter, stop!"

Unwilling to bear further witness to the desecration of those daisies, to the desecration of her neighbor's yard, she closed her eyes.

What was she going to do now? She couldn't just walk up to Logan's door, smile, and be like, *Hi, my dog is in your back yard, and he just took a massive dump on your daisies. Good news is that his business is done, so he probably won't pee on your foot again. Mind if I go get him?* This was just another thing to add to the growing list of how horrible of a neighbor she was.

"He's going to hate me." Tabitha tipped her head back and opened her eyes. The sky was bright blue with big, puffy white clouds, far too beautiful for the defilement taking place here on the ground.

"I got this. I'll just sneak over, get Dexter, and repair the damage he did without Logan ever knowing what happened. Simple."

Okay, well, maybe not *simple*, but how hard could it be?

Tabitha darted back into the house, stuffed a doggie poop bag into her pocket, and returned to the hole Dexter had dug. She placed her hands atop the fence slats and frowned. The fence was taller than her; how was she going to get over without tearing the planks off?

Taking a deep breath, Tabitha turned her head toward the overgrown flowerbed at the back of the yard. It was a shady area with a tree in the center that had flowers, ferns, and bushes growing around it. The flowerbed also happened to be raised a couple feet above the rest of the lawn, walled in by bricks and stone.

Bingo.

She moved over to the flowerbed and climbed onto the mossy stone wall. Once she was standing atop it, the top of the fence was just above her waist. From this vantage, she could see over a few of her neighbors' fences, could see their landscaping, their décor, their barbeques and patio furniture. But only one yard mattered.

She watched as Dexter, the naughty mongrel, moseyed over to Logan's patio and jumped up onto a wide, blue-cushioned chair. He turned about in a couple circles and lay down.

Tabitha glared at him. "You're lucky I love you."

He just looked at her and yawned.

Stepping closer to the fence, Tabitha leaned forward and looked over it. Logan didn't have a raised flowerbed on his side. Just a lovely, six-foot drop to the grass. "Oh, this is going to suck."

She grasped the top of the planks with both hands, tightening her hold carefully so she wouldn't end up with palms full of splinters, and swung a leg over the fence. She extended her leg down until her toes touched one of the wooden beams that spanned the planks on the other side. Unfortunately, due to her height, that left the top of the slats digging into her crotch and ass.

Tabitha winced. "So glad these are flat."

Pushing her weight down on her toes, she lifted her other leg over the fence, and once it was clear, she lowered that foot onto the beam beside the other.

"Okay. Nearly there, Tabby." Taking a deep breath, she let go of the fence and hopped down onto the grass.

Her feet slammed onto the ground. The impact was jarring enough that it made her teeth clack together; it was the only sensation she had time to register before her feet slipped out from beneath her, unable to find traction on the damp grass. Tabitha's eyes rounded, and she gasped. Her heart stopped as the world tilted. Then she hit the ground, and all the air rushed out of her lungs, stunning her, leaving her unable to breathe.

She lay there staring up at the sky, remaining entirely still, and she'd swear that there were little stars dancing above her.

Is this really how it ends for me? Killed by a three-foot fall into grass?

Her body jolted as the shock wore off, and she took in a deep, gasping breath, filling her lungs with sweet, sweet air. She clutched a hand to her chest, just to confirm that her heart was beating, and she was still alive.

"That dog *is* going to be the death me of," she whispered.

Get up, Tabby. How much more mortified will you be if Logan comes out right now and sees you like this?

With a grunt, Tabitha rolled onto her hands and knees, brushed a hand on her pants, and ran her finger through her hair to tug it back from her face. She carefully got to her feet, wiping clingy blades of grass off her jeans. The denim covering her ass was wet, and her shirt clung to her back. The slight breeze blowing against it made a shiver course through her. Tugging on the hem of her shirt, she unpeeled the damp fabric from her skin.

"I'll just have to do that one more time," she said with a cringe. "And hopefully not break my neck in the process."

Tabitha turned toward Logan's patio—toward the dog blissfully curled up on a cushy chair.

Dexter was so grounded. No treats for at least a month. It didn't matter how many puppy-eyed looks he gave her.

She hurried across the lawn to the house, pressing up against the siding. Dexter looked at her and tilted his head. His tail wagged.

She pursed her lips, giving him a narrow-eyed glare.

You are in trouble, she mouthed.

He just licked his chops.

She checked the window next to her; it was thankfully closed and covered by blinds. She ducked beneath it to be safe, and only as she was creeping closer to Dexter did she realize the sliding glass door ahead was open, with only the screen closed. Logan's baritone voice was coming from inside, along with another unfamiliar voice.

Damn it.

Feeling like the nosiest neighbor in history, Tabitha listened to the muffled conversation. At first, she wondered if it was simply a matter of poor acoustics making it difficult to decipher their words, but she soon understood that they weren't speaking English at all. It was a foreign language unlike anything she'd ever heard. There was a lyrical quality to it, but some of the words bore harsh edges that kept the language from being wholly musical.

Still, she couldn't help herself. She was brimming with curiosity. Brows creased, Tabitha eased closer to the door and peered inside. Her eyes widened.

The interior lights were off, and with the curtains drawn it was relatively dark within—which only made the glowing holo-gram stand out even more. The image was reminiscent of an old sci-fi movie redone in high definition—a man's disembodied head and shoulders in 3D, projected from Logan's coffee table. The man was wearing some sort of strange uniform she didn't recognize, and the tips of his ears tapered into points that would've put Legolas to shame. His eyes were glowing amber.

That alone wasn't so crazy. Maybe...maybe Logan was just a technophile or something, into really cutting-edge technology. Maybe he was playing a game. The latest in in-home 3D entertainment.

But then Tabitha's gaze shifted to Logan, who was seated on the couch in front of the hologram. He had been sitting back against the cushions, face tipped toward the ceiling, but as she watched, he leaned forward. He was shirtless, his sculpted muscles on full display, though she wasn't really able to ogle them like she would've liked. Because there were strange, tribal-like tattoos on his arms—*glowing* tattoos.

Okay, so...maybe he likes to wear glow-in-the-dark body paint while he's hanging out at home?

She caught a glimpse of his eyes and immediately understood that he was not wearing glowing body paint. His eyes were an even more intense blue than before, and they were putting out their own light, perfectly matching the color of the markings on his arms.

And his ears were pointed, just like the man in the hologram—though Logan's were adorned with a few gleaming piercings.

Tabitha couldn't move, couldn't take her eyes off Logan, as he stood up. Two things struck her immediately—his nipples were pierced, too, and he had a freaking *tail* flicking through the air behind him like he was an agitated cat.

No, not a cat. A lion. Complete with a tuft of fur at the tip of his tail.

He and the man in the hologram exchanged a few more words, and the hologram vanished.

Logan sighed and lifted a hand to the back of his neck,

rubbing it and shaking his head. There were dark claws on the tips of his fingers.

Just when she'd thought he couldn't possibly get any hotter...

What was she *thinking?* He...he wasn't human!

Maybe he's just a secretive but really, really serious cosplayer?

Damn it, Tabby, get the dog and get out of there!

Dexter, ever helpful, chose that moment to bark.

Logan's head snapped toward the door.

Tabitha's heart stopped. For an instant, all she could see of his face were those glowing orbs, so inhuman, so terrifying, so breathtaking. Ice formed in her veins.

Tail stilling, Logan spat a single word—one with which Tabitha was quite familiar.

"*Fuck.*"

He darted toward the door.

Tabitha let out a little cry that was *definitely* not a frightened shriek and shoved away from the house. Dexter leapt from the chair and ran in front of her as she raced back toward the fence.

The screen door slammed against its frame. "Tabitha!"

Arms pumping, breath short, and heart pounding, Tabitha pushed her ass faster than she ever had in her life.

Why did I never take that horror movie advice and work on my damned cardio?

Dexter, the traitor that he was, crawled through the hole under the fence, disappearing.

Tabitha threw her arms out, grabbing at the top of the fence as she lifted a foot to step on the lower support beam. She was almost there, just a little farther...

A powerful arm banded around her middle from behind. She gasped. As though her strength and weight were meaningless, she was plucked away from the fence. Both her feet were suddenly a long way from the ground.

Before she could even scream, a big hand clamped over her mouth.

I'm dead.

EIGHT

Curse words in half a dozen languages tumbled through Zevris's mind as he pulled Tabitha against him. She struggled wildly, kicking her legs and swinging her arms. Her breath was hot against his palm as she tried to scream.

He couldn't help but notice how well she fit against him—how her luscious backside was pressed firmly to his pelvis, as though it were meant to be there.

Damn it, if there is a right time for such thoughts, this is not *it!*

He knew what he had to do in this situation; he'd trained for this inevitability, had dealt with it in the past. He'd been exposed. He'd exposed himself.

That thought only had him cursing in his head again—the English phrase *exposed himself* was often used with a very specific meaning by modern humans, and he most certainly hadn't done *that*.

Zevris gritted his teeth and growled in pain as Tabitha grabbed a fistful of his hair and yanked. He turned his head sharply, rewarding himself with another flare of pain on his scalp, but thankfully broke her hold.

As her struggles intensified, he tightened his hold on her and said, "Enough, Tabitha. I am not going to harm you."

For a moment, it seemed as though she were complying. Her thrashing ceased, and she drew in a deep, ragged breath through her nostrils.

"Good," he soothed. "Just breathe, and—"

She released that breath in a scream so powerful that it nearly forced his hand away from her mouth. Her muscles strained, and her body trembled against him.

Zevris's brows fell low. He glanced from side to side and up at the nearby second-story windows, scanning his surroundings; he was tall enough to look over the six-foot-tall privacy fences, and no other humans were in sight. But it was only a matter of time before one of the neighbors was alerted to this situation and it became even messier.

Tabitha's muffled scream finally ended, and she relaxed. The reprieve was short lived. Not a second later, she resumed her struggles with renewed strength.

Releasing another growl, Zevris turned and carried her toward his dwelling.

As they reached the open door, Tabitha lifted her legs and spread them wide, planting one foot on the door frame and the other on the screen door. That stance only pressed her more firmly against him. This was not how he'd envisioned having her body flush with his; these were not the circumstances for which he'd longed.

Zevris pushed forward, and she poured surprising strength into her legs, halting his momentum. The weak frame of the screen door buckled under her foot, causing part of it to pop off the rails.

Though he could have easily overpowered her, doing so

would have placed her at risk of injury, and Zevris had not lied. He would never hurt Tabitha. He took a step backward, and her legs fell, one of her heels bumping his shin. Spinning around, he walked through the doorway backward.

Tabitha said something against his hand—he wasn't certain, but it sounded like a curse—and threw her legs up again, hooking her feet on either side of the doorway. Her resistance slowed Zevris for a moment, but she could not find strong enough purchase to stop him this time. Both her feet slipped, and again her legs fell, but not before he saw the angry red lines on the tops of her feet.

A pang of guilt struck his chest, yet he did not hesitate. He turned around again, putting his back to the door, and curled the end of his tail around the handle. With a twist of his hips, he dragged the glass door shut. A flick of his tail engaged the lock, and a signal from his neural transceiver activated the forcefields at every door and window in the residence along with the sound dampeners.

Now that his dwelling was secure, he took a moment to breathe. He should've been used to things going wrong so quickly, should've been accustomed to sudden bursts of action, but his stay on Earth had been so quiet, so peaceful, so uneventful, that he'd let his guard down.

Why had she been in his yard? Why had she happened to come just then, when he was uncloaked and speaking to his commander, the one time he'd forgotten to close the door?

A sharp pain on his hand swept those questions aside. Zevris hissed through his fangs as the pain intensified—he'd never imagined how much a bite from those relatively flat human teeth could hurt, but Tabitha was certainly demonstrating the potential now.

He dropped her onto her feet as he attempted to pry his hand from the viselike hold of her teeth, which had clamped down over part of his palm and the knuckle of his pointer finger. Zevris didn't realize his mistake until it was too late. Her new position meant her backside was no longer against his pelvis.

Tabitha twisted her torso aside and swung her hand backward. Her fist struck his scrotum—which was offered no protection by his sweatpants—with the force of one of those huge wrecking balls humans used to demolish buildings.

A supernova of pain blasted outward from the point of impact, so overwhelming that it dropped Zevris to a knee. Tabitha wrenched herself out of his hold and ran for the front door.

Again, when he'd yearned for her touch on his cock, he'd had something rather different in mind. He clenched his teeth and cupped his groin, trying to breathe through the pain as his runaway mate-to-be tugged on the doorknob and fumbled with the locks.

"Someone help me!" She pounded the door with her fists.

"Tabitha," Zevris rasped, bracing a hand on his knee and shoving himself back to his feet. His stomach lurched, and a tight, impossibly heavy lump of agony sank low in his belly. He forced himself toward her.

She turned her head and caught sight of him. Her eyes widened, and after a brief search, she grabbed the carved stone tray—meant primarily to hold house keys—from atop the stand beside the door and raised it as though it were a weapon. The keys that had been in the tray fell to the floor with a jangling clank.

"Stay away," she warned.

Zevris paused in the entrance of the foyer, placing a hand on the wall to steady himself as another wave of agony nearly made him double over. "I need you to calm down, Tabitha."

"And I need you to let me out. Now."

He trailed his gaze over her. Blades of grass clung to her bare feet, her shirt was slightly twisted, and part of its hem had worked its way under the waistband of her pants. Her hair was loose and wild around her heaving shoulders, and her face was flushed.

He'd wanted to see her like this, but he'd wanted it to be in the wake of their mating, not after he'd been forced to take her prisoner against her will. Not with that fear gleaming in her eyes.

Zevris clenched his jaw, and his nostrils flared with a heavy exhalation. "We both know I cannot."

"You can. Just...just open the door. Please. I never saw anything."

"Tabitha..." He took another step toward her.

She hurled the stone tray at him.

He shoved away from the wall. Even for beings as tough as falorans, the tray was heavy enough—and jagged enough in some spots—to have caused serious injury.

The tray *whooshed* through the air mere inches from his face, and his eyes followed it as it struck the wall, punching a deep gouge in the drywall, and fell to the floor with a heavy thud. It left a few noticeable dents and scratches on the floorboards. Flakes of the slate-like material lay scattered on the floor around the tray.

Brows low, Zevris returned his attention to Tabitha.

Her eyes were wide, her mouth agape. She looked from the tray to the hole in the wall and finally met Zevris's gaze. For a moment, she seemed on the verge of apologizing.

Instead, she bent forward and snatched the keys off the floor. He did not understand why, considering the keyholes were on the exterior side of the door, until she took the keyring in her palm and positioned the keys to jut out from between the fingers of her closed fist like metal claws.

A grin teased at Zevris's lips, but he held it back. *My mate has claws.*

Apparently, humans were adept at improvising weapons even when they were not combat trained. That was valuable information. But he didn't waste time considering it further—he didn't want any more damage inflicted upon his dwelling, didn't want any more damage inflicted upon his body, and most certainly didn't want any more damage inflicted upon Tabitha.

As she stood upright, Zevris darted toward her.

She gasped and thrust her arm out, swinging her little fist and its key-claws at him, but she wasn't fast enough.

Catching her wrist in one hand, Zevris tugged her extended arm out further, forcing her to take a stumbling step forward. His leg was there to meet hers. Tabitha cried out and fell face first, throwing her free arm out in front of her to brace for the impact.

Zevris spun so he was behind her, looping an arm around her waist to ease her fall. She landed lightly on her hand and knees. He lowered himself atop her, his pelvis once again pressed against her enticing backside, and forced her flat on the floor, pinning her in place with his body.

Before she could react, he shifted his hand to hers and pried the keys from her grasp. He tossed them toward the stand in the corner blindly. All that mattered was that they were out of her reach.

She wiggled beneath him, her ass rubbing against his groin and sending ripples of pleasure—laced with lingering pain—through his cock. He tightened his hold on her and pressed his face into her hair. Her scent enveloped him like a cloud, dominating his senses.

Heated blood rushed to his shaft, which throbbed and hardened with blossoming desire.

"Tabitha," he groaned and ground his erection against her.

Her breath hitched, and she stilled. "W-What are you doing?"

Zevris clenched his jaw. All he had to do was lift his head, and he could find an escape from her maddening fragrance, he could find some clarity. But he could not bring himself to do so. The feel of her silky, tousled hair tickling his skin and her soft, warm body beneath his was too delightful to end. He curled his tail around her calf.

Ah, no. Not like this. No.

He snarled and pushed himself back, taking not even a second to think as he lifted Tabitha over his shoulder and stood upright. She gasped and slapped her hands against his bare back, producing a sting as thrilling as it was painful. Zevris's tail darted up, coiled around her wrists, and forced them together.

"I will not harm you, Tabitha," he grated through his fangs.

As he climbed the stairs, she begged him to let her go, begged him to release her, swore she would never say a word about any of this. By the time he reached his bedroom—it couldn't have taken more than half a minute—his chest ached, and his gut was churning.

Karak'duun, I didn't actually want *to kidnap her!*

As unsuccessful as he'd been in wooing human females before now, he was fairly certain this was not the way to proceed. But he knew with equal certainty what was expected of him. Tabitha had seen him without his holoshroud activated. She had likely seen the *ultricar.*

She was a threat not just to him and his mission, but to the *Exthurizen,* to the faloran people. If she spoke to anyone about what she'd seen...

He would have had to reveal himself to her eventually, had things gone as he'd hoped. But that would've been after building mutual trust, after knowing she would safeguard his secret. Their relationship hadn't quite reached that point. All his training, all his experience, told him there was only one way to handle this for sure.

But Zevris refused to follow that course of action. He would not lose Tabitha. He would do everything he could to court her, to gain her trust, to make her see that he was not her enemy...

Zevris smoothed his palm up her thigh, stopping it just below her ass, and squeezed.

He would make her see that she was *his*.

He opened the hidden compartment behind the television and removed the adjustable restraints. They'd simply been part of his kit; he'd never anticipated using them, and he didn't want to use them now.

Don't humans sometimes like to be bound during mating?

He cast aside that thought. He had no idea if Tabitha enjoyed that sort of thing, and, again, this seemed a highly inappropriate time to be considering such matters. And he was sure that mating was the *last* thing currently on her mind.

Zevris carried her to the bed, unwound his tail from her wrists, and dropped her atop the bedding. She let out a startled little gasp as she bounced on the mattress. He leapt onto the bed before she could recover, straddling her and using his weight to hold her in place. When she slammed her hands against his chest to push at him, he touched a restraint to each of her wrists. Commanded by his neural transceiver, the bindings' material snaked around her pale flesh and sealed itself to make closed loops.

"What are you doing?" she asked, her voice rising in panic as she looked at her wrists. She bucked beneath him, but he didn't budge. "No!"

He leaned forward, drawing the loose end of the binding on her left wrist to the corner of the bed. She tried to pull her arm away, but she couldn't match his strength. He attached the restraint to the post on the slatted headboard. Tabitha's breaths came quick and hot, fanning across his chest. Zevris did his best to ignore the way her body felt beneath his, especially now that her full breasts were pressed against his abdomen.

Tabitha went incredibly still. "Logan, please don't do this."

He placed a hand on the headboard's upper rail, fingers trembling as he struggled to keep from crushing the wood in his grasp. "Zevris."

"What?"

"My name is Zevris Akkaran," he said, forcing himself back into motion. He drew the restraint on her right wrist toward the other bedpost. "Logan Ellis is an alias."

"What...what *are* you?"

The binding secured itself to the post. Zevris hesitated for another moment, closing his eyes. She was right here beneath him, in his bed, her body against his...

Muttering a curse, he shoved himself away from the headboard and rolled off Tabitha. He stood up and stepped away from the bed the instant his feet touched the floor. He didn't let himself look at her, not yet; not while her scent was still lingering in his nostrils, not while his skin still thrummed with her warmth, not while traces of that mysterious pheromone remained in his system.

"I am a faloran. My race comes from a planet very, very far from Earth."

"So you're...an alien."

He walked to the open compartment, tossed in the extra restraints, and closed the panel. "I am."

There was a soft rustling on the bedding, and Tabitha's bindings creaked against the wooden headboard. "Are you going to kill me?"

That question struck him hard, landing like a blow to the chest. He knew its impact was only intensified by it being wholly valid—and the fact that, were he following protocol, he would have killed her already.

He whipped his face toward her, and when he spoke, his voice was harsh and raw. "*No. Never.*"

Her brows creased, and the corners of her lips turned down as her eyes moved over him. "Are...you going to probe me?"

Zevris stared at her; she was laid upon his bed like an offering, arms spread to either side and hair fanned around her head. His cock twitched with want, and his skin tingled with the memory of how her body had felt against him.

How would she look were she unclothed? How would she look were she...open to him, thighs spread, sex bared, her lush breasts thrust forward, with desire gleaming in her eyes?

Oh, he wanted to probe her, but not in the way she had implied.

He drew in a deep breath and turned to face her fully, taking a step toward the bed. "Truly, Tabitha, I mean you no harm. We...can work through this situation together, if we both remain calm."

"You have me tied to your bed, Logan!"

"My name is Zevris," he corrected as gently as he could, "and this is not the way I wanted things to go between us. But my mission will be compromised if I let you go."

"What do you mean? What mission? Why...why are you here?"

Zevris tipped his face toward the ceiling and paced at the foot of the bed, his body assailed by alternating waves of tension and lust. His tail flicked back and forth in stilted motions. He was going against everything he knew in this, but if Tabitha was to be his mate, he needed to be honest with her.

"My people were devastated by a virus a few generations ago that killed most of our females. The effects of it have only strengthened over the years, and now we find ourselves facing eventual extinction. I was sent here to..." He halted, sighed, and swung his gaze to Tabitha. "I was sent here to make a human female my mate so we can learn whether your people are compatible with ours. My efforts have been unsuccessful thus far."

Tabitha stared at him silently, brows creased. "So...you're here, disguising yourself as a human, so you can...*breed* with one?"

"No, to *mate* with one," he corrected. "The, uh...breeding would potentially come later. Our scientists do not even know if it is possible."

"You have the technology to travel through space to get here and to disguise yourself as a human, and some high-tech tools"—she glanced up at one of her wrists, giving it a twist—"but you can't, like...make babies in tubes or something?"

"We cannot. For our people to reproduce, a mating bond must be made. It triggers a biochemical reaction that enables fertilization, and that reaction cannot be artificially replicated."

She sighed, closing her eyes briefly as she relaxed her arms. "What is a mating bond? Is that your form of marriage?"

He resumed his pacing, though his tail's movements were a little less erratic. "No. The mating bond is for life. It cannot be undone once it is made, and it is forged through a process some-what more intimate than the exchange of vows and rings."

Tabitha's gaze followed him. Thankfully, the fear he'd seen in her eyes had faded, leaving only wariness.

"If you're successful, and you make this bond and are able to impregnant a woman, what then? Are you planning to bring more of your people here, all disguised as humans?" Her eyes rounded. "Or are you going to start abducting people?"

Once again, Zevris halted, this time running a hand through his hair and letting the tips of his claws drag across his scalp. "I am not planning anything, Tabitha. We're not here to harm humans or start a war. We're not even supposed to be here at all, as underdeveloped civilizations are deemed off-limits by several intergalactic governmental associations.

"But my people's need is dire. My mission is simple, and it is as I have stated. And if my people intended to abduct anyone, don't you think it would have made more sense to do that early in the process, rather than leave me here for almost a year failing to make any sort of meaningful connection with Earth females until—"

He pressed his lips together, silencing himself.

"Until what, Zevris?" she asked.

Closing his eyes, he allowed himself a moment to relish the sound of his name from her lips, barely suppressing the pleasurable shudder threatening to course down his spine. When he opened his eyes, he met her gaze. "Until you, Tabitha."

Her eyes flared, and she balled her hands into fists, once more tugging on her restraints. "W-What do you mean *until me?*"

Keeping his gaze locked on her, Zevris moved to the bedside. He reached down, meaning to brush the backs of his fingers across her cheek, but she flinched away from his hand. He knew the pang of hurt in his chest wasn't justified; he had captured her and tied her to his bed. She had every right to pull away from him.

Curling his fingers into a loose fist, he withdrew his hand. "I was attempting to court you, Tabitha. I have encountered no female who has set my blood ablaze as you have, none who have captivated me as you have. I'd intended to ask you on a date, to follow your human customs, to gain your trust, and reveal everything to you in time, but circumstances have made all that impossible."

With her eyebrows furrowed, Tabitha drew her legs closer

and slowly pulled herself up, leaning her back against the head-board. "You...chose *me*?"

"Yes."

She leaned toward him, and some of her long hair fell over her shoulder. "Then just let me go. I won't say anything to anyone. I swear."

He shook his head. "You know too much, Tabitha. I can't let you go. You...are now mine."

She yanked on the bindings, baring her teeth. Her position thrust her breasts out toward Zevris, and he couldn't stop his gaze from briefly dipping to them.

"Damn it, Zevris, you can't do this! You kidnapped me, have me tied to your bed, and...and you just expect me to want to have your babies?"

"Eventually."

Tabitha gaped at him. "You're insane."

Zevris leaned over her, bracing himself on one hand while he caught her chin with the other. She struggled to pull away, but he held firm. "And you are beautiful."

She stilled, staring up at him.

"I want you, Tabitha. I crave to know your touch, thirst for your taste, and yearn to make you mine. I have chosen you to be my lifemate, and it is my mission to make it so."

She shivered, releasing a short, sharp breath.

Zevris lowered his face until it was mere inches from hers and stroked the shallow cleft in her chin. "I would never hurt you, but I can't let you go. Not yet."

"This is wrong. Just let me go. Please, Zevris."

He moved his thumb to her plump bottom lip and traced it, hungering more than anything to feel it against his own...but not until she was willing. "I will win you."

"People are going to wonder where I am. You can't keep me here."

"I must, Tabitha." Withdrawing his hand from her face, he pushed himself off the bed and walked toward the door.

He would have loved to remain here with her for hours, would have loved to talk with her until she understood the situation, until she understood that he had no choice—and that they could make something meaningful of this. But having to abruptly kidnap his human neighbor presented several other matters that now required his attention, and it was best to see to all of it sooner rather than later.

"Where are you going?" she asked, a hint of fear creeping into her voice.

"I will be back soon, Tabitha. Do not worry." Zevris opened the bedroom door.

Tabitha yanked on her restraints hard enough to shake the bed. "Let me go!"

He did not respond as he stepped out of the room and closed the door behind him. Her shouts, only faintly muffled by the door, followed him into the hall.

"Help! Someone help me!"

Zevris turned toward the door, leaning his forehead against it. Hearing her pleas was heart wrenching, and knowing that he was the cause for her fear, her distress, her helplessness...

His hand crept toward the doorknob.

"*Svesh,*" he growled, stilling his hand. He closed his fist, digging his claws into his palm, shoved away from the door, and walked down the stairs. How had he fucked this up so badly?

NINE

Frowning, Zevris crouched and brushed his fingertips across the gouges on the floor. They were deeper than he'd initially thought—not that he'd been very focused on the damage while it was being inflicted. He could perform the necessary repairs on his own, and, at worst, would have to make an extra trip to the hardware store. But those repairs were the least of his concerns.

Laying a rug on the floor and hanging a painting on the wall would suffice for the time being. He could mask the damage.

Just as he should've been masking himself.

He grunted, picked up the fallen stone tray, and rose to carry it over to the stand beside the front door. After returning the tray to its place, Zevris bent down to pluck his keys off the floor. He dropped them onto the tray with a heavy sigh.

His carelessness today—his carelessness as of late—was inexcusable. Perhaps he could have placed the blame upon Tabitha for trespassing and spying on him, but her actions shouldn't have made any difference. Had Zevris been maintaining the appropriate level of caution all along, she could've wandered the perimeter of his dwelling, looking into every window, listening at every door, and never would have seen or heard anything to alert her to his true nature.

No, none of this was her fault. Zevris was the fool who'd left the back door open while he was undisguised and speaking with the *ultricar*.

She was still yelling in his bedroom, calling for him, calling for help. After all the things he'd done, all the death and destruction he'd wrought in the name of his people, he'd never felt as monstrous as he did now. Dragging Tabitha into his dwelling and binding her to his bed seemed the most heinous act of all.

So why did some deep, primal part of him like it? Why did that part of him like having Tabitha beneath him, having her at his mercy, having her staring up at him with her cheeks flushed and hair tousled?

His feelings were a chaotic jumble, as they'd so often been during his stay on Earth. He hated what he'd had to do, and he felt guilty for doing it—and for not doing enough. He was frustrated with himself, with the mission, with the universe. Yet he still thrummed with desire for Tabitha. That undiminished want only further complicated his feelings.

This was what he'd wanted, wasn't it? Tabitha in his home, in his bed?

He followed a trail of scattered blades of grass and wet, incomplete footprints from the front door to the back, reversing the path of Tabitha's frantic flight through his dwelling. She'd surprised him; she'd made him proud. Though she was not a warrior, she had put up a valiant struggle, and had shown a strong spirit at her core that had only made her that much more attractive to him.

After tucking his tail into his pants, Zevris activated his holoshroud, deactivated the forcefield before him, and unlocked the glass door. It slid open smoothly, nearly silent. The screen door beyond it was another matter. Its warped frame jittered and scraped the rails as he tried to pull it closed, sticking so firmly after moving a few halting inches that he simply gave up and shoved it off the railing completely.

Stepping onto the patio, he set the misshapen screen door aside, closed the sliding door, and reengaged the forcefield.

The cool breeze was still flowing, gently rustling the vegetation behind his yard. Big, fluffy white clouds rolled across the cerulean sky, drifting leisurely; they were carefree. The sun was bright and clear but not hot, making everything seem more vibrant. It was a beautiful day on Earth, a peaceful one—at least in this little part of the world.

All Zevris had to do was step back inside and that sense of peace would be gone.

Tabitha's words echoed in his mind. *People are going to wonder where I am.*

He raked his fingers through his hair and growled. His lack of knowledge concerning Tabitha had been a source of limitless intrigue less than ten minutes ago, and now it was a liability. Friends, family, coworkers, neighbors, debt collectors, the mailperson—there were so many people she might have been connected to who would eventually notice her absence. Once the local authorities were tipped off, it would not be long before they knocked on Zevris's door to ask questions.

He'd need to learn as much as he could about her as quickly as possible, and he would need to use that knowledge to somehow keep up the pretense that nothing was wrong. He would have to somehow prevent the people who cared about her from becoming suspicious.

"That'll be simple," he grumbled. "As simple as this whole damned mission."

And yet his greatest concern was for Tabitha herself. How

could he make her comfortable, how could he best tend to her needs, how could he make this unfortunate situation as pleasant for her as possible—or at the very least, how could he mitigate the unpleasantness?

The only way for Zevris to have her, to keep her, to stay with her forever, was through a mating bond. It was only a matter of time before she became his mate, before they made that bond. There was no other choice. But that process would be far more enjoyable—and far faster—if he showed her that he would tend to all her needs. If he showed her that he cared for her.

If he was unsuccessful in those endeavors...what would *Exthurizen* Command do with a human who knew of the falorans' existence, of their presence on Earth, of their objectives?

Zevris knew the answer to that question, but he refused to acknowledge it. He would not let anyone harm Tabitha.

All uncertainty had to be cast aside. It made no difference that faloran scientists didn't know if humans could form mating bonds with falorans; it *had* to work. And Zevris only had thirty days to make it happen.

A foul odor struck his nose as he neared the flowerbed, halting Zevris in his tracks. He looked down to see several of his daisies uprooted and a large, fresh pile of feces in their place.

He gritted his teeth and swallowed the anger rising from his gut. As silly as it seemed, he was proud of his garden. He'd spent many hours kneeling in the dirt to plant seeds, bulbs, and seedlings, had read countless articles to learn which plants were best suited to this region and how to tend them, had fine-tuned the sprinkler system to ensure they received the water they required. He'd made extra trips to the Hardware Emporium to buy plants, fertilizers, and soil.

All that had started because his understanding had been that untended property drew unwanted attention, but he'd come to enjoy the work. Like woodworking, it was simple, soothing, and satisfying.

He'd not put in all that labor for a dog to dig up his flowerbed and shit in it.

Zevris strode to the fence, bracing his hands atop it, and peered over. Tabitha's yard was plain and unkempt. The grass, having been left uncut, was shaggy and overgrown in several places, and the raised flowerbed at the rear of the yard was brimming with vegetation—flowers, bushes, and weeds gone wild, all gathered around a central tree. With a little tending, the spot would've been lovely.

For a moment, he wondered what Tabitha had planned to do with her yard. Would she have planted flowers? Would she have tended her plants regularly? Would she have simply left it to the dog?

His eyes met Dexter's. The dog, who was lying on Tabitha's patio with his tongue lolling, tilted his head questioningly.

"You and I are going to need to reach an understanding," Zevris said. He scanned his surroundings, checking for onlookers, and drew himself over the fence smoothly.

Dexter did not move save to wag his tail.

Failed to protect his human, failing to protect his home. This is no guard beast.

Brows falling low, Zevris walked across the grass, approaching Dexter directly. The dog's ears perked, and his tail sped. Dexter and Zevris stared at one another for several seconds. A strange, faint itching sensation soon pulsed along Zevris's tail, the sort of feeling that almost compelled it into motion—as though he subconsciously longed to wag it, just like the dog was wagging his.

"No. I refuse," he said.

Dexter made a soft whining sound, keeping his big, dark eyes on Zevris.

"I also refuse to have a rivalry with an animal," he contin-ued. "You are my female's beast, and so you will defer to me as your master. Do you understand?"

The dog's tail thumped the concrete beneath him, and a tendril of drool oozed from his tongue to splatter on the ground.

"This world has driven me to madness," Zevris snapped as he walked past Dexter to Tabitha's back door. The screen was closed, but the glass door behind it was wide open.

Claws softly clacking on the concrete signaled that Dexter was following. Zevris twisted to look back at the dog, jabbing a finger toward the animal. "Behave."

If Dexter had any intention of complying with the command, he made no indication. Perhaps that was why dogs were considered humankind's best friends—they were just as headstrong and difficult to read as their human owners.

Leaning close to the screen, Zevris sniffed the air. Though there were traces of many scents inside her home—far more than he could identify, but most of which were pleasant—he thankfully did not detect the one that had thrown him into that lustful frenzy.

Zevris opened the screen door and stepped inside. Dexter sauntered in behind him, brushed past Zevris's legs, and continued into the kitchen, where he dipped his head to lap noisily from a water-filled bowl on the floor. Zevris slid the glass door shut and looked around.

Tabitha's walls were painted a different color than Zevris's, and the floorboards were a paler, warmer wood, but the similar-ities outnumbered the difference. The layouts of the two resi-dences were almost identical mirrors of one another.

There were numerous cardboard containers in sight; some were stacked neatly, some were open with flaps askew, some were flattened and piled haphazardly. Wadded papers and sheets of plastic were scattered about, as well. Zevris might have mistaken this for disorganization, but he realized quickly that she'd still been in the process of unpacking her belongings. He could see signs everywhere of her having been creating order out of chaos.

His gaze settled on her dining table. He stepped over to it, reached down, and plucked her phone from its stand at the center of the table. When he attempted to unlock the device, he was greeted by a screen asking for a passcode.

Releasing a huff, he roused his neural transceiver and initiated a connection with the phone. As simple as it was to hack human technology, Zevris didn't like doing so with his neural transceiver; human devices were especially vulnerable to malicious software, and he had no desire to have whatever garbage they flung through their virtual networks get stuck in his head. Who knew what viruses and corruptions could affect him?

Once the phone's code had been cracked, he severed the connection between the device and his neural transceiver and entered the code with his thumb. The display opened on Tabitha's home screen.

As Dexter's loud drinking gave way to eating of equal volume—and considerably more crunchiness—Zevris looked through Tabitha's phone. The busiest form of communication for her seemed to be her email, which was filled with order submissions, payment and shipping confirmations, and message notifications from various social media platforms. Her contacts list was small but well organized, and her message and call history were sparse, both consisting primarily of calls and text messages to and from a contact labeled *Mia Jones*.

There were no contacts marked as *Brother* or *Sister*, none labeled *Mother* or *Father*. Only one seemed to have any family connection—Nan. Zevris seemed to recall it being synonymous with grandmother.

Curious, he went to the text thread associated with Nan,

and frowned as he noticed the date of the last message—slightly over two years ago.

Nan had texted, *I'm so glad you stopped by this weekend, hon. Dexter misses you already! If you're still having trouble keeping up with those orders, let me know. I'm not too old to pitch in and teach you a thing or two more.*

Tell Dex I'm still mad at him for eating the turkey off my sandwich, Tabitha had replied with a little laughing face. *It was nice to be home for a little while. And I may have to take you up on that offer. Things are picking up! It's not enough to quit my day job or anything yet, but who knows? Maybe one day. Love you!*

Love you too, Nan had sent two minutes later, the words surrounded by pink hearts.

The last message on the thread was from ten days afterward, sent by Tabitha.

I know this is stupid, and all I'm going to do is sit here hoping that I'll get some kind of response, but...I really miss you. I really, really miss you, so much that I can barely breathe. I know you urged me to find my own way, to make my own life, but you were always there for me anyway, and I just don't know how to keep going without you. I miss you, Nan.

Zevris stared down at the screen, a tightness seizing his chest that he couldn't quite define. He'd spent his years as an *althicar* spying, infiltrating, sabotaging, and waging what the humans called *guerilla warfare* on numerous planets. He'd found compromising information of both political and personal nature on numerous targets, but he'd never felt this sense of wrongness in doing so.

He'd just intruded on something deeply private. On something no one was meant to see. As simple as that last message had been, he could not ignore the weight of emotion it bore.

Because that message—and the inactivity afterward—made it easy to infer what had happened to Nan.

Exhaling slowly, he exited the messages, locked the screen, and slipped the phone into his pocket. The tightness in his chest didn't fade as he resumed his search of the house; in fact, it only strengthened when he noticed the framed pictures on display. Several were of Tabitha and an older woman with grayish hair but the same green eyes. That older female appeared in a number of the other photographs in which her hair was light brown instead of gray, often alongside a young girl with blond hair and emerald eyes.

There was one in which the pair were standing in front of a huge, misshapen witch's head, looking as though they were about to be swallowed by the gaping mouth—though their exaggerated expressions could not hide the smiles in their eyes. Another showed the two on a beach with the ocean behind them, their hair swept to the side by the wind.

Realization struck him suddenly—the young female was Tabitha in her youth, and the older female must've been Nan. The happiness on their faces in all those pictures was in total contrast to the sorrow in that final text from Tabitha.

He picked up one of the picture frames and tilted it to eliminate the glare on its glass. The photo was of Nan and Tabitha—the latter clearly younger than she was now, but not by much—holding a little dog in their arms as it licked at Tabitha's face. The position of Tabitha's right arm suggested she'd been holding the camera that had captured the image.

Zevris looked at Dexter, who was lying on the floor near the food and water bowls. "You were cuter as a pup."

Dexter released a huff that flapped his lips before lowering his chin onto his paws.

Zevris placed the picture down carefully and swept his gaze around again. This time, it stopped on a small splash of green and pink over the kitchen sink—the cactus he'd gifted Tabitha, sitting on the windowsill. He smiled to himself. Perhaps it was of no real significance, but seeing his gift there, on open display, instilled him with a bit of pride and satisfaction.

He continued his perusal of her home with unbridled curiosity. As much as he felt like an intruder, as bad as he felt about what he'd had to do, he could not pass up this chance to learn more about Tabitha.

Her workroom was on the ground floor; he could tell by the smell as he approached the closed door. He only peeked in for a moment, glancing over all the supplies and containers that were neatly arranged on shelves along the walls. Even if the rest of her home was not quite put together, she'd made sure her workspace was prepared. Her passion for her work warmed his heart.

Zevris climbed the stairs and entered her bedroom. The tightness inside him now centered on a different spot—his groin. Despite all the other smells present, Tabitha's scent was so strong here that Zevris could do nothing more than stand in place and breath for several seconds, each inhalation heating his blood a little further.

He could not wait for his bedroom to take on her fragrance, could not wait for her to be the only thing he could smell.

Her bed was positioned with its headboard against the wall, centered between two windows. The bedframe was a distressed white and gray, with intricate flowers carved at the top of the headboard. The bed was neatly made, with white, gray, and purple decorative pillows laid atop the billowing white comforter. A pair of matching nightstands flanked the bed. One was topped with a lamp, the other with a violet vase of fake flowers. Her dresser stood against the opposite wall.

Two bookcases were situated along the wall beside the

door, with boxes stacked on the floor in front of them. Zevris walked to the boxes and opened one of the flaps, tilting his head as he surveyed the contents—books. That shouldn't have been surprising in itself, but it was the apparent subject matter of those books that stood out to him.

The covers bore images of males with naked chests and no heads, or of males and females together, clutching one another close, their expressions mixtures of possessiveness and pleasure. Other covers displayed inhuman characters—a male with a scorpion-like body; a tentacled, gray-skinned male holding a female; muscled, blue men with horns and tails; part-machine, part-animal males apparently called *Cyborg Shifters*.

He picked up one of the books, this one featuring an alien with green scales, four arms, and four eyes. He opened it to the middle and scanned the words. His brow furrowed as he read, and the heat that had been pooling in his loins intensified. He'd assumed there were written versions of those instructional mating videos, but what he was reading here went well beyond anything he'd seen watching pornography.

This was not merely describing sex between a male and female, it was describing their emotions during the act, describing their connection in terms far deeper than the physical. He read faster, turning to the next page.

Perhaps the task before Zevris was not so daunting as he'd believed. His female apparently found appeal in the notion of mating with inhuman males. A slow grin stretched across his face.

By the time he placed the book down, his cock was hard as stone, the result of his imagination having inserted himself and Tabitha into the scene. Perhaps he'd have to read a few of her books—he had a feeling there was more to learn within them than in any available porn.

I am here for a purpose, he reminded himself. His female

would need clean clothing and hygienic products if he was going to keep her in his dwelling.

Zevris snatched up an empty cardboard box from the floor and walked to her dresser, trailing his fingertips across the bedding as he moved. He set the box down atop the dresser and opened the bottom drawer, taking out articles of folded clothing to add to the box as he worked his way up—pants, skirts, shirts, socks, thin, silky tank tops, and pajamas. When he opened the top drawer, he paused.

The wide drawer was divided into two sections. One side was filled with bras of various colors. Some were plain, others were adorned with lace or floral patterns. These garments had cupped her full breasts, had touched her soft skin.

Her panties were on the other side, and they were even more varied than her bras. Some were cut smaller than others, some appeared nearly see through, some were lacy, some were patterned, and some were unadorned. He plucked a pair out and lifted it to his nose, drawing in a deep breath.

There was a clean, floral scent—her detergent, most likely—on the surface, but deeper than that, just barely noticeable, was a fragrance belonging wholly to Tabitha. He'd picked it up once before. It was the scent of her essence, of her sex. He groaned, and his cock hardened painfully further, stretching the front of his sweatpants as it throbbed.

He needed to get back to her.

But could he trust himself around her in this state?

He tossed several of her undergarments into the open box and was about to shove the drawer shut when something caught his eye. Removing those panties had exposed the items that had been hidden beneath them. He withdrew the objects, disrupting the remaining panties as he did so.

The first was small, about the size of his thumb, and its pink covering was soft and smooth. A thin wire dangled from one end, wrapped in a neat bundle, leading to a small controller. He pressed the button on the control. The plastic object vibrated with surprising power.

He knew what this was—it was a sex toy, used to bring females pleasure.

The other object was larger and heavier, immediately unmistakable in its nature. It was a piece of purple, semiflexible silicone in the shape of a human phallus, at least eight inches long from one end to the other. Like her panties, the fake cock carried the faintest hint of Tabitha's scent.

It had been inside his female.

Zevris bared his fangs and growled at the thing, knowing how foolish it was but unable to help his flare of jealousy. She was his to claim, his to mate, his and no one else's. A small voice in the back of his mind told him this was her property, that no matter his feelings, he had no right to destroy it.

Flexing his fingers, he extended his claws and tore the purple cock to pieces. He let the remains fall to the floor and kicked them under the dresser.

He was about to do the same with the small vibrator, but he stopped himself and reconsidered. Perhaps it would be of use at some point...

Zevris stuffed it into the box, tucking it away under her clothing. His female was a thirsty thing, and he was not averse to finding creative ways to satisfy her, but that would only come after he proved that he was the only source of pleasure she'd need for the rest of her days. She would never have use for one of these *toys* again—unless the two of them decided it would somehow enhance their mating.

Of course, he needed to earn her trust first. Considering that she was currently tied to his bed, possibly still screaming for help, he feared he had a long way to go on that front.

But he looked forward to the challenge.

TEN

Tabitha had glared at the bedroom door for a long time after Zevris left. She'd screamed herself hoarse calling for him, calling for help, but it had been to no avail. No one had come. She'd heard things from outside just fine—cars driving by, people conversing as they walked along the sidewalk, kids playing and laughing, a bouncing basketball, barking dogs. But no one had heard *her*. It was like she'd ceased to exist, like she'd become a ghost.

She growled, smacked her knuckles against the headboard, and immediately regretted it. She winced. The pain was sharp and radiating but slowly mellowed to a dull throb.

It was no worse than the pain she felt at her wrists, which also happened to be her own fault for fighting her restraints for so long. While she was still, her bindings were as flexible as silk ribbons, snug but not painful. Yet when she tugged against them, they became hard and firm, more like bands of steel—and the degree of that change seemed proportionate to the strength of her struggle.

There was nothing for her to do but sit there and stew.

Zevris's room didn't offer much in the way of scenery, and she was annoyed that she found that a little disappointing. The queen bed was draped with a plain blue comforter, the pillowcases were a mixture of white and blue, all tied together by the oak slatted headboard and a matching nightstand beside the bed, the latter of which had a small lamp set atop it. Even the dresser had the same oak finish. The walls were white, the carpet beige. There was a large flatscreen TV mounted on the wall, apparently hiding a secret compartment full of all sorts of alien devices that she didn't want anything to do with.

The decorations were minimal—a trio of smooth glass balls in varying shades of blue sitting atop a small granite slab on the dresser and two paintings on the walls, both of which were the sort of generic, almost abstract still-life paintings that could be found in the wall décor sections of most department or thrift stores.

His bedroom was neat and clean, but in a way that screamed *model home.*

Which made sense, really, considering he wasn't human. Of course he would've decorated based on some idealized version of the modern American home. But after a few minutes, it was boring to look at.

Couldn't he have at least turned on the TV or something?

With a sigh, she lay down and stared up at the textured white ceiling. Volatile emotions swirled within her, making her chest and throat tight.

I am not going to cry. Nope. It's not going to happen.

Except those damn tears escaped the corners of her eyes, anyway, and slid down her temples to dampen her hair.

She blinked rapidly to clear her vision.

Damn it, why'd it have to be Logan?

No, not Logan. Zevris. An alien.

Tabitha had never imagined a scenario in which she'd be

taken against her will and tied to a bed, much less by an alien. Aliens weren't supposed to exist!

At least...at least he'd promised not to hurt her.

She snorted. "No, he just wants a womb to fill with his baby batter."

But even as the words passed her lips, she knew they weren't wholly true.

I want you, Tabitha. I crave to know your touch, thirst for your taste, and yearn to make you mine. I have chosen you to be my lifemate, and it is my mission to make it so.

She couldn't deny the spark of surprise, hopefulness, and, strongest of all, desire his words had kindled within her. Zevris had chosen her—*her*—out of hundreds, thousands, millions of other women, many of whom were thin and pretty. Many of whom would've looked like the perfect partner standing next to him.

Because Zevris was gorgeous. How could he really want someone who looked like her, someone who'd made such a mess of everything?

He'd wanted to court her.

He said I was beautiful...

If only she'd been adult enough to have walked to his front door, if only she'd been brave enough to have just told him what Dexter had done and apologized for it, none of this would have happened.

But it would have eventually. Well, not exactly like this, but it would not have changed the fact that Zevris was an alien. An incredibly, mouth-wateringly, heart-throbbingly hot alien. She'd just found it out earlier than he'd intended.

Tabitha closed her eyes and groaned. She'd been reading romance books since she was a teenager, hundreds and hundreds of them, and some of her more recent favorites had involved alien abduction tropes. Like many women, she'd place herself in the role of the heroines. She'd fantasized about those heroes, about those males so obsessed with their female that they'd obtain her by whatever means necessary whether she had crash landed on an alien planet, was being sold at an intergalactic auction, or he'd abducted her himself.

But that didn't mean she wanted it to happen in real life...right?

That was fantasy, and this...this was reality. And in reality, a man wasn't supposed to kidnap a woman because she wouldn't sleep with him and he couldn't take *no* for an answer. Or, in her case...because she'd discovered he was an alien. It didn't matter how attractive they were, or if they had stupidly sexy, sculpted muscles, glowing F-me eyes, tattoos, piercings, and a tail.

Damn it, why did Zevris have to have a tail? She was such a sucker for tails. And for strong hands with long fingers and claws, and wicked fangs that could scrape her neck and send shivers straight to her core, and nipple piercings she wanted to flick with her tongue...

Tabitha snapped her eyes open. "Damn it, Tabby, stop it. He's your *kidnapper*."

But her body was already responding to her fantasies. Her nipples were tight and achy, and her sex clenched with the stirrings of arousal. Worse, Zevris's scent was wafting up from his bedding, filling her nose with sandalwood, musk, and cedar, turning her on even more.

She was totally blaming Dexter for this, the traitor. It was all his fault she was in this predicament.

The bedroom door opened, shattering the silence and stillness of the room. Tabitha started, heart leaping into her throat, and dragged herself back into a sitting position. Dexter raced in, panting excitedly, and jumped onto the bed. He barked and licked her face.

Tabitha turned her head away, sputtering against the onslaught of slobbery affection. "Dexter, stop!"

"Dexter, out," Zevris commanded as he stepped into the room carrying a large cardboard box. Once again, he appeared as he had when she'd first met him—human.

Dexter pulled back from Tabitha, looked at the alien, and whined. His tail stilled, and his ears drooped depressingly. Tabitha frowned, straining her wrist in an effort to pet him, to comfort him, but the bindings locked tight to keep her arm in place. The dog jumped to the floor and left the room.

Swinging the box into one arm, Zevris shut the bedroom door. "His understanding of English seems to be selective."

"Sounds like someone else I know," she retorted, leveling her gaze on him.

His nostrils flared with a huff, and his brows fell low. "Your tone implies that you are referring to me."

"*Let me go* is a pretty simple phrase, but you sure act like you don't understand it."

"I understand it, Tabitha, but I cannot comply. This situation goes far beyond the two of us."

Tabitha sighed and attempted to wipe the slobber from her face, but when the restraints again halted the motion of her arm, she scowled.

Bending her neck, she used her shoulders to wipe her face before settling back against the headboard. "Why did you bring my dog here, Zevris? What are you going to do to him?" Her eyes widened. "Is this because he dug up your flowers and pooped in your garden? Look, I'm sorry. I was trying to get him out of the yard and fix it before you knew anything but... Well, we all know how that turned out. Just don't hurt Dexter."

Zevris walked to the foot of the bed and set the box on the comforter, placing a hand atop the closed flaps. "Despite the grievous harm your beast has inflicted upon my flowers, I'm not going to hurt him. I would never hurt anything you love or hold dear. Dexter simply needs some discipline…and he cannot stay in an empty dwelling."

His reassurance calmed her. Despite the mischief Dexter always got into, she loved him to pieces.

She looked at the box, frowning when she recognized her handwriting on the side. *BEDROOM.* She narrowed her eyes. "What is that?"

"Some of your belongings." Zevris opened the flaps and folded them down. He began removing items from the box, placing them on the bed beside it—her makeup bag, toothbrush, toothpaste, deodorant, shampoo, face and body wash, lotion, shaving cream, and a razor. He'd even brought her a little box of tampons.

"You were in my house? You went through my things?"

He swept those items into his arms and scooped them off the bed. "I did."

Tabitha gaped at him. He'd responded so nonchalantly that she might've thought he rifled through people's belongings all the time. "How would you like it if someone went through your things? Your *private* things?"

"You are more than welcome to go through my things," Zevris replied as he walked into the adjoining bathroom and out of her sight, "as you are to be my lifemate."

"No, I'm not!" she called after him.

She heard him opening cabinets and moving things around, heard him grumble as something fell and clattered in the sink— her razor, by the sound of it.

He emerged from the bathroom a few moments later. His eyes settled on her, their blue impossibly vibrant even if they were no longer glowing. "You are, Tabitha. It can only be you."

Tabitha ran her gaze over him. He was still bare-chested, and his muscles were as toned and tantalizing as ever, but the tattoos and piercings she'd seen before were gone. She realized now that his face was different, too. His features were softer, still masculine but far more human, and his ears were rounded rather than coming to elvish points. The fangs she'd glimpsed as he'd spoken before were nowhere to be seen, and his fingers bore plain old fingernails rather than black claws.

Nothing about him looked alien anymore...but now that she'd seen under the mask, her brain insisted something was wrong about his appearance, even if it was just that he was too perfect.

"How are you doing that?" she asked.

He returned to the cardboard box. "Doing what?"

Tabitha motioned to him with her hand, waving her fingers up and down. "Looking human."

Zevris removed a piece of clothing from the box—a pair of her jeans—and set it down on the bed. "It's a holographic projection, of sorts. A relatively simple one, as our people are already fairly similar in appearance."

His body shimmered and blurred for an instant. The effect was strong enough that it made Tabitha feel like she'd gone cross-eyed; everything was in focus but him, and it was almost maddening to watch. When that blur cleared, something like those old wireframe computer images appeared on his skin, the lines arranged in interlocking hexagonal patterns that rapidly faded, section by section, until only Zevris—*alien* Zevris—remained.

Yep. Definitely hotter as an alien.

God, what is wrong with me?

"How...many of you are here on Earth?" she asked, trying to ignore the way her body reacted to the sight of him. His sweatpants hung low, revealing the grooves of his Adonis belt, which guided her eyes toward his...

"I am the only one you need to concern yourself with,

Tabitha." The way he said her name, half growling, half purring, sent a thrill up her spine. He continued removing clothing from the box, stacking her folded pants and shirts on the bed.

"Well, would you recognize each other if you ran into another...faeleon?"

"Faloran. And yes, we have measures in place for such occurrences. But it will not happen here on Earth."

"Why?"

He scooped up the pile of clothing and carried it to the dresser, setting it on top. He opened a drawer and shifted its contents. "Because that is the nature of this mission. We are operating individually, with no knowledge of one another. I must assume my comrades have their own designated areas of operation outside of my own."

Tabitha's gaze trekked down his muscular back to his ass, where it remained glued. The fabric of his sweatpants molded to his taut backside. She bit the inside of her lip. There was a slight bump at the top of his ass, and a hint of short, dark fur just above his waistband.

He's hiding his tail in his pants.

"Who were you talking to?" she asked. "Through that hologram, I mean."

"My commander." He placed her clothing in the drawer, pushed the drawer closed, and opened the next one up, moving his arms again as though clearing space.

He's...moving me into his house. My alien neighbor kidnapped me and is moving me into his house, and I don't know how I'm not freaking out right now.

Or maybe I'm so freaked out that I don't even realize it anymore?

Or maybe she believed him when he said he wouldn't hurt her, maybe she understood the mission he was on. That...

didn't mean she had to go along with it and become his mate, though.

But why not?

She hushed that voice faster than an ice cube could melt in a blast furnace. She was not going to go there.

Tabitha cleared her throat and forced her attention away from Zevris's ass to something safer. Like...the bland painting hanging on the wall.

Ugh, why does he even have that?

"What were you talking to him about?" she asked.

Zevris returned to the box and paused. From the corner of her eye, she saw him tilt his head and follow her gaze with his own. "Is there a problem with the painting?"

"It just so...*boring.*"

He frowned, walked to the painting, and lifted it off the nails that were holding it in place. Grasping it in both hands, he leaned his head back and scrutinized the painting, like he was some sexy, shirtless alien art dealer.

"Why?" he asked, glancing at her.

"There's no...life in it. No vibrancy. There's nothing wrong with it, not really, but it just...doesn't have any character. And it says nothing about you."

Zevris angled the painting slightly, as though to view it from a different perspective. "It doesn't say that I'm an ordinary human male in his early-to-mid-thirties with a comfortable career and room for a mate?"

Tabitha blinked at him. "No, it just says you're boring. And most people don't go into other people's bedrooms, so it's not like anyone would be able to see that thing and assume all that."

Brows falling low, he set the painting on the floor, leaning it against the wall, and turned to face her fully. "Firstly, it is common for humans to bring people they are interested in into their bedrooms. It happens in almost all your forms of entertainment. Secondly, I am not boring. I'm a faloran *althicar*, a soldier who has run covert missions on over a dozen planets."

"Are you seriously trying to educate *me* about human behavior?" She glared at him as unwanted jealousy simmered within her. "And just how many women have you brought in here that you were *interested in?*"

Zevris placed his big hands on the bed, mere inches from her thigh, and leaned toward her. The mattress dipped as more and more of his weight settled upon it. He held her gaze with his glowing, entrancing blue eyes. "One."

Tabitha swallowed thickly. "Why me? I...I'm sure you've met plenty of other women since you've been here. I can't imagine you'd have a hard time finding women who'd jump at the chance to sleep with you."

"You assume that I would want to sleep with any woman who threw herself at me." He stood upright and walked to the foot of the bed. "It is not merely a matter of fitting the right anatomical pieces together, Tabitha. I have met many human females in my time here. You are the only one who I have felt drawn to, and that draw is far too powerful to be ignored."

I refuse to feel flattered. I will not be drawn in by sweet words.

"I just thought, well, with the urgency of your people needing women—" Her words ended when she saw him lift a handful of her underwear from the box. He set them on the bed, followed by another handful. Warmth flooded her cheeks.

Zevris plucked up a lacy pair of black and hot pink panties, dangling them from the claw of his pointer finger. "I look forward to seeing these on you, though I'm even more excited about taking them off."

The fire in Zevris's eyes stole Tabitha's breath. Her pussy clenched, aching more deeply than she could ever have imagined possible.

He cocked his head, trailing his fiery gaze down her body. "I wonder what it is you are wearing beneath your clothes now."

"You...you can just keep wondering," she said, shifting on the bed to draw her knees closer to her chest and squeeze her thighs together. The movement caused something to roll from the pile of panties. The moment she looked at the object, mortification struck her, twisting her stomach into knots.

Oh no. No, no, no, no.

How could she have forgotten that her panties weren't the only things she kept in that drawer?

Zevris chuckled, dropped the underwear onto the pile, and grasped the little bullet vibrator between his forefinger and thumb. "I am intrigued by this." He turned it on. The sound of its vibrations was thunderous in the otherwise quiet room. "I think we'll find many ways to put it to use."

Unbidden, a scene played in her head—Zevris staring down at her with those magical blue eyes as he pressed the vibrator to her clit, his free hand kneading the flesh of her thigh before he slipped two of his fingers inside her, pumping in and out, just like she wanted him to do with his cock. The Zevris in her imagination watched with a hungry gaze as she came undone before lowering his mouth to her—

He turned off the bullet and leaned his head toward her, nostrils flaring as he sniffed the air. One corner of his mouth tilted up in a mischievous half smile. "Are you imagining the possibilities, Tabitha?"

"No," she lied, curling her fingers to press her nails into her palms.

A deep, rolling hum rumbled in his chest. "This was not the only surprise I found in your drawer. But your other *toy* is no more."

He dropped the vibrator onto the pile of underwear and

crawled onto the bed. "You'll have no further use for it, my mate. I will satisfy your needs from now on. If you require a cock for your pleasure"—he caught her ankle in one hand and dragged her down until she was on her back before drawing himself over her—"it will be mine. It will be my cock that fills you, my seed that floods your womb, my name you will utter in the throes of passion."

Tabitha stared up at him with wide eyes, her breath short and her heart fluttering wildly. Her body was on fire, and she was sure her cheeks were a color to match. She felt his heat radiating above her, felt his thighs as he straddled her, and couldn't help but feel the incredibly large tent he was sporting between his legs that was currently probing her belly.

"You're getting a little ahead of yourself, aren't you?" she said, proud that she kept her voice steady.

He inhaled again, and he was close enough that she felt his hot breath on her collarbone when he released it. "You are already mine, Tabitha. Your body knows it."

"I'm not going to be your...your breeder."

Zevris moved a hand to her neck and brushed his long fingers over her skin. The teasing scrape of his claws sent a thrill through her, and she tilted her chin up reflexively. He hooked his thumb beneath it, settling his fingers on her cheek. Their eyes remained locked.

"I want you to carry my young." He lowered his head until his lips were but a hair's breadth from hers, filling up Tabitha's whole world with his alien sexiness. "But more than that, I want you to be my lifemate. I want to touch you, to glide my hands over your body, to feel your soft skin and your alluring curves. I want to strip you bare and taste you, to lick every inch of you, to lap your essence from between your thighs like it is my altar and you are my goddess. I want to thrust my cock inside your pussy and feel your heat wrap around me. I want the air filled with your cries of pleasure, I want my name alone upon your lips.

"I want you, Tabitha. All of you. And soon enough, you will see that you are mine."

Tabitha caught her bottom lip between her teeth and curled her toes into the bedding as she shivered with temptation. Liquid heat pooled between her thighs, and she knew that her panties were wet with her desire. She felt hollow and needy, and the ache at her core had become the greatest agony she'd ever endured. No matter how hard she tried, she could not look away from his eyes. She was caught, ensnared, totally at his mercy.

And it turned her on.

He drew in a long, deep breath and lifted his head away, shutting his eyes as though in bliss. His lips stretched into a wide, sensual grin, flashing his sharp fangs. "Your scent is the most delicious, maddening thing I have ever smelled, Tabitha."

Opening his eyes, he looked down at her. His gaze was feral, predatory, sensual and hungry, dangerously seductive, but his grin soon faltered. His brow creased with strain, and his jaw tensed, lips pressing together. His next breath was ragged and unsteady.

Zevris shoved away abruptly, sliding off the bed to stand at its foot. The room seemed impossibly, unbearably brighter for a few seconds without his body over Tabitha, and the air seemed too cold and thin for her to catch her breath.

She watched, flustered and speechless, as he closed his hand around his thick cock, his features tight with desire and agony. He groaned, the sound ending in a guttural growl. When he lifted his hand, he returned his attention to the cardboard box, scooping out an armful of her bras.

He bunched them together with her panties and carried them to the dresser, quickly putting them away, before he snatched up the box and upturned it over the open drawer. Several pairs of her socks tumbled out into the drawer.

Between his bare chest, taut ass, and the undiminished bulge in his sweatpants, Tabitha wasn't sure where to look—every part of him was delicious.

Zevris stepped to the door and reached for the handle.

That was enough to snap Tabitha out of her trance. "Where...where are you going?"

He closed his hand on the doorknob and looked at her over his shoulder. His eyes gleamed with lust. "To prepare food for my female."

He opened the door and slipped out into the hallway, turning slightly to fit through the gap and granting her one last glimpse of his outlined cock before he was gone. The door closed softly, but the sound of it was deafening in the relative silence.

And all she could do was lie there, stunned, her body aching with unfulfilled need.

Alien one, Tabitha nothing.

Tabitha groaned and turned her eyes toward the ceiling. The haze that had clouded her thoughts slowly lifted.

What was wrong with her? She shouldn't have wanted him, shouldn't have craved him like this—he'd *abducted* her. She should've been kicking and screaming, demanding he let her go, fighting him tooth and nail. But every time he touched her or spoke to her in that husky, growly voice, she was like putty in his hands. Even if he could mask his true appearance, he couldn't mask the raw yearning burning in his eyes whenever he looked at her.

Was she so starved for affection that she could forgive what he'd done?

Yes. Yes, I am.

She could admit it. She was twenty-six years old, lived by

herself, had no boyfriend, and the only family she'd ever had passed away two years ago. Tabitha could admit to herself that she was...lonely. And she truly didn't think Zevris was a bad guy—or a bad alien. Everything he'd said had seemed sincere and honest, and if it was a matter of his whole species dying out, could she blame him for doing whatever he needed in order to save them?

But that didn't mean he could take her choice away. That didn't mean he could just take...*her*. She refused to go down without a fight. So what if he was mind-numbingly, panty-wettingly sexy? It didn't change the fact that he'd kidnapped her and tied her to his bed!

She was his captive, and she needed to remember that.

ELEVEN

The fork Zevris was holding clinked against the plate. "You need to eat, Tabitha."

Tabitha kept her face turned away from him, trying to remain strong even though she felt a little like a kid throwing a tantrum after being told to eat her veggies. Though her means of resistance were limited at the moment—refuse to look at him, refuse to speak to him—she had to use whatever weapons she could in this battle.

But it was hard to ignore the mouth-watering aromas of buttery garlic steak, mashed potatoes, and cheesy broccoli.

Her alien had gone all out.

No. Not my *alien.*

Zevris growled. "I will tolerate neither the *silent treatment* nor the *cold shoulder*, female. And I will not remain idle while you make yourself suffer to spite me."

As amusing as it was that an alien knew those terms, Tabitha didn't allow it to show. She turned her face toward him, tilted her chin down, and gave him a look that said, *What are you going to do about it?*

Or at least that was what she hoped it said.

His dark brows were low, angled down toward the bridge of his nose, and his eyes were locked on her. He was sitting on the edge of the bed with a plate of food on his thigh and his tail laid beside him, its tip—with its tuft of black fur—flicking as though in agitation.

"This does not need to be unpleasant, Tabitha."

Zevris's expression also sent a clear message—*Whether I end up feeding you or fucking you, I will have my way.*

And it was equal parts thrilling and irritating that she knew either of those options would be far from unpleasant.

She pressed her lips together and looked back at the wall. It was at that moment that her stomach decided to growl.

Zevris caught her chin and turned her face back toward him. "I am aware that humans can survive for several weeks without food, but I will not allow you to reach anywhere near that point. You are hungry. You will eat."

Tabitha clenched her jaw. A few missed meals weren't a big deal. She could hold out for a few days, right? She could hold out until she either found a way to escape or convinced him that this was crazy, and he really ought to let her go...

But she already had that nauseous, hollow feeling in the pit of her stomach, a wonderful addition to the discomfort of her sore, dry throat and raw wrists. She'd missed lunch today, having been too busy unpacking before Mia's call—and now that she thought about it, she'd skipped breakfast, too. As much as it seemed like it should have, a cup of creamer with some coffee splashed in didn't count as a meal.

She *was* hungry, and Zevris's food looked and smelled delicious. Nan had taught Tabitha to cook years before, and Tabitha considered herself a pretty good cook, but when was the last time she'd had a real, home-cooked meal? When was the last time she'd taken that time for herself?

When was the last time anyone had done so for her?

Keeping hold of her chin, Zevris lifted the fork with his other hand, moving it toward her lips. The piece of steak impaled on the prongs was red and juicy, just the way she loved it. But she jerked her chin away.

"Tabitha..." Zevris's voice was at once commanding and concerned, laced with both warning and desire.

How could anyone put so much feeling into saying a name?

"I'm not a baby, Zevris. I can feed myself."

So much for the silent treatment, Tabby.

"Oh? Do you plan to hold the fork with your toes, female?"

She glared at him.

Zevris sighed. "The situation is not ideal. I am attempting to make light of it."

"I can see how it'd be easier for you to joke about it. You're not the one tied to a bed."

He lowered the fork to the plate and ran a hand through his hair, producing a faint scratching sound. It took Tabitha a moment to realize that was the sound of his claws grazing his scalp.

"If you untie me, I'll eat," she said.

"Will you eat before or after you attempt to stab me with the fork?" he asked.

She couldn't tell whether he was being serious or teasing her. "I'm not going to stab you."

Zevris stared at her for what felt like a long, long time, but it couldn't have been for more than a few seconds. He seemed to be searching her, and there was a strange light in his eyes that almost seemed like a hint of...desperation.

Like he was desperate to trust her.

"Releasing you from the bindings does not mean you are free to go, Tabitha," he said.

"I'm just asking you to untie me, Zevris. I'm sore and stiff, my arms hurt, and my hands have been asleep for a while now."

His frown deepened. His gaze lingered on her for another moment before he turned and set the plate on the nightstand, beside the other plate he'd brought up—his meal, presumably, though the food was untouched.

Zevris turned back to her and climbed onto the bed, looming over her on his knees. It put his groin just below Tabitha's eye level, and it took everything within her to stop herself from leaning forward and flicking her tongue across his toned abs. Unlike the bodybuilders she'd seen, Zevris wasn't completely bare of hair. There was a nice, dark, happy little trail leading down from his navel that disappeared beneath the waistband of his pants. She was eager to see what it led to.

His scent washed over her as he reached across to her arm. He settled his fingertips on her forearm and slid them up toward the binding around her wrist, and the tingling that trailed in their wake had nothing to do with her arm being asleep. That simple touch was the tender caress she'd always dreamed about, so gentle and yet so powerful that it stole her breath.

When he touched the restraint, it released her wrist abruptly. She hissed as her arm fell, but Zevris caught it and eased it down slowly. Her shoulder ached from the change in position.

Zevris brushed his thumb over the red skin that had been rubbed by the binding. "Ah, Tabitha. Why didn't you tell me sooner?"

She watched as he continued to tenderly soothe her wrist. "I didn't think it would have made much difference since *let me go* didn't work."

"You are my mate. I don't want any harm to come to you," he said, a hint of a growl in his voice. With his free hand, he released her other arm, his touch again gentle, his frown only deepening as he stroked the newly revealed raw flesh. "I had not realized your skin would be so delicate. I should have known better."

Her heart clenched at the guilt and pain written upon his face. She shouldn't have felt pity for him when he'd been the one to tie her to the bed. And yet...

She bit back the words she'd been tempted to speak to comfort him.

"Thank you," she said instead, withdrawing her arms from his hold to bring her hands together and rub away the sharp, stabbing tingles assailing them.

He returned to his place, sitting on the edge of the bed facing her, but his gaze lingered on her wrists. She glanced down at them, too, subconsciously covering the irritated flesh as best she could. Zevris settled his big hand over hers. His palm was warm and rough, but his touch was still so light. His were practiced hands—the hands of a craftsman, of a soldier, strong and sure, and she'd be lying if she said she didn't want them all over her.

"Look at me, Tabitha."

She complied without thinking.

His face was hard, serious, and his frown remained firmly in place. "I have not earned your thanks. When I have given you pleasure, when I have given you security, when I have given you happiness, you may thank me."

Warmth flooded her cheeks, but she arched a brow. "You're still so sure."

"I have never been more certain of anything."

The way he was looking at her, the way his eyes glowed, it was getting harder and harder for Tabitha to convince herself he was wrong. In some ways, this almost felt like those moments that so often happened in movies—the intense stare that led into a passionate kiss.

She was definitely not ready for that.

Yet.

Tabitha tore her gaze away from his and twisted to the side, stretching her arm out to grab one of the glasses of water he'd placed on the nightstand with the plates. With her hand still regaining feeling, the glass nearly slipped from her grasp. She tightened her hold on it and brought it to her lips. The ice water instantly soothed her parched mouth and throat, so cold, refreshing, and delicious that she couldn't stop. She drank like she'd just spent days trekking across a scorching desert.

Before she knew it, only the ice remained. The cubes clinked together as she lowered the glass.

She glanced aside to see Zevris still staring at her. Fortunately, some of the intensity in his gaze had been eased by the slight smirk on his lips.

She lowered the glass. "What?"

That smirk took on a roguish edge. "My female is even thirstier than I'd thought."

Tabitha's brows furrowed. "Did you just... Did you seriously..." She shook her head. "Nope, we're not going there."

"No, we aren't. Not yet." Zevris plucked the glass from her hand, leaned forward, and placed it on the nightstand. He picked up both plates and sat upright again, holding one to her. "But soon you will learn that I can quench your thirst and satisfy your every hunger."

"Well, you certainly quenched my thirst—for *water*," she said, taking the plate. She grabbed the fork with the piece of steak still attached to it and waved it at him. "And now, you are satisfying my hunger. For *food*. That's as far as this goes."

With what she hoped was a sense of finality, she brought the meat to her mouth, bit down on it, and slid it off the fork.

The steak hit her tongue with an explosion of flavor that made her close her eyes and moan. She chewed, relishing the tender meat and its buttery garlic sauce, wanting the bite to last forever while simultaneously craving the next. She'd rarely had steak since moving out on her own—it was too expensive when you were on a budget—and she couldn't recall ever eating one that tasted this good.

"Oh my God, how did you learn to cook like this?" She opened her eyes and was about to stab another piece of meat when she glanced up at him. Her hand froze.

His expression had softened, but his eyes were just as intent on her as ever—as though he were as invested in her reactions as she was in the taste of the food.

"The internet," he replied. "I was not here long before I tired of preprepared food, and I feared the sodium content would kill me. That, and it seemed like knowing how to cook was a valued trait in a potential mate."

Tabitha chuckled. "I thought the saying was that the way to a *man's* heart is through his stomach. I guess it works the other way around, too."

She stilled, realizing what she'd said only after the words had been spoken.

"That the way to a man's stomach is through his heart?" Zevris asked, frowning.

"Um, yeah. That." She bit back her smile, though it was harder to do once the food was in her mouth.

Zevris settled his plate on his thigh and scooped up some mashed potatoes with his fork. "I've been able to puzzle out the meaning of many such phrases, but I think I'm missing something with this one."

"It's nothing. Why don't you, uh, tell me what you do as a soldier?"

He narrowed his eyes, keeping them on her as he slipped

the food into his mouth. His jaw—his perfect, stubbled jaw—worked as he chewed. "You're evading. You realized some meaning to what you said that you hadn't considered, and now you're trying to shift my attention away from it."

"I am not. I'm just enjoying this delicious food," she said, taking another bite.

His eyes rounded for a moment, and he grinned, giving her another glimpse of those wicked fangs. "That's what it is. *Heart* is figurative in that saying." He leaned closer to her. "You were implying that you love my cooking, and that it would lead you to loving me."

"You can think whatever you want. I admit nothing...except yes, I love your cooking. But only your cooking!"

Zevris chuckled and leaned back again. He speared a chunk of meat and wagged his fork at her, much as she'd done to him before. "That's a start."

Tabitha watched him chew, studying the muscles of his square jaw, the strong tendons on his neck, and his bobbing Adam's apple. Was there no part of him that she didn't find appealing? She tore her gaze away and focused on her food.

After a few more bites, she stopped caring about etiquette and simply ate for the sake of filling her belly. It was only when a couple pieces of steak and a tiny pile of mashed potatoes remained that she set her fork down, unable to take another bite. She instinctively reached for her glass, having forgotten that she'd drank it all—but it was heavier than it should have been when she picked it up. Her brows creased as she looked at the glass to find it half full. A glance at Zevris's glass, which was a little less than half full, filled in the blanks.

He'd poured some of his water into her glass without her noticing. As simple as a thing it was, it was also incredibly sweet and thoughtful.

"Are you finished eating?" Zevris asked.

She nodded as she brought the glass to her lips, drinking slower this time.

He took her plate, stacked it atop his own—which damn near looked like he'd licked it clean—and placed them on the nightstand. Tabitha watched him over the rim of her glass, unable to look away from the graceful play of muscles beneath his tanned skin.

How was he even real? How was any of this actually happening?

She set her glass down. Now that her hunger and thirst had been satisfied, there was another need making itself known, growing stronger by the moment. She glanced toward the bath-room door.

"I...need to use the bathroom," she said, shifting her legs to take some of the pressure off her full bladder.

"Of course." He waved his arm toward the bathroom.

Tabitha eased toward the edge of the bed and slid her feet to the floor. Every little ache and bruise from her fall from the fence and their tussle earlier made itself known as she stood up. She walked past him, her gaze flicking toward the bedroom door.

"You may shower while you're in there," Zevris said.

She stopped and looked at him, wrinkling her nose. "Are you saying I stink?"

Not that she'd blame him if he said she did. After every-thing that had happened today—including sitting on his bed for hours in damp, dirty jeans—she was sure she didn't smell like roses.

Zevris tilted his head. Somehow, the gesture drew her attention to his pointed ears, and for an instant she longed to nip at one of them or trace its tip with her tongue.

"I have smelled nothing on a dozen alien worlds that approaches the sweetness of your fragrance, Tabitha," he said.

"And to be clear, I am not referring to any perfume you might wear, or the smell of your antiperspirant, soap, or shampoo. *Your* scent is a lure I will never be able to resist."

Tabitha bit the inside of her bottom lip. Her cheeks felt warm, but they weren't the only part of her that was flushed. She squeezed her thighs together. Why did he have to say things that made her heart quicken, her stomach flutter, and her core pool with desire? Why couldn't he have been cruel so it would be easy to hate him?

She brought her fists to her mouth, brows drawn as indecision warred within her.

"Tabitha?"

Lowering her arms, she met his gaze. "Please, Zevris, just let me go home. I won't say anything to anyone, and maybe... maybe we can go about this the right way. You can—"

"I cannot." He dropped his elbows onto his thighs and leaned forward, bowing his head and shaking it. "I can't risk it. Can't risk you."

Tabitha pressed her lips together. She didn't know why he thought she'd be in any danger, but it hurt that he didn't trust her. She recognized the ridiculousness of that—he had no reason to trust her, just as she had no reason to trust him. They barely knew each other.

Her feet were in motion before she could consider what she was doing. She spun and ran to the bedroom door, closing her hand around the knob.

Zevris uttered a word she did not recognize—but which was undoubtedly a curse of some sort—and was behind her in an instant. She'd barely turned the knob when his big arm banded around her middle and swept her back against the solid muscle of his torso, breaking her hold on the door.

She struggled against him as her feet left the ground. "Damn it, Zevris! This isn't right. I'm not your prisoner!"

He took a step forward, pinning her against the wall with his body. Tabitha gasped, hands flat on the wall, as she felt something hard and thick probing just above her ass. There was no doubt in her mind what that was.

Zevris leaned his head down so his mouth was close to her ear. "No, but you are mine all the same, *Nykasha*. Now you can either behave and shower yourself, or"—he smoothed one of his hands down her side and slipped it up under her shirt, making her belly quiver with the touch of his palm—"I can undress you right here, right now, and we'll take one together."

"You wouldn't!" She squeaked when the tips of his fingers dipped behind the button of her jeans.

"I'm having trouble finding a reason not to, Tabitha." He pressed his nose into her hair, running its tip along the rounded shell of her ear. "I would be happy to wash my female, especially between her—"

"I'll do it!" She bucked her backside against him.

Apparently, that was a mistake; Zevris groaned, and murmured in a deep, husky voice, "Pity."

For a moment, his already hard body tensed further, and then he pushed away from the wall, lifting her again as he spun around. He set her neatly on her feet and released his hold on her.

She didn't look back at him as she darted to the bathroom, swiftly shut the door, and locked it.

TWELVE

Panting, Tabitha turned and pressed her back against the door. Her eyes locked on the large window above the jacuzzi tub. She crossed the room, stepped into the tub, and shoved up the black blinds, revealing a frosted glass window. She pushed up on the window panel. When it didn't move, she flipped the locks and tried again. It refused to budge.

She growled, smacking her hand against the glass. The sound made by the impact was oddly dull and resonant.

His front door hadn't opened either, even though she'd sworn she'd unlocked it. The deadbolt had been undone, the knob had turned freely, but the door had simply refused to move. It was like some invisible force had held it in place.

Was he using some sort of super high-tech device to secure the windows and doors? Considering how convincingly his technology could mask his true appearance, she didn't doubt he had some kind of alien security system in place. She had a feeling that this glass wouldn't break no matter what she hit it with—but she was tempted to try, regardless.

Of course, even if she did manage to break the glass, there

was a fifteen-foot drop to the ground to deal with afterward. Not that she'd have the pleasure of falling—she knew Zevris would be all over her before she could squeeze her ass out the window.

Shoulders sagging, Tabitha pressed her forehead against the cool windowpane.

Why couldn't he trust her a little? Tabitha wasn't against being with him—she was drawn to him, she desired him, even more so now that she'd discovered he was an alien. But...not like this. Not by force. He could've let her return home and dated her like a normal human being. Like he had been trying to do before, well, *this*. She would never have told anyone what was behind his mask. She just wanted to take it slow, wanted them to get to know each other, wanted him to be sure she was the one he really desired.

She'd been used, betrayed, and dumped by guys who she thought cared about her. The connection she felt she and Zevris shared...it had already greatly surpassed what she'd had in her past relationships. This felt real, like he was the one. But she wasn't naïve enough to believe that this lust was love at first sight. She just didn't want him to regret this, she didn't want him to feel like he had no other choice because she'd been too damn curious. She just...didn't know if she'd survive the rejection and heartbreak.

With a defeated sigh, Tabitha turned and looked around.

The layout of his bathroom was similar to hers, though his seemed a little larger—and his jacuzzi tub was definitely bigger than hers, shaped like a triangle rather than an oval. For an instant, Tabitha imagined herself stretched out in his tub, surrounded by a mountain of bubbles with the scent of lavender filling the air. She imagined arms wrapping around her, and large, rough palms cupping her breasts before sliding down her belly toward her pussy to stroke her clit with those long, dexterous fingers.

She groaned. "Damn it. For real? Stop it, Tabby."

She forced that image out of her mind—secretly tucking it away for later—as she perused the rest of the bathroom.

It was a mixture of neutral colors, with large, light gray tiles on the floor and built up along the side of the tub. The brown walls bisected by a strip of white tiling with smaller squares of light and dark gray scattered through it.

The walk-in shower next to the tub had a fancy showerhead, a built-in seat in one corner, and it looked large enough for three or four people to stand in comfortably. The glass wall separating it from the rest of the bathroom was crystal-clear and borderless. A wide, double-sink vanity stretched across one wall, with a big mirror above it. The toilet was tucked in a little alcove in the corner.

Like the rest of the house, there was minimal décor here; a couple generic pictures of flowers, a couple pillar candles on wicker candle stands, and plush brown towels hanging from the towel rack.

Tabitha climbed out of the jacuzzi and moved to the vanity. Her bright pink toothbrush was in the toothbrush holder next to his blue one, her deodorant stood next to his, and her hairbrush lay beside his comb on a small, rectangular silver tray. She took a quick peek inside the drawers and cabinets to discover her other toiletries neatly mixed in with Zevris's.

Both at Nan's and when she was rooming with Mia, Tabitha had had her own bathroom, her own space. Sharing with someone felt so domestic, so intimate. So...right.

Nothing seemed out of the ordinary here. All perfectly normal, all perfectly natural, like it was just a bathroom shared by an everyday, average guy and his girlfriend. Except...

She stepped over to the toilet and lifted the seat.

The toilet was spotless. Not a speck of urine anywhere.

Okay, so not an *everyday, average* guy. But she'd already known Zevris was none of those things.

Tabitha blew her hair out of her face and lowered the seat. How could he be any more perfect?

After a glance at the door to make sure it was still locked, she flicked on the fan and hurriedly used the toilet. When she was done, she washed her hands, brushed her teeth, and undressed, folding her clothes and setting them on the counter. Her skin pebbled with goosebumps in the cool air as she turned on the shower. Once the water was nice and steamy, she stepped into the shower and closed the door behind her.

She groaned as the hot water struck her body, closing her eyes and relishing the heat. As soothing as it was, however, it couldn't hold back the wave of exhaustion that struck her in that moment. Days of packing, moving, and unpacking, followed by the fight she'd put up today, had drained her severely... All she wanted to do was fall into bed, cuddle in a blanket, and sleep.

Tabitha opened her eyes. The shower's glass was all foggy now, creating the illusion that she was in her own comforting, secluded space. She reached for her shampoo but halted her hand before she could take hold of the bottle. Tilting her head, she regarded Zevris's shampoo. She picked up his bottle, opened it, and sniffed. It smelled of spices and musk, but it wasn't nearly as good as the man himself.

She'd never smelled anything as masculinely divine as him. If she could replicate his scent and make it into a soap, she'd make a fortune.

Closing the bottle, she returned Zevris's shampoo to the shelf, grabbed her own, and continued with her shower.

When she was done washing and rinsing herself, she turned off the water, wrung out her hair, and opened the shower door to grab a towel. The towel was surprisingly soft and large—large enough to wrap around her entire body without leaving the annoying gap her shorter towels always did. She dried off and stepped out onto the rug.

Tabitha froze.

Her clothes were gone. In their place was her black satin and lace camisole and those black and hot pink panties Zevris had picked out of her underwear pile, both folded neatly.

"I'm going to kill him." She clenched her fingers around the towel. "You pervert!"

Despite the closed door between them, Zevris's laughter carried to Tabitha clearly; it was deep, rich, and rolling, at once good natured and tantalizingly wicked.

"I'm going to double kill him."

Tabitha pressed her lips together as anger simmered within her, but that furious heat was swiftly accompanied by heavy dread and self-loathing.

Zevris had come into the bathroom.

Zevris had come into the bathroom while she'd been showering! The locked door hadn't stopped him at all, and she'd neither seen nor heard him.

But he...he'd seen her. He'd *seen* her.

It didn't matter that his vision of her must've been distorted by the foggy glass, the shadow of her body was enough.

She opened her towel and looked at herself in the mirror, focusing on every imperfection; the extra roll on her sides, her not-so-flat stomach, the silvery stretch marks marring her belly, hips, and thighs. Old, hurtful words, words she'd tried so hard to forget, echoed in her head.

Just wanted to see what it was like with a fat girl.

You're too soft and jiggly. You're lucky I got it up to begin with.

Her last boyfriend had even hooked up with other women

because Tabitha just hadn't been enough for him. Or, in his words, she'd been *too much*. Too big.

Tabitha shoved back those memories, that old pain, crammed it all into a mental box and buried it as deep as she could. There was plenty to worry about in the present without digging all that crap up.

She pulled on the panties and cami and wrapped the towel around herself, tucking the end in tight. Once her hair was brushed, she stepped out of the bathroom.

Zevris was sitting on the end of the bed, his long legs spread and his torso leaned back, propped up on his arms. He'd removed his sweatpants, leaving him clad only in a pair of green boxers. Almost every little bit of him was exposed for her viewing pleasure. His tail lay atop the bed, curled to one side, its tip flicking lazily.

Tabitha stilled as she ran her gaze down his body. His thighs and calves were muscular, and even his freaking feet were perfect with their long toes and short black claws.

"Why are you wearing the towel, Tabitha?" he asked, his voice low and teasing.

She snapped her eyes up to meet his. He had one eyebrow arched, and his lips were slanted in a crooked smile.

"Because *someone* took my clothes," she said.

"I left clean clothes in their place."

Heat engulfed her cheeks. "They can barely be called clothes." She glared at him. "And I locked the door. You shouldn't have even come in!"

"My female required clean clothing to wear after her shower. I simply acted to accommodate her needs." He ran his gaze over her body slowly, deliberately, and it was so hot and heavy that she almost felt it on her skin. "Take off the towel, *Nykasha*."

Tabitha tightened her grip on the towel, shook her head, and took a step back. "No."

Zevris sat forward, abdominal muscles rippling, and stood up. His eyes remained on Tabitha as he stalked toward her, his stride smooth, graceful, leisurely—like a predator advancing on prey that could not escape.

She backed away as he neared, but it was only a moment before her back was against the wall. He placed his hands on the wall to either side of her, caging her in, once again reducing her whole world to nothing but him. No one had ever made her feel as tiny and petite as he did. She tilted her head back, locking her eyes with his.

He lowered a hand to her shoulder, where he hooked the thin strap of her cami with his claw. "Take off the towel, Tabitha."

"No," she said again, her voice much weaker than it had been a moment ago.

"Hmm."

Faster than she could perceive, he grasped the towel and snatched it off her as easily as if she hadn't been holding it at all. His movement produced a little burst of air that fluttered the hem of her cami around her hips and caressed her now bare thighs.

Zevris swept his gaze down slowly, dragging it over her body, his eyes flaring brighter as they moved. "Fuck."

As he tossed the towel aside, something thin but strong looped around Tabitha's lower back and drew her against him. She only realized it was his tail when the soft fur at its tip brushed her outer thigh. Zevris dropped his hands to her backside. Her breath hitched, and she slapped her palms against his chest, planting them firmly, but she knew she couldn't separate their bodies even if she used all her strength.

He palmed her ass with both hands and groaned as he squeezed.

She opened her mouth to protest, but all that emerged was a gasp as Zevris lifted her off the floor. His hands slid to her upper thighs, guiding her legs to move around his waist, and they complied as though they'd wanted for nothing more. She threw her arms around his neck, telling herself it was just for the need of something to hold on to.

Zevris spun around and strode toward the bed. His tail brushed over her calf, reaching for something behind her, but she could not look away from him to see what it was doing. There was a brief flutter of fabric from the bed—like the covers being swept aside—and then Tabitha was falling backward.

She landed atop cool, soft sheets, and her damp hair fanned around her. Zevris didn't let her go. He came down over her, his hips still wedged between her thighs, bracing himself with one hand on the mattress beside her head.

He raised his other hand, settling it on her elbow, and slid it up her forearm slowly. His touch was gentle but firm, and it spread thrilling sparks across her skin. That hand continued higher and higher until it finally reached her wrists, which were still crossed behind his neck. Zevris grasped both her wrists in his big, strong hand, ducked his head slightly, and guided her arms down.

Though she longed to touch his chest, to run her fingers over the ridges of his muscles, she let her arms fall, settling them on the bed to either side.

Zevris reared back and stared down at her. His gaze was so bright, so intense, so heated and hungry, that Tabitha swore he was about to devour her. He placed his hands on her sides, his thumbs close enough to Tabitha's breasts that her breath caught in her throat. As he trailed his hands down toward her hips, palms rasping over the satiny cami, he released a low, apprecia-tive growl. Desire pooled in her core.

His touch was even lighter than before—it was outright teasing her now, especially with the fabric of her cami sepa-rating their skin. But his hands were not the only things teasing her. His cock, long, thick, and as hard as steel, was pressed against her pussy, throbbing rhythmically.

He...actually wants this. Wants me.

Tabitha's nipples stiffened, their outlines immediately visible through the cami. She lifted her arms to cover herself, but they froze when Zevris growled again and shook his head.

"No, *Nykasha*." He leaned down, slipping a hand under her head to twine his fingers in her hair. His lips were within an inch of hers when he stopped. "There will be no hiding. You are beautiful beyond words, Tabitha."

His hold on her hair tightened, and he tilted her head back, exposing her neck to him. His face moved closer still, so close that the tip of his nose brushed along her jaw, and he inhaled deeply. "And your scent is ambrosial."

When he exhaled, his warm breath fanned across her skin, only amplifying the heat at her core. Tabitha's heart raced, and little tremors coursed through her body. She raised her knees, and she barely bit back a whimper as the length of his cock settled deeper into the cradle of her sex. There was something different about the way his shaft felt, something...alien.

Zevris released a heavy breath, body tensing, and rasped, "Let me have you, Tabitha." He lifted his head and met her gaze. "Let me make you mine."

Her thoughts were clouded with lust, and her body burned with need. Her core clenched. Subtly, she tilted her pelvis, causing his erection—with its strange bumps she felt through their underwear—to brush her clit, sending a tiny bolt of pleasure through her. She was so, so wet. One little word was all it would take, and he'd be inside her.

In fact, she was pretty sure she'd come right now if he commanded her to.

"My *Nykasha*," Zevris rumbled. He rolled his hips, grinding his cock along her pussy and stroking her clit.

She gasped, eyelashes fluttering as she arched her back.

"Say yes," he coaxed as he pumped his hips again. He bared his fangs, his face contorting with a snarl of tortured pleasure. "Let me inside you."

Yes.

That word danced on the tip of her tongue. She wanted to concede, to give in to him, to let him use her body as he wished and welcome the consuming pleasure, but this wasn't right. They were moving too fast. Not only was he keeping her prisoner, but he was skipping the whole getting to know you phase. What about building trust and affection? What about...love?

Tabitha deserved more than this. She *wanted* more than this.

"No," she whispered.

Zevris's fingers closed just a little tighter on her hair, and his hips stilled. He dipped his face so his stubbly cheek was against her neck and sighed. She felt his jaw muscles tense and relax several times. Slowly, mirroring the reluctance she still felt herself, he eased his pelvis back slightly, eliminating most of that sweet, maddening pressure on her clit.

He turned his face, brushing his lips against her neck and making her breath hitch, before pushing himself up on one arm. His eyes still held that lustful fire as he looked down at her, but his expression had softened. Gently, he took hold of her forearm and guided it over her head, his thumb stroking the tender spot where her wrist met her palm.

"Very well, Tabitha," he said.

She felt his fingers move, but she was so transfixed by his eyes, by his continued nearness, that she didn't realize what he was doing until he curled his hand around her wrist, pressing something familiar against her skin.

Tabitha jerked, pulling her arm, but it remained in place—held fast by the binding once again on her wrist. She glanced up at it before returning her gaze to Zevris, hoping her feeling of betrayal was strong enough to make her eyes burn a hole through him.

"Easy," he soothed. Still holding her wrist, he guided her arm—slowly—down to her side. To her astonishment, the binding stretched along with it.

She shoved against his chest with her free hand and bucked beneath him, trying desperately to ignore the way his cock was still nestled against her pussy and the unwanted pleasure it was causing. "Damn it, Zevris! Why?"

"Because it is safest for both of us if you are right here tonight." He reared back, sliding his pelvis away from her fully as he rose on his knees.

She snapped her legs together, feeling exposed, feeling stupid, feeling horny and unfulfilled. "What are you talking about?"

"I didn't miss your threat in the bathroom. You said you were going to kill me. Twice."

Was that a spark of mirth in his eyes now? Was he teasing her over this?

Tabitha glared at him. "I'm not going to actually kill you. Though now I'm having second thoughts." She gave her wrist another useless, angry, defiant tug. The binding went taut immediately.

"Do not fight it, Tabitha. You'll only do yourself more harm." He slid off the bed, giving her full view of his massive erection, which was barely contained by his boxers—and the wet spot on the fabric of said boxers.

Tabitha squeezed her thighs together even tighter. Facing burning, she reached down and grabbed the blanket, pulling it over her like a shield. "You know, this isn't how you go about wooing a lady."

Zevris chuckled. "I am aware. But to be fair, I was attempting to woo you in a more traditional human manner before events took this turn, and I'd planned to continue. Did you...like it?"

She peeked at him over the blanket, which she'd tucked under her chin. "Like what?"

"The cactus." The tiny frown that brought down his lips was almost enough to melt her heart again—*almost*.

Her brows creased. "The cactus was you trying to... I thought it was a housewarming gift."

"Don't human males give flowers to females they are romantically interested in?"

"Well, yes, but they're usually a bunch of fresh cut flowers. Not potted flowers or, you know...a cactus. Not to mention the way you just kind of thrust it at me and ran off in a panic. I mean, usually the guys sticks around after he's given his girl the flowers."

"It wasn't my intention to flee," he said with a wince before running his fingers through his hair. "I...chose that cactus because it reminded me of a plant that grows on my home-world...and because out of all the cactuses on display, it was the only one with a pink flower."

"Why the pink one?"

He dipped his chin toward her. "Your nails. The note you left. The pink made me think of you."

Tabitha looked down at her nails. "Oh." He'd paid attention to so little a detail? "Guess you discovered my favorite color."

Zevris hummed thoughtfully. "I plan to discover many things about my female."

A soft sound came from where he was standing—a barely audible rasp of fabric sliding over flesh. Somehow, Tabitha knew exactly what that sound meant, but she turned her face toward him anyway as though seeking confirmation.

Her eyes flared. He was bent down with his back toward her and his boxers around his ankles, granting her a perfect view of his taut ass and his tail swishing nonchalantly back and forth.

Look away, Tabby! Just. Look. Away.

Tabitha did not look away. "What are you *doing?*"

He plucked his boxers off the floor. "I prefer to sleep naked."

"But you can't...you can't—"

Zevris stood upright and turned to face her. He said something, she knew he did, but Tabitha didn't hear his words because there he was, in all his delicious glory.

All his *huge*, delicious glory.

She'd known he was big, had seen his thickness through his pants, had felt it against her pussy, but seeing it... His cock was long and thick, with a defined crown. At a glance, it could've been mistaken for a human's. But then there were the nubs running from the edge of his crown down to his base—a line of them on his underside and another on top.

Those were what she had felt when he was grinding against her.

Textured for her pleasure.

Heat flooded her core as she imagined all the spots those nubs would stimulate inside her. She gripped the blanket tighter as she rubbed her thighs together against the growing ache of need. And as she continued to stare, Zevris wrapped his fingers around his cock and gave it a stroke to its base. A drop of seed oozed from its tip, and Tabitha had the urge to lick it clean.

He grunted and stilled his hand. His shaft pulsed in the air. "I see my mate approves of her male."

Her gaze snapped up to his face to find him wearing a naughty grin.

Way to go, Tabby. What was it he called you? Thirsty?

Yeah. She could seriously go for a nice, tall, hot alien drink right about now.

Trying to keep a straight face, she looked him dead in the eyes and said, "I've seen bigger."

His grin faltered for a moment before he threw his head back and laughed. "I assure you, Tabitha, this is exactly the right size to fulfill your every desire."

He turned off the light. Tabitha couldn't see anything for a moment, but her eyes quickly adjusted to the diffused glow streaming in through the closed blinds—from the house lights across the street, most likely.

It helped that Zevris's eyes and tattoos gave off gentle glows of their own, granting him an ethereal air and giving his skin a blue cast as he moved around the bed. He grasped the blanket and gave it a sharp tug, pulling it from her grasp. Her eyes widened as he climbed onto the bed, stretching himself out behind her.

"What are you doing?" she screeched, scooting away.

Zevris wrapped his arm around her waist and pulled her back, tucking her body against his. He slipped his other arm under hear head. "I am going to sleep with my mate."

"But you're naked!"

"Mhmm." His cock, now pressed along the curve of her ass, twitched.

"And hard."

"Since I first laid eyes upon you."

Tabitha groaned, turning her face slightly against his arm, unsure if she should be mortified or flattered. She'd never been in a situation like this before, had never had a man focus *all* his attention on her.

It's just a dick, Tabby. It's not going to bite....right?

Zevris pulled the covers over them, likely with his tail, as his arms hadn't budged. His leg slid over hers, and his tail stroked her calf.

His musky, seductive scent enveloped her, cocooning her just as fully as his body had. She refused to admit just how wonderfully she fit with him like this. She was his perfect little spoon.

"What about Dexter?" she asked.

"I took him out while you showered," he rumbled, and she felt the vibrations from his chest against her back.

"I hope he poops on your floor."

He chuckled, creating more of those thrilling vibrations. "I'll be sure to watch my step in the morning." Zevris pressed his lips atop her head and drew in a deep breath. "Sleep, *Nykasha.* You'll need your energy if you mean to continue your resistance tomorrow."

Tabitha couldn't stop the smile that spread across her lips.

She closed her eyes, not expecting to fall asleep any time soon despite her exhaustion. She was tied to an alien's bed, locked in his house, and his arms were around her, holding her close, and she was so aroused...

But her awareness soon faded. She didn't know if it was truly just her weariness or Zevris's warm, secure, soothing presence that lulled her to sleep.

THIRTEEN

Tabitha floated in a dreamlike haze that was somewhere between sleeping and wakefulness, disoriented but oddly content. She felt herself rising toward consciousness, and she didn't fight it, even though she wasn't yet aware enough to understand where she was or what was happening. All she knew was that she felt...good.

Good and aroused, like her dreams had been filled by a sexy alien man who knew more ways to please a woman than there were stars in the sky. She just couldn't recall a single one of them. But her body remembered. She was warm and aching, and her clit throbbed with the aftermath of the climaxes she must have had in her dreams.

She took in a deep breath. The air was scented with that alluring blend of musk, sandalwood, amber, and cedar.

Tabitha released a soft moan and stretched, only to go still when she felt the solid mass wrapped around her—and more prominently, Zevris's long, thick, hard cock wedged between her thighs.

Everything from the day before came back to her in a rush, forcing aside the ignorant bliss that had carried her out of sleep.

She started, meaning to pull away, but the muscular arm around her middle tightened, holding her in place.

Zevris groaned and shifted his arm, sliding his hand down her belly to her pelvis until the tip of his middle finger was a mere half an inch from her slit. Tabitha sucked in a breath and froze again. Could he feel the flare of heat that his touch had sparked between her legs? Could he feel her wetness, or the clenching of her core?

But his hand did not move once it was in place; it remained there, pinning her against him, against his throbbing cock.

"Do not move," he murmured. "Anything more and I may well spill."

Tabitha caught her bottom lip with her teeth as her heart quickened. She was tempted to undulate against him, to tease him, to show him what it felt like, to force him to come so she could feel his seed upon her thighs.

But she couldn't bring herself to do it. No matter how much she wanted to move, no matter how much she wanted to lift her hand and touch him, her own doubts and self-consciousness held her back. She wasn't a seductress, wasn't one of those bold women who took whatever they wanted. Tabitha wasn't even sure what she wanted.

Oh, I know what I want, and he's tall, tan, and alien. Just... not like this.

At least say something, Tabby. Don't just lie there.

But all she could bring herself to say was, "Wouldn't want to, uh...soil your sheets. That'd be an unnecessary load of laundry, am I right?"

For real? Did I just say that? What the frick, Tabby?

Then she realized that she'd just said *load*, and her cheeks went up in flames.

He laughed, tilting his head down to brush his nose against her hair. She felt his breath on the back of her neck, nearly as hot as her combined embarrassment and arousal.

Was there a word to describe that feeling? *Embarrousal? Arousassment?*

She turned her face against his bicep. "Kill me now."

"Ah, Tabitha." He inhaled deeply and released it as a slow, shaky breath before moving his hand away from her pelvis and flattening it atop the bed.

She dared not move as he carefully extracted his shaft from between her thighs. Tension thrummed in his body, radiating from him in waves. She had the sense that all she'd have to do was squeeze a little, and he'd lose control. The thought of having that sort of power over him was exciting...empowering.

As soon as he was free, he sighed heavily and gently slid his arm out from beneath her head. She twisted to watch him roll onto his back and kick the blanket off himself. His engorged cock stood straight up in the air, its head glistening with precum. Being this close, Tabitha noticed something she hadn't last night—there were two larger nodules on the underside of his shaft, just below his head, positioned like a natural frenum piercing.

Zevris wrapped a hand around his shaft. He groaned as he slid that hand down to the base and squeezed, making his cock twitch and seep another droplet of precum from its tip.

Tabitha's eyes widened when he continued moving his hand, sliding it up and down in slow, rhythmic motions.

She turned to face him fully and scooted back, but the restraint around her wrist only allowed her to go so far. "W-what are you doing?"

His half-lidded eyes were upon her as he continued pumping his fist, his movements gradually gaining speed and force. "Easing my discomfort." The corner of his mouth curled up devilishly. "Unless you'd like to ease it for me, *Nykasha?*"

Tabitha shook her head sharply, but she couldn't look away. She watched, transfixed, her arousal growing with each second. Her nipples were hard points against her cami, and the aching throb between her thighs made it difficult to remain still. Every time a drop of seed oozed from his cock, she wanted to lean forward and taste it, to run her tongue from his base to his tip and take him into her mouth.

His ragged breaths, taken through his bared fangs, punctuated each downward thrust of his fist. His eyes did not leave her; their glow seemed stronger than ever.

Tabitha's hand crept down of its own accord, moving toward the source of her discomfort. She gripped the hem of her cami before her fingers could pass her waist, squeezing tight enough to make her knuckles ache, and refused to relinquish her hold.

Zevris growled, his free hand grasping a fistful of the bedding as his back arched. His hips lifted off the bed, and for an instant, his shaft swelled, those nubs looking more pronounced. A spray of seed erupted from his cock, wetting his hand and belly. He grunted, and his movements were erratic as he continued pumping his fist, coaxing out spurts of seed until there was nothing left.

Her core clenched, feeling hollower than ever before. She released a harsh breath as she tore her eyes from his shaft to meet his gaze.

He grinned at her, flashing those sexy fangs, as his chest rose and fell with his heavy breaths. Though he'd just come, the hunger in his gaze was more intense than before—as though he'd sharpened his appetite rather than satisfied it.

"Did you enjoy the display, *Nykasha?*" he asked.

Tabitha glared at him. With a growl, she grabbed the pillow

behind his head and yanked it out from beneath him. He chuckled as his head fell to the mattress, but the sound was cut short an instant later when she swung the pillow at his face. It struck with a dull but satisfying *thump*.

Zevris raised a hand—his clean hand, fortunately—and plucked the pillow off his head. His grin hadn't faded. "Despite this unjustified assault, your scent tells me you enjoyed it thoroughly."

Oh, my God.

She reached for the pillow again, but her fingers had barely brushed the pillowcase before he sat up and jumped off the bed, laughing. As annoyed as she was, Tabitha couldn't help but run her gaze over him as he tossed the pillow onto the bed and strode toward the bathroom door. His seed was trickling down his abs, the muscles of his forearms were tight and even more defined than normal, and his tail was swinging languidly. And, of course, his cock was still fully erect.

But there was just a hint of stiffness to his movements; was it lingering tension, or an enduring struggle for control?

He disappeared into the bathroom, and the shower came on a few moments later. Tabitha lay back down with a heavy sigh. She was so damned aroused. Her body thrummed with desire and heat, and squeezing her thighs together did nothing to alleviate her discomfort—in fact, it only made that ache worse.

As she listened to the water running in the bathroom, she was tempted to slip her hand beneath the covers and quickly finger herself just to find some relief. All it would take was a few strokes on her clit...

But she knew that wouldn't be enough. Any time she'd masturbated when the need struck her, it had always been so... unfulfilling. So hollow. So detached from what she'd truly craved—the romantic connection that made everything so much richer. Someone who...loved her.

More than once, she'd wondered if things would've been easier if she were more like those one-night-stand types of people, the ones who just enjoyed sex for the sake of sex.

But that just wasn't her. She always got too emotionally invested. She didn't want sex for the sake for sex, she wanted...someone.

Tabitha wanted Zevris.

If only he wasn't keeping me prisoner and tied to his damn bed.

She grabbed the pillow and drew it over her face. "Ugh!"

It couldn't have been more than ten minutes before the shower turned off, and only a few more had passed when the bathroom door opened, but the need throbbing at Tabitha's core had made it feel like a hundred years had passed.

She shifted the pillow aside to peek at Zevris. He was staring at her with an arched brow and a crooked smile. Unsurprisingly, he was still very much naked. At least it looked like his cock had finally softened—not that it was all that much smaller while flaccid.

As though sensing her thoughts, his shaft twitched and began to harden right before her eyes.

"Is there anything you want me to do for you, Tabitha?" he asked as he stepped to his dresser. His tail swished behind him. "Anything I might help you with?"

Tabitha knew exactly what his question implied, and the answer she longed to give resounded in her head.

Yes! Touch me!

Instead, she simply glared at him and kept her mouth shut.

He shrugged and opened the top drawer. "Very well."

Zevris dressed himself with the nonchalance of someone who didn't have an audience—or who didn't care that he had an audience. Boxers, socks, a button-down shirt, and, after flattening his tail along his leg and curling its end around his calf, a pair of jeans that hugged his ass like they were molded just for him.

"Isn't that uncomfortable? Keeping your tail in there like that?" she asked.

"No. But it isn't really comfortable, either." He walked to the bedroom door as he buckled his belt.

Tabitha's brow furrowed, and she set the pillow aside, pulling herself up to sit as he reached for the doorknob. "Wait, where are you going?"

Zevris paused and glanced back at her. His eyes skimmed over her chest and back to her face, and his jaw muscles ticked. That tension she'd sensed in him so often again reasserted itself.

"I need to make sure Dexter didn't poop on my floor," he said finally, turning the knob and opening the door. "And my mate will need sustenance."

"Zevris," she said as he turned away and stepped through the doorway. "Zevris, wait!" She hurriedly moved toward him, only to be stopped short when the binding went taut on her wrist. "You can't just leave me here!"

His only answer came in the form of the door closing behind him.

Tabitha growled, snatched up the pillow, and threw it at the door. "I am soooo going to kill him."

Tabitha's comment brought an amused smirk to Zevris's lips, but it could not quell his rising desire. He very nearly pressed himself back against the bedroom door, very nearly raked his claws over the wood, very nearly tore open his pants and took his throbbing cock in hand again.

As though her warmth and beauty had not been alluring enough, as though the feel of her body against his had not been tempting enough, he'd awoken to Tabitha moaning softly in her sleep, rocking her hips in the throes of a dream. The scent of her arousal had been thick in the air; a trace of it still seemed to linger in his nose even after he'd showered and left the room.

He wasn't sure how he'd kept himself still until she'd roused, wasn't sure how he'd managed to pry himself away from her afterward, but he knew one thing with certainty—if he allowed himself to sway even a fraction of an inch toward the bedroom, he would not be able to stop himself.

He would be helpless but to go to her, and he would have her.

Zevris forced his legs into motion, hurrying to the stairs.

Each time his foot came down upon a step during his descent, he felt a jolt in his aching groin. He had his teeth gritted and his fists clenched by the time he reached the bottom of the stairs. His shaft was straining against his jeans, pressing unrelentingly against the denim, and his tail was coiled around his leg with crushing strength.

Tabitha had looked so stunning in his bed. Her eyes had been dark with lust despite the intense gleams that had shone within them, and her tousled hair, hanging freely about her shoulders, had begged for him to comb his fingers through it. That satiny top had molded to her breasts and perfectly outlined her nipples. The way she'd fidgeted, the way she'd bitten her lip, the way she'd pressed her thighs together as though yearning to be filled...it had all nearly driven him mad with want.

He tugged on his boots and propped a foot on one of the lower steps, leaning forward to tie his bootlaces.

A series of soft clicks sounded on the floorboards in the hallway, drawing steadily nearer to Zevris. He pulled the knot on his bootlace tight, lowered his foot the floor, and straightened to find Dexter in the hall.

Dexter stared at Zevris with dark, expectant eyes, his tail wagging erratically from side to side as though in muted anticipation.

Zevris frowned down at the animal. He still wasn't sure what to make of Dexter—or of any dogs, for that matter. He knew they were descended from wild beasts called wolves, knew that humans had trained and domesticated them over many thousands of years, knew that they had a reputation for loyalty. Sometimes, they even seemed to show intelligence well above that of most Earth animals, at least in Zevris's limited experience.

What of Dexter? Was he loyal to Tabitha? Dexter had been the reason Tabitha snuck into Zevris's yard yesterday afternoon, and he had abandoned her when she'd been discovered. The dog had seemed unbothered by his master's absence and had seemed equally indifferent to Zevris's presence on Tabitha's property afterward.

There was a tiny chance that the dog had been leading Tabitha to what she truly wanted, but the notion seemed too foolish, too hopeful, to hold any weight.

"It does not smell like you defecated in my dwelling," Zevris said as he walked toward the kitchen, "but I suggest you mind your claws. My tolerance for further scratches on my floor is quite low."

Dexter walked behind him at an unhurried pace, claws clacking on the floorboards in casual defiance of Zevris's suggestion.

Perhaps it could be attributed to his lingering arousal and lack of fulfillment, but Zevris couldn't find it in himself to be angry at Dexter. The animal had an undeniable, indefinable charm.

"We both need some fresh air. Do you want to go for a walk?"

The dog's ears perked, and his tail rose, swinging with greater speed and enthusiasm.

Zevris activated his holoshroud. For some reason, the faint hum of the hologram shimmering into place sent a shiver through him, sparking a brief but potent flare of pleasure in his groin.

Gritting his teeth, he picked up the leash he'd taken from Tabitha's home—he'd filled one box with things for her, another with things for the dog—and clipped it to Dexter's collar. He wound the loop at the end around his hand. Dexter was already pulling on the leash in his attempt to get to the front door as Zevris turned to pluck a pet waste bag out of the little box.

With the bag in his pocket, he walked to the door—or, more accurately, allowed Dexter to lead him to the door. He deactivated the security field and had a moment of hesitation as he stepped outside, turning his head and glancing toward the stairs. Though he'd attempted to treat the situation with some humor, he could not deny his guilt at having Tabitha trapped here alone, once again bound to his bed, as he was stepping out freely.

He forced himself forward, closed the door, and locked it, sending the command through his neural transceiver to turn the forcefield back on.

Dexter started down the walkway, glancing back to give Zevris a big canine grin.

Matching the dog's pace, Zevris followed Dexter along the sidewalk and through the quiet neighborhood, scanning his surroundings closely and offering smiles and waves to the few people he passed. The rising sun bathed everything in a lovely golden glow that granted the world an almost surreal quality.

But his mind remained preoccupied with Tabitha.

What the fuck am I doing?

His reasons for taking her captive and keeping her

restrained were only sound justification so long as he didn't think about them too much. In truth, he was failing in more ways than he could count. This whole situation with Tabitha was sloppy no matter how he looked at it, especially from the standpoint of this military operation.

She was *it*—she was the only one he had any chance of forming a mating bond with. The only one he desired to make that bond with. And, despite his projections of confidence, he had no idea if that would even work. He wanted it with every bit of himself, but he recognized that his willpower was not enough.

Dexter increased his pace to a run as they rounded the corner onto the main road, where the sidewalk was backed only by landscaping and fences. Zevris jogged behind him without much thought; the physical exertion neither distracted him from his thoughts nor eased them.

He only had thirty days to show definitive progress in his mission.

Twenty-nine, now.

The realization that one day had already passed created a sinking feeling in his gut. One day down. At this rate, he'd need a thousand days to win Tabitha over. He had a feeling that he gladly would have spent a thousand years in his efforts to woo her, but he didn't have that time, and neither did she.

However much she seemed to want him, there was something significant holding her back...and he couldn't help but guess that it was result of his own foolishness.

Being forced to take her captive had encouraged him to be far bolder in his advances, though he knew that would have happened eventually, anyway—Tabitha was the only female to have ignited that spark within him. But the mating bond, as he understood it, went far beyond the physical, just as his desire for her went far beyond the physical.

Trust. That was the key here, wasn't it? He needed to show her that, despite his actions, he trusted her, and that he was willing to let that trust grow. He also needed to demonstrate that she could trust him in turn. That would mean—

Zevris's thoughts were interrupted when Dexter slowed and turned into the grass, nose to the ground. Zevris watched as the dog sniffed, wandering in circles with tail wagging until he finally found a spot.

Dexter turned, squatted, and took a huge shit—all while staring up at Zevris.

"As long as it's not on my floor," Zevris muttered. "Or on my furniture. Or in my garden, or in my truck. You know what? Let's just say you ought to keep it to the grass, and we shouldn't have any problems."

Once the dog was done, Zevris used the bag to pick up the still-warm droppings and tied it shut. His mind shifted back to more important matters as he and Dexter, resuming their jog, turned down another street that would take them around the edge of the neighborhood and eventually back to Zevris's dwelling.

It was time to admit what he'd known all along—Tabitha was right. Keeping her strapped to the bed was wrong, and it was no way to woo a mate. She deserved so, so much better than this, and even if his mission ultimately failed and no mating bond could be made between them, he would not let his relationship with Tabitha be part of his failure.

He couldn't release her, not yet, but he could do what humans so often spoke of regarding romantic relationships. He could compromise. He could shift the dynamics of their current situation in a more favorable direction, even if he could not yet bring himself to change it completely.

Dexter was panting happily by the time they returned to Zevris's dwelling. Zevris dropped the waste bag into the trash can and brought the dog inside, giving Dexter a pat on the side as he unclipped the leash. He closed the door behind him and reengaged the security field.

The dog trotted into the kitchen and sat on the floor in front of his food dish. He settled his expectant gaze on Zevris once again.

"Breakfast sounds good." Zevris untied his boots, kicked them off, and placed them on the mat beside the door before walking into the kitchen. He poured the suggested amount of dog food into Dexter's bowl, washed his hands at the sink, and turned to face the fridge, dragging his fingers through his hair.

He'd learned to cook initially during his *Exthurizen* training, many years ago. It had been a survival skill. Eating food was a necessity, and preparing it had been only about keeping his body sustained, not about taste. But in his time on Earth, he'd learned to prepare many flavorful foods. He had the stores to make any number of dishes for Tabitha, and her enjoyment of the meal he'd prepared last evening was both inspiring and encouraging. He'd been fortunate with his choices.

What else did she like? What did she like for breakfast, specifically? There were certain foods humans seemed to eat only at certain times of the day, and no meal seemed quite as restricted as breakfast.

All he knew was that he wanted to both provide for her and surprise her.

Zevris rolled up his sleeves, created a prioritized mental task list, and set to work. Since he didn't know a specific food she liked, he would make a variety of foods and allow her to have her pick.

He moved with the sort of efficiency, confidence, and focus he'd rarely applied outside combat, waging a battle in which his greatest foes were eggs, sausage, bacon, batter, and toast. The kitchen was soon filled with the mouthwatering aromas of cooking foods, reminding Zevris of his hunger. Dexter, having apparently finished his dog food, sat watching intently, occasionally leaning his nose forward and sniffing. His attention seemed most often turned toward the sizzling sausage links and strips of bacon.

When the food was done, Zevris set it all out on the center of the table, covered everything with whatever lids and trays he had that would fit to keep them warm—and, just as importantly, keep Dexter from getting into anything. He set two empty plates, each with an accompanying knife, fork, and spoon, down in front of two of the chairs, and stepped back to survey his work. It was a strangely heartening feeling to have the table set for two after so many meals alone.

Only one thing was missing.

"Stay down," he said, pointing at Dexter. "Behave, and there'll be something in it for you soon enough."

Dexter tilted his head, releasing a soft whine. His tail thumped softly on the floor.

Zevris walked backward for several steps, keeping his finger directed at the unmoving dog, before he finally turned and went upstairs, taking the steps two at a time. He felt lighter already. This couldn't atone for what he'd done, but this was a start toward making it better, wasn't it? This was a start toward courting his mate properly.

His mouth stretched into a smile as he opened the door and stepped into the bedroom.

That smile fell the instant his eyes met Tabitha's furious glare.

She was sitting up against the headboard with her thighs squeezed together and his pillow pressed over her lap with her free hand, but any arousal that had been on her face before had fled her expression, leaving only fury in its wake. He understood what he'd done immediately and cursed himself for being so foolish.

He'd been gone for twenty minutes walking Dexter, and then had spent another thirty preparing breakfast. All while Tabitha, who hadn't relieved herself since the night before, had been stuck in this bed.

Zevris had left her aroused, unfulfilled, and unable to empty her bladder.

His brows fell low, and his lips sank into a tight frown as itching heat spread just under his skin. All his plans of easing her discomforts and making this as pleasant an experience as possible seemed meaningless now.

She said nothing as he crossed the room and moved to the bedside, and he could not keep his gaze upon her. Shame had clamped around his chest like a vise, tightening a little more with each second, crushing his lungs and making it difficult to breath.

But he felt her eyes upon him. Felt their heat. And he could not blame her for it.

As soon as he was at the bedside, he touched the binding, sending the remote command to release it.

"Tabitha, I—"

She swung her legs off the bed, stood up, and thrust the pillow against his chest hard enough to make him rock on his heels. Before he could muster another word, she stormed into the bathroom and slammed the door shut with a thunderous bang.

Zevris winced, sucking in a breath through his fangs. This was not the new start for which he'd planned.

Tossing the pillow on the bed, he walked to the door and lightly rapped upon it.

Tabitha responded with a growl fierce enough to have given most predators pause.

He couldn't keep the smile from his face. Tabitha was complicated, and there were still many things about her that he didn't understand, but he adored her vitality, her spirit. He was grateful that he'd not broken it through his stupidity.

"I'm sorry, Tabitha." Though his words were nothing but sincere, they felt strangely empty; he knew they could not make up for any of this. "When you are ready, come down to the kitchen."

She made no further response. Zevris lingered in front of the door, searching for something more to say, but there were no simple words to fix this. He could only hope that she'd come.

Tail coiling around his leg tight enough to hurt, Zevris left the bedroom and went downstairs to await his mate.

FOURTEEN

"I suppose we're bonded by being recipients of that glare," Zevris said, folding his arms across his chest and leaning his backside against the counter. "And we were both deserving."

Dexter glanced up at Zevris without lifting his head. He was lying on the floor now, chin on his paws, doing his best to look contrite and pathetic. He'd had his paws on the table and was sniffing at the covered plates when Zevris came downstairs only moments ago. The dog and the faloran had exchanged a long, heavy stare before the dog had dropped down on all fours, sauntered away from the table, and assumed his current position.

Zevris sighed and shifted his attention to the table. With all the improvised coverings, the arrangement wasn't quite as impressive as he'd thought. It looked...haphazard. Sloppy. Like it had been an impulsive decision, executed without any true plan, thrown together on a whim.

Even if that was all true, that was not the image he wanted to present.

He pushed away from the counter and stepped over to

Dexter, crouching. The dog turned his eyes up toward Zevris, looking even sadder and more apologetic than ever.

"Stay put," Zevris commanded. "Do not touch the food."

Dexter's tail thumped on the floor once and went still.

Though the answer was not satisfactory, Zevris accepted it. He only needed a minute or two. Rising, he hurried to the back door, deactivated the security field and disengaged the lock, and slid it open.

After a final warning glance at Dexter—who was facing away now but had his ears perked—Zevris stepped out into the back yard. He jogged to the fence, checked for any onlookers, and climbed over into Tabitha's yard. Her back door was still unlocked. As he slipped inside, he reprimanded himself again.

This place was her home, and the items within were her belongings. It was inconsiderate of him to leave it unsecured and vulnerable. He'd have to remedy that today.

But for now, his goal was simple and clear. He walked into her kitchen, plucked the potted cactus off its windowsill perch, and returned to his dwelling.

As Zevris entered his kitchen, his pace slowed, and he arched a brow. Dexter was still lying on his belly with his head down, but Zevris could've sworn the dog was at least a couple feet closer to the table. Eyes narrowed on the animal, Zevris brought the cactus to the table, set it down, and shifted the food-laden plates in an attempt to find a more symmetrical layout.

After a minute or two of fiddling, he stepped back. It was far from perfect, but it would have to do. He was already stretching his limited selection of flatware as far as it could go.

Zevris glanced down at Dexter again. Those big, dark eyes, so sad and sorry, were almost enough to convince Zevris that he'd been the one who'd done wrong and not Dexter.

They were almost enough to convince him the dog hadn't moved a few inches closer.

Zevris returned to the counter, leaned his backside against it, and propped his hands on the countertop to either side of his hips. He eyed the dog skeptically.

Dexter released a huff that made his lips flap.

With a huff of his own, Zevris turned his gaze to the hallway. Would Tabitha come down? She must've been hungry, but she'd also been furious with him. It was quite possible that her anger would outweigh her appetite, and she'd avoid him for the rest of the day.

Not that he'd allow that to happen.

Twenty-nine days...

He understood that she needed space, that she needed time to adjust to this situation, but he didn't have much time to waste. Absently, he drummed his fingers against the granite countertop. His tail twitched against his leg. How long a wait was long enough?

Despite all the deadly tasks Zevris Akkaran had undertaken, despite all the times he'd faced his own potential death, nothing filled him with as much dread as the thought of Tabitha Mathews deciding she didn't want to see him again.

"If she doesn't come down soon, the food will be cold, and I suppose you'll get your feast." He glanced at Dexter and frowned. The dog was unquestionably closer now, his snout within a few inches of one of the table's legs.

Upstairs, the bedroom door opened, and Zevris heard Tabitha's light footsteps as she made her way down the stairs. Dexter lifted his head and turned toward the kitchen's entryway.

The end of Zevris's tail curled, and his heart thumped a little faster.

Tabitha hesitantly appeared a few moments later.

She looked freshly showered, with her damp blonde hair woven into a large braid that fell over one shoulder. She wore blue jeans that clung to her shapely legs, socks, a white shirt that said *Too Hot To Candle* across the front, and an unbuttoned maroon cardigan.

Even like this—in what must've been her everyday attire—she was stunningly alluring.

Dexter scrabbled to his feet and hurried toward her, tongue lolling and tail wagging faster than Zevris had ever seen. The dog barked and lifted his front paws onto Tabitha, who beamed a smile down at him, catching his face between her hands.

"Hey Dex," Tabitha said, voice high and happy. She scratched him behind his ears. "Did you miss me?"

The dog barked again, rubbing his head affectionately against her before sitting at her feet.

Tabitha straightened, her smile fading as she studied the spread on the table before she raised her gaze to meet Zevris's. "No breakfast in bed?"

"I'm more than willing to take you back to my bed if that's what you desire."

She narrowed her eyes on him. "You do, and I'll gouge your eyes out with a spoon."

Blood thirsty female.

Zevris couldn't stop the corner of his mouth from quirking up. "So long as you are the last thing I see, I wouldn't mind."

Tabitha snorted.

Pushing away from the counter, Zevris walked to the table. He drew out a chair for her. "Come. Sit."

She stared at him for a moment longer, her fingers toying with the cuffs of her sweater. Finally, she closed the distance between them and sat, allowing him to push her chair in. Dexter followed, plopping down next to Tabitha, looking hopeful.

Zevris pulled out his own chair and leaned over the table, removing the coverings on the various plates of food. "I wasn't sure what you would prefer. Help yourself."

Her brows rose as she looked over the spread, but her gaze paused and lingered on the cactus. The corners of her lips lifted into a small smile. She reached out, picked up a strip of bacon, and fed it to Dexter, who noisily gobbled it down.

"So this is what you were doing while my bladder was in danger of exploding?" she asked.

He deserved the sting inflicted by her words. "Yes. I focused so much on fulfilling this need that I lost sight of the others." Zevris gathered the spare plates and covers and carried them to the counter, where he set them down. "Again, I am sorry. Hopefully, this will make it up to you, if only in small part."

"Are you going to tie me to the bed again?"

Zevris drew in a deep breath, returned to the table, and sat down. "No."

"Are you letting me go?" she asked hopefully. *Too* hopefully.

"No. But"—he hurried to add when her features fell—"I wish to make a compromise."

Tabitha's brow creased, and she turned her head slightly, giving him a suspicious look. "What kind of compromise?"

"Eat. Some of it's likely getting cold already."

She looked back down at the table. Finally, she picked up her fork and used it to transfer a pancake to her plate, followed by a small pile of scrambled eggs, and two strips of bacon. She drizzled syrup onto the pancake.

"I'm listening." Tabitha glanced at him as she took a bite of her eggs.

Zevris piled food onto his plate, barely looking at what he was taking. "I've already explained why I cannot let you go,

Tabitha, but I want to do all I can to make you feel like...a guest, and not a prisoner. I will not restrain you again. You may move about this dwelling freely, without restriction, but you cannot leave. My being here *must* remain secret."

"Zevris, please just let me go home. I swear I won't tell anyone."

"I believe you, *Nykasha*, but I cannot take the chance. Not yet. If it were merely a matter of me being discovered, I wouldn't care. But this mission is larger than me, and the consequences of me being discovered could be dire for my people."

Tabitha stared down at her plate, absently pushing her food around with her fork. She didn't take another bite.

"Four weeks," Zevris said.

She looked up at him and frowned. "What?"

"I want you, Tabitha. More than anything I've ever wanted." His heart pounded, his chest grew tight, and his mouth went dry, but none of that stopped him from continuing. "I have met more females than I can count since coming to this planet. Of them all, only you have this pull on me. From the moment we met, I knew you were it. You were mine.

"I know how much it is to ask, but allow me four weeks to convince you. To court you, to win you, to...earn you. And to make you see that you want me, too. Just...give me time, Tabitha. Give me a chance."

Tabitha searched his eyes. "And...after the four weeks?"

"If I have failed, you are free to go."

And you will never see me again.

Zevris placed his free hand on his thigh, curling his fingers as he gritted his teeth. The tips of his claws pricked his flesh through the denim. Would he be able to leave her? Would he be able to live without seeing her? It was insane to have grown so attached to this female already, to have come to crave her so much, but he understood on an instinctual level that he needed her.

And part of his mind was already formulating plans to disappear, to use his years of experience to evade the military force that had charged him with this very mission, just so he could be with Tabitha.

"And you are to never speak a word of my true nature, my people, or my mission to anyone," he continued, "for doing so would put your life in danger."

His female was silent for a long while. He wished he could read her thoughts, wished he knew what troubled her, knew her doubts, her fears, her wishes, her desires.

"So, four weeks to convince me, and you promise not to tie me up again?" she asked.

Not unless you ask me too, Nykasha.

The very thought of Tabitha submitting to him like that, of agreeing to be bound to his bed so he could do with her as he pleased, had his cock hardening.

"I will not bind you, but you will still share my bed."

Her cheeks flushed, and Zevris knew she was thinking back to this morning, when she'd watched as he'd pleasured himself.

His gaze bored into hers. "I will not force myself upon you, Tabitha. I will only take what you give freely. But I will not relent. I will do everything I can to have you beneath me, to have your taste upon my tongue, to make you *mine.*"

Tabitha looked away, her cheeks turning that adorable shade of pink, but not before he caught the flash of want in her eyes. She reached up with both hands to fiddle with the end of her braid.

Zevris forced himself to take a bite of food, barely tasting it. Eager as he was for her to answer, for her to agree, he wanted her to do so in her own time.

"And, um...your mission," she said. "It's to...form a mating bond, right? To...impregnate me?"

"Technically, it is to determine whether those things are even possible between our species. But yes. Those are the objectives." He leaned forward. "Regardless of my mission, even if that bond is not possible between us, I want you for my lifemate, Tabitha."

Though he knew, deep down, that the bond *would* work. It had to work—he would accept no other outcome.

She took a deep breath, exhaled slowly and quietly, and returned her gaze to him. "Okay. I will give you four weeks."

He grinned.

"On the condition that you bring my supplies, equipment, and computer here so I can continue my work," she added.

"Anything you need, I will obtain for you. Any comfort you desire."

"What about my phone? And will I be able to record my videos, interact with my customers, ship out orders? Talk to my friends?"

"I..."

I haven't thought about all that.

"I will move your equipment and supplies after breakfast," he said, "but the phone and the computer...I need time for those, Tabitha. Granting you that access would put me at great risk."

"What if I prove you can trust me?"

"Just give me time, *Nykasha*," he said again, gently. "We *will* get there."

Tabitha glanced down at Dexter, gave him another strip of bacon, then looked back at Zevris. She smiled. "Okay. I accept."

Relief and excitement flooded Zevris, surging so quickly and powerfully that he felt like he would burst. All he could do was grin at her like a damned fool.

Tabitha Mathews, you are mine.

FIFTEEN

AT LEAST A HUNDRED new scents had taken up residence in Zevris's dwelling, each one vying for dominance over the rest but none managing to achieve that goal. He was handling the plethora of smells better than he'd anticipated. He wasn't sure whether that was because they'd only been introduced a few at a time as he'd brought boxes full of supplies over or because the jumbled smells cancelled each other out, but it didn't matter.

All that mattered was visible before him.

He was standing in the doorway of his spare first-floor room, shoulder leaned against the doorframe, watching as Tabitha arranged her workspace. She was focused and efficient, yet at the same time had grown quite relaxed. She'd made several amusing comments as she'd sorted the scents and colors, and she'd stopped more than a few times to open a container, sniff its contents, and make a pleased hum.

She was in her element now, and though he couldn't bring himself to interrupt her, he found her passion and excitement astoundingly arousing. But if he were being honest with himself, there wasn't *anything* about her that he didn't find astoundingly arousing. His gaze dipped down to her luscious ass.

He was going to have to learn how to live with a permanent erection, because his cock refused to ease. The damned thing was making Dexter look well behaved.

At least he could be thankful that the scent that had affected him the day he'd given her the cactus was either absent or overwhelmed by the others. In his current state of arousal, that smell would've been too much to bear, and might very well have pushed him to break his word to her.

Reminder of that event, of his loss of control, brought a frown to his face. He didn't know of any aphrodisiacs with so powerful an effect on falorans, especially not any that worked by scent alone. Learning what he could about it would be prudent—both to report back to the *ultricar* and to prevent himself from being overcome by it again.

Reluctant as he was to disturb his female's work, he needed to ask while it was fresh on his mind. "Tabitha?"

She looked up at him as she opened another box. "Yeah?"

"The day I brought you the cactus, there was a strong scent in your home. What was it?"

Her brows creased. "I'm...not sure. There's usually a lot of strong scents going on while I'm working."

"It was extremely prominent. It seemed floral, but not a flower with which I am familiar. You had spilled it on your apron."

"Oh! That was lily of the valley." She smiled sheepishly as she returned her attention to the box, taking out bars of soap and stacking them neatly on the shelving he'd installed. She kept them together based on their colorations and designs. "I hadn't been expecting company, so I was kind of...in the zone. When you rang the doorbell, I was walking with the bottle of scent, and Dexter jumped up in front of me. It startled me, and

I dropped the bottle. Some spilled on the floor, but most of it wound up on me.

"Why do you ask?"

Just curious might have been the easiest answer, but his cock chose that moment to throb, making a deep ache resonate through his lower belly as though to remind him of what had happened.

"It had an...unexpected effect on me."

Tabitha looked at him, tilted her head to the side, and lowered her eyebrows. Her gaze dipped down his body. Her eyes flared, and she quickly turned away, skin flushed. Her motions were noticeably quicker as she resumed stacking soap on the shelf.

She'd seen his erection.

He chuckled. She was not unaffected by him, and he found her reactions adorable. She was a shy female when it came to sex. He couldn't wait to see pleasure brighten her eyes, couldn't wait to watch her come undone beneath him, couldn't wait until she gained the confidence to take all the ecstasy she craved from him.

"Is that, um...why you ran off?" she asked.

"Yes. It seemed best not to involve you in my...condition at the time."

Tabitha tucked a stray strand of hair behind her ear. "I wondered why you ran off like that."

Zevris smiled, and that ache in his groin intensified. In that moment, he longed to walk up behind her, wrap her braid around his fist, and tilt her head aside to skim his lips and fangs across her delicate skin. To nip at the ear she'd just bared, to trail his tongue along her jaw, to taste her lips with his.

He was beginning to wonder how long he could resist his desires even without the effects of the lily of the valley clouding his mind.

"I never intended to flee," he said, voice sounding just a touch strained to his own ears.

She pressed her lips together for a moment, dropping her gaze. "I didn't mean to run from you, either. Well"—she reached into the box and removed another stack of bar soap—"not the first couple times, anyway. You know, before I saw your, erm..." She mumbled something, the words so low and muffled that they were difficult to make out with any real certainty.

But to Zevris, they'd sounded suspiciously close to *sexier side*. He told himself that first word must have been *alien*, not *sexier*, though he wasn't quite convinced by that explanation, however probable it seemed.

His tail swept from side to side behind him. It felt good to have someone around whom he could be undisguised. He'd not had to hide that he was a faloran during every operation he'd conducted, but he'd always had to keep his presence mostly hidden. Being himself, being out in the open, even if it was only with her, was a refreshing and welcome change.

Tabitha owned a collection of books about human females being taken by aliens as mates, and her desire for Zevris was apparent almost every time she looked at him. He would use that to his advantage as often and heavy-handedly as he could.

He pushed away from the doorframe and was about to enter the room—with imaginings of his imminent seduction of Tabitha coursing through his mind—when his pocket vibrated. Zevris halted.

The vibration did not repeat, but it didn't need to. He knew it had come from Tabitha's phone. She'd received a message of some sort, and he would need to address it in order to deflect any potential suspicions.

He could not do so in front of her.

"I'm going to take Dexter out back," he said after a moment's pause. "I'll return shortly."

Tabitha turned her face toward him. Zevris didn't miss the way her eyes dipped along his body before they met his gaze. She smirked. "Okay. I don't plan on going anywhere, so...see you in a few."

He snickered, appreciating her humor. It was clear that she wasn't entirely satisfied with the arrangement they'd made—not that he was, either—but she'd been so much more vibrant in the hours since breakfast.

He hoped he would witness such excitement and joy on her face every single day, until all his days had been spent.

Forcing himself to turn around, he walked away from the room. Every step was heavier and quicker than the last. As he neared the back door, he called for Dexter.

The dog bounded down the hallway to join Zevris at the sliding glass door. As soon as the door was open, Dexter darted outside, lowered his nose to the ground, and sniffed around.

Zevris closed the door and reengaged the forcefield. With a single glance back to ensure Tabitha wasn't watching, he strode along the patio to a spot where he'd be out of sight, only taking her phone out of his pocket when he was away from the windows.

The screen flashed on, displaying a text message from Mia.

Zevris glanced over at Dexter, who had his front paws over the concrete curbing that separated the flowerbed from the grass.

"No," Zevris said firmly. "Keep it in the grass, Dexter."

Dexter released a drawn-out whine that ended with a huff. One paw at a time, he backed away from the flower bed.

Returning his attention to the phone in hand, Zevris tapped on the message and entered the passcode.

Mia's name had a small picture beside it, a woman with

brown hair and skin. She'd texted, *Everything good, Tabby? Hope Dex didn't get you in too much trouble yesterday!*

Frowning, Zevris scrolled up, scanning the messages previously exchanged between Tabitha and Mia. Fortunately, both women seemed to use relatively proper English in their communications. It might have broken his brain if he'd had to mimic the texting style of the last female he'd dated.

Dropping the conversation back to the latest message, he typed out a reply. *Sorry, Mia! Dex was trying to dig under the fence, so I had to get him inside. Then I just got so caught up with unpacking I totally lost track of time.*

Zevris lifted his gaze to Dexter. The dog sniffed the ground in the center of the yard, moved a few steps, and stopped to sniff again.

The phone vibrated as Mia's reply appeared. *Don't worry about it, Tabs! I know you're busting your sexy butt over there. Just remember to stop and take some time for yourself when you're done. Bubble bath, glass of wine, a romantic book, and maybe some one-on-one time with your old pal Big Buck.*

Zevris's brow furrowed as he read the message a second time. There was a little picture accompanying each of the things Mia had listed—a bath with bubbles rising over the rim, a goblet of red wine, an open book, and, for some reason, what appeared to be an eggplant after *Big Buck.*

Who was Big Buck, why would Tabitha have one-on-one time with him, and what did eggplants have to do with it?

He moved his thumbs, meaning to type a response, but how could he reply when he had no idea what she meant? His eyes fixated on that eggplant. It was almost reminiscent of the long, purple sex toy he'd discovered hidden under Tabitha's underwear.

Zevris clenched his jaw, growling low in his chest. Was *that* what Mia was referring to?

Another message popped up before he could stew on that any further.

OMG, you'll never guess who came by last night.

Before Zevris could even type *who*, Mia texted again.

Cody fucking Everton!

Can you believe that he had the nerve to come looking for you? He looks totally different, like he's on roids or something. He gave me a bunch of BS about how he was really sorry and just wanted to see how you were doing, that he'd been thinking about it the whole time and he wanted to make things right with you. He did his best to look pathetic, but his inner asshole came out when I said you weren't here.

So he was all like "where is she, then?" I told him you moved out and that you moved on, and that you had a boyfriend that made him look like a wet sack of potatoes. I think he was about to go full dickhead on me, but Josh stepped up and made him leave.

Again, Zevris wasn't sure how to respond; again, Mia sent another message before he could.

Ridiculous how your asshole ex who did nothing but treat you like shit thinks he can just walk back into your life, probably because he got his dumbass dumped or something and thinks he's too hot for you to resist. I'm so glad you broke it off with that douche.

Another growl rumbled up from Zevris's chest. *Ex* was typically used as shorthand—ex-boyfriend, ex-girlfriend, ex-husband or wife. Tabitha had been in a relationship with this Cody Everton. That alone was infuriating enough, but to know that the man had mistreated her nearly threw Zevris into a rage. He forced himself to breathe, slowly but heavily, through his nostrils. He needed to send a text back before Mia grew suspicious.

Me too, Zevris replied. *He doesn't deserve me, and I deserve a whole lot better than him.*

He winced, wondering if that was too bold, too out of character, but Mia responded with what looked like a pair of clapping hands.

You're damn right, girl! Anyway, enough about that piece of human garbage. Any more news on your smoking hot neighbor? I neeeeeeeeed pics, Tabby! Did you man up and ask him out yet?

A grin stretched across Zevris's lips. Had Tabitha told Mia about him? Had she expressed her interest in him? He couldn't help the swell of pride that filled his chest at that notion.

Well...we actually had breakfast together this morning, he typed, his grin only widening at the memory. *He'd definitely make an excellent mate.*

Frowning, he deleted that last line; it wasn't how most humans—or Tabitha—would've phrased it. He only sent the bit about breakfast.

Mia's reply came with a flare of fireworks across the screen. *Damn, Tabby, get down with your bad self!*

I need to get going, Zevris typed. *Got a lot of work to do today if I want to get everything on track. I'll talk to you soon, okay?*

Ooooooh, you're lucky. I love you, Tabby. Go get to work! But I expect full, explicit details ASAP. Love ya!

Love you too. Zevris sent that last message and was about to press the lock button on the phone when he stilled his thumb.

His frown deepened as he closed the message application. There was a social media app right there on Tabitha's home screen, taunting Zevris. Though Tabitha had mentioned she made and shared videos online, she didn't strike him as the type of person who publicized much of her life. Going into that app wasn't likely to tell him much about her.

But there was someone else he wanted to see.

He pressed on the icon, and as soon as the app loaded, he pressed the magnifying glass to initiate a search. He gritted his teeth as he entered the name, straining to keep his thumbs from slamming down on the screen.

The name Cody Everton yielded no results—at least not any who were located within several hundred miles. After a few seconds of thought, Zevris navigated to Tabitha's block list. Surely enough, Cody Everton was there, having the distinction of being the one and only profile Tabitha had blocked.

Zevris locked Tabitha's phone, returned it to his pocket, and took out his own phone to perform another search. Somehow, he knew just by the man's picture that the first Cody Everton on the list of search results was Tabitha's ex. Zevris tapped the name.

His jaw muscles only tensed further as he scrolled through Cody's profile. The man had posted numerous pictures of himself, many of which were in expensive looking shirts and ties. He seemed to never have his sunglasses off, even when indoors. But scattered through those were pictures of Cody in athletic wear or without a shirt, flexing in front of mirrors or in the middle of a gym. He was tall, with brown eyes and blond hair that was pulled up in a bun atop his head, and his body was muscular and toned.

The self-taken images were broken up by posts of what Cody must have considered wisdom—platitudes pertaining to things like positive mindsets, hard work, and not complaining unless one could offer a solution for the problem. Sprinkled throughout were also what Zevris assumed to be jokes, though he found no humor in them.

Zevris tapped on the photos tab and scrolled down. There were numerous images of Cody with different women, several of which were marked with captions like *Feeling so blessed* or *So happy to have met the love of my life!* As he delved deeper, he noticed the changes to Cody's body in reverse—the man must've packed on a significant amount of muscle over the last couple years.

Zevris had scrolled through hundreds of images when his finger halted, and fire flared in his belly. Because there, buried deep in all the bullshit, was a series of pictures of Cody and Tabitha.

Zevris's hand tensed, and he had to exert most of his willpower to ease it so he didn't break his phone. In most of the pictures, Cody seemed to be the one holding the camera. He was often angled to be in front of her, giving himself prominence. In the earlier pictures, Tabitha was smiling, looking happy, but that changed over time. She looked shyer in the later photos, like the light had faded from her eyes. In the last few, she appeared to be uncomfortable, avoiding the camera.

The blend of fury and jealousy that boiled inside Zevris was as volatile as a star on the verge of exploding. Seeing his mate with another male was more than he could bear, but knowing that male had treated her poorly, had failed to care for her and cherish her as she deserved, filled him with a murderous rage he'd rarely felt outside of traveling human roadways at rush hour.

If he ever encountered this Cody Everton face to face, there'd likely be one less male on this world before everything was done.

He forced himself to exit the application and lock his phone, stuffing the device in his back pocket before he could be tempted to open it again. The past didn't matter; he couldn't let it matter. Cody and any other males she'd dated had had their chances. Now was Zevris's time.

Tabitha was his. All he needed to do was win her over...

And Mia had given him a good idea to pamper his female and help her relax.

SIXTEEN

Tabitha sat on Zevris's sofa with her elbow propped on the armrest and her head cradled in her palm. Dexter lay next to her, his head in her lap, as she absently petted his back. It was late, and her belly was full after another delicious dinner. The food had tasted all the better because she hadn't had to cook it. Zevris had insisted on catering to her. He'd even shooed her out of the kitchen when she'd offered to clean up afterwards, and once he'd finished, he'd taken Dexter out before disappearing upstairs. So here she sat.

Despite the circumstances of her being here, she felt...good. It'd been a good day.

Well, apart from him leaving her tied to his bed and on the verge of peeing herself for over an hour that morning. But she had forgiven Zevris for that incident shortly afterward, while she'd taken her shower. His expression when he'd released her from the restraint had been so contrite, so ashamed, and his apology so sincere... She knew he hadn't done it on purpose.

The day had passed faster than Tabitha thought it would, and true to his word, Zevris had allowed her free rein of his home. She'd explored, but there hadn't been much to discover. His house really was decorated like a model home, furnished tastefully but sparsely enough that it left room for prospective buyers to envision themselves living here. It was nice, but there were no personal touches, there was no décor that showcased his personality, there was no real vitality. Just the basics. This place said nothing about the man who lived in it.

What was his favorite color? What did he enjoy? What were his hobbies?

Did aliens even have hobbies?

Of course they have hobbies, Tabby. He's still a person.

Well...Tabitha was determined to find out what they were. The time she'd spent with Zevris today had only further endeared him to her. He was kind, thoughtful, and funny, and he flirted with her at every opportunity. She wasn't used to that kind of attention from men, and most definitely not from any who looked like Zevris. But she found that she wanted to take the time to get to know him.

Four weeks.

Could things actually work between them? Once those four weeks were over, could she actually agree to become his... lifemate, after so short a time? He must've been sincere in his proposal, in his attraction to her. Why bother going through all this trouble if he didn't really want her? And if what she saw in his eyes every time he looked at her was real...

Tabitha's entire body flushed, and she turned her face into her hand.

Now that it was night and bedtime was fast approaching, she didn't know what to expect. But if this morning had been any indication, well, she'd be struggling against a whole lot of temptation pretty soon.

Take it slow, Tabby. You have four weeks. Don't rush into anything you're not ready for.

"He wants babies, Dex," she whispered, looking down at her dog.

Dexter raised his eyes to meet hers, and his ears perked.

"Oh, don't you look at me like that. Four weeks is a little soon to be asking me for babies, don't you think?" Tabitha scratched the top of Dexter's head. "Isn't it supposed to be first comes love, then comes marriage, then comes a baby? The key word in all of that being *love?*"

Dexter rubbed his face against her belly, his tail wagging.

Her brows shot down, and she pushed his nose away. "Whose side are you on, anyway?"

God, was she even ready to be a mother? Would she make a good one? She'd never known her birth mother. Amanda Davidson had abandoned Tabitha when she was an infant, leaving her in the care of her father, Luke Mathews—who had also soon run off on his child, leaving Tabitha in the care of his mother. Nan had been Tabitha's mother in every way that mattered. She had set the example for Tabitha to follow.

Tabitha would do everything in her power to make sure her baby was happy and knew it was loved.

Though there was no rush for a baby to begin with...

You have four weeks, Tabby. Better get used to the idea, especially because you know you're going to get in too deep.

"That's *if* we're even compatible," she said quietly, frowning.

But she was already falling, and she had a feeling it would be just like he'd said—even if the mating bond thing his people made didn't work with her, she'd want him anyway.

Yet would he truly still want her if that was the case? His race was dying, and his mission came down to popping out some super-attractive alien babies to save his people. If she couldn't produce, what reason would he have to stay with her?

Four weeks. I can stop myself from falling head-over-heels in love with him for at least that long, right? I can enjoy this, but be strong...

She frowned. The faint pang in her heart suggested that no amount of self-encouragement would change the truth. She'd never wanted anyone as much as she wanted Zevris, and she'd never been as scared of her desire as she was now.

"Tabitha," Zevris called from upstairs.

The sound of his voice startled her from her thoughts. Dexter lifted his head and regarded her, his tail flicking uncertainly.

Tabitha swallowed back her surprise, stuffed her doubts into the dark hole she'd dug for them in the back of her mind, and replied, "Yeah?"

"Come upstairs. I have something for you."

Is it his throbbing dick?

Her cheeks heated instantly—not merely because of the nature of that thought, but because of the little flare of excitement it sparked at her core.

What was wrong with her? What kind of spell had he put her under?

But once that initial thought had faded, a tiny lump of dread formed in her belly. Though he'd given her his word, she couldn't shake the frustration and helplessness she'd felt while tied to his damned bed. That little voice in her head, the one that questioned *everything*, told her there was always a chance he was about to do it again, anyway.

Trust. She needed to *trust* him.

"Just a sec," she called. Standing, she turned to Dexter, rubbed the sides of his face with her hands, and kissed the top of his head. "Goodnight, Dexter."

She released him and made her way to the stairs, looking up to find Zevris waiting for her at the top, wearing only his jeans and looking down at her with that wickedly sexy smile. The light was off in the little hallway at the top of the steps, and the glow of his tattoos cast his sculpted muscles in an ethereal radiance that rocketed his sex appeal off the charts.

As she walked up the steps, her anxiousness, as well as her anticipation, grew.

"Hi," she said nervously when she reached him, clutching the banister like a lifeline.

His smile tilted slightly. "Hi."

"Was there something you wanted to show me?"

"There is." He settled his hand atop hers, taking gentle hold of it and lifting it away from the banister, and he didn't release it as he walked into the bedroom. With only the lamp on the nightstand turned on, the room was cast in a dull light that made it feel smaller and more intimate.

Her heart raced as she looked at the bed, but he led her past it until they were standing before the closed bathroom door.

Reaching forward, he took hold of the doorknob, turned it, and glanced at her over his shoulder. "Close your eyes."

Tabitha arched a brow but couldn't stop her smile as she did as he asked, "Should I be worried?"

"My goal is to ensure you never have to worry about anything, Tabitha."

The door latch clicked. A moment later, the soothing smell of lavender washed over her, strengthening as Zevris led her into the bathroom.

He released Tabitha's hand and settled his palms on her waist, startling her, but she didn't open her eyes. She felt his big body at her back, felt the strength of his hold, the slight prick of his claws through her clothing. A thrill raced across her skin, making it prickle with goosebumps.

Zevris turned Tabitha gently, moving his body with hers, and lowered his head. His breath tickled her ear as he whispered, "You may look."

Tabitha opened her eyes and gasped softly.

The lights were off, but the bathroom was bathed in a warm orange glow from the numerous tealight candles arranged around the bathtub and on the counter. Bubbles rose over the rim of the tub, shimmering in the candlelight. Flower petals of several different colors were scattered along the edges of the tub, between the candles, along the vanity, and on the floor. Real flower petals.

A bottle of wine and a wine glass were set beside a folded hand towel at one corner of the ledge running around the tub, with one of her romance books sitting atop the towel.

She twisted slightly to look back at him, and Zevris lifted a hand to his hair, combing his claws through it.

"The candles and the wine are yours," he said, just a hint of sheepishness in his voice. "I've not yet gone to the store to purchase things for you. I will compensate you for them."

Tabitha looked back at the candles. They were simple, easy, cheap things to make, and usually sold alongside her more elaborate decorative candles. She couldn't be mad at him for using them. Especially not when he'd been thoughtful enough to have gone through the trouble of setting this up for her.

When had she last taken time for herself? When had she *ever* taken time to pamper herself and relax?

"You did this...for me?" she asked.

"I did." Zevris released his hold on Tabitha and stepped around her, stopping in front of the tub. He picked up the wine bottle and jabbed his thumb claw into the cork. He shifted the bottle to a sharper angle, twisted his hand, and tensed the muscles of his arm. The cork came out with a soft *pop*.

He poured the wine into the glass and set the bottle down again, placing the cork beside it. "You've worked hard, Tabitha, and I've not made the last couple days easy on you. You deserve relaxation. You deserve luxury."

Zevris turned to face her, lifting one of his large hands to her cheek. His fingertips slipped into her hair, grazing her scalp with the tips of his claws, and he angled her face up toward his. "Think of me as you read your book." Lightly, he brushed the pad of his thumb across her lower lip.

Her lips parted, and she felt herself swaying forward infinitesimally, so close to sucking his thumb into her mouth, to pressing herself against his hard body.

He dropped his hand and walked around her, leaving her briefly stunned.

"I will be thinking of you, *Nykasha*," he said just before the door closed.

Tabitha was suddenly alone in a room so quiet she could hear the whisper of tiny bubbles popping.

"Four weeks," she breathed, clutching the front of her shirt and pressing her hands against her belly as though that could alleviate the growing ache deep in her core.

She turned back toward the bath. No one had ever done anything like this for her. Of course, she knew he was just doing this to win her over, and, well...

It was working.

Tabitha switched on the fan, removed and folded her clothes, and set them on the corner of the counter, far away from the burning candles. Using one of her hair clips, she wound her braid up and pinned it atop her head before returning to the tub.

She brushed her fingers over the petals scattered along the side and smiled. She could just imagine him outside, hurriedly picking them off his flowers, which he must have done when he'd taken Dexter out earlier. Had he fetched the wine and the book at the same time? The wine had been in her fridge, ready for her to drink in celebration once she'd finished unpacking.

Guess I don't have to worry about unpacking for a while, though.

She chuckled to herself and carefully climbed into the tub.

The water was hot, but not scalding—it was absolutely perfect. She lowered herself into the water, lay back, and closed her eyes with a sigh, relishing the heat. The gently popping bubbles surrounded her, and the scent of lavender, fresh and sweet, soothed her senses.

Opening her eyes, Tabitha picked up the wine glass. She breathed in the fruity aroma of the Pink Mascato before taking a sip. The wine's bubbles tickled her tongue, and the sweetness filled her mouth. She took another deeper drink before setting the glass down, refilling it, and picking up the book.

Tabitha couldn't help but laugh as she looked at the cover. It was a headless torso with tanned skin that matched Zevris's.

Think of me as you read your book.

And she found herself helpless but to obey. Not long after she'd cracked open the book and begun reading, Tabitha had increasing trouble focusing on the words. The text soon lost all meaning. All she could think about was Zevris.

She pictured him as he'd been that morning, lying naked beside her with his clawed fingers wrapped around his cock, pumping his fist up and down, gradually gaining speed. His expression tense, his blazing eyes fixated on her, his breath coming in ragged bursts.

Her memories of the way the light in his eyes had flared as he came, the way he'd kept his gaze upon her even as his body was in the throes of his climax, and that bestial growl he'd released were vivid. All that had stoked the fires inside her to an inferno—both then and now.

He'd made it clear that she'd been the only thing on his mind, that she'd been what had driven him wild, that she'd been all he needed to work himself to completion. And his lingering gaze afterward had told her his appetite was far from satisfied.

Tabitha closed the book, set it aside, and took another long drink of the wine. She bit her lip and glanced toward the bathroom door. Zevris was just on the other side. She'd be spending another night in his bed, lying against that gorgeous body, with his arms wrapped around her. How would she find sleep when her body was crying out for pleasure? When she craved his touch, his lips, his tongue, his...cock.

She needed to take the edge off, to find some relief from the desire thrumming throughout her body, from the ache between her thighs that was worsening with every minute.

Closing her eyes, Tabitha took in a deep, calming breath, and slowly slid her hands up to her breasts. She cupped them, kneaded them, and tweaked her nipples, creating a piddling, unsatisfying whisper of pleasure.

Brows creasing, she imagined Zevris's hands in place of hers. She imagined his palm smoothing down her belly, his fingers brushing through the small patch of hair before he reached her pussy. Imagined his fingers spreading her, skimming along her folds, dipping inside to gather her slick before moving up to her clit. Those fingers gently circled that spot, again and again, moving rhythmically, allowing her to become accustomed to his touch before increasing in speed.

Tabitha's breath caught, and she bit her lip harder. The water diminished the sensation, but it was there, building and building...

She snapped her thighs together around her hand as she came, sealing her lips to keep from crying out. Her body tensed, her core contracted, and she moaned quietly as a flash of pleasure shuddered through her.

Tabitha breathed slowly through her nose as her muscles relaxed and the quivering of her pussy eased. Her skin felt flushed and warm—too warm. Rather than assuage her need, she'd only sharpened it. The orgasm had been stale, unsatisfying, passionless.

Pulling her hand free, Tabitha frowned. She knew what was missing.

Zevris.

It wasn't his hand touching me, no matter how hard I imagine it.

Her hands were smaller and didn't possess his strength, her fingers didn't have his calluses or his claws. And her body damn well knew it.

With a sigh, Tabitha drained the rest of the wine from her glass, pulled the tub's plug, and stood up. Water and bubbles sluiced off her. She reached for the towel hanging close by and used it to dry off before wrapping it around her body. Once the towel was secure, she moved to the sink.

Between the wine and the bath, her body was languid, and warmth lingered on her skin. But the relaxation hadn't eased the heavy ache of desire in her core.

After a groan, she brushed her teeth and unbraided her hair, letting it fall in waves around her shoulders. She glanced at her pile of folded clothes before sweeping her gaze around the bathroom. Zevris had either forgotten to set out pajamas and underwear for her or had purposely left her without.

She'd bet on the latter.

She didn't feel like putting her clothes back on only to take them off again in a moment. She'd just have to go get panties and pajamas herself.

Tabitha blew out all the tealights, plunging the room into darkness. She felt her way to the door. As soon as her fingers bumped the doorknob, she wrapped her hand around it, opened the door, and stepped into the bedroom.

Zevris's eyes were upon her immediately, as fierce as ever.

The covers were drawn down, and he was sitting on the bed with his back against the headboard and his hands intertwined over his lap. He'd removed his jeans and was currently wearing only a pair of black boxers. Tabitha found herself both grateful that he had those on and disappointed that he wasn't naked.

His gaze raked over her slowly, up and down and back again, so intense that Tabitha swore she felt its caress on her skin. Zevris was looking at her like he could see straight through her towel—and like he yearned for what he saw.

He swung his legs over the side of the bed and stood up. His eyes didn't leave her for even an instant as he walked around the bed and approached her. She remained still, clutching the towel in her fingers. She had a sense of déjà vu, that this had happened before, but she knew this time would be different.

Zevris stopped in front of her and lifted a hand. The pads of his fingers brushed her shoulder as he caught some of her dangling hair, stroking it with his thumb. "Did you think of me, *Nykasha?*"

SEVENTEEN

BEFORE TABITHA COULD RESPOND, Zevris leaned a little closer, and his nostrils flared with a deep inhalation. A deep growl vibrated in his chest, and his pupils dilated. "You did."

Tabitha's sex clenched, and slick gathered in her pussy as his deep voice resonated within her. She shivered; it had nothing to do with the slight chill in the air.

"I did," she admitted, dropping her gaze.

He swept her hair back over her shoulder and slid his hand up to her neck. His touch was everything she'd craved from him —firm, confident, callused. He curled his fingers around her throat and pressed his thumb beneath her chin, tilting it up and forcing her to meet his gaze.

His eyes searched hers. "But you found little satisfaction."

Not a question, but a statement.

Cheeks burning with shame, Tabitha caught her bottom lip between her teeth and nodded once.

Zevris gently pried her lip free using his claw and soothed it with gentle strokes of his thumb. He raised his other hand and skimmed his claws along her arm, making her flesh tingle delightfully. "Let me give you the pleasure you desire, Tabitha."

Tabitha's lips parted, and she released a shaky breath. That ache in her core intensified, spreading outward to her breasts to harden her nipples.

Zevris slipped his hand into her hair, clutched it at the roots, and tilted her head to the side before lowering his face. He brought his mouth to the place where her neck and shoulder connected and brushed his lips over her skin, at first in a caress, then more firmly in hot kisses. She felt his warm breath and the wet flick of his tongue, felt his tail as it slid up and down her calf, as it teased the sensitive spot behind her knee.

Tabitha's breath quickened. His touch was electrifying, and his mouth made her flesh buzz with pleasure in places she'd never thought possible. She felt drugged, lulled into euphoria, unable to resist his allure. "Zevris..."

"It does not mean you are accepting me as your mate," he rasped. "I only wish to pleasure you. To feel you tremble beneath my touch, to taste you upon my tongue, to revel in your cries of ecstasy."

She curled her toes into the carpet, barely containing a whimper. Then he nipped her with his fangs.

Her pussy contracted with sudden, unbearable need. Tabitha gasped, her body rocking toward Zevris, and she released the towel with one hand to clutch his forearm. The mingled pain and pleasure of his bite was overwhelming.

She tried to come up with reasons to stop this, to stop him, but those reasons vanished as swiftly as they came. She didn't know if it was the alcohol clouding her judgement or if it was simply the haze of lust, but in that moment, she didn't care. He'd offered to give her pleasure, and Tabitha...she *wanted* it.

She wanted him.

Like he'd said, this didn't mean she was taking him as a mate, it didn't mean she was making an important life decision on a whim, it didn't mean she was committing to anything... To anything but pleasure, anyway. This was just a single moment she could embrace.

"Yes," she whispered.

Zevris groaned, sliding his arm around her and settling his palm on her lower back, just above her ass. His body tensed around her, and he drew her just a little closer. He grazed the tender flesh of her neck with his teeth as his mouth worked its way up behind her ear, sending thrills through her that made her eyelids flutter shut.

His tail coiled around her leg and squeezed. She could feel the hard stab of his erection against her belly. She leaned into him, sliding her hands along his sides, running her fingers over his muscles, feeling his heat. His scent enveloped her; she greedily breathed him in.

He drew back from her abruptly and crouched, dropping one arm behind her legs. He rose in a smooth motion, sweeping her feet out from beneath her and lifting her against his chest.

She gasped, eyes wide, and looped her arms around his neck, her body stiffening as though he might drop her at any moment. "Zevris!"

He chuckled as he carried her toward the bed, seemingly without effort—like she weighed no more than a feather. "Get used to calling out my name, *Nykasha*. You will do so many times before the night is through."

She turned her face toward him. He was grinning wide, his eyes were glowing, and there was a thick strand of hair dangling across his forehead, granting him a rakish appeal that made her heart lurch madly.

Zevris laid her atop the bed gently, and Tabitha couldn't help but compare this to a groom carrying his bride to their bed.

He climbed on after her and braced himself over her with his hands to either side of her shoulders. The humor in his eyes faded, and was replaced by a smoldering blend of ravenousness, awe, and lust.

He lifted a hand and brushed the back of a claw over her eyebrow and down the side of her face. Drawing his hand back up, he trailed that claw down from the center of her brow, along the bridge of her nose, and over her lips, which he then stroked with his thumb.

Tabitha slipped her tongue out, touching its tip to his thumb, tasting the saltiness of his skin. His expression went taut, and his eyes darkened.

Leaning back, Zevris spread Tabitha's hair out around her before he moved his palms to her shoulders. He slid both hands lower still, following her collarbone until he'd hooked his fingers under the towel to either side of the spot where she'd tucked the corner in.

Tabitha swallowed thickly. Her brow creased, and she clutched the bedding beneath her, suddenly wishing she'd drank more wine; the alcohol's effects seemed to have already faded. She could *really* use some more of that liquid courage right now.

What if he didn't like what he saw? How could she handle watching as the hunger in his eyes faded or, even worse, turned to disgust?

His tail stroked her leg and said softly, "Ah, *Nykasha*, you've much to anticipate, but nothing to fear."

Zevris tugged on the towel, loosening it, and peeled it open, revealing her naked body beneath.

A different sort of heat flooded Tabitha, this one born of shame and embarrassment. She looked away from him, unwilling to witness what she feared most. Unwilling to see his expression change. She drew up her knees, pressed her thighs together tight, and moved her arms to cover herself.

Zevris growled and caught her wrists in his hands, spreading them apart and pressing them to the bed on either side of her head. Her eyes widened as she returned them to Zevris.

His fangs were bared, and his eyebrows were low. "You will not hide your body from me, Tabitha."

He slowly smoothed his palms up her arms to her breasts, cupping them both. Her breath hitched as he stroked his thumbs over her pearled nipples, sending bolts of pleasure straight to her core.

"You have no reason for self-consciousness or shame," he said as his fingers kneaded and caressed her flesh. "I feel I have waited an eternity to see such beauty, and my wildest imaginings could never have done it justice."

Zevris clasped one of her breasts and lowered his head, taking her budded nipple between his lips. He sucked it into his mouth, teasing it with teeth and tongue, sending shivers of delight along her spine. A soft, whimpering cry—perhaps his name—escaped her lips as she moved her hands to his head. Her hips undulated of their own accord. Her pussy clenched, and her clit throbbed.

He released her nipple from his mouth and took it between his forefinger and thumb, continuing to stroke the sensitive flesh. "You deserve adoration. Deserve to be worshipped. Deserve to be pleasured in ways no human or faloran has ever dreamed." He pinched her nipple, making her breath hitch. "Your body was made for pleasure, Tabitha. Made to be pleasured by me."

He took her other nipple into his mouth and sucked, hard enough to make her moan and scrape her nails against his scalp.

Zevris growled against her breast, and his fangs pricked her skin, but he did not bite. For an instant, she wanted him to. She wanted him to claim her in that way, wanted him to mark her, wanted him to do whatever he pleased to her.

He lifted his head, releasing her nipple with a wet pop, and pressed a kiss between her breasts before drawing back to trail more kisses down her belly. His hands followed the shape of her body, tracing her waist and the flare of her hips. They paused there as his thumbs brushed over the silvery stretch marks on her thighs. There was no disgust in his eyes as he looked up at her—only that same hunger.

"You are beautiful, Tabitha. And your scent..." He lowered his head until his nose brushed the dark blonde curls over her sex, closed his eyes, and drew in a deep breath. His lips drew back in a snarl. When he opened his eyes again, they were feral and ravening. "It's fucking divine."

He placed his hands on her knees and pushed her legs apart, baring her pussy to his lustful gaze. A low sound reverberated in his chest, a blend of a growl and a groan, as he spread her thighs wider and positioned his body between them, not looking away from her sex for even an instant.

A shiver crept along Tabitha's spine, sending little tingles out through her limbs. The heat of his gaze made the air in the room feel so much cooler, so much colder, so unbearable. She needed his touch to soothe it away. She needed his warmth to suffuse her skin.

His hands slid to her inner thighs, and he absently kneaded her flesh, his fingertips occasionally tracing her stretch marks, as he stared. Tabitha's heartbeat grew steadily faster and louder. Impossibly, the ache between her legs deepened. She raked her nails over the sheet, struggling to keep from squirming, struggling to ignore the tightness low in her belly.

Why wasn't he *doing* anything? Was he hesitating now because he realized that he'd made some mistake?

That old, embarrassed heat flared in her chest and raced up to her cheeks. She couldn't fight it anymore; she squeezed her thighs together.

"No," Zevris growled, forcing her legs apart so wide that they were flat on the bed. He lifted his gaze to meet hers. There was a hardness in his blazing eyes now, a commanding gleam, as unwavering as his strength, as deep as a canyon.

She couldn't have disobeyed if she'd wanted to.

"I am barely holding myself back, *Nykasha*." His eyes dropped as he lifted his hand from her leg, leaving only the pads of his fingers in contact with her flesh, and trailed it toward her pussy. Her thigh quivered. Jolting thrills sparked beneath his fingertips, enhanced by the soft scrape of his claws.

Tabitha clamped her teeth over her lower lip and watched, barely breathing, as his fingers inched closer to the source of her discomfort, toward the blazing furnace at her core.

Zevris brushed his fingers along her sex, his touch light, delicate, reverent.

Tabitha gasped, stomach clenching against a flare of pleasure.

"So beautiful," he rumbled. "There's nothing in the universe so lovely."

She only realized after he'd spoken that he'd been looking up at her again.

This was really happening. He *really* wanted her.

And God, she wanted him, too.

He lowered his gaze, fingers trailing up and down her pussy in a slow, tender caress. After a few moments, he positioned one finger to either side and spread her open. Somehow, that hunger in his eyes sharpened. His jaw tensed; it was her only warning before he dropped his mouth to her pussy, sucked her clit between his lips, and lapped at it with his tongue.

"Zevris!" Tabitha's hand flew out, and she grasped his hair

as her head tilted back. Her lips parted in a silent cry. It was like an electric current lighting up every nerve in her body with pleasure. She whimpered, curling her toes into the bedding, conscious thought fading against the overpowering sensations. It was almost too much, too fast.

Zevris released her clit and soothed it with his tongue, which swirled with gentle, slow strokes. She flattened her back on the bed and stared at the ceiling, stunned. His fingers clutched her thighs, again pricking her with those claws, but she didn't care. All that mattered was what he was doing with his mouth.

Panting, Tabitha looked down. Her eyes locked with his. Zevris between her thighs, with his inhuman expression and his alien eyes casting a soft blue glow upon her skin as he licked her was the most erotic sight she'd ever seen. Her pussy clenched as the sensations within her intensified, and her awareness of everything but Zevris faded further with each wave of pleasure.

Soon, her body was moving of its own accord, undulating against his mouth, seeking more, *needing* more.

He lifted his face suddenly, turned it, and brought his fingers to his mouth. In one quick motion, he snapped his teeth down on the claws of his index and middle fingers, biting off the sharp tips. He spat the pieces aside.

When he dropped his mouth to her pussy, he dragged his tongue over her from bottom to top in one wide swipe. He groaned and lapped at her again and again, licking up her essence, flicking her clit with each pass, and making her thighs tremble.

He moved his tongue to her opening and thrust it inside. A moment later, he replaced his tongue with a finger, pumping it in and out of her in slow, bold thrusts.

Her pussy clenched around that digit, and Tabitha moaned, rocking against him.

"You're so hot and wet, *Nykasha*," Zevris said huskily. "Your body wants this. Wants me. It yearns for what only I can give you."

He inserted a second finger and thrust them deep inside her. Tabitha nearly leapt out of her skin as he stroked *that* spot. He pumped his fingers again and again, each time harder and faster than the last, wringing soft, breathy cries from her. She dropped her hand from his head to gather the bedding in her fists. Liquid heat flooded her, enhancing the pleasure that was coiling at her center.

Zevris grinned. "Ah, my mate, you are beautiful in your pleasure. You were made for it." He kissed her clit, then flicked it with his tongue.

"*Nngh*," Tabitha cried, eyes squeezing shut, hips bucking. "Zevris, please!"

"You were made to be mine, Tabitha." Zevris pressed his mouth over her clit, sucked it between his lips, and lavished it with his tongue, while his fingers continued to piston ruthlessly.

She writhed, head thrashing from side to side, back arching, but he held her firmly in place, refusing to let her escape, forcing her to accept everything he had to give. She could not control the passionate sounds that came from her any more than she could control her body's response.

The ecstasy gathering at her core wound so tight that it stole her breath. For an instant, the pressure was immense, crushing, torturous. Then it burst outward, suffusing her with indescribable pleasure. She came violently, crying his name, as she was swept up in the maelstrom of sensation.

Heat consumed Tabitha, and her pussy clamped down on his fingers, but he did not stop their motion, and his mouth continued its merciless assault. Her cries escalated as he made her come again and again.

It wasn't until her final climax faded and she lay there with her chest heaving that Zevris slowed his fingers. After a few moments, he withdrew them entirely and replaced them with his tongue. He growled as he drank from her, lapping greedily, as though she were the most decadent treat and he refused to miss a drop.

Tabitha trembled, still feeling the echoes of her orgasms. Every time Zevris's tongue flicked her clit, her breath hitched, and her belly fluttered. When she finally gathered the willpower to open her eyes, she looked down to find him watching her, his gaze darkened by fiery, possessive need.

Her lips stretched into a pleased smile, and she sighed contently.

Zevris chuckled. He lifted his head, and that wicked tongue slipped out to lick his lips clean. He turned his face and kissed her inner thigh before smoothing his palms to her hips and drawing himself up.

She had no idea what to say. *Thank you* sounded too much like he'd done her a service, and she refused to look at it that way. *That was amazing* just sounded cliché. *You just rocked my freaking world* was too embarrassing. But they all would've fit what she felt. Her first and only time receiving oral had been from her ex-boyfriend, Cody, and he'd made her feel disgusting in the process—*he* had been so disgusted that he hadn't continued. But this... Tabitha had no words for what this had felt like.

"What thoughts are running through your mind, Tabitha?" Zevris asked as he ran his hands up her sides, pausing at her breasts to caress her nipples with his thumbs.

Tabitha's mind went static for a moment, and she could have kicked herself for the words that spilled out. "My ex hated doing that."

Zevris snarled, expression hardening, and his lips peeled back to display fangs that had only minutes before been teasingly grazing her skin. He moved to lie beside her, wrapped his strong arms around her, and tugged her body against his. His tail swept along her leg to coil around her ankle.

Her wide eyes met his, and she flattened her palms on his chest. "Sorry! That was...*so* stupid to say. Especially after... after..." She buried her face against his neck, heat flooding her cheeks. "I didn't mean to ruin the moment."

"You did not ruin the moment, *Nykasha*," he said, settling his cheek on her hair as he smoothed a hand along her arm. "My anger is only for the way you've been mistreated. *He* ruined something for you, something precious. And if I were ever to encounter him"—his muscles tensed, a growl sounded in his chest, and his claws pressed against her skin—"I would ruin him."

It shouldn't have—it really, *really* shouldn't have—but Zevris's threat to her ex-boyfriend pleased her immensely.

Tabitha smiled to herself and traced her fingertip in a circle around his nipple and over the silver bar piercing it. Zevris shuddered and groaned, grinding his hard cock against her belly.

She stilled her hand. "Sorry."

Of course he was aroused. He'd just given to her without receiving anything in return.

"I could...help you with that?" she offered.

He exhaled heavily, his hot breath flowing over her hair, and his chest rumbled. "No. Tonight was for you, Tabitha. Your pleasure is what I craved most."

Part of her was disappointed that he hadn't accepted her offer, while another part of her warmed at his words.

Taking things slow, Tabby. Remember?

Zevris drew back, curled a finger beneath her chin, and lifted her face, forcing her to meet his gaze. "If you want to help me, Tabitha, sleep. For come tomorrow, I *will* drink from you again."

He pressed a kiss to her forehead and drew her head back down. He reached behind him, turned off the lamp, plunging the room into darkness, and pulled the covers over them.

She'd never been so eager for morning to come.

EIGHTEEN

A GRIN STRETCHED across Zevris's lips as he scrubbed the pan; his mind was far away from the breakfast he and Tabitha had just shared and the dishes he was cleaning. Today had been the second day upon which he'd awoken with his mate in his arms, and it had been the sweetest of the two by far.

Of course, some portion of that sweetness must have come from the hint of flavor that had been lingering on his tongue—Tabitha's essence.

Seeing Tabitha naked and lost in pleasure, her inhibitions shattered, had defied description. She'd been more dazzling than a comet with a glittering tail, more radiant than the brightest star, more entrancing than the most vibrant, sparkling nebula.

As he rinsed the pan, his cock ached and throbbed, torturously restrained by his jeans. His craving had only strengthened since last night.

It would have been easy to curse himself as a fool for declining her offer of *help*—and he had cursed himself, over and over again, especially this morning while his cock had remained hard enough to have whisked the eggs he had cooked for breakfast. But he'd made the right decision. Pleasing her last night hadn't been a transaction, and he would have done it even if there was no chance of ever winning her over.

The question of trust had loomed over him, also—specifically his lack of trust in himself. Had he given in, there was no telling whether he would've maintained self-control, whether he could have stopped himself at tasting and touching.

Pleasing Tabitha had brought him no relief, but plenty of satisfaction. The taste he'd had of her was more than worth the torture.

Waking up with her body, so warm and soft, tucked against him had instilled Zevris with a bliss he'd never imagined possible. He knew the circumstances were far from ideal, knew she hadn't slept with him entirely of her own free will, but he knew also that he wanted to wake with Tabitha in his arms every morning for the rest of his life.

And she seemed to want it, too, even if she wasn't yet at the point of admitting as much.

He placed the pan in the drainboard and moved on to the spatula.

Zevris hadn't had a place to call home for more than half his life. He'd not even had the luxury of sleeping in a bed during many of his assignments, and every one of the beds in which he had slept had been empty. There'd been no one to hold, no one to hold him, and even when he'd had comrades in the field...he'd been alone. He'd accepted that as normal for so long because it was. He'd suppressed his yearning for more, for someone to hold in his empty arms, for someone to...love.

For Tabitha.

Even if he'd not known of her existence until a week ago, he knew, somehow, that she was the one he'd always awaited. She was the one he'd always been meant to find.

This small taste of something more, of life with Tabitha, had been so spectacular that he wasn't sure he could go back to the loneliness.

Using his thumb, he scrubbed at the egg clinging to the spatula. He paused when he caught sight of his trimmed claws. Unbidden, his tongue slipped out and ran across his lips.

Though he had brushed his teeth and eaten since last night, he swore he still tasted a trace of Tabitha's essence on his lips. His cock twitched, and the denim of his jeans was suddenly far too tight, crushingly restrictive, and so abrasive that even the fabric of his boxers offered no protection. Tabitha was the sweetest thing he'd ever smelled, and her taste was even more sublime. No flavor on any of the planets to which he'd ever journeyed compare to hers.

Karak'duun, it had been so difficult to stop himself from waking Tabitha this morning by burying his face between her thighs. Even with as much as he'd drunk from her last night, his thirst was not quenched, his hunger was not sated; he would never have his fill when it came to his female. He would always want more.

But he hadn't wanted to startle her, hadn't wanted to scare her, hadn't wanted to push the boundaries they were still determining and experimenting with. She'd agreed to his offer of pleasure last night. That did not mean she'd want it this morning. Even if he knew Tabitha was his, even if his body recognized it, even if it was a fact emblazoned on his heart, she'd not come to that understanding yet. Pushing too hard would scare her away.

Knowing all that, it had still been an immense struggle to stop himself. Somehow, he'd managed to simply lie there, holding her as she slept, relishing her warmth as he fought to ignore his arousal.

His discomfort had proven worthwhile when she'd roused

in the morning and gifted him with the brightest, sexiest, most endearing smile in all existence.

Zevris clenched his jaw and took the soapy scrub brush to the spatula, battling back the urge to press his pelvis against the counter. It wouldn't alleviate the pressure. Only one thing could do that.

Only one *person* could do that.

"I could get used to this," Tabitha said from the table behind him.

A flare of hope shone bright within Zevris; dangerous as it might've been, he didn't try to extinguish it. As he rinsed the spatula, he asked, "Used to what?"

"A man doing all the cooking and cleaning. If you want to woo a woman, this right here is how you do it."

He placed the spatula in the drainboard, turned off the water, and glanced over his shoulder while he dried his hands on a dishtowel.

Tabitha was sitting with an elbow on the table, chin in hand, and the fingers of her other hand wrapped around her steaming mug of tea. Though she'd been awake for at least an hour, her eyes were still half-lidded, shining with a contented, dreamlike gleam.

They were also very clearly fixated upon Zevris's backside.

He grinned and arched a brow. "My eyes are up here, female."

Her lips stretched into a slow smile. "I know. Just enjoying the view."

Zevris's tail twitched, and he lifted it higher. "Oh?"

Tabitha laughed, finally looking up to meet his gaze. "Have I mentioned that I really like tails?"

With a snicker, Zevris turned to face her, leaning back against the counter's edge—but making sure to keep his tail in motion. There were already several ideas drifting through his mind on how to take advantage of the information she'd just shared, and each of them only made his grin widen.

"Noted, *Nykasha*. I look forward to helping you like them even more."

Her eyes dipped to his groin, and the deepening red on her cheeks told Zevris that she knew very well what was on his mind. Tilting her chin down, she looked at her mug; her smile didn't fade.

Dexter, currently lying on the kitchen floor, abruptly lifted his head. He turned toward the living room with his ears perked. A moment later, he got to his feet and made his way into the other room, lured by the sound of another dog barking somewhere outside.

"So...do you get money from some kind of alien hacking technology, or do you actually work for a living?" Tabitha asked, glancing back up at him. "You know, like us normal humans do?"

Zevris decided not to comment on her abrupt change of subject; he needed a distraction himself if he ever wanted the pain in his shaft to wane. "If I had to do things the way normal humans do, I'd have had to work for a few decades just to afford a home. My understanding is that preparations have been in a place for some time before my arrival. Human funds had been acquired and pooled, likely through hacking, so me and the other operatives could focus on our mission. In theory, I have access to unlimited funding...though abusing that access would bring dangerous attention my way.

"But I have taken on a job, so to speak, as part of my cover, and it has brought me income. I try to use that money for any necessities before tapping into the rest."

"What do you do?" she asked, tilting her head.

Motivated partly by pride and partly by a yearning to share

this part of himself with her, he replied, "Would you like to see?"

She straightened in her chair, and her brow creased. "You're...letting me go outside?"

Zevris cringed and shook his head. "Only if you consider my garage *outside*."

"Oh."

"But...perhaps we could eat dinner on the patio this evening? It's been pleasant enough outside as of late."

She smiled brightly. "Really?"

That smile struck him hard; it was almost enough to make him tell her to forget the whole *no-outside* rule, to tell her that he'd take her anywhere she wanted to go, anywhere in the world, right now, protocol be damned.

Yet he could not bring himself to tell her any of those things. Not yet.

"Really," he said. "For now, how does a harrowing journey to the garage sound?"

Tabitha eyed him with mock skepticism. "I don't know... I mean, I've seen a couple garages in my time, and none of them were all that exciting."

Zevris smirked and walked over to her, holding out a hand. "But none of those garages belonged to alien special agents, did they?"

She chuckled. After taking a drink from her mug, she set it back down on the table and placed her hand in his, allowing him to help her to her feet. "It's not every day I get to have an alien take me to his garage."

He absently brushed the pad of his thumb across the back of her hand. Her skin was so warm and soft, her hand so small, so perfect in his. He wanted Tabitha's hands all over him as much as he wanted to run his all over her.

Reluctant as he was to do so, he released her, knowing that

he could not long withstand the thoughts her touch brought to mind.

"This way," he said, walking into the hall.

Tabitha followed him, looking at him expectantly when he stopped at the door in the laundry room and that would let them into the garage.

He flicked the light switch to turn on the garage lights. "I must warn you, Tabitha—prepare yourself. For I may have made what you are about to see sound far more interesting than it truly is."

She side-eyed him. "As long as you don't have any other captives in there, and you have nothing nefarious planned for me, then we're good."

He tilted up a corner of his mouth. "That depends entirely upon your definition of *nefarious*."

She ducked her head, but not before he caught her grin. Clearing her throat, she tucked her hair behind her ear and waved for him to continue. "Show me what secrets you are hoarding."

As he reached for the doorknob, doubt fluttered in his gut. He'd sold many of the things he'd crafted, had made a few custom-ordered pieces, but he'd never taken anyone he knew into his workshop. He'd never shared this side of himself with anyone. And, though he felt his skills had greatly improved since he'd begun this craft, he knew there was still so much for him to learn.

That unattained knowledge had been a factor in keeping him interested in this work, but now... Would she see his lack of experience in the pieces he'd made? Would she see the same beauty in the wood that he saw, would she even care?

Regardless of those doubts, he was still eager to share this with her. Perhaps his passion for woodworking was not quite as strong as hers for making soap and candles, but there was a connection between them in their dedication to their crafts, wasn't there?

He turned the knob, opened the door, and stood aside. "After you, *Nykasha*."

She smiled and walked through the doorway.

Tabitha stepped down onto the garage floor, moved forward another pace, and stopped, her eyes wide as she surveyed her surroundings. "Oh, wow."

Zevris paused on the step, easing the door closed behind him. He wondered what this room looked like through her eyes. It had become familiar to him, comforting both in appearance and smell. His tools were arranged so they'd be in the places he was most likely to need them, the floor was swept clean, and many of his projects, both completed and in progress, were on open display. Of course, things were rarely so tidy while he was working, but something about the contrast between the resting order and the working chaos was cathartic for him.

She moved farther into the room, lifting her hand to touch the varnished surface of the dining table sitting in the center. She traced the wood grain with her fingertips, then moved her fingers toward the middle of the table, where Zevris had used small stones and resin to create a swath of blue running through the wood like a river.

"You made this?" she asked, awe in her voice.

"I did."

"This is gorgeous."

That quickly, the Zevris's doubt was crushed by a swelling of pride.

She stepped away from the table and walked to the tall oak bookcase against the wall that held his smaller works—little chests, keepsake boxes, jewelry boxes, and bird houses. Many were unfinished, waiting for his skill to catch up with his ambition, but a few were already varnished and painted, and some were even adorned with simple carvings, engravings, and embedded stones.

Zevris moved closer to her, flattening a hand on the dining table as he watched her.

Tabitha reached for one of the keepsake boxes, but she stopped her hand midway and looked back at Zevris. "Can I?"

"Feel free. If any of it breaks from being touched, I must not have done a particularly good job."

She smiled and picked up the box, carefully opening the lid. "My Nan had a keepsake box like this when I was little. It was filled with raw and polished gemstones and rocks she'd collected over the years. I used to take them out and spread them on the floor thinking she was the richest woman in all the world. They were like diamonds to me, all sparkling and beautiful. I thought the white quartz crystals *were* diamonds. On my seventh birthday, she bought me a keepsake box of my own so I could keep special little souvenirs from our vacations in it. Every year, I'd add something new.

"This box is going to collect wonderful memories for someone someday."

Zevris's chest ached as he walked over to Tabitha. She'd not said anything to him about her Nan's passing, and he might not have understood the wistfulness of her smile and tone had he not found out on his own. "Do you still have your box?"

"Yeah, I do. It's just still packed away." She closed the lid gently, running her finger over the design carved into it. "This reminds me of the tattoos on your arms."

"My people use such adornments often. On buildings and clothing, on furniture and household items. On ourselves. They're considered an artform unto themselves, and the true artists make my attempts look pathetic in comparison."

"Do they have any meaning?" she asked, turning her face up toward him.

"They do, though the most intricate of them can be quite difficult to decipher at times. Each has at least one word at its core, woven into the design."

"So, what do your tattoos mean?"

He raised his arms to draw up the sleeve of his t-shirt and glanced down at the design on his flesh. "They say that I have been banished. They're the markings of an exiled faloran."

Tabitha reared back. "What?"

"The nature of my assignments as an *althicar* are often such that they must not be linked back to the Azmus Protectorate. I haven't truly been banished, but were I ever captured or killed, these markings would have given our leaders grounds to deny any involvement in my actions. Upon honorable completion of my service, these markings will be changed to reflect the risks I undertook in service to my people."

She stepped closer and touched her fingers to one of the markings on his bicep. His skin tingled beneath her fingertips, thrumming with faint, electric energy. The marking glowed a little brighter.

"So if you're killed in the line of duty...you're treated like you were just some criminal acting on his own? They don't bring fallen soldiers back to their families?"

"An *althicar* is no typical soldier. I understood the dangers when I volunteered." He lifted both his gaze and his hand, brushing the backs of his fingers over her cheek as he looked into her eyes. "I am far more concerned with what I do with my life now than what happens after I am gone."

She smiled softly. "What makes them glow?"

"It is a reaction between our biochemistry and the substance used to create the markings. It's supposedly similar to the process that makes our eyes glow, but I can't pretend to really understand the science behind it." He looked back down at the marking and willed its glow to cease; it was like flexing a phantom muscle, maddeningly intangible but nonetheless effective.

She smoothed her palm over his upper arm. "That's amazing! Even your eyes dimmed."

But he knew his eyes had brightened again when he lifted them back to her face; they were clearly reflected in her eyes.

"So what does the symbol on this mean?" she asked, returning her hand to the keepsake box.

Zevris touched a fingertip to the lid, tracing the carving. His finger lightly brushed hers. "It means something like...*dear* or *treasured*."

Tabitha gifted him with that smile he was coming to adore so much. "What's the word in your language?"

"*Nyka*."

Her brow creased, and she tilted her head. "That sounds pretty close to what you've been calling me."

Zevris chuckled, once again running his finger along hers. "*Nykasha*. It means *beloved one*."

"Oh." She averted her eyes, and her cheeks pinkened as she placed the box on the shelf. "It's...a beautiful word. Especially the way you say it."

Reaching out, he caught Tabitha by her hips and drew her close. Her breath hitched, and she braced her hands on his shoulders.

"You are beautiful, Tabitha," he said, walking her back until she bumped into the workbench. He leaned closer, so his lips were next to her ear, dropped his voice low. "And I've a thirst I'm desperate to slake."

Tabitha drew back to look at him with wide eyes. "H-here?"

"No," he rumbled as he hooked his fingers under the waistband of her leggings and panties. He drew them down slowly, relishing the feel of her soft skin, until they were bunched around her knees. When he glided his hands back up, he cupped her ass and lifted her off the floor. She gasped, bending toward him to brace herself, her hair brushing his face.

He sat her on the edge of the workbench. "Here."

Grabbing her leggings and panties, Zevris yanked them the rest of the way off her legs and tossed them aside before wedging his body between her thighs. He settled his hands on her knees and smoothed his palms over her skin, feeling her flesh pebble under his touch.

She stared up at him, pupils dilating, eyes hungry.

Her scent, her *need*, called to him, and he inhaled deeply, filling his lungs with it. His cock, already hard and throbbing, strained against his jeans with enough strength and urgency that it seemed likely to tear the denim apart at the seams.

"Are you wet for me, Tabitha?" Zevris tilted his head down, brushing his nose through her fragrant hair. He curled his thumbs over her inner thighs. "Do you yearn for more? Are you aching to have my tongue between your thighs, licking that sweet pussy?"

Her lips parted, and her grip on his shoulders tightened.

He pushed her legs open wider. "Let me hear you say it, *Nykasha*."

"Yes," Tabitha breathed.

That word, so simple, so brief, so softly spoken, was the most moving, powerful thing he'd ever heard in any language. The desirous flames that had been burning within him since the moment he'd first seen Tabitha roared, building to a consuming inferno.

But he could not give in to it, not yet. Not until Tabitha's *yes* meant *everything*.

Zevris slipped a hand between their bodies and dragged a finger through her slit. He closed his eyes and groaned, nearly spilling in his pants. She was so hot and wet.

He worked his finger over her, all the gladder that he'd bitten off the tips of his claws to be able to touch her like this. When he stroked her clit, Tabitha's breath caught, and she shivered. Her sex blossomed beneath his touch, and her essence gathered like dew upon those delicate petals.

Taking in another lungful of air perfumed by her scent, Zevris drew back from Tabitha. He was nearly trembling as he ran his gaze down to where he was caressing her. His finger glistened with her arousal. Zevris met Tabitha's gaze as he raised that finger to his lips, and he did not look away as he took it into his mouth, sucking her sweetness onto his tongue.

"You are so fucking delicious," he growled.

Her eyes flared.

Zevris dropped to his knees. He would worship her as the goddess she was. Drawing her legs over his shoulders, he grasped her ass in both hands, tugged her toward him, and covered her sex with his mouth.

"Zevris," Tabitha gasped, looking down at him with half-lidded eyes.

Desperate, hungry, burning from within, he swept his tongue over her and drew in her nectar. He groaned as her taste struck him fully, overloading his senses. His cock pulsed wildly, longing for freedom, for relief, for Tabitha's slick heat.

He flicked his tongue up to her clit. She jolted, one of her hands coming up to grasp his hair. Even the sting on his scalp did nothing to alleviate his need. His tongue danced around her little bud, teasing it, coaxing out more of her essence. He listened to her soft mews, her breathy moans, her little gasps, loving them all the more because he knew they were only the build-up to something deliciously thunderous and wholly erotic.

"Zevris...I... *Mmph.*" Tabitha's head fell back, her hair a curtain of gold draped over his workbench.

"Let me hear you, *Nykasha*. Let me hear you scream." Zevris speared her opening with his tongue, rubbing his nose against her clit.

She moaned through closed lips, and he felt her straining, felt her holding back. He would not tolerate it.

He slid his tongue up along her slickened flesh and poised a finger at her entrance. "Everything, Tabitha," he snarled. "Give it all to me."

"Please," she whimpered, trembling.

Zevris thrust his finger into her sex and closed his lips over her clit, sucking it into his mouth and lashing it with his tongue.

She cried out, her grip on his hair tightening as she drew him closer and gyrated against him. Her channel clamped down on his finger, so fucking tight, so fucking needy, so fucking perfect that seed seeped from his cock. He stroked her, thrusting his finger deeper as he worked her clit.

Tabitha tensed for an instant, her toes pressing into his back. Then she shattered, his name tearing from her lips in a ragged scream as she bowed over him, her body quivering. He gripped her ass tighter, holding her against his mouth, unrelenting in his assault, unwilling to let her escape. More of that delicious essence flooded her.

Zevris withdrew his finger from her sex, replacing it with his tongue, and gently eased her down from the heights to which he'd brought her as he lapped up her sweetness.

Her soft moans turned into pants as she caught her breath.

He waited until she'd loosened her hold on his hair and sat up before he pressed a kiss to her clit and drew back to look at her.

Sitting there on his workbench table, bare from the waist down with her skin flushed, her golden hair flowing around her, and her green eyes bright but half-lidded, Tabitha was the sexiest, loveliest thing he'd ever seen. This was a view of which he'd never tire and would forever cherish.

Zevris lowered her legs from his shoulders one-by-one, braced his hands on the edge of the workbench, and stood. He grimaced. The ache in his groin was bone deep. He'd gone weeks, sometimes months, without relieving his urges in the past, but now, after having met Tabitha, he felt like he couldn't go ten minutes without being nearly overwhelmed by need.

He released a slow, measured breath and placed a hand upon her thigh. He idly stroked her soft flesh with the pads of his fingers, trying to ignore that the feel of her made his desire flare just a little more, that it made his cock just a little harder. "I could drink from you all day, *Nykasha*, and be left greedy for more."

Her eyes flicked between his searchingly. Placing her hands on his chest, she smoothed her palms up to his shoulders. "Help me down?"

A low growl rumbled in his chest. For a moment, he was tempted to drop to his knees again, to return his face to her pussy, to hear her cries of pleasure. But, somehow, he managed to move his hands to her hips, lift her off the table, and set her gently on her feet.

Zevris took a step back, meaning to collect her discarded leggings, but Tabitha's hands curled into fists, clutching his shirt. He halted and arched a brow at her.

She dropped her hands to his belt and worked the buckle loose as she leaned close to him, her head tilting back and lips curling into a seductive smile. "I'm feeling a little...parched myself."

He clenched his jaw and drew in a sharp breath as a jolt of pleasure-tinged pressure coursed through his groin. Her hands moving down there might have been the cause of the sensation, but her words had heightened it beyond his ability to fathom.

She unbuttoned his jeans and drew the zipper down.

"You don't have to, *Nykasha*," he said, taking loose hold of her upper arms.

Some of the pressure on his shaft eased, but the relief was infinitesimal, and now it was laced with uncertainty.

He'd never had this done to him. Though he'd seen such acts performed before coming to Earth—and had seen them countless times in those sexual instruction videos—he'd never participated, and he'd never even dreamed of it before Tabitha. There were too few female falorans for him to have ever expected a mate of his own, and his profession had offered him plenty of distraction from any such urges.

"I know," Tabitha said, pushing his jeans down his hips. Her eyes locked with his. "But I want to."

She lowered herself to her knees and dragged down his boxers. His cock sprang free, and Zevris hissed, his body stiffening, when her hand closed around his base. She was still for a moment, but his shaft twitched in her hold. That pressure was so immense that he was certain he'd spill his seed right then.

Tabitha pumped her hand, stroking him slowly. Zevris groaned, belly quivering with the unexpected, overwhelming pleasure of her touch. Seed beaded at the tip of his shaft.

Tabitha's tongue slipped out to wet her lips. Bracing her other hand against his thigh, she looked up at him as she brought her mouth down on his cock, closing her lips around the crown.

"*Fuck!*" Zevris growled as his hand reflexively darted to her head. He buried his fingers in her hair and breathed, harsh and fast, through his fangs. He bucked his hips, forcing his cock deeper into her mouth. Tabitha gasped, and his chest fluttered with alarm, but she didn't pull away. Instead, she tightened her grip at the base of his erection and sucked.

"Tabitha," he rasped. Nothing had ever felt so good. Her

mouth was hot and wet, creating the most exquisite suction, and every tiny movement seemed likely to be the one that would make him burst.

She drew back, trailing her tongue along the underside of his shaft. He shuddered with pleasure each time it ran over one of his nodules. Finally, her tongue reached his tip, swirling along the slit to gather his seed. Her moan reverberated through him, making his balls draw up tight and a thrill shoot through his spine.

"Ah! Fuck..." Zevris threw out his other hand to brace himself on the workbench, needing it to hold himself upright. His grip on Tabitha's hair tightened, and it took all his willpower to keep from thrusting his hips, to stop himself from fucking her face as badly as he wanted to fuck her.

She sucked him deep, her eyes never leaving his as she worked his length. Though she could not take all of him into her mouth, she used her fist to make up for it, pumping it in time with her lips.

The pressure within Zevris built to a torturous level, and the pleasure grew along with it. The sensations were so strong, so intense, that he couldn't tell whether he'd spill his seed or if his mind would shatter into countless pieces as fine as stardust first. Either way, he would be undone.

And he didn't want her to stop.

His own touch had never brought him even a sliver of this pleasure. What Tabitha was making him feel was well beyond anything he could've dreamed, was beyond his comprehension, was beyond not only this world but the whole universe.

He couldn't even begin to imagine what it would feel like to truly be inside her.

His lips peeled back, exposing his fangs as he took in ragged breaths. In his lust-hazed delirium, only Tabitha remained—her bold, confident movements, as unrelenting as his own had been moments ago; her soft lips and hot, tight mouth and the occasional scrape of her flat teeth along his shaft; the cloud of her aroused fragrance engulfing him.

She tightened her fist and sucked harder, rubbing her tongue against the nodules on the underside of his crown.

Zevris's mind—and his self-control—shattered.

He lifted his hand from the workbench, taking hold of her hair on both sides of her head, and pumped his hips. Each of his thrusts was punctuated by a snarl, and each struck him with a surge of pleasure.

Tabitha dropped her hand from his shaft, bracing herself with her palms against his thighs. Staring up at him with those big, gleaming, lustful eyes, she curled her fingers, digging her blunt nails into his skin.

Everything within Zevris tightened at once, the pressure suddenly so immense that he couldn't talk, couldn't breathe, couldn't *think*.

A roar tore up from his chest as pleasure burst through him. His cock pulsed, and his seed erupted into Tabitha's mouth. She made a sound of surprise, but she quickly swallowed, sucking on him again, coaxing out more seed.

His torso sagged forward as waves of ecstasy blasted through him, but he kept his hips moving erratically. By the time she'd milked him for everything, his arms and legs were trembling, and his breath was coming in strained pants.

Tabitha pulled back, and his cock slipped free from her mouth. Loosening his grip on her hair, Zevris reached down and grasped her chin, tilting her face up toward him. He swiped his thumb over her swollen bottom lip, rubbing his seed into it. She licked his thumb before she took it into her mouth and twirled her tongue around it.

Zevris inhaled deeply; the air was scented heavily with their arousal, but the smells were separate. He yearned for them to be combined, for them to come together to form a new fragrance that was unique to them—the scent of their mating bond.

He growled and pulled his thumb free to brush the backs of his knuckles over her cheek. "Ah, Tabitha. I cannot wait to make you mine." He sank into a crouch before her. "Until then..."

She giggled, offering no resistance as he gently laid her back and spread her thighs wide.

He grinned down at her. "Until then, I'm going to drink my fill."

Zevris lowered his head, and his female's laughter quickly gave way to breathless moans of pleasure.

NINETEEN

Though Tabitha's eyes were on the TV screen and the movie it was playing—*The Princess Bride*—most of her attention was elsewhere. Elsewhere, of course, being Zevris.

She was lying on the couch with her head on his lap, and he was gently combing his fingers through her hair. It was such a simple, soothing thing, and she nearly shivered in delight every time those fingers touched her scalp. It meant the lightest, teasing scrape of the claws on his ring and pinky fingers and the brush of the rough, callused fingertips of his index and middle fingers; he'd kept those claws trimmed short, just for her.

His other hand was resting possessively on Tabitha's side, its fingers occasionally stroking or creeping tantalizingly close to her breast, and he had his tail draped over her waist, the fluffy tuft at its tip curled against her belly.

Tabitha couldn't fully ignore that Dexter was on the couch, too, or that he was lying on top of her feet, but that didn't matter. At least her feet were nice and warm. Not that she'd been wanting for heat over the last week.

This whole situation—lounging on the couch, watching a

movie with an alien—was so unreal, so unbelievable, and yet so...*normal*. This was what her life had become, and, well...it was good. *Really* good.

She'd spent a week here in Zevris's home, and the routine they'd fallen into was equal parts mundane and out of this world. Every morning, Zevris had woken her with pleasure. Whether it was with his fingers, mouth, or tail, he'd ensured she started each day in a happy place. He'd not once asked for anything in return—but that hadn't stopped her from reciprocating.

And oh, did she love to reciprocate. She loved the way he trembled under her touch, the way he tasted on her tongue, and most of all, the way he lost control. Zevris coming undone was the sexiest thing she'd ever seen. It made her feel powerful. And when he pleasured her...he made her feel beautiful, made her feel wanted, made her feel like she mattered.

He made her feel *loved*.

After her daily wake-up call, he would cook breakfast, letting her relax afterward with a cup of coffee or tea as he took Dexter for a walk, and often shared the bathroom—and the shower—with her as they got ready for their day. They'd spend some of the day apart, Zevris in his garage workshop and Tabitha in the room he'd given her to use for her own business.

On the first day of this arrangement, his power tools had been so loud that she'd cranked up her music to drown them out. As soon as he'd realized, he'd apologized, and installed some sort of device that muted the noise—but she'd kept playing her music anyway. Just yesterday, as she was singing along and moving her hips, he'd snuck up behind her, drawn her away from the table, pressed her up against the wall and used his hand and tail on her until her cries of pleasure were louder than the music.

The unexpected breaks he took during the day had become

something she eagerly anticipated, to the point that she'd taken a few herself. She loved watching him work, watching the way his arm muscles bulged when he lifted something heavy, the way sweat glistened on his golden skin, especially when he'd remove his shirt. Of course, her going into the garage often led to him carting her out so he could have his way with her.

Tabitha could have sworn she was turning into a nymphomaniac. But Zevris seemed to crave her as much as she craved him.

Aside from the sexy times, she loved just being with him. He would've catered to her every whim if she allowed him to, but she didn't want a slave. She wanted a partner. She loved it more when they cooked dinner and cleaned together. She loved talking with him, joking with him, listening stories of the planets he'd been to and the missions he'd conducted—though she knew he left out a lot of details, particularly the gory ones.

She had told him about how her parents had abandoned her when she was a baby, had told him about Nan, had told him about how she'd gifted Dexter to Nan for Christmas one year and how small, innocent, and adorable he'd been. She had told him how she'd come to love making soap and candles, told him about her friend Mia and Mia's now-fiancé, Josh, and how close they all were. No matter what the subject was, Zevris listened with unwavering attentiveness, as though he was absorbing every little tidbit he could regarding Tabitha.

No guy had ever treated her like Zevris did. Hell, no man had ever even *looked* at her like he did—like she was the most precious thing in all the universe.

Tabitha was...happy. Even though it had only been a week, and even though he'd technically kidnapped her, she'd never felt so happy.

And it was getting harder and harder not to just...love him.

Was she crazy? Hadn't she been hurt in the past by

allowing herself to get so caught up in a relationship too quickly? She'd blinded herself to the warning signs just for want of companionship, had justified or ignored the poor treatment she'd received for so long, foolishly thinking it would save her from the inevitable hurt. She'd made the mistake of believing that pouring her all into a relationship meant she'd get the same in return.

But this felt different. Zevris was different. Everything he did and said seemed genuine. She knew exactly what he wanted from her, knew the mission he was on, and knew that his desire for her went lightyears beyond that mission. What she had with Zevris felt real.

Tabitha felt as though she was already *in* love with him. An alien.

And they hadn't even kissed yet! She kept waiting for him to kiss her, for him to initiate that bit of intimacy that was somehow both more innocent and yet more meaningful than what they'd done so far, but he seemed to be waiting for something, himself. Despite the way they'd pleasured one another, she knew he was holding back significantly.

Was Zevris waiting for her to lower her defenses, for her walls to come down, for her to embrace him fully?

She didn't know how much longer she would be content with only hands and mouths. It was *amazing*, and she never wanted him to stop, but she knew it wouldn't be long before she needed more. Before she needed all of him.

Before she accepted *everything* he had to offer.

But was she ready for that?

"Inconceivable!" declared Vizzini on the TV.

The word jarred Tabitha from her thoughts; its timing had been so perfect that it was difficult to believe it hadn't been a response to what she'd been thinking.

But Inigo leapt to her rescue. "You keep using that word. I do not think it means what you think it means."

Seven days ago, falling in love with her alien captor had certainly seemed inconceivable. Now...it felt inevitable.

Zevris laughed, a deep, rich sound that seemed to come straight from his gut.

Smiling, Tabitha turned her head to look up at him. "That one hit your funny bone just right, huh?"

"It speaks directly to my experiences in communicating with humans. English is one of the most convoluted, confusing languages I've ever encountered."

She chuckled. "Yeah, English doesn't always make sense."

"It has its moments of beauty, though." His eyes dipped to her, flaring with that blue light that made her feel all warm inside.

Tabitha turned her attention back to the movie. This was one of her all-time favorites, something she'd wanted to share with Zevris just like Nan had once shared it with her, but again, she couldn't focus on it. "Zevris?"

"Hmm?"

She looked up at him. "Take me on a date."

His hand in her hair stilled, and the one on her side tensed. Even his tail seemed to stiffen and coil a little tighter. He frowned, and a crease formed between his eyebrows. "Tabitha..."

She pushed herself up onto her knees to face him, placing one of her hands on his chest and the other on his shoulder. Dexter, clearly annoyed that she'd pulled her feet free from beneath him, huffed.

"You trust me, right?" she asked.

Please say you trust me.

She could not bear to have her heart crushed by him telling her *no*, not after everything they'd shared.

He looked into her eyes, expression tight, and was silent for several seconds, seeming to search for something. She could feel the tension in him; she knew his struggle. His duty to his people, to protect them and their secrets, against his feelings for her.

Tabitha's chest constricted when he parted his lips and drew in a soft breath.

"I do," he said.

The air left her lungs in a rush.

The enormity of Tabitha's relief was so strong that she nearly sagged against him. She lifted her hand off his chest and reached up to stroke his jaw. His stubble was abrasive against her fingers, and she couldn't help but recall all the times she'd felt it against her thighs.

"Then take me out on a date," she said. "A *real* date. Somewhere in public, around people, like...like a normal couple. I want this to work between us, and I need to know that I'm not just a prisoner here, that you can really, truly trust me with your secrets, like a partner. Like...a lifemate."

Zevris sighed and lifted a hand, raking his fingers through his hair. "And I suppose *I* need to know that a date can be a pleasant experience."

Tabitha arched a brow at him. "Do I want to ask?"

Though she had no right to be, she was jealous of every single woman he'd taken out since he'd come to Earth. Had he looked at them like he looked at her? Touched them as he had touched her?

Had he...kissed them?

"No, and I would rather forget." He dropped his hand from his hair and cupped her cheek. "You are the only female who matters to me, and you stand high above all others. Even when you threw a stone tray at me and kicked me in the groin, my experience with you was far more pleasant than any date I've been on."

"I won't apologize for that." She stared at him, trying to keep a straight face, but couldn't help the laughter that slipped out. "Okay, never mind. I'm sorry. Well, sorry, but not sorry. You *were* kidnapping me."

Zevris chuckled and shook his head. "You don't need to apologize. I admired you for the fight you put up. It was admirable. I am still sorry you were placed in a position where you needed to fight at all."

Tabitha looked over her shoulder to glance at Dexter. He raised his eyes to meet hers. She smiled at the puppy-dog look he gave her.

She turned back to Zevris. "I can't say that I'm mad with where we ended up. I'm...happy, Zevris. You make me happy. I would just like this thing we have between us to be...real."

"It is real, *Nykasha*." He tucked her hair behind her ear, brushing his fingers over the rounded shell before following it down to her jaw to capture her chin. His lips curled into a smile that was at once soft and sexy. "And I will do all I can to help you feel it, too."

Tabitha smiled widely. "So you'll take me on a date?"

Zevris wrapped his arms around her and dragged her onto his lap, guiding her legs to either side of him so she was straddling his thighs. He squeezed her ass with both hands and looked at her with those hot, hungry, loving eyes.

"As you wish," he said, echoing her favorite line from the movie playing in the background.

Giddiness flooded her. It was hard not to read a very specific meaning into his words, especially given what they were watching.

She leaned forward, pecked a kiss on his cheek, and threw her arms around him, hugging him tight. She took in a deep breath, loving his combined scents of musk, sandalwood, and cedar; any one of those would always make her think of him. "Thank you."

Again, Zevris stilled. His body heat seemed to intensify for a moment, and then he moved his hand, sliding it up her back to tangle his fingers in her hair. He drew her head back to look into her eyes again. Somehow, his gaze was even more intense than before. "Anything for you, *Nykasha*."

TWENTY

A DATE. *I am finally going on a date with Zevris.*

Tabitha had been excited about this moment since she'd asked him to take her on a date two nights ago, but now that the time had come, she was anxious. Everything had been perfect between them here in his house. Would he be different in public? Would he...would he be embarrassed to be seen with her?

She worried her bottom lip as she stared at herself in the mirror, double-checking her makeup and hair. Her black eyeliner and mascara paired with the neutral tones of her eyeshadow to really make her green eyes pop. She hadn't worn makeup for over a week, so it was strange to see herself in it again, much less feel it on her skin. Her hair was pulled back into a loose, flowing ponytail with long strands framing her face.

Tabitha released a long, slow breath from her mouth.

Now to figure out what I'm going to wear.

With her towel securely wrapped around her body, she

stepped out of the bathroom and into Zevris's bedroom. Her steps slowed when she saw what awaited her.

Lying across the foot of the bed was a long, red chiffon spaghetti strap dress and a pair of black heels.

"Zevris," she whispered.

She neared the bed and ran her fingers over the dress's soft fabric. She never would have purchased a dress like this, never would've even considered wearing something like this. It was so...bold and sexy. It was made for a woman who was confident in her body—which Tabitha had never been.

Just try it on, Tabitha. What can it hurt?

With a grin, she moved to the dresser, selected a pair of lacy red boyshort panties and a strapless bra, and slipped them on. Picking up the dress, she stepped into it and shimmied it up her body, struggling briefly with the back zipper.

It fit perfectly.

The dress was cinched at the waist, and its plunging neckline showed off plenty of cleavage. There was a slit in the skirt on one side from the thigh down, baring her leg with each step, and her shoulders and arms were completely uncovered. It made her feel...exposed.

She frowned as she hugged herself, running her palms over her arms. She'd always been self-conscious about her arms. For a moment, she considered putting on a cover-up, and for an even briefer moment, considered changing entirely into something more comfortable and less revealing.

No. Zevris had left this for her as a gift. She'd wear it tonight, for him, and hope he liked what he saw.

After pulling on the heels and running back to the bathroom to put on some matching red lipstick, Tabitha took a deep breath, stepped out of the room, and headed downstairs. She heard the light scrape of a chair moving over the kitchen floor as she reached the bottom of the steps.

When she turned into the hallway, Zevris was approaching her, his strides long and leisurely. The instant his gaze fell upon her, his gait faltered. He came to a stop in the middle of the hallway, his eyes wide and covetous as they trailed over her body from head to toe and back again. Though his holographic disguise was already in place, making him appear human, she swore there was a hint of blue light in his eyes.

He wore a charcoal gray suit jacket over a white button-down shirt and matching slacks. The clothing was tailored perfectly to him, accentuating his wide shoulders, narrow waist, and long legs. His usual scruff had been shaven clean; she'd known he wasn't one of those guys who needed a beard to look masculine, and this only hammered that fact home.

You could cut diamonds on that jawline.

Tabitha pinched the sides of her skirt and lifted it outward, smiling at him a bit awkwardly. "Thank you for the dress and shoes. Do you...like it?"

He closed the remaining distance between them, angling his face down to keep his eyes locked on her, and placed his hands on her shoulders. He smoothed his palms down her arms slowly, causing a shiver to run through her. An appreciative growl rumbled in his chest. "Maybe we should stay in tonight..."

Tabitha laughed and shook her head, trying to ignore the pulse his growl produced in her clit. "Heck no. We are going out."

Zevris caught his lower lip between his teeth and drew in a soft, hissing breath, eyes smoldering. "I don't know if I'll last until we make it back."

The way he looked at her—as though the mere sight of her was enough to make him climax—made an ache bloom in her core. She was sure her panties were wet already.

Tabitha pressed a finger to his chest and trailed it down his abdomen toward his groin. "Behave and you won't have to wait until we get back." She grinned playfully. "I've...never fooled around in a car before."

His eyebrows shot up briefly, and as they sank, his lips stretched into a wide smile. He moved one of his hands to her hip. "I'll be sure to save room for dessert."

She blushed. It didn't matter how many times they'd been intimate; it was still so strange to hear a man—especially *this* man—flirt with her like this, and for her to flirt right back.

"Are we ready to go?" she asked, thrumming with excitement.

"No. Not yet." He stepped back, withdrawing his hands from her, and reached inside his jacket. "Turn around."

Tabitha arched a brow but did as he commanded.

He stepped up behind her; she didn't hear his movement, but she felt it, and tantalizing heat radiated along her back. His hands brushed over her shoulders, and something small and solid fell against her collarbone. As his hands swept back, she realized what he was doing.

Zevris gently shifted her hair aside, and his fingers tickled her neck as he fiddled with what must've been a latch. When he was done, he placed his palms over her shoulders, and a delicate chain settled into place around her neck.

Looking down, Tabitha raised her hand to touch the pendent hanging between her breasts. It was a heart-shaped emerald on a white gold chain. Simple, elegant, lovely.

She knew Zevris had the funds to purchase her all these gifts but...he didn't have to. He could have taken her out anywhere and she could have worn what she already owned. But he wanted this night, this date, to be something special. He wanted *her* to feel special.

Her eyes burned with tears. "I...I don't know what to say."

"You don't need to say anything, Tabitha." He let her hair

fall back into place, the pads of his fingers brushing the back of her neck as he did so. Stepping in front of her, he caught he chin and lifted her face, forcing her to meet his gaze. "It reminded me of your eyes."

She sniffled and tried really hard not to cry—it would ruin her makeup. "You really are a romantic. Did they teach you that before you came here looking for a mate?"

He shook his head with a chuckle. "I could have been taught everything my people know about humans over the span of many years, and it wouldn't have been enough to figure out your courtship rituals. I simply want to please my mate."

My mate.

He'd called her that since the beginning, but more and more she felt like it was the truth. That she was his.

She smiled and reached for his hand, lacing her fingers with his. "Are we ready to go now?"

Zevris returned her smile, tightening his fingers around hers, and dipped his chin. "Now we are ready."

⸻

Tabitha glanced at her drink again. Though the glass itself was nothing out of the ordinary, its contents had drawn her eye several times since the server had delivered it. The liquid bled from red to pink to yellow, and, nestled amongst the ice cubes, were a few pieces of strawberry and a thin slice of lemon. The glass's rim was crusted with glittering sugar. It was the fanciest glass of strawberry lemonade she'd ever seen.

It was also the most delicious drink she'd ever tasted, and she was making it last—she was determined to relish every single drop.

The lemonade symbolized the restaurant as a whole for Tabitha. She swept her gaze around the place for the hundredth time. Her eyes were drawn in every direction, wanting to take in everything, though there was no single feature that particularly called her attention. Everything was in harmony. This was easily the nicest restaurant she'd ever been to.

The lighting was relatively dim but quite atmospheric. Soft, warm yellow and orange lights dangled from the high ceiling in short strings and tastefully minimalistic fixtures. Much of the décor, including the walls, booths, and floor, were colored dark; blacks, deep reds, and browns abound. Rather than all that darkness making the space seem oppressive or grim, it served to make the warm glow over each booth and table all the more welcoming and comforting. It certainly made the booth Tabitha and Zevris were sharing feel far more private and intimate despite all the other patrons seated nearby.

Conversations from the other diners created a gentle hum in the air, backed by music that was either some sort of unobtrusive jazz or light classical. She couldn't tell which—and couldn't really bring herself to focus on it too much, anyway.

But her favorite feature was the tall windows that spanned the entirety of one wall—the wall against which their booth was positioned. Those windows looked out over the Willamette River, which was sparkling with the reflected light from the surrounding city as though its waters were laced with molten gold. This view would've been lovely at any time of the day, but it was particularly magical now, when the sky was dark.

Still, she'd have to convince Zevris to bring her back to the area during the day sometime soon so they could walk along the river while all the trees were wearing their autumn colors. Dexter would love it, too.

Her smile softened. Fall hadn't even begun, but here she was already planning ahead—already planning to be with Zevris when the trees were all gold, red, and brown.

A big, warm hand settled over hers, its touch gentle despite the roughness of its calluses. She looked at Zevris.

He smiled at her. Even in his human disguise, even under this low lighting, his eyes were such a clear, vibrant blue. "What are you thinking about, *Nykasha*?"

"I was...thinking about you, me, and Dexter walking along the river."

Zevris glanced out the window. "We'll have to plan for it. And, at some point, I think I'd like to see what Earth looks like in places that don't have quite so many people."

Tabitha glanced to the side to make sure no one was near when she lowered her voice. "You said the cactus reminded you of your home planet. What was it like?"

He leaned closer to her, lowering his voice as well. "I don't remember very much, to be honest. The area in which I lived was all low, rolling hills with those cactus-like plants and a great many others you would think looked quite strange. Few things grew tall, but many grew quite wide. In the rainy season, those hills would become more like islands amidst marshes that teemed with vegetation and life. I left as soon as I reached adulthood to join the *Exthurizen*...to become a soldier. And I have not often thought of my homeworld in the time since."

She turned her hand beneath his so they were palm-to-palm. "Did you always want to be soldier, or did you ever dream of doing something else?"

"I never really *wanted* to be a soldier," he said, brushing his fingers across her wrist.

Even though they were invisible, she felt the tips of his claws against her sensitive flesh, and their touch sent a delightful thrill along her arm.

"But I never could imagine myself as anything else," Zevris continued. "My people have been in decline for so long, and I simply wanted to do my part. Science, engineering, and mathematics were never my strengths, so I decided early on that I would become a soldier. More, that I would join the *Exthurizen* and become an *althicar*, that I would do my duty and face whatever danger I needed to face in order to safeguard what remained of my kind.

"And...I was good at it. The lifestyle came naturally to me, and I excelled, becoming one of the youngest *althicars* in recent history. For"—he blew out a breath and glanced toward the ceiling as though searching—"nearly eighteen Earth years, I have served. It has been that long since I last saw my homeworld."

"I can't believe I haven't asked you this before, but how old are you?"

"Thirty-six Earth years." With a wink, he added, "Though Logan Ellis is thirty-two."

Tabitha smirked. "You're ten years older than me. I always liked older men."

His brows fell low, and he leaned closer still. There was a predatory, carnal glint in his eyes. "You don't anymore, *Nykasha*. Only one male, and he is no man. He's a faloran."

Tabitha pressed her thighs together beneath the table at the pure possessiveness in his voice. "I still have three weeks to decide," she teased.

Now it was Zevris's turn to smirk. "You act as though you haven't chosen already."

She chuckled. "Still so sure of yourself, I see." Her smile faded into something softer as she looked at their hands and lightly brushed her fingers along his calloused palm. "Do you miss it? Your homeworld?"

He also dropped his gaze. For what felt like a long while, he was silent, his face more unreadable than ever before. "I miss the idea of it. I miss what it should've been to me...what it should be. But I have been away for so long...it has not felt like home in my heart for a long, long while."

His eyes flicked aside, looking beyond Tabitha, and his expression changed to something far more neutral—a friendly but guarded look. He sat back, withdrawing his hand from hers. Tabitha glanced to the side to see their server.

"Your food is ready," the man declared, flashing them a wide smile as he lowered his arm and set the dish in front of Tabitha. "Baked salmon and saffron rice for the lady"—he turned toward Zevris and placed the other plate down in front of him—"and the rib-eye steak, medium rare, for the gentleman. Is there anything else I can get you?"

"I'm fine, thank you," Tabitha said with a smile.

"No, thank you," said Zevris.

"Then enjoy!" The waiter gave them a slight bow and walked away.

The lemon-and-spice scent of Tabitha's salmon wafted up to her, making her mouth water. As she unwrapped her silverware from the cloth napkin, she glanced at Zevris. "Do you still have family there?"

"I'm sure I've some blood relations somewhere on my homeworld, but no immediate family."

Tabitha placed her napkin on her lap and frowned. "I'm sorry."

"You don't need to be sorry. I accepted long ago that I was likely to never see that world again, and I've made peace with it. Especially now. Earth is more a home to me than anywhere else I've ever been." Zevris took up his knife and fork and cut into his steak. "Speaking of Earth...I've seen so little of it. You mentioned vacations with your Nan. Where did she take you? What places have you seen?"

Thoughts of Nan were always bittersweet. Tabitha missed

her sorely. The woman had been her mother, had been there for Tabitha's entire life, and then was simply...gone. But the memories... It was in those memories that her grandmother would always be alive, and Tabitha would cherish them forever.

She smiled. "We never left the states, but we visited *so* many places. We took a lot of road trips during the summers. I remember one when I was maybe twelve, Nan said we were going to the Grand Canyon. I was really excited until I realized how long a drive it actually was. And it wasn't even so much the drive itself, but how bland the scenery was. There's a lot of dry, desert landscape once you go far enough east to get out of the forests, and it was boring as heck for a twelve-year-old.

"But Nan kept me pretty entertained. She had this digital music player hooked up through the cassette player in the car. I think there were only twenty songs on it, but we sang our hearts out to every one of them, over and over, and it just got funnier every time. Our voices were hoarse by the time we got into Nevada.

"I was in awe when we got to Las Vegas. I mean, it was nighttime, and there was *nothing*, just dark, barren land, and then bam! It was like a sea of light in the distance. It was like...Christmas."

Zevris tilted his head. "Like Christmas? Isn't Christmas a holiday?"

Tabitha reached for her strawberry lemonade. She felt the grains of sugar against her lips as she took a drink. "It is. And during Christmas, people usually decorate their trees and homes with lights. In some neighborhoods, there are so many lights it's as bright as day."

"Ah, yes. I saw lights like that on some of the houses in our neighborhood last winter."

"Vegas was like that, just lights everywhere the eye could

see, but it wasn't decorated for any holiday. That's just what Las Vegas is. It's flashy and bright. It's also known as Sin City."

She speared a flaky piece of salmon on her fork, bringing it to her mouth for a bite.

He slipped a piece of meat into his mouth and chewed thoughtfully. "Unless sin has a meaning of which I'm not aware, it doesn't sound like Sin City is any place for a child."

She chuckled, covering her mouth with a hand until she'd swallowed her food. "That's at least partially right. I...saw a few things that made Nan hurry and cover my eyes. But there are plenty of things for kids, too. She took me to see *Cirque de Soleil* and *The Phantom of the Opera*. I'm still irked that Christine never chose the Phantom."

Zevris chuckled too, and his eyes gleamed with not only their usual hunger, but joy. "You'll have to show me what those things are at some point. If there is one thing humanity excels at, it's creating entertainment. I came into your culture thirty-five years behind my peers."

Tabitha grinned, but it softened as she ran her eyes over him. Zevris was gorgeous. His eyes were bright and alive, his dark hair was swept back with a couple rogue strands curling over his forehead, and the warm light overhead created contrasting shadows that made his cheekbones sharper—that made them look more like his natural face. And she was the only one on Earth who'd seen behind his mask, the only one who knew his true appearance, who knew of those now-familiar attributes that made him impossibly more appealing.

She'd never dreamed she would be sitting in such a fancy restaurant on a date with a man like Zevris. She absently reached up with her free hand and touched her emerald pendant.

"Have I told you how handsome you look?" she asked.

His grin was that rakish, lopsided one she loved so much. "So, my female approves of her mate?"

Tabitha looked up at him from beneath her lashes and lifted her foot, brushing the toe of her shoe up and down his leg beneath the table. "Your female very much approves of her male."

Though it was barely audible over the soft hum of conversation, Tabitha heard Zevris's growl. It went straight to her clit and nipples, making them ache.

"Behave," she whispered, unable to stop a teasing smile from turning up the corners of her lips.

"You willfully tempt me and then tell *me* to behave?" His grin took on an even more devilish slant as he tilted his chin down to stare at her from beneath his dark eyebrows. "Every day, *Nykasha*, you show me more reasons why you're meant to be mine."

Yep. Panties officially wet.

Tabitha's breath quickened, and her heart fluttered at the promise in his eyes. She took another drink, this one deeper, longer, but it did nothing to cool the fire burning in her core.

Who was she kidding? There was no way she was going to last three more weeks.

Lust doesn't equal love, Tabby.

And she had to remember that he was looking for a womb. His whole race was looking for wombs.

But if it really is that simple, why all this? Why all the effort?

She knew, deep down, despite her reservations and insecurities, that he really was seeking a lifemate. She just... Was she really ready for that? Was she really ready to become a mother so soon? A couple weeks ago, she wasn't even thinking about getting into a relationship, and now she had to think about having a baby?

But boy did her ovaries burst every time she saw him.

What would their child look like? Would they have pointed ears? Fangs? An adorable little tail?

As they continued with their meal, Tabitha finished her tale about the Grand Canyon and told him about the other trips she'd taken, including her those to New York City, Niagara Falls, and the beaches of Florida. She had him laughing when she described the time she and Nan had gone down to Disneyland in California and got lost in Los Angeles. After finally figuring out where to go, they'd hit a massive traffic jam and been forced to sit for hours on the expressway. It was the first time she'd ever heard her Nan swear.

The conversation flowed easily between them. Apart from Mia and Nan, no one had ever shown so much interest in Tabitha and her life, no one had ever listened to her stories so attentively, had ever made her feel so heard.

The waiter returned at some point to clear away their empty plates. The food had been so good that Tabitha had been tempted to lick her plate clean. He left them with a dessert menu and told them to take their time in deciding.

Tabitha perused the menu out of curiosity. Unsurprisingly, almost everything sounded delicious. "The cheesecake is tempting, but I don't think I could eat another bite," she said, sliding the menu toward Zevris. "You can get something if you want. Don't let me stop you."

Eyes locked on her, Zevris slipped a finger beneath the menu and flipped it shut. He pressed the pads of his fingers down atop it, turned it, and slid it to the edge of the table. "I already have plans for dessert, *Nykasha*."

Tabitha blushed under that heated stare and the promise in his voice.

When the waiter returned, Zevris paid for their meal. He helped her from her seat and, rather than walking ahead of or behind her, remained at her side as he guided her through the restaurant, his hand resting possessively just above the curve of her ass.

She looked up at him in surprise. He met her gaze and smiled. There was no shame on his face, no embarrassment, just pure want and tenderness in his eyes. Zevris was walking with her as though he were proud that she was his date.

As though he was claiming her for all to see.

As though she was *his*.

TWENTY-ONE

Cool night air swept over Tabitha as she stepped out of the restaurant and onto the sidewalk, sending a shiver down her spine. Tonight, the breeze carried just a touch of winter, which was totally unacceptable—she refused to let fall be skipped over before it had truly begun. The chill wouldn't have been so bad were it not for the pleasant warmth she'd left behind in the restaurant and the fact that she'd not brought a coat or a cover-up.

She hadn't wanted to cover this dress, not with how Zevris looked at her in it. Not with how beautiful he made her feel.

Zevris released the door he'd held open for Tabitha and moved to her side, placing his hand once again on her lower back. She loved the feel of it there, but there were more than a few other spots she was eager for him to touch tonight.

They turned and walked down the sidewalk. The street was bathed in a yellowish-orange glow cast by the streetlamps and businesses along it. It was that particular quality of light, artificial but somehow charming, that seemed to settle upon most cities after dark. Each of the many trees lining the sidewalk cast multiple shadows, none of which were very deep or dark. The cars parked along the curb to either side of the roadway gleamed with reflected light, just like the river was somewhere behind Tabitha.

Parking had been the only real issue this evening, not that she'd considered it much of a problem. They'd had to park a few blocks away from the restaurant. Zevris had woven along the nearby streets in search of a spot to fit his pickup truck, muttering about the lack of parking places like a man who'd lived in a big city all his life.

She'd laughed a few times at the things he'd said, especially when he'd refused to find a parking garage, saying that the whole concept was criminal. Why, in a place where such methods of transportation were all but required, should someone have to pay to register their vehicle, to be licensed to operate that vehicle, to fuel and maintain that vehicle, and then have to pay to turn it off for a while, too?

That Zevris had laughed along with her had proven that his grumpiness was only on the surface, and that he'd not let anything so trivial as difficulty finding a parking spot put a taint on their evening.

There were a few other pedestrians out and about, including a well-dressed couple walking toward the restaurant Tabitha and Zevris had just left. Of course, everyone else out here seemed to have had the foresight to wear a jacket.

Tabitha shivered again, folded her arms across her chest, and rubbed her upper arms with her palms.

Zevris stopped, hand falling away from Tabitha's back.

She took another step before drawing to a halt and turning toward him. "What's wrong?"

He unbuttoned his suit jacket, took hold of the lapels, and drew it down his shoulders. Tabitha's brow furrowed. She meant to question him again, but the words had died on her tongue, and she found herself suddenly quite transfixed on the way his dress shirt molded to his muscles as he removed his jacket.

She'd never seen anyone—at least outside TV and movies—look so powerful, so predatory, so sinfully sexy in a suit.

Without a word, he closed the short distance between them and swept his jacket around her shoulders. The interior of the jacket was silky and warm, cocooning her in his residual heat, which was amplified when he smoothed his hands down from her shoulders.

Well, there go my ovaries.

His palms came to rest just above her elbows, and as grateful as she was for the warmth of the jacket, she wanted so badly for it to be out of the way so he was touching her skin directly.

"Thank you," she said, catching the edges of the jacket.

Zevris lifted one of his hands to her face, brushing the backs of his fingers across her cheek and granting her the lightest scrape of his claws in the process. It produced another shiver in her—but this one was the *best* kind.

He tilted his face down toward her. "I should have considered the temperature before we left."

"It's not your fault," she said a little breathlessly. She could lose herself in those impossibly blue eyes...

"To be honest, Tabitha, the idea of covering you up couldn't have been farther from my mind when we left." Gently, he guided her to face the direction in which they'd been heading. But now, instead of placing his hand on her back, he wrapped his arm around her shoulders, drawing her against him, sharing his heat as they resumed walking.

She'd seen it in his eyes when she'd first come down the stairs wearing this dress—he'd been so fired up that he'd practically been undressing her with his gaze.

"Well...you'll be uncovering me soon enough, won't you?"

He chuckled and produced a low growl. "Not soon enough."

Heat rushed to her cheeks and pooled between her legs.

Zevris had awakened a new side of her, had brought out the sexuality she'd learned to so carefully guard during her life. Her last relationship, especially, had taught Tabitha that women who looked like her didn't get to be overtly sexual, didn't get to say what they wanted out loud, didn't get to do anything without being judged.

She'd known those lessons were wrong when she'd broken up with Cody. Zevris had taken those lingering ideas, had taken so many of those doubts she'd carried for so long, and ground them to dust beneath his heel, wearing that sexy, fanged grin of his all the while.

Tabitha leaned into Zevris's solidness as they walked, drawing the coat snugly closed around herself. Besides the warmth, the best part of this was that his masculine scent was now surrounding her in a haze, at once arousing and soothing.

They turned onto a side street, and the atmosphere changed immediately. The trees were a little thicker here, the streetlamps spaced a little farther apart, and tall apartment buildings stood on either side of the road. The shadows were deeper, the patches of light less abundant and welcoming. Though several of the apartment windows were lit from within, many more had blinds drawn or were dark.

This was the kind of street that would easily have been creepy and unsettling to traverse were Tabitha alone. But she wasn't alone, and she wasn't frightened, not while she was with Zevris.

Apart from the usual city sounds—most of which were from cars driving on out-of-sight roads—it was quiet. For this little while, it was easy for Tabitha to imagine that she and

Zevris were the only two people in the world, that they were walking beneath a sky dusted with sparkling stars, that they could look up there and he'd point skyward and say, *That one's where I'm from, but this is my home now.*

Any other time, with any other man, she would've felt silly about such imaginings. She didn't now. Not with Zevris. She felt...fulfilled. Happy. Like she could dance on air.

Unfortunately, the world would soon remind her that it was, indeed, full of other people.

She and Zevris walked another block, crossed the street, and turned at the corner. The new street was like the last, with the dark, looming apartments and trees on either side and vehicles parallel parked up and down its length, but one key thing set it apart—Zevris's truck was one of those vehicles, awaiting its owner at the end of the block.

Voices drifted to Tabitha from down the street—masculine voices, talking and laughing. Her eyes caught on something ahead. It was the tiny orange ember of a cigarette as someone took a drag from it. Only then did she notice the four men standing in the shadows against the building, two leaning against the wall and two standing on the sidewalk. At least three of them were smoking.

Zevris had already shifted his course so he and Tabitha were as close to the curb as they could be without walking face first into a tree, apparently aiming for the gap between the group of men and the parked cars.

The men looked toward Zevris and Tabitha, one of them taking another drag of his cigarette. Despite the shadows, it was impossible to miss their leering grins. Though none of them were as big as Zevris, they all looked solidly built and athletic.

"Well, aren't you two fancy," one of the men said.

Tabitha leaned just a little more firmly against Zevris, already feeling that old, familiar, uncomfortable heat creeping into her cheeks. She recognized the man's tone. There'd only been a couple kids in school who'd truly bullied her, and that was the exact tone of voice they'd used when doing so.

"Surprised his coat's big enough," said another man.

She moved her feet a little faster, hoping Zevris would pick up his pace. They were so close to his truck, so close to moving on with their evening.

She felt the men staring at her as Zevris led her past them. A couple of the men snickered.

"Ever seen a cow in red?" the first man asked.

"Trying to attract a bull, maybe," replied another.

"Target's sure big enough." The third man grunted and made a drawn-out mooing sound.

Tabitha tensed and pressed her lips together as ice flowed through her veins. Her chest was tight, and it was difficult to breathe as she fought the sting of tears. She *knew* that man's voice. She knew who he was.

Cody fucking Everton.

Don't you dare cry, Tabby. It doesn't matter what they say, doesn't matter what he says. They don't matter. He doesn't matter.

"You could park a truck on that ass," the fourth man said.

Zevris slowed his pace.

No, no, no! Don't slow down, please. They won't stop, and I don't want to see him.

The second man laughed. "Your dick would get lost if you tried, Tad."

"*You'd* get lost if you tried, Vance," Tad replied. "We'd have to send in a rescue team."

Zevris halted. He was still for a few moments before he hooked a finger beneath her chin. Tabitha resisted when he tried to tip her face up. After this perfect evening, he didn't need to see tears in her eyes. He didn't need to see how this affected her.

Because damn it, it shouldn't have.

But it did.

She wanted to tell him it was okay, to just keep walking, but she couldn't find the words. She'd heard all the insults before, and she'd moved on from Cody years before. She should've been above the hurt. But it always seemed to catch her off-guard, and she never came up with the perfect comebacks until long after the confrontations were over.

If she were to write down everything she'd thought of to say to Cody *after* she'd dumped him, she could've filled a five-subject notebook. Of course, her mind refused to produce even one of those things now.

"I don't fully understand what their words mean," Zevris said in a voice that, though low, already held a dangerous edge. "Are they referring to you when they say *cow*?"

Tabitha reached for his hand and tugged him forward. "It's nothing. Let's...let's just go home."

Zevris pulled her back toward him, caught her chin with his fingers, and forced her to look up at him. He searched her face for a second or two, and his eyes hardened. "There are tears brimming in your eyes, *Nykasha*. Are these men insulting you?"

Her bottom lip quivered before she could stop it. "It's nothing," she repeated.

His brows fell low, and he clenched his jaw. His hold on her chin tightened infinitesimally. "It is not nothing if it has hurt you."

Zevris gentled his touch, stroked her jaw, and released her to turn toward the men. Menace radiated off him, and though it could've just been a trick of the poor lighting, Tabitha swore his shirt looked tighter—or his muscles larger. He stalked toward the men.

Tabitha's eyes widened, and she wrapped her hands around his arm, pulling him to a stop. "Zevris, don't. Let's just go. They're not worth it."

"But you are," he said gruffly, his eyes catching hers briefly before he shook her off and guided her behind him.

"What's it like banging that, man?" Cody asked, thrusting his hips as he held his hands out wide in front of him. "I know from experience that a little cushion for the pushin' can be good once in a while, but isn't she taking that a little too far?"

Those words hurt more than anything else Cody or his friends had said. It hurt because Tabitha knew he was referring to her, it hurt because he'd not even made any indication of having recognized her, it hurt because, again, his words should never have affected her since she'd moved on from him long ago. But it was like a wound that had never fully healed, and he was tearing it right open.

Zevris turned his head from side to side as though scanning his surroundings—or surveying a battlefield. His attention settled on the men again; the two who'd been leaning against the wall had stepped forward to join their companions, and they all wore smug grins.

"I will allow you one opportunity to apologize to my female," Zevris said.

That only roused more laughter from the men.

"Shall I take that as your response?" Zevris asked.

"You should take your heifer and get the fuck out of here," the man named Vance said, his humor giving way to aggression.

"Listen to her and walk away," said Tad. "We will fuck you up."

Zevris released a heavy breath. Tabitha stepped back, worrying her lower lip. She knew he was stronger and faster than anyone she'd ever met, but her list of acquaintances wasn't exactly brimming with well-trained athletes and elite warriors. Was he really going to fight four men at once?

Was he really going to fight her ex?

She didn't want Zevris to get hurt, couldn't stand the thought of it, but at the same time...a small part of her wanted to see him put these jerks in their places. An admittedly larger part wanted to see *Cody* put in his place.

"You don't know who you're fucking with," Cody declared. His gaze flicked past Zevris, landing on Tabitha for an instant before moving away again. His eyes immediately rounded and returned to her. "Oh, shit. Tabitha?"

Her cheeks flamed, and she could barely force air through her throat. This was one of those moments. She could've told him off in front of his friends, could've finally shown him just how little she thought about him, just how pathetic he really was.

"Tabitha? This is the fat chick you used to fuck?" asked Tad.

"Yeah." Cody's expression darkened with embarrassment as he looked away from her. "Pussy is pussy, right?"

"I'd let her suck my dick," said Vance.

"She never dressed up like that for me," Cody grumbled.

"Just leave us alone, Cody," Tabitha said, her words strained. She touched Zevris's back and lowered her voice to a whisper. "Please, Zevris. Let's just go home."

Cody frowned, running his gaze over her again.

That threatening aura pulsing from Zevris only intensified, belied by his slow, smooth movements as he bent his arms up and unbuttoned his shirt cuffs. "Keep back, *Nykasha*. This will not take long."

"This guy for real?" Tad asked.

"Fuck yeah," the man who'd first spoken growled. "Been

holding back in the ring all week. Finally gonna have a chance to let fucking loose!"

The men who'd been smoking took final drags on their cigarettes and tossed them to the ground, stomping them out with their shoes. There was unsettling eagerness in their eyes as they stepped forward to close the distance between themselves and Zevris. A couple of them were rolling their shoulders as though limbering up.

Cody looked at Tabitha again for just an instant, his expression uncertain before hardening more than ever.

Zevris didn't budge from his place. The nearness of his foes didn't seem to alarm him in the slightest; he rolled up his sleeves one at a time with nonchalance. But Tabitha knew when he spoke that his leisurely demeanor was only surface deep. His voice bore an undercurrent of fury that made his alien accent more pronounced.

"You are warriors, then?" he asked.

"Brent is the former Pacific Northwest Amateur MMA champ," said Vance, "and the rest of us aren't far behind."

The first man who'd spoken, Brent, stepped even closer to Zevris, nearly bumping chests with him. He stared up with an aggressive gleam in his eyes.

"Good." Zevris lowered his arms to his sides.

Tabitha retreated another step, wishing she had a phone or that she could bring herself to look away to find help. But what would that mean for Zevris? Wouldn't it put him at risk of being discovered if the police became involved?

All she could manage was one thought, extremely loud and clear—*kick their asses, Zevris.*

Cody laughed; it sounded forced. "Got a tough guy here. Hits some weights at the gym and thinks he's badass."

Sounds like Cody's doing some of that classic projection.

Just like that, the hurt and embarrassment that had seized Tabitha lost some ground to her anger.

"Probably needs to if he wants to lift his date," Tad remarked.

"What's more embarrassing," Brent said, "that he's out with a fat chick, or that he's about to get his ass ki—"

The former champ's head snapped aside, and he flew back into his friends, who spat curses and exclamations into the air. Tabitha's brain caught up with the situation a second later, only then registering that Zevris had moved—he'd punched Brent so fast that she'd missed it.

The other men grabbed hold of Brent, whose legs now seemed about as sturdy as wet noodles. Zevris was amongst them in a flash. He hit Tad and Vance before either could defend themselves, sending them reeling. Cody released the semi-unconscious former champ and charged at Zevris, dropping low to throw his arms around Zevris's middle and slam his shoulder into the alien's abdomen as though to tackle him.

Zevris leaned forward instantly and wrapped his arms around his attacker's chest. He slid back a couple feet before coming to a halt; Tabitha had the sense that, were he wearing something other than dress shoes, he wouldn't have given half as much ground. He reared back, wrenched Cody off his feet and high into the air, flipping him over in the process, and slammed him down atop Brent.

It was just like a move she'd seen wrestlers do on TV those times she'd watched with Josh and Mia, but this was all the more impressive knowing that those wrestlers were working together to make their moves look powerful. Zevris didn't need a willing opponent to show off his unrivaled strength.

Both men, now sprawled on the ground, groaned in pain.

The other two men had recovered, and they rushed at Zevris in tandem. Tabitha's breath caught in her throat. Tad and Vance unleashed a series of lightning quick punches and kicks, coming at Zevris from two different angles. Apart from the handful of wrestling shows she'd watched, she didn't know much of anything about fighting, but even she could tell these guys knew what they were doing.

That should have been the moment when her worry for Zevris hit its peak. That should have been when her heart stopped along with her breath, when terror constricted her chest and pressed in on her from every direction.

Zevris dodged their blows for a couple seconds at most. Then his foot slammed into Vance's chest, knocking him back with a pained grunt. Tad swung his fist at Zevris, mistaking the alien for being off guard.

Zevris caught Tad's wrist, slapped a hand on his shoulder, and flung him aside with seemingly little effort. Tad's feet left the ground. His momentum was halted by the door of a nearby car, which buckled inward as his shoulder and face slammed into it.

Brent had managed to get onto his knees. His eyes looked a bit glossy, and he still seemed unsteady. He lunged forward, striking Zevris in the backs of his legs. Zevris fell, but before Tabitha could even reflexively panic, he somehow rolled backward and caught Brent's arm, wrenching it behind the man's back. Zevris landed with one knee on the ground and the other pressed on the center of Brent's back, pinning the man face first on the concrete.

Cody had regained his feet nearby. He shook his head sharply.

"Fuck, *fuck*, my fucking arm," Brent groaned, slapping the ground with his free hand.

"Fucking bastard," Cody muttered.

Zevris's face snapped toward Cody, and for an instant Tabitha was granted a surreal view of her male's face. His eyes gleamed with reflected light like those of a predatory cat, and his teeth were bared in a ferocious snarl.

Cody swung his fists at Zevris. Zevris dodged the first two punches as though he were avoiding an irritating gnat flying at face. His hand darted up for the third punch, catching Cody's fist and halting the blow entirely.

Tabitha could just barely make out the muscles of Zevris's forearm flexing in the darkness.

Crying out in pain, Cody dropped to a knee and grasped his arm with his opposite hand as though to alleviate the pain. "Fuck you and that fat—"

Zevris's fist cracked against Cody's face with a crunch. Cody's head snapped backward, and faintly glistening blood oozed from his nose. When he swayed forward again, he let out a wet cough and spat thickly onto the sidewalk.

Seeing Cody be shut up like that brought Tabitha some satisfaction, even if it was petty.

Tad dragged himself away from the car he'd been thrown into and staggered to his feet. He stumblingly charged at Zevris from behind.

"Zevris, behind you!" Tabitha clenched the fabric of his jacket in both fists tightly enough to make her knuckles ache.

Zevris twisted around, pivoting on his knee—the one still pressed down atop Brent—to face the new attack. He kept hold of Cody's fist, causing Cody to fall forward onto the sidewalk.

Tad leapt at Zevris, raising a knee.

What came next happened so fast that Tabitha couldn't be sure what she'd seen. It looked like Zevris swung his free arm aside like a club, striking Tad in the legs well before that knee could connect. The man's legs were swept one direction, forcing his torso to pitch in the opposite. Before he could even hit the ground, Zevris caught hold of the Tad's shirt, tugged him closer, and headbutted him, forehead to forehead.

Zevris eased the unconscious man onto the ground with surprising gentleness.

He stood up then, momentarily pressing his weight down upon Brent and coaxing out another agonized groan. Releasing Cody's fist, Zevris clamped a hand on the back of his neck, pulled him up, and dragged him toward Tabitha.

Brent and Vance scrambled way, leaving Cody and the unconscious Tad behind.

Cody's head lolled, and he mumbled something—likely more curses—before managing some intelligible words. "You fucking win. Lemme go."

"Our business is not yet concluded," Zevris growled.

Tabitha had never heard such formal words spoken with such a savage edge on them.

He stopped in front of Tabitha and lowered Cody enough for the man's knees to accept his weight. She glanced questioningly at Zevris, but his attention was focused on his foe, and that intensity still thrummed from him.

"Apologize to her," Zevris commanded.

Cody lifted his head. His nose was definitely broken, and his eyes looked like they were already swelling. But there was more in them, something she'd never seen—fear. Perhaps even a hint of humility.

Zevris shoved the Cody's head back down and forced him onto hands and knees. "You don't get to look at her. You have not earned that right. Apologize. Now."

"I'm sorry," Cody murmured. "So fucking sorry."

Zevris's hand flexed.

Cody groaned. "Damn it, I'm *sorry*! Sorry I...I treated you like shit, Tabby. Sorry for all the things I said, everything I did. So, so fucking sorry."

Tabitha's breath fled her as her wide-eyed gaze flicked between Cody and Zevris. This...this had all really happened.

Zevris had stood up for her, had beaten the crap out of these men because they'd mocked her and called her horrible things, had forced Cody to apologize to her for the first time ever, and though she'd never condoned violence...she was really freaking turned on right now.

He cares for me. He really wants me.

Unceremoniously, Zevris cast the man away. Cody rolled onto his side, features contorted in agony. Zevris scanned their surroundings briefly, took hold of Tabitha's wrist, and began walking—*fast*.

Her heels clicked on the sidewalk as she jogged to keep up with him. Thankfully, his truck was within sight. Despite having won the fight and getting Cody to apologize, Zevris was still brimming with tension, and she had a feeling that there was far more aggression simmering within him than what he'd already let loose.

She kept silent as they reached the truck. He opened the passenger door for her and helped her inside, but he didn't look at her. Once she was settled in the seat, he closed the door, rounded the truck in quick strides, and threw open the driver's door.

The truck rocked as he climbed inside, and he slammed the door shut far harder than he had hers.

But Tabitha refused to let this ruin their night. The rage on his face as he'd fought for her honor had been unmistakable, but there was so much more to what he'd done. There'd been so much restraint despite his bristling fury. She understood the truth of it now that they were out of the situation—he could have killed those men with minimal effort. She wouldn't have been surprised if he'd exerted more energy holding himself back than he would have if he'd opened the flood gates and let his rage flow freely.

He could have simply ignored them. As he'd admitted, he'd

not really understood what the men had meant beyond their insulting tones. But it had been her pain that had set him off.

Screw waiting three more weeks. Tabitha knew what she wanted.

She wanted Zevris to be hers.

TWENTY-TWO

THE STEERING WHEEL creaked as Zevris tightened his grip on it. His jaw was clenched with teeth-shattering force, and the muscles of his arms were so tense they ached—in no small part due to the exertion of preventing himself from crushing the steering wheel outright. Somehow, he kept himself from slamming the accelerator to the floor.

He'd already done enough to risk drawing unwanted attention tonight.

Fire roiled inside him, accompanied by a sinking sourness in his gut. His breaths came in harsh bursts that seemed even to him more like the snarls of an agitated beast. Unspent energy thrummed in his limbs, coursing to the tips of his fingers, toes, and tail before racing back to his thumping heart. He'd never been so affected by combat, not even the first time he'd killed.

An *althicar* always conducted himself with precision, control, and deliberateness. He'd maintained that through every mission he'd ever undertaken, had prided himself on it. But tonight, he'd been dangerously close to losing control.

I did lose control. The instant I turned to confront them.

He'd never had to operate under such restrictive rules of engagement—and he'd never fought in defense of a female's honor.

But this wasn't just any female. This was Tabitha. *His* Tabitha.

How could he not have lost control? Those men had said hurtful things to Tabitha, deeply hurtful things, and they'd done so without provocation. Zevris could have ignored any insult they might've hurled at him, but he could not tolerate anyone insulting his mate.

And when he'd turned to face those men, when he'd finally looked them in their eyes, he'd realized that he knew one of them. Cody Everton. Tabitha's ex-boyfriend.

A low growl rumbled from his throat, and he squeezed the steering wheel tighter.

"Zevris?" Tabitha softly inquired.

His lips peeled back, and a shaky, hissing breath escaped through his teeth. His words pained him before he even let them out, but they were necessary. "Not now."

He couldn't trust himself at the moment—he didn't even feel like himself.

Because even though he'd managed to avoid killing those men—thus protecting his cover by a razor-thin margin—he'd *wanted* to. Even now, he was battling the urge to turn the vehicle around, to go back to the scene and track those men down—to track *Cody* down. The pain that man had caused Tabitha had not yet been avenged. His suffering had been too brief, too limited. Zevris craved true justice, and he was sorely tempted to truly finish what Cody and the other men had begun.

It was either that or give in to an even stronger urge—to pull over on the side of the road, tear Tabitha's dress off her luscious body, and claim her *now*.

The drive back to Zevris's dwelling passed in a blur. He was aware of the road before him, of the countless headlights and taillights of other vehicles, of shadowy trees and lit-up buildings, was even more acutely aware of the silence within the cab of his truck, but he navigated based purely on instinct.

It felt like either a thousand years or ten seconds had passed when he pulled into his driveway.

"Stay," he commanded as he shoved open his door and climbed out of the truck. He closed the door behind him, barely stopping himself from slamming it, and drew in a deep breath.

It did little to ease him.

Zevris walked around the front of the vehicle to the passenger side and opened Tabitha's door. Somehow, he kept his hand steady when he held it out to her.

She placed her fingers in his hand and looked at him curiously as she stepped down. As soon as she was clear of the door, he closed it as gently as he could manage.

The feel of her warm, soft little hand in his was nearly too much to bear. He released it, turned, and stalked toward the front door of his dwelling, the heat of his desire roaring in its war against the heat of his rage.

Zevris stabbed the key into the keyhole and turned it hard enough that he felt the metal flex. His lack of care only fed into his frustration. Tugging the key free, he opened the door and stepped inside, standing aside to allow Tabitha through behind him.

"Zevris?" she said as he closed the door. She reached toward him. "I want to—"

"I can't, Tabitha." He twisted his torso, avoiding her touch, and strode past her. It pained him to do so. "Not now."

He deactivated his holoshroud, barely feeling the hum that swept over him.

Dexter padded into the hallway, stopping to stare up at

Zevris and Tabitha eagerly. He made a drawn-out half-yowl, half-whine, and turned to hurry over to his empty food bowl and nudge it with his nose.

Zevris walked into the kitchen, grabbed the bag of dog food, and poured some food into Dexter's bowl, forcing his hands to move slowly and steadily so he didn't make a mess that would only agitate him further. After returning the bag to its place, he stalked along the hallway.

The crunching of Dexter gobbling down his food filled the otherwise quiet residence.

Tabitha was standing halfway down the hall, looking at Zevris. Unable to make eye contact with her, unwilling to trust himself, he moved past her.

Her fingers wrapped around his arm, bringing him to a halt. Zevris turned to face her. Before he could say another word, she caught his face between her hands, pulled his head down, and slammed her mouth against his.

Zevris's eyes widened. Her kiss was like being struck by lightning, its electric current making every muscle in his body lock tight, but instead of inducing pain it pulsed with sizzling pleasure. His cock stirred, jolting with the sensation of her lips caressing his, instantly growing hard.

Tabitha was kissing him. His *mate* was kissing him. Her mouth was soft and warm, her breath sweet.

But it wasn't enough.

Zevris brought a hand up and shoved his fingers into her hair, cradling her head as he slanted his mouth across hers. She released a startled breath, her lips parting, and it was all the invitation he needed to deepen the kiss.

He moved forward, leaning into her. She moved with him until her back bumped the wall. Once she was trapped there, he dropped his hands to her ass and lifted her off the floor, pinning her body with his own.

Tabitha's fingers delved into his hair. She moaned against his lips, wrapping her legs around his waist as he drew her pelvis against his. He plundered her mouth, his tongue sweeping against hers, stroking it, coaxing it into a sensual dance.

Karak'duun, she was so fucking sweet.

She arched her back, pressing her breasts against his chest, and ground her sex along his cock. He growled, flexing the fingers of one hand to clutch her ass tighter while he slid the other hand along the bare skin of her left leg, which was exposed by the slit in her dress.

The fragrance of her arousal struck him fully then, drawing a groan from deep within him.

Tabitha broke the kiss, and Zevris opened his eyes. Her lips were red and swollen, her eyes bright and glistening with desire, and she was panting softly.

"Make love to me, Zevris," she whispered.

He gritted his teeth, staring at her in disbelief. Though he'd yearned to hear those words for what felt like eons, though he wanted her more than anything, it was the last thing he'd expected to hear from her. After the way things had gone tonight, the way their date had ended...

Fangs bared, he tipped his forehead against hers and squeezed her thigh, unable to stop a low growl from sounding in his chest. All that heat and restlessness was still roiling inside him, stronger now than ever. He rasped, "You know what that would mean, *Nykasha*."

Tabitha slid one of her hands down until her fingertips were caressing his jaw. "Yes. Make me yours. I *want* to be yours." She tightened her legs around him, forcing his shaft, which was trapped within the confines of his pants, to press more firmly against her. "I want your cock inside me. I want your seed." She brushed her lips over his. "I want your babies."

"Tabitha." It was all he could say, the only thought he could form in a mind overwhelmed by the power of her words.

Zevris crushed his mouth to hers, his kiss hungry and demanding, and she returned the kiss with a ferocity that matched his own. He knew in that instant that he would never find the right words to express all he felt—and he knew, also, that he didn't need to say anything.

His body was ablaze, consumed by torrents of desire, need, and lust. He craved his female with every atom comprising him. He needed to be inside her, needed to fill her with his seed, needed to forge his mating bond with her. He needed to make Tabitha his in every way.

But he would not take her here; he wanted her in his bed.

Clutching Tabitha close and keeping his lips against hers, he carried her upstairs and into his room, kicking the door shut behind him. He didn't break the kiss until he'd laid her atop his bed. He straightened to look down at her. She'd never been more radiant, more alluring, but her dress—which he'd so admired on her earlier—now served only as a barrier between him and what he wanted most.

Zevris did not hesitate. He extended his claws, grasped her dress, and shredded it down the middle, tearing the pieces apart.

Tabitha gasped, eyes rounding. "Zevris!"

"I'll buy you another," he growled as he slipped a finger into the valley between her breasts, hooking it under her bra. He sliced the bra open between the cups, letting it fall atop the tattered dress, and tore it all away to flutter to the floor.

He cupped her bare breasts, squeezing their yielding flesh. Her nipples, already hard, pressed against his palms, begging for more. He caught them and rolled them between his forefingers and thumbs, watching Tabitha's face as she moaned.

Unable to resist, Zevris leaned down, captured one of the

pink buds between his lips, and sucked it deep. Tabitha cried out. She grasped his hair as she held him closer, whimpering when he grazed his fangs over her tender flesh. His palm kneaded and teased her other breast as he sucked her nipple, and soon she was writhing beneath him, undulating her hips, and panting.

"Oh God, Zevris, please," she begged.

He released her nipple and raised his head. Their eyes locked.

He trailed his hands down her sides, wanting to be slow about it but finding that almost impossible. His claws cut through the lace of her panties at her hips, and he tore the fabric away.

Zevris ran his hands down her legs, almost shuddering in his need. He spread her knees wide. His cock was throbbing in his pants, feeling close to bursting, and his chest was so tight he could barely breathe.

Now his mate lay before him, body bare in all its glory. Her eyes were even brighter than before, her cheeks were red, and her sex was already glistening with arousal.

If true perfection were possible, it was lying before him now.

"So beautiful," Zevris said as he removed her shoes, letting them fall to the floor one by one. He reached between her thighs and dragged his finger through her pussy, gathering her slick. "And already so hot and wet for me."

Tabitha shivered, her thighs quivering, as Zevris lifted his finger to his mouth and slipped it between his lips.

That taste of her shattered what little control he'd maintained. Part of him longed to descend upon her with mouth and tongue, to devour her as he'd done so often already, but that was not his strongest craving.

Standing straight again, he kicked off his shoes and tore his shirt open, yanking it down his arms. Tabitha pushed herself up onto her elbows to watch with heavy-lidded eyes as he unbuttoned his pants and shoved them, along with his boxers, down. When he stood, kicking his clothes aside, her eyes locked upon his cock. She licked her lips.

Zevris grasped his shaft at the base and squeezed. His tail flicked restlessly behind him. "I can wait no longer, *Nykasha*."

Tabitha slowly dragged her eyes up his body to meet his gaze. She smiled, scooted back toward the center of the bed, and spread her thighs wide. "I don't want to wait."

He climbed onto the bed and crawled between her legs. Keeping her gaze upon him, Tabitha lay down and smoothed her palms up Zevris's chest and shoulders as he positioned himself over her. Zevris braced himself with one arm on the bed beside her head, reached down to clamp his hand around his shaft again, and shifted his hips forward.

He ran the head of his cock up and down her slit, coating himself in her slick, before lining up with her entrance.

"You're mine now, Tabitha," he growled, thrusting inside her with a fierce snap of his hips.

She gasped, tilting her head back. Her fingers curled into his shoulders, digging her blunt nails into his flesh.

Zevris hissed at the burst of torturous pleasure that rocked him. He slammed his hand down beside her head. He wasn't even fully inside her yet, and it was already almost overwhelming.

Staring down at her, he clenched his teeth and pumped his hips again and again, forcing her pussy to stretch around him, forcing her body to accept more and more of him. She was hot, wet, and tight, so very tight, and her pulsing sex clutched at him, eager to draw him deeper.

When his cock was finally fully sheathed inside her, Zevris groaned and buried his face in her hair, inhaling her lavender and vanilla scent. His muscles were tense, and he squeezed the blanket in one of his fists; he was on the verge of spilling, but he refused to do so this soon. As much as he wanted to claim her, to solidify their bond with his seed and irrevocably mark her as his, he needed this to last.

He *wanted* this to last.

Tabitha's hands swept over his back and shoulders in soft caresses, spreading tingling warmth across his skin that only deepened the ache in his loins. She turned her head and pressed her lips to his jaw, to his neck, leaving little kisses and teasing him with flicks of her tongue along his ear.

It was more than he could resist. Zevris lifted his head, caught her hair in one hand, and angled her face up toward him. The instant her eyes met his, he slammed his mouth over hers in a fierce kiss and drew his hips back. He drove them forward again, hammering his cock even deeper than before.

Tabitha released a choked cry; Zevris greedily swallowed the sound. Spurred by her reactions, by his overwhelming lust and desperate need, he pumped into her repeatedly, his frantic pace only increasing. A ragged snarl accompanied each of his thrusts, joining her muffled moans to create a savage, sexual song all their own.

Her nails wildly clawed at his back as she undulated her hips, meeting his thrusts.

The pressure in him grew to a maddening degree. His discomfort was only rivaled by the waves of pleasure accompanying it, which were more potent than any he'd ever felt.

Zevris broke the kiss, baring his clenched fangs as he reared back so he was on his knees. He caught her legs and pushed them up, opening her wider and providing himself more leverage that made him sink even further into her body with each powerful stroke.

Though his lips throbbed in the absence of hers, he found

the sight worth the sacrifice—his Tabitha was tantalizing and sensual with her hips angled up toward him, her full breasts and their pearled nipples bouncing, her lips parted in pleasure, and her half-lidded eyes blazing through a haze of lust and pleasure. She was everything he could have ever wanted.

Grasping her hips, Zevris pistoned into her, guttural sounds escaping him with each movement of his hips. His mate writhed beneath him, clutching at the bedding before moving her hands to her breasts as her breathless moans rose in pitch.

He looked down at where their bodies were connected, watching his cock, glistening with her essence, enter her pussy again and again. Something primal swelled in his chest at the sight. He was inside his mate, staking his claim.

Tabitha was *his*.

"Zevris, Zevris..." she panted, turning her face into the blanket.

Suddenly Tabitha's body locked, and her sex convulsed. With a cry, she arched her back and squeezed her eyes shut as liquid heat flooded her.

Her climax shattered whatever dams had held his at bay. His every muscle flexed at once, curling his body toward her, and his fingers pressed into her skin, pricking her with their claws. His tail stiffened, stretching straight behind him. He jerked her toward him hard, burying himself as far as he could in her heat just as he exploded inside her.

Zevris roared as his seed blasted into her. He forced himself to keep moving, to maintain the slide of his shaft against her tight, quivering inner walls and thus prolong the ecstasy that had crashed down upon his mind. His eyes closed of their own accord. The pleasure was staggering, forceful, relieving, and enthralling, it was consuming; it was everything. It was *her*.

He fell over Tabitha, wrapping an arm around her as he continued to grind his pelvis against hers, his tail twitching with every spurt of seed, until he hadn't a drop more to give and his trembling had subsided. But he did not withdraw from her. Instead, he pressed firmly into her, unwilling to let any of his seed seep out.

They lay like that together, panting, their bodies hot and coated in perspiration, their thumping hearts gradually easing. Her hands leisurely petted his back; he stroked the tip of his tail up and down her calf. Pleasure had suffused him, and it was slow to fade. He'd never felt so languid, so satisfied.

Zevris took in a deep breath. His nostrils flared, and his heart quickened slightly—Tabitha's scent was sharper and fuller than ever, bearing an impossible new sweetness and just a hint of something more. And it was strengthening by the moment.

He raised his head to look down at her. She opened her eyes and peered up at him.

The faintest glimmer of blue flashed in her eyes.

He moved a hand to her cheek, sweeping back loose strands of her sweat-dampened hair, and watched in awe as tiny blue flecks appeared amidst the green of her irises, so subtle at first that he doubted whether they were real.

"What is it?" she murmured, brows creasing slightly. She shifted her gaze as though searching his face, and those flecks briefly lit up with reflected light, like stars being born and fading in the space of an instant.

Zevris's lips stretched into a wide smile. There was a warmth in his chest, a remnant of the raging fires that had been burning in him before, but it was soothing now, fueled by elation rather than fury or unmitigated lust.

No, it wasn't merely elation. He understood somehow, on a deep, instinctual level, that the warmth he was feeling was his connection to her. It was their mating bond.

He took in another breath, and he finally realized what had

changed about her fragrance. It wasn't merely the smell of sex in the air; Tabitha's scent had taken on a hint of his own, creating something new but immediately familiar. It had become *their* scent.

Zevris caught her chin. His eyes bored into hers. "You are mine, *Nykasha*."

TWENTY-THREE

Tabitha smiled and stretched as she roused from her slumber. The warm, hard body against her back and the big, strong arm draped over her middle were absolutely perfect. She and Zevris were right where they belonged. His breath tickled her hair against the back of her neck, and his tail was coiled possessively around her thigh. There was also something hard and thick pressed along the curve of her ass.

Her lashes fluttered open. The dim morning light glowed through the slats of the blinds. From the corner of her eye, she could just spy the shredded remnants of her dress on the floor. She felt a faint pang of disappointment at the loss, but it swiftly faded as she recalled the vehemence with which Zevris had looked at her last night. His blue eyes had been aglow with barely restrained lust.

Pfft. Restrained? My alien unleashed his inner beast.

And that first time hadn't been the only time. He'd taken her—quite thoroughly—twice more, the final time with her on top, sitting astride him. She had never imagined she could take a cock so deep. He'd lifted her up and driven her down upon him as though she weighed nothing, all while his tail had stroked her clit.

She didn't remember when she'd fallen asleep last night. It must have been sometime after she'd collapsed upon his chest, panting and utterly exhausted; her thighs were still sticky with his cum. Though she'd not felt it then, she was sore now in muscles she hadn't even known existed, but the most prominent ache was still between her legs. Her pussy clenched at the memory of Zevris's cock.

Down girl.

Were it not for what Zevris had done, for the way he'd confronted Cody and his friends in her defense, she might have wondered if she was jumping into this too quickly. She waited for the regret, for the dread, for the second thoughts that always weighed upon her when she made rash decisions...but none manifested.

Tabitha wanted Zevris. She knew that with certainty. He was caring, considerate, funny, and sexy as hell. He'd stood up for her. He was also genuinely attracted to *her*. His every glance at her, his every caress, and every powerful thrust of his shaft had shown her that. Why would she let someone like him slip through her fingers?

Zevris stirred and clutched her a little tighter, rubbing his face against her neck. His hand slid down to rest over her belly. He took in a deep breath and released it in a low purr before seeming to calm and settle back into sleep.

Though his touch was relaxed and comforting, having his hand on her stomach reminded Tabitha of why he was here in the first place.

Would she get pregnant? Was she already pregnant? Was it even possible between their two species?

She moved her hand down to rest next to his on her belly.

What would it feel like to have life growing within her, to have *his* baby?

Again, she waited for that voice to tell her that this was a bad idea, that she wasn't ready, that she barely knew Zevris, but her mind was quiet and calm. She had no regrets. Everything felt...right. Better than right. It felt perfect.

You are mine, Nykasha.

Tabitha closed her eyes. His voice was so clear in her mind that it was as if he'd spoken those words aloud right now.

The connection she felt to Zevris was so deep and powerful it almost defied explanation. It was so much more than the pleasure they'd shared, so much more than his touch or his embrace, so much more than her adoration for him—more, even, than her burgeoning love.

But Tabitha knew what that something more was, even if she couldn't understand it.

This was the mating bond he'd talked about. It had begun as a warmth in her core when he'd first filled her with his seed, but even then, she'd recognized it as something separate. Because unlike that fullness in her womb, this warmth had spread through her veins, suffusing her body from the inside out, making her heart flutter and her skin thrum.

Now it was a steady sensation, a grounding force, dependable and calming; it was the antithesis of loneliness. She felt Zevris through that sensation just as surely as she felt his body against hers. This new warmth...it was *him*. Like some part of his soul had nestled inside her, like it had wound itself around her heart and would never let go. And now that it was there, she wanted to feel it forever.

But there was another sensation, more urgent and far less welcome, that made her restless and uncomfortable when all she wanted to do was simply lie in Zevris's arms.

Her bladder was full to bursting.

Tabitha groaned and reached for the edge of the bed, gently pulling herself away from Zevris. He growled and yanked her back, tightening his hold as he skimmed his lips and fangs over her neck and shoulders, sending a thrilling shiver through her.

"Does my mate hunger for me?" he asked, his voice deep and husky from sleep. He pressed his hips forward. His cock slipped between her thighs to run along her pussy. "I hunger for her."

Her nipples tightened, tender and achy from his ministrations last night, and that spark of desire thrummed low in her belly. But it only enhanced her discomfort.

She pressed her forehead to the pillow and groaned again. *Stupid bladder.*

"Zevris, unless you get kicks out of golden showers, I suggest you let me go," she muttered into the pillow.

"I would enjoy any shower with you, *Nykasha.*"

Tabitha burst out laughing. "Uh, no. We'll skip *that* particular shower."

His hands cupped her breasts, and he rolled her sensitive nipples with his thumbs. It sent a jolt of pleasure straight to her clit.

Stupid, stupid *bladder.*

"We can shower *after,*" he rumbled in her ear nipping it with his fang. His tail unwound from her thigh to slither higher, brushing along her pussy.

Tabitha started. "Zevris, I have to pee!"

He froze so thoroughly that it was like he'd been dunked in a vat of liquid nitrogen. An instant later, he lifted his arm away and withdrew his tail. His voice had lost some of its early morning gravel when he said, "I'm sorry. I didn't realize."

She knew without asking that he was thinking about how he'd kept her tied to his bed for hours while she'd *really* had to pee, that this was an echo of that same guilt, but she considered the two situations entirely different.

Tabitha twisted to face him. Though his gaze burned with that ravenous light, it was softened by his slight frown and furrowed brow. He looked so adorable and sexy while he was all sleep rumpled.

She chuckled and leaned closer, pressing a quick kiss to his lips. "It's fine. I'm not dying."

A corner of his mouth tilted up. "Good. You're not allowed to."

Tabitha smiled and pulled away. This time he let her go. She slipped out of bed, aware of every muscle that had been worked last night—and especially aware of the tenderness between her legs. As she walked to the bathroom, she felt Zevris's gaze on her naked body as though it were a physical thing. If he were any other person, she would have been embarrassed, would have sought to cover herself up, but he'd shown her plenty how much he desired her. *All* of her.

When she reached the bathroom doorway, a thought occurred to her. She cringed and glanced back at him. "You miiiiight want to check on Dexter. He hasn't been out since we left for dinner last night."

Zevris's expression fell. "*Svesh.*"

He rolled out of bed so fast his legs got tangled in the blanket and he dropped to the floor. He released a longer stream of alien words that Tabitha assumed were all curses. As he stood up and angrily kicked at the bedding that had tripped him, tail flicking erratically in agitation, Tabitha couldn't help but admire the view of his toned ass—even as she covered her mouth to hide her silent laughter.

She slipped into the bathroom and closed the door behind her. Her need to pee had become unbearable.

After she relieved herself, she took a quick shower and

brushed her teeth. It was only as she rinsed her mouth that she glanced up at her reflection and noticed the glimmer in her eyes. Brow creasing, she leaned closer to the mirror. Her breath hitched.

Streaked within the green of her irises were strands of faintly glowing blue. She turned her head from side-to-side. The blue flickered as her eyes moved in and out of the direct light, but it was so soft either way that it was barely noticeable unless she was actually looking for it.

Was this...part of the bond? Zevris had never told her that there would be physical evidence of it. She touched the outer corner of her eye.

"I guess if anyone asks, I can say I'm wearing contacts."

It was such a strange thing, but she...liked it. The change was pretty, like she had glitter in her eyes, but more than that, it was proof of her bond with her mate.

My mate.

I have a mate!

Grinning, Tabitha stepped out of the bathroom and got dressed; Zevris must have gone downstairs.

She snatched the blankets off the floor and laid them on the bed. As she was about to leave the room, something caught her attention on the nightstand. For a moment, what she was seeing didn't register; she had to do a double take to be sure that it was real.

Her cell phone was lying on Zevris's nightstand.

Tabitha's eyes flared. It'd been over a week since she'd last had her phone.

She picked it up and tapped the screen, expecting it to be dead, but the time and date appeared. The phone was fully charged. With a smile, she put in her passcode, and her phone unlocked. There was a single missed text.

Strange. I would've expected more by now.

She clicked on the message icon.

Sooooo, how did the date go? Did you get your sexy thang on? You did have sex, right? Give me the deets! Mia had written.

How did she...?

Tabitha scrolled up, and her smiled dropped. There were whole conversations between *Tabitha* and Mia that had taken place throughout the week.

"Are you *serious*?"

She wasn't surprised that Zevris had a way to bypass her passcode—the man was an alien with super crazy techy stuff. But this...

Growling, Tabitha stalked out of the bedroom and hurried downstairs. She heard Dexter barking from the back yard, so she made her way to the back door, slid it open, and stepped outside.

Dexter was running circles in the grass, keeping within the borders made by the low concrete curbing around Zevris's planting beds, his tongue lolling happily. But Tabitha's gaze only lingered briefly on the dog.

Zevris was standing at the edge of the patio, and he turned to face Tabitha as she shut the door. He was in his human disguise, wearing nothing but a pair of jeans, low-slung around his hips, granting her full view of his golden, sculpted muscles in the morning light. His hair was disheveled, and his jaw was shadowed with stubble. His lips curled into a smile that made Tabitha's knees weak.

He met her gaze; his eyes were bright despite the hologram masking his true appearance, and they still held that lustful gleam. *F-me* didn't cut it. His were full on fuck-me eyes, and they were only for her.

Yes, please.

Damn it, Tabitha, you're supposed to be angry at him right now!

She pressed her lips together and glared at Zevris as she held her phone up with the screen facing him. "What is this?"

Zevris's smile took on a sheepish slant. "Your phone."

"You know what I mean, Zevris."

He sighed and lifted a hand, combing his fingers through his hair and dragging back the wild strands that had been dangling over his forehead. "Those are the messages I've exchanged with Mia, pretending to be you."

"These are my *private* conversations, Zevris." She flicked through the messages, stopping on one he'd sent two days ago. "You even told Mia we were together!"

"I gave her as little information as I could, and didn't say anything untrue," he replied.

"This is wrong on so many levels. You don't snoop through people's phones, especially the phone of someone who is your... your mate! It's an invasion of privacy and it shows you have absolutely no trust in that person."

He closed the distance between them smoothly, dipping his chin to keep his gaze upon her. "I trust you, *Nykasha*. That's why you have your phone back. I should have done so sooner. I was simply acting to protect my mission and prevent suspicion. Mia is someone you care about. I did not want her to worry." He reached up and caressed her jaw, his lips spreading into a grin. "I was also confident in my skills. I knew you were mine the moment I saw you, Tabitha."

Tabitha opened her mouth to scold him some more, paused, and closed it. She couldn't be mad at him for that...could she?

Ugh. I should be, damn it, but I'm just...not.

She understood why he'd done it, and, well, none of what he'd told Mia was actually wrong. Tabitha and Zevris were together.

They were mates. He'd just...announced it a little prematurely.

How crazy was this? She was mated to an alien. Her alien from next door.

Knowing she was likely wearing the biggest, goofiest grin ever, she stepped closer to him, rose on her toes, and pecked a kiss on his jaw. "You're lucky I like you so much."

"I certainly am." Zevris put his hands around her waist and drew her against him. He stared at her, a ravenous gleam in his eyes. "I missed breakfast in bed this morning. Shall I have it on the patio, instead?"

Dipping his head, he captured her mouth.

Tabitha moaned and slipped her arms around the back of his neck. He dropped his hands to her ass, taking a handful of each cheek, and squeezed as he clutched her closer, inserting a knee between her legs.

She gasped as he ground his knee against her pussy, and he took that opportunity to sweep his tongue into her mouth. Tabitha clung to him as he devoured her. His lips were hot, and his tongue was demanding. Whispers of pleasure bloomed within her core, making her clit throb with need.

Dexter barked, startling Tabitha. She pulled her head away and watched as Dexter chased a squirrel.

"The universe seems determined to block my cock today," Zevris grumbled, tightening his hold on her.

Tabitha burst out laughing. "You know what cockblocking is?"

"I am living it, female."

She snickered and rubbed her nose against his. "Well, consider it punishment for going through my phone and pretending to be me."

Leaning back slightly, she brought her phone into the space between herself and Zevris, tapped the camera icon, and switched it to the selfie lens. She extended her arm and angled the phone toward them. "Now stoop your pervy butt down and smile!"

Laughing, Zevris did as she commanded, hunching his back to get his face into the frame. Once they were both smiling up at the camera, she took the picture. She turned to reward him with a kiss on his cheek and pulled away.

But he stopped her before she could escape, keeping one hand on her ass while the other smoothed back loose strands of hair from her face. He leaned close, staring into her eyes. An awed gleam joined the desire blazing in his gaze. "The blue is more pronounced today."

She smiled up at him. "Will they get brighter?"

"I don't know. I've never seen the change as it happened." He gently brushed the pad of his thumb just below her eye. "But I hope it won't. I'm rather fond of your eyes as they were."

Her heart fluttered, and the warmth in her core radiated outward to heat her whole body. "I love the blue." She reached up and caressed his cheek. "I'm now yours."

A growl vibrated in his chest, and his gaze dipped. Tabitha knew right away that he was going to kiss her again. Before he could, she withdrew, stumbling back toward the patio door.

"Tabitha..."

She wagged her finger at him. "Punishment. The blocking of the cock. Remember?"

Zevris dropped a hand to his groin, squeezing his very pronounced bulge through his jeans. "This punishment will not extend beyond our morning meal, female."

She grinned, unable to look away from his hand. "We'll see."

Tabitha caught her lip with her teeth. No, it probably wouldn't last much longer. She was dying to have him between her thighs, to have him filling her, stretching her, but she could punish him in other ways. She could lick and suck him close to completion only to stop at the last moment and leave him on the verge of spilling. Though that'd be torturing herself, too...and, well, she didn't want that. She longed to have him thrusting into her with all the ferocity burning within him, and she knew that her *punishment* would only make their coming together all the more passionate.

As though reading her mind, Zevris said, "I'll keep this punishment in mind, *Nykasha*, when you're crying my name in pleasure and begging me for more."

With a laugh, Tabitha retreated into the house. Her body was thrumming with arousal; she knew it wouldn't be long before he made good on his promise.

Reaching up, she touched her cheek. It was sore from how much she'd been smiling lately. She couldn't recall ever being this happy. She turned her phone toward her and brought up the picture she'd just taken with Zevris. Her smile softened.

There was something in his eyes and in his smile, something so powerful and deep that she couldn't deny its presence even if it seemed far too soon to be there. That light, that brightness, that joy...Zevris looked like a man in love.

And she saw the same thing mirrored on her face.

She lightly brushed her finger over the image before opening her messages.

Maaaaaybe, she typed out to Mia, adding a winky face with the tongue sticking out.

The blinking dots appeared on Mia's side of the messenger immediately, followed by, *Don't you DARE hold out on me!*

Tabitha chuckled. *I don't kiss and tell.*

She attached the picture of herself and Zevris and pressed send.

Mia promptly responded with, *OMFG!!!! He's so fucking hot!!!!!!*

A gif of a woman fanning herself appeared right below, then another of a woman fainting.

Girl, you better have jumped that man's dick and rode it to kingdom cum, Mia wrote.

Tabitha couldn't stop laughing as the conversation continued to scroll with gifs—a train ramming a too-small tunnel repeatedly, cream spurting out of a long, narrow pastry, the old school finger in the fist-hole, and multiple images of people thrusting their hips and humping.

On a serious note, Mia texted after the spammage, *you look absolutely gorgeous, Tabby. I'm so happy for you.*

Tabitha smiled and turned to look out the patio door. Zevris was running across the lawn, playing with Dexter, his lips stretched in a grin and muscles flexing. He was gorgeous.

And he's mine.

TWENTY-FOUR

Tabitha swayed her hips to the music as she laid out her next batch of soap bars, arranging them in neat rows. Their fragrance washed over her—wisteria and cyclamen with a touch of fresh rose and a few subtler citrus notes. The bars were colored a harmonious blend of vibrant yellow and sunny orange with pear green swirled along their upper edges. Between their scent and coloration, they were reminiscent of summer.

She smiled as all those special summer things flitted through her mind—warm breezes, blue skies, fragrant flowers. Lemonade and barbeques; swimming in lakes, ponds, and pools. Hot neighbors who turn out to be even hotter aliens in disguise.

Okay, so maybe that last thing wasn't necessarily linked to summer...but she had met Zevris during the end of summer. That had to count, right? That was good enough to redeem summer a little after years of sunburns and boob sweat.

With the soap bars in place, Tabitha sorted through her stacks of ingredient cards until she found the proper bunch.

Humming along with the song playing in the background, she paired each bar with a card.

Though it was still four weeks before she'd have her booth at the farmer's market Autumn Harvest Fair, she wanted to have everything ready to go well in advance. That was how she and Nan had done it every year. Selling homemade items at that event had been as firmly ingrained a tradition for the Mathews women as Thanksgiving turkey and presents on Christmas morning.

As always, those thoughts of Nan were bittersweet. Nan had loved the Autumn Harvest Fair—not just for selling her creations, but because there was so much to see, taste, and buy.

Tabitha reached for one of the little poly bags, but her hand stilled atop the pile. She drew in a deep breath and blew it out quickly, wrestling back her sorrow.

She'd missed the Harvest Fair that had happened a few months after Nan's death. The thought of going without her grandmother had been too much; Tabitha's pain had been too raw, the hole in her heart had been as vast as the Grand Canyon.

The fair had been strange the following year. Tabitha's booth just hadn't felt the same; the fair itself hadn't felt the same. Of course, Tabitha had recognized that *she* was what had changed. All the people, some of whom she'd seen at the fair every year since she was a little girl, had been just as friendly, the foods and smells and festivities had been just as wonderful, the fall weather had been just as pleasant.

It had all just been missing something without Nan there to enjoy it, too.

But this year was different. Tabitha wasn't going alone, and she was far more excited and eager than she was melancholy. With Zevris alongside her, selling his woodwork, everything would be great, and she'd get to have the added enjoyment of introducing a newbie to the farmer's market.

Four weeks...

She'd lived with Zevris for nearly a month now, and already couldn't dream of life without him. It seemed unreal. They'd filled that time with so much, had created so many amazing memories. How could she not be eager to create a lifetime's worth of memories beyond those?

They'd gone out several times for breakfast, lunch, and dinner at various restaurants in and around Portland. They'd gone hiking, had strolled through parks, had walked Dexter along the Willamette, had visited local sights and had braved a few tourist traps. They'd even gone to see a couple movies in the theater and had spent one evening watching a hilarious mystery rom-com play.

She'd enjoyed every outing with him, especially those during which they'd just...spent time together. As much as she loved sharing those experiences with him, Tabitha and Zevris didn't need movies or shows for entertainment, didn't need food to converse over in order to enjoy one another's company. Simply being with him and talking to him was a joy; everything else was a delicious bonus.

She finally plucked up one of the little bags, sandwiched a bar of soap between an ingredients card and a business card with her logo and information on it, and slipped the soap into the bag. She'd packaged thousands of soaps like this over the years, and now that she was moving, her hands did the work automatically. What was that called? Muscle memory?

I have a few muscles that are aching with the memory of Zevris...

Heat flared low in Tabitha's belly, and she pressed her lips together. She had work to do. She was *not* going to walk out into the garage to jump her man's bones.

At least not right this second.

As she continued bagging soap bars, her eyes flicked toward her computer desk in the corner. She smiled to herself. Sitting prominently atop the desk was a wooden keepsake box with alien symbols carved on the lid, the very box she'd examined when Zevris had first taken her into his workshop.

The heat in her belly shifted up into her chest, and her heart melted a little more. He'd gifted her the keepsake box this morning, and it would've been a wonderful gift on its own, but there'd been more to it—when she'd lifted the lid, she'd discovered that it wasn't empty.

Zevris had placed an eclectic collection of items inside the box, each of which pertained to something they'd done together. There was a napkin emblazoned with the logo of the restaurant he'd taken her to on their first date, a ticket stub from the first movie they'd seen together in the theater, a tiny twig from the giant stickwork heads they'd visited in Orenco Woods Nature Park. He'd put in the teeniest, most perfect little pinecone she'd ever seen from a hike they'd taken in the Tillamook State Forest. There was also a bookmark from Powell's Books, her favorite bookstore in Portland; she still felt bad for him having had to carry what must've been a hundred pounds of books when they'd left that place.

But he hadn't acted as though they strained him in the slightest, and he'd even said one of the most romantic things he could have ever said to her when they'd first walked into the store.

Buy as many books as you want.

Those items and the others he'd included each spoke to a memory Tabitha and Zevris had made, and there were already so many of them. It was still hard to believe it had only been four weeks...

She paused, counting back the weeks, and her eyebrows

rose. She hadn't been with Zevris for *about* four weeks or *almost* four weeks.

It had been *exactly* four weeks since he'd made his offer to her. Today was the twenty-eighth day. This would have been the day upon which she made her final choice, the day she would've had to either commit to being his mate or demand a return to her old life.

He'd given her four weeks.

Tabitha snorted. Her pussy had only lasted one week.

Once she'd finished packaging her soaps, she turned to get the twine, and her eyes caught on her bottles of fragrance. There, sitting in the front row, was a bottle labeled *Lily of the Valley*. It was the fragrance she'd spilled the day he'd given her the cactus, the day he'd run off because it had apparently had some *unexpected effect* on him.

A devious thought entered her mind.

Tabitha plucked the bottle down from the shelf, grabbed a swab stick from the nearby jar, and opened the bottle. The fresh, floral, springtime scent filled her nose. Using the swab, she took some of the fragrance and dabbed a little bit behind her ears—and some between her breasts just for good measure.

She was curious to see firsthand what effect it had on her alien.

Tabitha tossed the swab in the trash, returned the bottle to the shelf, and grabbed the twine to start tying off the soap bags. Her music cut out while she was working, giving way to her ringtone. She picked up her phone.

The screen showed an incoming call from Mia. Tabitha tapped the answer button and put it on speaker. "Hey!"

"We set a date!" Mia squealed.

Elation bubbled within Tabitha. "Really? When?"

"Next year, August first."

Tabitha groaned as she tied the twine into a pretty knot.

"You just had to pick the hottest month of the year, when we're all going to be sweating like pigs."

"But we'll be *beautiful* sweating pigs."

"Bring on the boob sweat!"

They laughed.

"Have you picked your colors yet?" Tabitha asked.

"You will be happy to know that I've chosen some very flattering colors. Dusty blue and burgundy."

"I love you."

Mia laughed. "Did you really think I was going to pick orange?"

"Yes!"

"I was *thiiiiiis* close."

Tabitha grinned. "Liar."

"Okay, you're right. So I wasn't." She snickered. "Wouldn't want my ladies to be sweating pumpkins. Anyway! How are things going between you and Logan?"

It was so strange to hear Zevris being referred to by that name now. Though it had been the name he used when he'd first introduced himself, it...wasn't him.

Tabitha's grin softened into a smile as she thought of him. "Things are...amazing. They're really, *really* amazing."

"Wow. What is that I hear in your voice?"

"What?"

"Are you...in love?"

"Mia, it's only been a month."

But even as Tabitha said those words, she knew they were meaningless. What did time matter? If you truly felt something for someone, something as powerful and consuming as love, what did it matter if it had been a week, a month, a year? Maybe it had only been a month, but she felt like she'd known him forever.

Zevris's touch made her heart flutter, the sound of his voice filled her with warmth, and the way he looked at Tabitha made her feel like she was the only important thing in all existence. He'd pampered her, yes, but it was about so much more than that. He made her feel cherished. He made her feel empowered, made her feel beautiful. His thoughtfulness and attentiveness had helped her become a better version of herself—the happiest Tabitha ever. And the thought of not being with him, of losing him...it made her heart clench and filled her with dread.

"There is such a thing as love at first sight," Mia said. "Though in your case, it might've been *lust* at first sight."

Tabitha laughed. "There was that. I won't lie."

"Well, I can't wait to meet him. You know," Mia's voice lost its playfulness, "Cody never deserved even a second of your time. None of the guys you were with ever did. And I saw it. Even Josh, who can be so oblivious sometimes, saw it."

"I saw it, too," Tabitha said, frowning as she set the twine down and flatted her hands on the table. "I saw it, but I just... didn't want to believe it. I couldn't believe that someone who was supposed to care for me could be so cruel. And I hate that I was desperate enough to stay with him as long as I did. But Logan isn't like that. He...he sees me, Mia."

"Yeah, I've seen it in the pictures you've sent. That man has it hard for you. I'm happy for you, Tabby."

Oh, Mia, you have no idea how hard *he has it for me...*

"Thanks. I'm happy, too." Tabitha shifted her weight onto one foot as she straightened and reached for her phone. "But I miss you! It feels like we haven't seen each other in forever. We'll have to meet up sometime so I can introduce you and Josh to Logan. We can do a double date and—"

A pair of strong arms looped around Tabitha's middle from behind, and Zevris's solid chest pressed against her back an instant later. He tipped his head down, brushing her hair with his face, and inhaled.

Zevris's hold tightened, and his body went rigid. "Tabitha..."

The low timbre of his voice sent a shiver down Tabitha's spine and made her pussy clench.

She grinned; she was in trouble. "Mia, I gotta go."

"Wait, was that him?" Mia asked quickly. "Oh, fuck. Don't tell Josh, but I think I just came hearing his voice."

"I'm about to come myself. Byeeee!" Tabitha tapped the *End Call* button and set the phone down.

Zevris inhaled again, chest swelling behind her, and groaned. Even though they were both dressed, there was no missing the feel of his hard, throbbing shaft against her lower back. "*Nykasha*, what have you done?"

"*Nooooothing.*"

He smoothed his hands down her belly to her thighs, where he gathered the material of her skirt. His fingers gripped her inner thighs, trapping her skirt in his palms, as a shudder wracked him. His breath was ragged when he said, "You lie."

Faster than Tabitha could respond, Zevris yanked her skirt up over her hips, pressed a palm to the center of her back, and shoved her forward, bending her over the table. She gasped, splaying her arms to either side. There was a flicker of fear inside her—maybe she'd gone too far—but it sputtered and died as quickly as it formed, leaving only excitement in its place.

This was Zevris. Her mate. She trusted him wholly and knew he'd never hurt her.

He kicked her feet apart, spreading her legs wider, and hooked his fingers under the waistband of her underwear. It bit into her skin for an instant as he pulled on it before the lacy material gave way, tearing apart with a thrilling *riiip*.

Then his fingers were *there*, dragging through her slit. Tabitha moaned and arched into his touch.

Zevris growled, spreading her slick over her pussy before positioning two fingers at her entrance. "Is this what you wanted, Tabitha?"

He thrust them into her.

Tabitha cried out and clutched the table. There was a brief burn with the stretch, but it was quickly overcome by pleasure. She was wet, but she just hadn't been prepared for the force he'd used. And he didn't stop there; he thrust his fingers into her again and again with hard, powerful pumps, each one coaxing a whimper from her.

Warmth pulsed through her body as her ecstasy built. She tried to move, to push herself up, but Zevris pressed her back down, his palm like a fiery brand on her back. He twisted his fingers inside her, sending a jolt of white-hot pleasure through her as he stroked her G-Spot.

Her sex tightened around his fingers, and liquid heat flooded her. "Zevris!"

"Do you like this, *Nykasha*?" he asked, voice rough. "By how wet you are and the sexy little sounds you're making, I'd say you're enjoying this very much."

Suddenly his fingers were gone, leaving her empty and right on the verge on coming.

"No! Oh God, Zevris, no, don't stop," she begged.

"Oh, I'm not stopping, Tabitha. I won't be stopping for a long, long time. You've ensured that."

The broad head of his cock pressed against the entrance of her pussy. Not a moment later, he surged into her, filling her so completely that the breath fled her lungs.

Ecstasy speared her, blasting through her in waves that consumed her entire body. She surrendered to him utterly. Her sex spasmed, clamping down on him as if to draw him in further still, and her legs trembled. A series of fervent cries escaped her as she came.

Zevris growled low and savagely bucked his hips, shoving himself deeper. His cock expanded within her, and he shuddered. Heat flooded Tabitha's core in scalding spurts that prolonged her own release.

She felt so full of him, and the delicious stretch caused by his shaft only added to her pleasure.

He curled his fingers, grazing her back with his claws, before flattening his hand and sliding it up. It trailed over her neck and delved into her hair, taking hold of it in his fist.

He gently drew back on her hair, lifting her torso off the table. His other hand moved to her front, gripping the neckline of her dress. There was another exciting *riiip* as he tore the dress down the middle. Her bra was destroyed immediately after, falling away to be forgotten. Zevris cupped one of her bared breasts and kneaded it. His callused palms were delightfully rough against her sensitive skin, and her clit throbbed in time with his fingers as he pinched and twisted her the sensitive, rosy peak.

Zevris moved his hips again, thrusting in and out of her with short, shallow pumps. Tabitha moaned and rocked against him, aching for him to push harder, faster, deeper, but he maintained his leisurely pace. She felt every single one of those nubs on his cock as they dragged along her inner walls. Her essence and his seed trickled down her thighs, but she didn't care. All that mattered was the man behind her.

Utilizing his grip on her hair, Zevris turned her face toward him. He gently kissed her temple, her cheek, the corner of her mouth, then grazed his nose along her jaw. Tabitha reached a hand up to cup his cheek.

"Ah, *Nykasha*, consider this your punishment. You're going to burn right along with me."

Releasing her hair and breast, he dropped his hands to her hips, drew his pelvis back, and slammed forward, driving his cock in hard and deep. Tabitha released a strangled cry and slapped her palms down on the desk, but she had no time to recover.

Zevris was a beast, relentlessly pounding into her, using his hold on her hips to jerk her back to meet his every thrust. It was a frenzy of motion, of guttural grunts and snarls and flesh slapping against flesh. It was wild, passionate, and untamed. It was pleasure that bordered on pain. It was a delicious torment, and all she could think was, *More, more, more.*

Pleasure coiled within her, winding tighter and tighter. Her skin was abuzz with sensation. Tabitha felt him everywhere—not just his hands on her skin, not just his legs pressing against hers, not just his merciless shaft filling her, but at her core, in her heart, suffusing every fiber of her being. He was in her blood, in her soul. He was part of her—and she was part of him.

"Zevris," she whispered; his name flowed from her lips in a plea, in a benediction. She needed more, needed it all.

"Come for me, Tabitha," Zevris growled. "I want to feel your pussy clench around me. I want to feel your body demand my seed. I want to feel your hunger."

Tabitha bit down on her bottom lip to silence her cries, clutching the desk like it was her lifeline. Her breasts swayed, her thighs and ass slapped against him with all his ferocity, and the maelstrom gathering in her core intensified.

"I-I can't," she rasped. It was too much, it was inhuman; his alien prowess shone through in every brutal thrust of his hips.

His grip strengthened, and his claws pricked her flesh. "You can. Let me hear you, *Nykasha.* Let me hear your screams."

Something slithered around the outside of her upper thigh —his tail. Its tip brushed over the hair above her sex before settling against her clit. Its touch, which had been whisper-soft, grew immediately firmer, pressing down with the same precision and confidence he'd demonstrated time and again with his fingers and tongue. Another burst of pleasure struck her, stronger than the last.

Tabitha jolted. "Ah!"

She felt like she was hurtling skyward, soaring higher and higher, but she wasn't *there*, couldn't get there.

His tail vibrated against her clit.

All that pleasure exploded outward in a blinding torrent; Tabitha shattered. She barely heard her own ragged cry as her mind broke apart under the force of her pleasure, barely felt her nails rake the tabletop. But she did feel Zevris—every inch of him, hot and hard, driving into her unrelentingly.

Her knees buckled.

Zevris wrapped an arm around her middle and cinched her up against him. He came with a roar, his cock expanding for an instant before his seed blasted inside her womb, filling her with heat. His primal roar brimmed with pleasure, with triumph, with conquest, and it only intensified the vibrations of his tail, combining with the jerking of his cock to coax her to another peak.

Tabitha rode those waves of ecstasy for a delicious eternity, her pussy spasming and contracting, greedily working Zevris's shaft to take everything he had.

When his thrusts finally faltered, and her awareness languidly returned, she found herself with her chest on the table and her head cradled in her arms. She was panting, her breaths disturbing the hair that had fallen into her face. Beads of sweat trickled over her skin. Her body felt loose and sated; she'd been ridden hard, but well-loved.

Zevris's hands slid up, gliding over her sides in soothing caresses. He leaned over her, placing kisses along her spine as he massaged her back, her sides, her shoulders, her arms. But he did not withdraw from her—and his shaft remained hard as steel.

"Mmm," Tabitha moaned, arching against him.

Zevris grunted and smoothed one of his hands down to her hip. He drew his pelvis back, but instead of pulling out, he thrust into her again.

Tabitha rocked, gasping at the sudden flare of pleasure. She pushed up on her hands and looked at him over her shoulder, eyes wide. "Again?"

His fangs were bared, his eyes blazing, and his sculpted muscles glistened with a sheen of sweat. He pumped his hips a second time, using his hold on Tabitha to pull her against him with more force. His snarl stretched into a sinful grin. "Again. You started this, *Nykasha*. Now I'm going to finish it. Over and over and over..."

TWENTY-FIVE

Tail flicking lazily on the bed beside him, Zevris hummed in satisfaction and drew Tabitha's body a little more firmly against his. He smoothed one of his palms up and down her back, following the line of her spine, while the other kneaded and caressed her thigh, which he held over his midsection. She was warm, soft, and languorous in the wake of their lovemaking. She had a hand settled on his chest, fingers tracing lazy, abstract patterns.

He couldn't ignore the fact that her inner thigh was pressing down on his throbbing shaft, pinning it against his belly. It was a pleasurable feeling, even if it was a teasing one. That stimulation, however small, would've been unbearable half an hour ago, and he would've been helpless but to act upon it. But he was finally regaining some semblance of control after hours and hours of being lost in a maddening haze of lust.

He'd lost count of how many times they'd mated since he'd walked into her workroom and been hit by that lily of the valley fragrance.

Zevris lifted his head off the pillow and glanced down at

Tabitha. Though the bedroom lights were off, and night had long since fallen, he could see her clearly—especially with the gentle blue glow cast upon her by his eyes and tattoos.

Her hair was disheveled, spread over his arm, shoulder, and chest. Her pale skin was not without markings—faint red lines and spots where his claws and fangs had scratched and nipped, a few dull purple bruises on her hips and thighs in the rough shapes of his fingers. Though he'd not broken her skin, and she'd assured him she was unhurt, he'd apologized for those marks.

She'd told him they were sexy. He agreed; Tabitha looked well and thoroughly loved.

"I couldn't get up if I wanted to," Tabitha murmured.

Zevris chuckled. "Do you want to?"

"Nah"—she flattened her hand on his chest—"I'm good. Just can't move."

He slid his hand up her thigh and cupped her ass, giving it a squeeze. His arm pressed her leg down harder on his cock, creating another spark of pleasure. "If I need more, you won't have to. I've plenty of energy left for the both of us."

She snorted and nestled closer to him. "Not sure how. Have you slept at all?"

"I have not." He lowered his head, looking up at the ceiling and the shadows cast across it. They'd come to bed hours ago, and he'd woken her three times—no, this had been the fourth— to deal with his enduring need.

Tabitha was not a faloran, and she lacked the strength and endurance of his people, but she'd kept up with him through- out. A few times, she'd even outpaced him, showing a wild side that had her flat little teeth nipping at him and her blunt nails raking his flesh. They'd slowed down as the day wore on, their frenzy gradually giving way to gentler lovemaking.

She'd yet to voice a complaint, though he knew she was

exhausted. He'd done his best to resist, to let her sleep, but the need had still been too great. That lily of the valley scent was merciless.

They'd showered together that afternoon, washing away all traces of that fragrance while making love a couple more times, but its effects had lingered long after. Just as the first time, that smell had been enough to set him off for a great while.

"Do you regret using that scent on me?" he asked, lips curling into a smile.

Tabitha took in a deep breath and let it out in a contented sigh. "Hmm...no. I'm a *very* happy participant, and now I can brag about having a freaky sex marathon. But I didn't realize just how badly it would affect you. Can I be sorry about that but not sorry?"

Zevris laughed and shook his head. "You can be whatever you like, *Nykasha*. It was much more pleasant this time around than the first."

She chuckled, smoothed her hand up his chest, and cupped his jaw, brushing her thumb along it. "Well then, I guess you won't mind if we do that again sometime. Maybe I'll even give you some forewarning."

He turned his face toward hers and pressed a kiss to her forehead. "Isn't the surprise part of the fun?"

She smiled up at him, and those blue streaks in her eyes lit up briefly. He couldn't be sure whether it was reflected light, or if her eyes produced their own faint shine, but they'd seemed particularly bright while he'd mated with her—not just the blue, but the green, too.

Zevris lifted his hand from her thigh, brushing some of her golden hair out of her face. "How were you not claimed before I met you?"

Her smile faltered before disappearing completely. "A lot of guys just don't like girls like me."

He stroked the small cleft in her chin. "Human males do not like intelligent, resilient, humorous, beautiful females?"

She smiled again, and he saw the way her eyes softened at his words. "They don't like fat girls."

Zevris growled, flashing his fangs. "They are fools." He moved his hand back to her thigh and clutched it. "Your size is perfect, and it is only one of a great many traits that encompass you. I do not need lily of the valley to look at you and be consumed by desire. From the moment I first saw you, I knew you were the other half of my heart, that you were what I needed to finally be content, to be complete. There is no one on this planet or any other who is like you."

"I see it when you look at me. I feel it." She quickly tilted her head down, but not before he glimpsed the tears glistening in her eyes. She pressed a kiss to his shoulder. "Thank you, Zevris."

"Ah, *Nykasha*," he said, smoothing his hand along her back. "I am sorry you haven't been treated as you deserve. But that time is behind you now. You have me. And if you ask it, I will find every person who ever mistreated you and ensure they become at least as apologetic as Cody Everton."

Tabitha laughed. "No. He doesn't matter. None of them do. And I...I'm glad for everything that's happened. If any one thing had been different, who knows if we would have ever met?"

Even trying to consider the myriad of decisions and occurrences that had eventually brought him to Earth, to Oregon, to this town, this street, and this house just before she'd moved in next door, was enough to drive Zevris insane. She was right—even the tiniest difference in anything in either of their lives could've been enough to ensure they never met. But at the same time...

"Perhaps it is illogical, but I *know* I would have found you eventually," he said, flattening his hand on her lower back and spreading his fingers. "It would have taken longer, perhaps, but I would have found you. Because everything in me says you were always meant to be mine."

She lifted her head and looked down at him, her long hair falling to one side. Her glittering eyes roved over his face. There was a seriousness in her gaze now. She reached up and brushed her thumb over his bottom lip, running it back and forth. "I love you, Zevris."

Heat blossomed in his chest and spread outward, and suddenly his every nerve was alight, hypersensitive to every spot his skin was touching hers. The weight and feeling behind Tabitha's simple words were immense.

He knew humans tended to throw that word, *love*, around freely—often enough in some cases to dilute its meaning. But he also knew that wasn't what Tabitha was doing. She'd never said those words to him before now, and though she'd given him countless meaningful looks, though she'd spoken to him so often with honesty and conviction, he'd never seen so much emotion and solemnity in her eyes.

Love was not a concept unique to humans; falorans had a term that represented the same thing, that carried the same weight. He didn't need the translations loaded into his neural transceiver to decipher the meaning of this. He didn't need to watch human entertainment to puzzle it out. Love was exactly what he felt for Tabitha.

It was...everything.

Cupping the back of her head, Zevris lifted his own and captured Tabitha's lips with his. He poured everything he felt for her into that kiss, charged it with all those powerful, complex emotions, with all the longings, desires, hopes, and fears that he harbored inside himself but could not fully voice.

His heart thundered and his pulse pounded. Unbidden, his cock twitched, but he ignored it.

When he finally broke the kiss, his lips were tingling, and his breath was ragged. He met her gaze and held it. "I love you too, Tabitha."

The smile that lit on her face outshone every star. It was more beautiful than any smile from anywhere across the entirety of time and space.

He dragged her back down to lay beside him, tucking her against his side with her head resting on his shoulder.

She rubbed her cheek against his shoulder and was quiet for a time before asking, "What now? It's been four weeks. What happens from here?"

Zevris frowned. His mind had turned to that question repeatedly over the last month, but he'd not allowed himself to dwell upon it for long. "Honestly, Tabitha...I don't know. I was assigned a specific mission. In theory, my involvement would end once my objectives are complete."

She tensed against him. "So, what? Either I have a baby and you leave...or I don't, and you leave?"

"No," he growled, clutching her tighter against him. "No. I will remain on Earth regardless, *Nykasha*. No matter my orders, whether we have a child together or not, my place is here. With you. That is never going to change, Tabitha. You have my vow on that."

"What about your people, your mission? The...the military? Won't they come?"

"If it comes down to me having to defy orders, yes. They will. But I have spent half my life eluding detection by a great many military forces, and I know all the methods my people would employ. They would never find us. I don't believe it will come to that, though, Tabitha. The mating bond is a sacred thing to my people."

Tabitha's body relaxed. "And we are bound. So they won't take you from me. Does our bond...guarantee that we're compatible to...have a baby?"

Zevris slid his hand to her belly. Even now, his seed could be taking root inside her, growing something precious and rare—a child. Their child. Just the thought of her carrying his baby had his cock throbbing anew with the need to be inside her, to ensure that she was filled with his seed again and again, that she had every possible chance to conceive.

"No. But my people cannot reproduce without a mating bond in place, and no faloran has ever made that bond with another species before. And our scientists have said your kind and mine are genetically compatible. There is no guarantee, and I do not wish to give you false hope...but I think the chances are strong."

She settled her hand over his, squeezing it gently. "Good. I've kinda...well, I've really grown attached to the idea."

Zevris's tongue slipped out and ran across his lips as her words pooled molten desire in his loins.

Tabitha sighed and slid her leg down his body. Freed from her thigh, his cock sprang up immediately. He hissed through his teeth.

"Do...you want me to help with that?" she asked, gesturing toward it.

"No," he said with a chuckle. "I'll survive this time, and you need rest. I've broken your slumber too many times already tonight."

She was silent, and he could *feel* her eyes on his shaft, could feel her debating with herself, and just the thought of her closing her mouth over his cock or taking it into the inferno that was her body had seed oozing from its tip.

"Tabitha..." he warned in a low voice.

"I've got the energy if you do," she said, and he could hear the grin in her voice. "Besides...we have a baby to make."

Zevris growled and rolled himself onto her. He positioned his body between her legs, bracing one hand next to her head to hold himself up. Sure enough, she was grinning up at him.

"*Nykasha*, you will be my undoing." He grasped his cock, lined it up with her pussy, and thrust his hips hard.

Tabitha's lips parted with a gasp. Her head tilted back, and her lashes fluttered, but she did not close her eyes or look away from him. Her sex gripped him; agonizingly exquisite, blisteringly hot, and tantalizingly wet. She fit him so fucking perfectly.

He groaned and circled his hand around her neck like a collar, using his thumb to keep her face tilted up toward him as he slowly pumped in and out of her, angling himself so the nubs on his cock dragged along her clit.

She panted, her breaths short and needy, and her inner walls quivered around him. He knew she was sensitive, knew she was tender, and knew she was close to reaching her peak.

Tabitha slipped her arms around his neck and wrapped her legs around his hips. "I love you," she rasped.

Those words again sent a thrill through Zevris that filled him with raw, volatile heat. His rhythm changed, becoming more urgent, and soon he was pounding into her with fierce snaps of his hips. He could not hold himself back.

"And I love you." He slammed his mouth down over hers and kissed her deep, swallowing her cries, her moans, her whimpers.

All that pleasure created by the joining of their bodies, all that ecstasy created by friction and touch, was overwhelming on its own, but it was cocooned by something stronger now. Their admission of mutual love had wrapped everything in an extra layer that made it more potent, more powerful, more meaningful.

This was his home. *This* was where he belonged—with Tabitha, his mate, now and forever.

And he refused to let anyone take her from his side.

THOUGH HIS EYELIDS WERE HEAVY, and the full weight of his weariness had settled over his body, Zevris had yet to fall asleep. A glance at the nearby clock told him it was thirty-seven minutes after three o'clock in the morning. This part of Earth was relatively quiet and still, and it would remain so for at least a couple more hours. The only sound in the bedroom was that of Tabitha's slow, steady breathing.

Karak'duun, she felt so good tucked against him. His blood still ran hot, and the ache of desire still pulsed in his loins. It would have been so easy to take her again, to pull her atop him and tease her sex before pushing his cock into her slick heat.

But he refused to submit to those urges. He refused to rouse his mate again. He'd known she was exhausted, and it had been proven beyond a doubt after their last round of lovemaking. After he'd withdrawn from her and rolled onto his back, Tabitha had curled up against him, laid her head on his shoulder, and fallen asleep within seconds.

Zevris lifted his head to look down at Tabitha. Her face was angled up toward his, cheek resting on his chest. Her warm breaths fanned delightfully across his skin. She looked so serene like this, so carefree. He wanted to ensure that she always looked so at peace; that was his new mission in life, the only one that mattered.

As slowly and gently as he could, he moved a hand to her face and traced her features with the pad of his finger. His whisper-soft touch followed her delicate brow, ran down along her adorable nose, glided over her cheekbone and down to her full, pink lips.

She didn't stir.

He had no doubt that she would make use of that lily of the valley scent sometime in the future, and he would not try to stop her...but he would make every effort to spare her the full ferocity of his desire for so prolonged a period. Even he felt the exertion; he could only imagine how tired and sore she'd truly been.

"Ah, my sweet, sweet *Nykasha*," he rasped, sweeping his finger down to her chin.

The last thing he wanted to do was leave the bed. Everything was perfect while he was here holding her. All the troubles of the universe were far away and out of mind, all the dangers had been chased away, and the darkness was warm and sheltering rather than mysterious and threatening.

But he knew it was time. He'd known it all day—well, all *yesterday*—and had done his best to put that knowledge aside for as long as possible. There'd been no need to delay this, no need to avoid it, but he'd done so regardless. Perhaps it had been out of some notion that it would preserve this amazing situation between himself and Tabitha—the longer Command had to wait for the news, the longer Zevris had with her undisturbed.

With even greater care than he'd exercised in his touch, he extracted himself from their mutual embrace. Several times, he paused, breath caught in his throat, as she made a little sigh or shifted infinitesimally, but in the end she did not wake. She simply curled the blanket around herself tighter and slept.

Zevris didn't allow himself to linger, knowing he could easily have spent hours just watching her sleep. He swung his legs off the bed, stood up, dragged on a pair of boxers, and walked to the wall-mounted television.

He eased the television aside and opened the secret storage compartment. Just as he'd expected, the comm disc had that blue light glowing. Command was ready for his report. In a few hours, it would have been exactly thirty days since Khelvar had informed Zevris of his looming extraction.

Plucking up the disc, he closed the compartment and exited the bedroom, quietly closing the door behind him. Though the walk downstairs couldn't have taken more than ten or fifteen seconds, the thoughts suddenly swirling through his mind made it feel like an eternity.

The uncertainty hanging over Zevris and Tabitha was more troubling than anything he'd ever faced. They both knew better than to bet everything on hopes and dreams, they both knew that life exceled at finding ways to be cruel and ruin plans. There were no guarantees.

Except that last sentiment no longer seemed correct. Even if nothing else in the universe was guaranteed, his love for Tabitha was. He knew that with a certainty he'd never believed possible. It was seared into is heart, his soul, his entire being.

But he could not be sure of his superiors' plans. As far as he knew, he was the only faloran to have formed a mating bond with an alien female. This was historic, unprecedented. That hadn't mattered to him, yet it was true all the same. Zevris and Tabitha were likely the first mixed-species couple in faloran history with a chance to produce offspring.

What did it mean for his people, for their society, their civilization? What did it mean for Zevris and Tabitha?

He walked into the living room and sat on the couch, placing the comm disc on the coffee table.

Dexter, who'd been lying in his dog bed near the back door, stood up and padded over to Zevris. The dog hopped onto the couch, curled up against Zevris's legs, and rested his head on Zevris's thighs.

Smiling, Zevris patted Dexter's side and scratched between his ears. Dexter kept his head down, but his tail wagged happily. Zevris's tail was in motion too, but its movements were erratic, jerky, and stiff, born of agitation rather than excitement.

This should have been an easy report to deliver, one in which he could pride himself. He'd made significant progress. Yet it was difficult to be anything but worried when he had no idea what Command's next step would be.

Releasing a huff through his nostrils, Zevris combed his fingers through his hair, leaned forward, and activated the comm disc.

The *ultricar's* holographic likeness appeared moments after the disc scanned Zevris's identity.

"Zevris." Khelvar's eyes flicked up and down, and he said in Faloran, "You look exhausted."

With a soft, amused snort, Zevris shook his head. "You look a bit worn out yourself, *ultricar*."

"I'm older than you, *althicar*. That gives me an excuse to look like shit. What's yours?"

This was almost too much like a pair of old friends catching up after a long time apart, and it didn't make the situation any easier. Zevris considered Khelvar his closest friend—and in many ways, even a father figure—but that was not the relationship that mattered between them now. This was an *althicar* reporting to his superior regarding an extremely important mission. A mission that could affect the fate of their entire species.

"I've simply been performing my duties," Zevris said. "I have information to pass on. There is a fragrance here that has had severe effects on me. *Convallaria majalis*, known in English as lily of the valley."

"What effects?"

"Dramatically increased sexual drive and urges, to the point of being almost uncontrollable. I have never encountered so potent an aphrodisiac. After smelling it for no more than two or three minutes, I was forced to...deal with those urges for the better part of nearly two Earth days."

Khelvar frowned. "I will pass the information on to our researchers. Is that why you look so weary?"

"In part. I have formed a mating bond with a human female," Zevris said.

Khelvar's eyes rounded, and the faintest smile touched his lips—more like the ghostly memory of a smile than a true change of expression. "And is there a child expected?"

"Not yet. We've been...working toward it."

"This is excellent news, Zevris. You will need to keep me informed of the progress on that front." The *ultricar* looked away, as though toward some other screen or source of information. "We'll have to mobilize the extraction and medical teams that have been on standby. They're going to want to monitor the vessel, and should she conceive, they'll keep track of—"

"Khelvar, with all respect, she is not a vessel."

The *ultricar's* brows fell, and he swung his gaze back toward Zevris. "I understand you've bonded with this human, *althicar*, but as far as the *Exthurizen* is concerned, she is a vessel. The most important vessel in existence."

"Have you formed a mating bond with a female, Khelvar?" Zevris demanded.

"You know I haven't, Zevris, but that's beside the point."

"No, it is not. Until you have, you cannot truly understand. She is my mate. I know that there is data to be collected, but I will not allow her to be treated like a test subject."

Khelvar's features softened infinitesimally. "I mean you no disrespect, *althicar*. What you've managed may well be the hope we need for the survival of our race. But we cannot afford any attachment to this female. It's too important that we know what's possible so we may replicate it."

"You knew when you sent us on this mission that we'd grow attached to the females we eventually bonded with, Khelvar. She is my *lifemate*. And her life is here on Earth, her place is here on Earth. She will not have it unreasonably disrupted, and she will not be taken from it. Nor will she be taken from me."

The *ultricar's* expression darkened. "It's not your place to make demands, *althicar*."

"It is, *ultricar*. And should it not be enough to know that the bond is possible? Forcing these females to become little more to us than wombs will only provoke their hatred, will only make them fight us. Should we not be treating them as our most treasured possessions rather than vessels? Let *them* make the choice to stay or go. After all my years of service, after all our years of friendship, after all I have done, you can allow me this much."

Khelvar dropped his gaze, lifted a hand, and raked his claws over his cheek. Dexter made a barely audible whimper in response to the sound of Khelvar's rasping claws.

"I cannot promise you anything, Zevris," Khelvar said after a long while, "but I will do what I can."

"I know you will, Khelvar. And you know that I will do what I can to keep her safe if I disagree with the *Exthurizen's* response."

For several tense seconds, Zevris and Khelvar stared one another in the eye, neither blinking, neither speaking, neither wavering.

"Mind your comms," Khelvar finally said, looking away. "I will be in touch soon."

The hologram disappeared, plunging the room into sudden darkness that left Zevris blind for a moment.

Something thick and heavy sank in Zevris's gut, and his chest was tight, making his breaths short. He'd never wanted it to come to this. He'd never intended to essentially threaten his commanding officer, his friend, his surrogate father—a threat that basically extended to his entire race. He was gambling the hope of his species on the safety and happiness of a single human female.

Dexter crawled across Zevris's lap, planting the majority of his weight on the faloran, and leaned his head forward the lick Zevris's hand.

Zevris smiled down at the dog and absently petted him. He had no doubt that Khelvar understood the situation—if they did not do as asked, Zevris would withhold Tabitha and all related data from them. He would take that hope away from them if they could not meet his simple demands.

And he refused to feel guilt for it.

He would always choose Tabitha first, no matter the situation.

TWENTY-SIX

"These are some of my favorites," Tabitha said as she placed the soap bars into the paper shopping bag. "Though my favorite seems to change every day."

"Oh, I can imagine," the woman replied. "You have so many that look and smell so good, it was hard to choose."

Chuckling, Tabitha slid the bag across the folding table that served as her sales counter. "We're out of so many bars, too. The fair's been so busy that we can barely keep up. But if you check the website, you can find a full list of what we have available, and order whatever you like."

"Oh, I will *definitely* be doing that"—the woman picked up the bag—"and my husband will just have to deal with it."

"Any wise man would," Zevris said from behind Tabitha, brushing his hand down her arm. She barely suppressed a delighted shiver.

"You two are the cutest couple." The woman leaned a little closer to Tabitha and whispered, "Even if I'm totally jealous of you."

Tabitha laughed along with the woman. No matter how

much she'd smiled over the last two months—and it had been *a lot*—she still managed to smile enough to make her cheeks hurt just about every day. "Thank you."

"And thank you. Have a great night." The woman's eyes flicked toward Zevris. "I know I would."

Tabitha smiled. "You, too. And have a happy Halloween!"

By now, she'd become used to women—and even some men—ogling Zevris, and she'd learned to ignore the little flares of jealousy it caused her and focus instead on her pride. Because he was hers, without question.

She turned toward Zevris and grinned up at him. He'd moved to lean against one of the display tables, one hand braced upon it and the other with its thumb tucked behind his belt. His jeans were faded, fitting him snugly in all the right places, and his black vest and boots had just enough wear on them. The green bandanna around his neck was almost the exact shade of her natural eye color. He had the sleeves of his white, button-down work shirt rolled up to reveal those strong, toned forearms.

Tabitha stepped up to him and lifted a hand, tipping his cowboy hat backward. "Have I told you yet that you make one fine ass cowboy?"

She'd been surprised when he'd chosen this as his costume for Halloween, but apparently one of the random movies they'd watched—an old spaghetti western with a grizzled, loner hero—had resonated with him.

She'd never been into cowboys until she'd seen him step out of the bathroom in his current attire.

"Mighty kind of you, ma'am," he said, tipping his hat back into place. He looped an arm around her and drew her against him, leaning down to whisper in her ear, "And I can't wait to devour this sexy little pussy."

"I'm a pussy *cat*," she giggled, her sex clenching in anticipation of what she knew would come the moment they got home —if they even made it home before he started.

"I know what I said," he replied with that sly grin. His hands spanned her hips, fingers flexing. Though they were unseen, Tabitha could feel his claws teasing her flesh through her black bodysuit and tutu.

"Mmm, this kitty could go for a little cream herself," Tabitha whispered back, grazing the bulge in his pants with her fingers.

Zevris shuddered, drawing her even closer against him. That bulge grew beneath her touch.

Okay, so maybe it wasn't a matter of whether they'd make it home before starting—it was whether they'd even make it out of this booth.

"Hey, Logan, got a question for you," said Hank, the man from the neighboring booth.

Zevris tensed, and a low, rolling chuckle vibrated in his chest.

Tabitha's face heated. She'd forgotten they weren't alone. But that seemed to happen often while she was with Zevris; all the world simply fell away when she was in his arms.

Zevris placed a kiss atop her head and drew in a slow, deep breath through his nostrils. "To be continued, *Nykasha*."

He stepped back, the light scrape of his claws as he withdrew his hands creating delicious tingles across her hips that stoked the fire in her core. It took most of Tabitha's willpower to keep from squeezing her thighs together and bunching her skirt in her hands; it wouldn't have helped that ache at all.

"What do you need, Hank?" Zevris asked as he walked to the other side of the booth.

Hank was standing at the tables between the two booths, his handmade wallets, belts, and other leather items on one side and Tabitha and Zevris's candles, soaps, and woodworks on the other. Zevris had kept his stock limited to what he'd deemed relevant to Tabitha's business—candle and soap holders, towel racks, a few wooden bowls and platters, and a few keepsake and jewelry boxes. He'd made many of the items over the last few weeks.

"Well, Tabitha gave me that printout she had of the other stuff you make," Hank said, holding up the stapled sheets of paper in one hand.

As simple as it was, that printout had already garnered Zevris some business. It had been the best they could do on short notice, as neither of them had thought about it until they were loading up their goods on the first morning of the fair, two days ago.

"Anything you like?" Zevris asked.

Hank smiled and turned the paper toward Zevris, pointing to a photo. "Well, yeah. I think my wife would really like a table like this, but I was wondering if you could do some custom etching on it."

"What'd you have in mind?" Zevris braced an arm on the table and leaned down as Hank held the paper forward.

"It's our fortieth anniversary coming up, so I was hoping maybe to get something to commemorate that."

Tabitha couldn't help but smile, too, as the men talked. Though she'd been out with Zevris many times over their two months together and had seen him interact with other people smoothly and naturally so often, it was still a wonder to her that he could do so at all. Yeah, he worded things strangely sometimes, and he didn't understand many cultural references, but most people never would've noticed during most brief, everyday conversations.

After a few moments, she turned her attention toward the rest of the fair.

Music played somewhere in the distance, and she could

faintly hear the mechanical sound of rides accompanied, of course, by delighted screams from adults and children alike. There were black, orange, and yellow ribbons tied to posts, and bunches of dried cornstalks, hay bales, and pumpkins decorated the wide walkway. Though it was close to closing time, people still milled about, browsing vendor booths and playing games.

Halloween was a couple days away, but it had come to the fair early—kids dressed in costumes were making their rounds to fill their bags and buckets with candy, several of them carrying huge caramel apples or giant bags of cotton candy.

The sky was painted with splashes of pink, purple, and orange as the sun set. Tabitha picked up her phone and tapped the screen. It was nearly five-thirty. The vendor portion of the fair was set to close at six, and the food and rides would close an hour later.

Movement drew Tabitha's attention forward. Two little girls had stopped in front of her table. The younger of the pair, who looked about six years old, was dressed in a soft, pink, poofy dress with glittery wings and a tiara, and the other, who was maybe eight or nine, was dressed as a ninja with plastic sais sheathed at her waist.

"Can we have a piece of candy?" the ninja girl asked, pointing to the big bowl sitting on Tabitha's table.

Tabitha smiled. "Of course!"

The princess turned to the other girl and whispered, "Supposed to say trick or treat."

Tabitha chuckled and picked up the bowl, which was only about a quarter full, casting a glance at the girls' parents, who were standing a short distance away. "That's okay. Here." She held the bowl out to the girls, and they both peered into it. "Tell you what. Since we're closing soon, you can each take a handful."

"Really?" the ninja asked.

"Yep. As big a handful as you can."

With giant smiles on their faces, they each shoved a hand into the bowl, candy trickling from their fists and onto the table and ground as they attempted to stuff it into their buckets. Their mother stepped forward to help them pick up the fallen pieces.

"Thank you," the woman said with a smile.

Before they left, the princess turned back to Tabitha. "I love your ears."

Tabitha grinned and reached up to touch the fuzzy cat ears on her headband. "Aww, thank you. Do you love cats?"

The princess smiled brightly. "I do!"

"Me too. And I love your dress."

"Come on, Jessica," the princess's mother called.

"I have to go! Bye!" The little girl waved and ran off to join her family.

Tabitha watched them go and was suddenly struck with a sense of longing. What if she and Zevris had a little girl? A girl with long black hair, bright blue eyes, and an adorable little smile. Or a boy who was an exact replica of Zevris?

She turned her face toward Zevris to find him still talking with Hank. As though sensing Tabitha's gaze, he glanced at her and sent her a smile that made her heart flutter and her breath quicken.

A few more people stopped by to browse, sniffing soaps and candles, picking up various woodworks and commenting on the beautiful designs carved into them. Tabitha and Zevris made a couple more sales before deciding it was time to start packing up.

She couldn't wait to get home. After three days of working the booth and long hours of standing, her feet were killing her. She was also starving and wanted to hit one of the food trucks

—and maybe snag a bag of cotton candy—before the fair closed.

Based on Zevris's speed in getting everything put away in their boxes and containers, Tabitha guessed he was in a hurry to get going, too. Though he was more likely to skip right to dessert...

"Do we have everything packed?" Zevris asked as he placed a wooden tray in a box.

Tabitha cast another glance around the booth. The tables were bare, and she didn't see anything on the grass beneath them. All that remained was the empty stack of plastic tubs that had been full of soaps and candles at the start of the fair. Only one full bin remained. "I think so."

Zevris stacked the boxes and tubs together, managing to fit all of it on the dolly; it had taken them several loads to haul all their stuff to the booth on the first day. She and Nan had always done pretty well at these fairs, but sales over the last three days had exceeded all her expectations.

Tabitha folded up the tablecloths, stuffed them in one of the bins, and waved to Hank, who was packing his own wares. "Bye, Hank! See you next year!"

He raised his hand to wave back. "It was good to see you, Tabby. Miss your grandma. Angie was a good lady."

"She was the best," Tabitha said with a smile. She held back the tears despite the sting in her eyes. It had been wonderful to see so many return customers from years past, many of whom had said kind things about Nan. Of course, she'd seen several of them last year, too, but it had been a little harder to take with Tabitha's grief having been so fresh at the time. Tabby was just happy her grandmother had been so loved.

She joined Zevris, walking alongside him back toward the truck. At her guidance, they took a detour down the fair food street, where you could find just about any food in its deep-fried form, along with countless other treats.

One of the first trailers they came to was selling a variety of sweets—cookies, deep-fried candy bars, candied apples, caramel popcorn, and beyond. Tabitha bought the big bag of pink cotton candy she'd been craving.

She opened the bag, pinched the top of the pink fluff, and pulled out a large piece. Bringing it to her mouth, she bit off a small portion. The sugary cotton candy melted on her tongue. "Mmm. I haven't had this stuff in years."

Zevris stared at the cotton candy with a lip curled. "It looks like the insulation installed in walls and attics. What is it made of?"

"Pure sugary deliciousness. Here." She held the candy up to his mouth. "Try some."

He eyed her with open skepticism for a moment before leaning his head forward. He caught a little piece between his teeth and tore it off, his tongue slipping out briefly to draw the candy inside. Immediately his brows went up.

"Good, huh?" she asked with a grin.

Before she could even guess what he meant to do, he snatched the bag from her.

"Hey!" She laughed and grabbed at it. "No hogging it!"

Grinning himself, Zevris held the bag out of her reach. "You have plenty right there. This is my share."

Tabitha lowered her arm and stepped back. "Fine. Enjoy your...*dessert*." She popped the rest of the piece of cotton candy she was holding into her mouth, licked her fingers clean, then turned and walked away.

The boxes and tubs on the dolly rattled as Zevris hurriedly caught up with her.

"I've decided to be a magnanimous conqueror and return the spoils of war to their rightful owner." With a bit a flourish, he presented her the bag of cotton candy. "I am not so short-sighted as to believe this sweetness can compare to that which I truly desire."

Tabitha laughed and took the bag. "I knew you'd see it my way."

They shared the cotton candy as they walked along the paved street, though Tabitha stopped eating after a few more bites when a scent she couldn't place wafted over to her. It was faint at first, but it was very distinct—and, as she walked forward, it grew increasingly unpleasant. She swallowed thickly as her stomach turned. She took several slow, deep breaths, trying to calm her stomach, to calm herself, but the nausea only worsened.

She came to a sudden stop. "I...I think I'm going to puke."

As soon as the words left her, her stomach lurched, and she ran for the nearest trash barrel. All that delicious cotton candy—along with what remained of her lunch—came back up. She clutched the sticky sides of the trashcan and gagged again as the smell of garbage and vomit filled her nose.

Zevris was there in an instant, his big hands gathering her hair and sweeping it back. He said her name, and probably said some other things, but she didn't really hear him. Her focus was elsewhere.

Nope. Not gonna puke again. I'm okay. Just gonna stand up straight and keep walking...

That thought had barely finished before she retched again, emptying what little had been left in her stomach.

Tabitha whimpered. Why did throwing up have to hurt so much?

The only good thing about this was the soothing hand on her back, which Zevris was moving in gentle circles.

"Tabitha," he said, his deep voice laced with worry, "what's wrong?"

She spit, cringing at both the disgusting taste in her mouth and the mess in the trash barrel. If she didn't move away from the garbage—and the stench wafting from it—she was definitely going to puke again...and she didn't think she had anything left to come up.

"I'm okay," she said. "I think I just smelled something that didn't agree with me." She slowly straightened and raised a hand, using the back of it to wipe her mouth. She hated to do it, but she had no choice but to clean that hand on her skirt.

Zevris caught her wrist before she could do so. She glanced at him to see him reach up with his free hand and tug off his bandana.

His frown was heavy, and his brow was furrowed. He first cleaned off her hand, then used another corner of the bandana to wipe away the tears that must have spilled down her cheeks. Tabitha could just imagine what she looked like right now. The makeup she'd worked so hard on to perfect her sexy cat look was likely running and smeared.

Once he finished wiping her cheeks, he dabbed at her lips. "I have not seen you react so strongly to any smell, and you work with many potent ones."

"The smell from one of these concession stands just hit me wrong. I'll be okay." Her stomach clenched again, giving her pause, but at least it didn't force her back over the disgusting trash can.

Ew.

He shifted his arm, wrapping it around her back, and led her to a bench in the grass off the side of the road. Fortunately, it was right by a trailer where funnel cakes were being cooked. The scent wasn't nearly as appetizing as it would normally have been, given what had just happened, but at least it wasn't making her stomach churn.

Once she was sitting, he hurriedly wheeled the dolly over, set it down, and strode to the funnel cake vendor.

Tabitha stared at the ground, sitting slightly hunched over with one hand braced on her thigh and the other clutching her stomach, which was now achy and crampy.

Zevris's boots entered her field of view a little while later, and she lifted her gaze to find him holding a bottled water out to her. "Drink, *Nykasha*."

"Thank you," she said as she took the water bottle. She brought it to her lips and took a drink. That first mouthful tasted like vomit, so she used it to rinse her mouth and spat it into the grass. A hint of that nasty taste lingered when she took a second drink, but she forced the water down, guzzling nearly half the bottle in one go.

Zevris cupped her chin when she lowered the bottle and brushed his thumb over her jaw. "Stay and rest. I'll get everything taken down and loaded into the truck."

Tabitha frowned. "Are you sure? I can help—"

"No. My mate feels ill, and she will rest."

She pouted up at him, but she knew he was right. With how her stomach felt, she wouldn't have been much help and would only have slowed him down. "Okay."

He bent down, pressed a kiss to her forehead, and stepped back. "I will return shortly."

Zevris stroked her cheek again before his hand fell away. He took a couple steps backward, keeping his gaze on her as though he anticipated having to race back to her side, and finally turned to walk away, grabbing the dolly as he moved.

Slowly sipping her water, Tabitha watched him until he was out of sight. It wasn't long before the bottle was empty. She turned her attention to the people walking by, offering a few smiles when they cast glances at her. The last thing she wanted was for someone to come and offer her help or ask if she was all right.

An announcement came through the loudspeakers, declaring that the fair would be closing in half an hour.

She took out her phone and checked her messages. There was a text from Mia, which Tabitha opened, and she smiled at the attached picture. It was of Mia and Josh, hair whipping in their faces, with the ocean in the background.

Below it was a text that said, *We're SO doing it on the beach tonight.*

Tabitha chuckled and typed out a reply. *Beware of sand getting in uncomfortable places.*

The dots appeared a moment later, preceding Mia's response. *Are you speaking from experience?*

Tabitha's thoughts immediately went to the day she and Zevris had taken a trip to the coast. Barefoot, they'd walked hand-in-hand along the beach under silvery moonlight, listening to the sighing of the wind and the waves. Things had turned...steamy. He'd sat on a big driftwood log, taken her onto his lap, and had made love to her right there.

It had been like a scene straight out of a romance novel— except for the fact that, even though his feet were the only part of either of their bodies touching the ground, sand had still worked its way into a few sensitive spots.

Maaaaaybe, Tabitha wrote back, adding a winky face.

Tabby, I am loving this new sex goddess you've become.

Tabitha's smile grew. Ever since she'd met Zevris, he'd made her feel worthy, beautiful, and loved. She had never felt as sexy as he made her feel. He was damned good for her self-esteem. She'd rocked this kitty costume with confidence because Zevris's eyes had locked on her the moment she stepped out of the bathroom as though he wanted to rip it all off and throw her on the bed.

She tucked her phone away to wait. Thankfully, her queasiness was gone by the time Zevris returned. The sun had set, the sky was dark, and the fair's lights—which would be going out soon enough—were brighter than ever.

"I'm sorry I took so long, *Nykasha*," Zevris said as he jogged the last thirty or so feet to reach her. He crouched in front of her, placing a hand on her knee. "How do you feel?"

Tabitha smiled. "Better. Actually, I'm kind of starving."

His lips stretched into a smile, and he shook his head. He gestured in the direction from which they'd come. "Was there anything back that way that sounded appetizing to you?"

"Eh... I lost my appetite for fair food. Let's just pick something up on the way home."

"Anything you'd like." Zevris leaned forward, slipped one arm behind Tabitha's back and the other behind her knees, and scooped her up off the bench effortlessly.

Tabitha's eyes widened, and she let out a squeak, throwing her arms around his neck. "Zevris!"

She glanced around. A few of the remaining fairgoers glanced her way. Suddenly, she was plagued with imaginings of what all those people were thinking.

Did her ass look too big?

Was she too fat to be carried this way?

What was a guy like him doing with a chubby girl like her?

"Everyone is looking at us," she whispered.

"And?"

And? That single word pulled her attention back to Zevris. She looked at him, met his gaze, and was reminded that he only had eyes for her.

And?

And who the hell cared?

What did the other people matter? All that mattered was right here in front of her. All that mattered was this man, her mate, the man who loved her. All of her, imperfections included.

Tabitha tipped her forehead against his and closed her eyes. "I love you."

Zevris hugged her closer. "And I love you, *Nykasha.*"

"Just do me a favor?"

"Hmm?"

"Don't smell my breath till I have a chance to brush my teeth."

He laughed, the sound rumbling from his chest and into her, kindling that delicious heat at her core. "It's a little late for that. But don't worry. I would still love you even if you smelled like the trash can you emptied your stomach into."

Tabitha buried her face against his neck and laughed. "You say the sweetest things."

Damn, I love him.

TWENTY-SEVEN

Tabitha woke with the feeling that something was wrong. This wasn't like other mornings, during which she'd drifted on a sea of contented grogginess until finally crawling onto the beaches of awareness; she was instantly awake and alert. There was a prickling sensation on her skin, and a heavy, ominous feeling in her gut.

She didn't know what was wrong or why she felt this way. Everything had been...perfect. Despite that bout of sickness at the fair the evening before, the last night had passed without incident. Tabitha and Zevris had shared dinner, a shower, and some pretty amazing shower sex before they'd collapsed into bed.

She swallowed thickly and snuggled against Zevris, tucking her head beneath his chin. He inhaled deeply and let it out in a rumble as he pulled her closer. Tabitha closed her eyes, intending to go back to sleep.

But the reasons for her wakefulness resurged an instant later with much, *much* less subtlety.

Tabitha's eyes flared open, and she shoved hard against

Zevris, making him grunt. Throwing off the blanket, she scrambled out of bed, slapping a hand to her mouth as bile rose in her throat, and sprinted to the bathroom.

She barely made it to the toilet before everything she'd eaten the night before came back up. She clutched the sides of the bowl as she retched, again and again, her stomach clenching in pain.

Tabitha wasn't aware of Zevris's approach, but he was suddenly there with her, pulling her hair back out of her face, crouching beside her, stroking her back with one of his big hands. When she lifted her face during one of the brief respites from retching, he flushed the toilet, wiped her lips with a tissue, and immediately resumed his gentle ministrations.

She groaned and lay her head on her arm, closing her eyes. Tabitha felt miserable. She was bare-assed naked, kneeling on the bathroom floor, vomiting her guts out. Even worse than that? Zevris was there to witness it all.

Not my finest hour.

Zevris brushed the backs of his fingers over her clammy forehead. "You are ill, *Nykasha*."

It wasn't a question, just a statement, leaving her no room to disagree or deflect. Maybe *I'm fine* had worked last night, but she knew it wouldn't anymore.

Tabitha opened her eyes and looked up at Zevris. He was wearing that concerned frown again, and his brows were low with a crease between them, just as they'd been last night. But there was more now; despite the gentleness of his touch, she could feel the tension in him. For the first time since she'd met him, there was a gleam of fear in his eyes.

"This is twice now, Tabitha, in twelve hours," he said softly. "I do not like this. Tell me what I can do for you. Tell me what we need to do to help you get well."

Maybe this wasn't her finest hour...but she'd changed her mind about his presence being a bad thing.

Yet apart from vomiting, she didn't feel like she was sick. There was a little queasiness left over, but now that she'd emptied her stomach, the unpleasant sensations that had awoken her were fast fading.

She scratched food poisoning off the list of possibilities, as she was sure she'd be feeling more miserable than this. And she didn't feel feverish or achy like she usually did when she was coming down with the flu. The only other thing she could think of was...

Can it be?

No. It was too soon...wasn't it? And they didn't even know if it was possible.

Not knowing doesn't mean it's not possible.

It'd been at least a month and a half since they'd first had sex, and not a day had passed since then during which they hadn't made love.

I haven't had my period.

Anticipation swept in to fill the space left by the dread that had woken her, making her stomach flutter and her chest tight.

"Tabitha," Zevris said, combing his fingers through her hair, "tell me what ails you."

Tabitha smiled up at Zevris. "I'll be fine."

He scowled. "Tabitha, *this* is not fine."

She lifted her head and sat back on her heels, shivering now that her skin wasn't flushed with heat. She didn't want to tell him yet, not until she was sure. She didn't want to get his hopes up. Knowing what his people were suffering, knowing the reason he'd come to Earth, it seemed to cruel to even suggest it without being certain.

"I'm feeling better already," she said. "I'll go to a walk-in clinic today just in case, but I'm sure this is just...an upset stomach, or something simple. The kind of thing that's over and done in a day or two, no problem."

Both his frown and the crease between his brows deepened. "We will go this morning, as soon as you are dressed."

"*I* will go alone."

"Tabitha," he growled.

She reached out and placed her palm on his chest, only then realizing that he was also naked—though for once, he wasn't sporting a massive hard-on. "I'm fine, Zevris. I promise. You don't need to come with me. I'd like to do this myself, and you have a coffee table to get to work on for Hank, right? You told him you'd have it ready before his anniversary in a few weeks."

"You are more important, *Nykasha*. I need to know you are fine."

"I am fine, Zevris. Trust me. And I won't be gone for long."

He clenched his jaw. "You will go as soon as they open?"

Tabitha could tell it was taking everything within him to keep from arguing the point further, to keep himself from ignoring her wishes and going with her regardless.

"I'll brush my teeth, take a quick shower, and be out the door as soon as I'm done getting ready," she said.

He was silent for several seconds, staring at her as though searching for something.

She brushed her thumb across his skin. "Just think about how happy you'll be to see me...and all the things we can do when you're ready for a break from your work."

"Fine," he finally said. His expression communicated what he'd not spoken aloud—*but I don't like it.*

Tabitha might have lied. Just a little. A teeny, tiny white lie. Barely even a lie at all, really. She had brushed her teeth, showered, and stepped out the door as soon as she'd finished dressing, just as she'd promised.

But she hadn't gone to the clinic.

Definitely a lie, Tabs.

She glanced up at the gas station she was parked in front of. Grabbing her purse from the passenger seat, she set it in her lap, took out her cell phone, and searched the internet for *early signs of pregnancy*, clicking the top link.

Missed period was the first on the list, followed by nausea and vomiting, and tender breasts.

Now that she thought about it, her breasts—particularly her nipples—*had* been more sensitive. So much so that she'd nearly orgasmed a few times recently just from Zevris sucking on and playing with them.

As she read further, mentally checking off each box that seemed to apply, she grew more and more certain that her suspicions were right.

"I still need to be sure."

Putting her phone away, she took a deep, calming breath. She opened her car door, locked it, and shoved it closed before making her way into the convenience store. It was busy inside, with several people lined up at the counter despite there being two clerks at the registers. Everyone was in their morning rush for gas, coffee, or breakfast. The rich aroma of coffee was strong, but thankfully didn't trigger her stomach. It actually smelled really good; good enough that her empty stomach rumbled in hunger.

She walked down the center aisle, glancing back and forth at the items on the shelves until she found the section she was looking for.

"Please let them be here," she whispered as her eyes

skimmed over lip balms, travel-sized medicines, nail clippers, and tiny sewing kits dangling from pegs. Finally, at the very bottom, she spotted her quarry—a rectangular box with bold print that said, *Pregnancy Test.*

Tabitha snatched it off the peg and took her place at the back of one of the lines. Though the line moved smoothly enough, time seemed to pass increasingly slower as her anxiousness grew. When she reached the register and set the test on the counter, she felt like all the world was staring at her, but she didn't care. She had nothing to be ashamed of.

She paid quickly and stepped away in search of the restrooms, finding them at the back of the store. She entered the women's room, which was thankfully single occupancy, and locked the door.

"Moment of truth, Tabby."

Hanging her purse on the door hook, she opened the pregnancy test box and pulled out the wrapped test stick and the instructions, reading over the latter. She'd seen plenty of people do these in movies and TV shows. How hard could it be to pee on a stick?

Easier than trying to pee in a cup, that's for sure.

"Okay. One line not pregnant, two lines pregnant. Easy."

Tabitha tore open the test, removed the cap, and moved to the toilet.

After doing her business, she recapped the stick, set it down on the sink, and washed her hands. She lifted her phone out of her purse briefly to note the time.

The instructions had assured her there would be results in five minutes.

"And now...the wait."

She returned to the sink, looked at herself in the mirror, tucking back a few loose strands of hair, and forced herself to breathe slow and deep.

Five minutes was nothing; more often than not, five minutes passed in the blink of an eye. Scroll through a few posts on social media? Boom! Five minutes gone. Try to find something intriguing to stream on TV? Boom! *Twenty* minutes, gone.

Tabitha absently drummed her fingers on the sink, nails clicking against the porcelain. When her eyes started drifting toward the test stick, she forced herself away, pacing the small space instead.

She stopped to check her phone again.

One minute had passed.

"Ugh."

Not going to look. I am not going to look yet.

The remaining minutes felt like years, and Tabitha seemed to develop a plethora of new nervous ticks during that time. She tapped her foot on the floor when she stopped moving, she picked at her fingernails, even caught herself about to chew on one. She wrung her hands, she fiddled with a lock of her hair, and ultimately reverted to her old, reliable favorite—she worried her bottom lip.

Anticipation and anxiousness warred in her stomach in a nauseating torrent not wholly unlike the sensation that had woken her this morning. She'd never been so happy, excited, terrified, and nervous at once.

When she felt like enough time had passed, she stepped to her purse and reached inside only to stop her hand once it had closed around her phone. She closed her eyes, blew out a breath, and counted to thirty.

Opening her eyes again, she took her phone out of the purse and pressed the button to activate the screen.

Four minutes. How could it only have been four minutes?

The clock changed from eight fifteen to eight sixteen.

She dropped her phone into her purse and darted to the sink fast enough to have put the Flash to shame.

Tabitha stared down at two blue lines.

Two lines. Pregnant.

"I'm pregnant," she breathed.

Her lips stretched into a wide smile, and she placed her hand on her belly. "I'm pregnant! Oh my God, we're compatible!"

Tabitha snatched the test stick off the sink and moved to the door. She stuffed the stick into her purse, pulled it down over her shoulder, and made her way outside.

Once she was in her car, she took out her phone, opened up the messages, and was about to text Zevris before she stopped herself. She wouldn't tell him over the phone. This was something she had to tell him in person, and she could only imagine how breathtaking his smile would be when she did.

Setting her phone on the seat, she started the car, reversed it out of the parking space, and drove it out onto the main road.

She was thrumming with excitement, with anticipation, with...with...with *love*. Tears prickled her eyes. She'd been so unsure, so indecisive in the beginning, but now she knew without a doubt that this was what she wanted. His baby.

Their baby.

And she couldn't wait to tell Zevris.

"He's going to be a *daddy*," she said with a wide grin as she came to a stop behind the car in front of her at a red light. She could barely sit still as she anxiously waited for the light to turn green. She couldn't get home fast enough. Tabitha just knew Zevris was going to make a perfect father.

Once the light changed, and the cars in front of her started moving, she pressed her foot down on the gas pedal.

As her car entered the intersection, she flinched at the loud blare of a horn to her left. She turned her head, and her eyes widened. A car had run the red light and was speeding toward her.

I didn't even get to tell him. He'll never know.

The car crashed into Tabitha's driver's side door, turning her world into a chaotic jumble of crunching metal, shattered glass, and agonizing pain before finally...blessed darkness.

TWENTY-EIGHT

AFTER HE'D RUN through a brutal set of exercises that left his limbs trembling and his skin coated in sweat, taken Dexter out back, and showered, Zevris still couldn't bring himself to go out into the garage to work. It simply didn't feel right; how could he devote adequate attention to anything while he was worried about Tabitha?

She said she will be fine. I must believe that.

But that thought—and her assurances—provided him little comfort. Humans dealt with a multitude of illnesses every day. Though most of those ailments were minor, easily overcome by human immune systems, some were not...and large numbers of humans succumbed to disease daily. No matter how many times he tried to shove that knowledge aside, it kept returning to the forefront of his mind. So many of the threats on this planet were ones from which he could protect her, but infection and disease...

Even the Azmus Protectorate's greatest scientific minds had been unable to stop the plague from ravaging their species across all corners of the universe. What could Zevris do that they could not?

I am making this situation harder on myself by pursuing these thoughts.

He wandered into the kitchen. There was a pulsating, ominous feeling in his gut, constantly tightening and loosening, resurging whenever it seemed on the verge of fading away, sometimes so strongly that it crept up into his chest and throat.

Dread. He knew the feeling, had experienced it before, but never to this degree—not even the many times during which his life had been in immediate danger.

The dwelling seemed too quiet now. He'd grown accustomed to having some sort of sound filling it, whether it was Tabitha's thumping music as she worked, her happy conversation, or her humming as she performed mundane tasks.

Dexter walked into the kitchen from the living room. His tail was down, and he stared up at Zevris with those big, sad eyes. Tabitha called them puppy dog eyes and considered the expression to be a masterful manipulation technique. Zevris was inclined to agree; she'd utilized a similar look on him a few times to great effect.

"She'll be back soon," he said as he strode to the fridge and tugged the door open.

With a short, soft whine, Dexter padded over to join Zevris.

"I'm not overreacting," Zevris muttered. "She's fine, and so am I."

He scanned the refrigerator's contents, barely registering what any of them were. Each item seemed less appetizing than the last.

Had his appetite not already been killed by worry, Tabitha's absence would have finished it off. Sharing meals with her had become a beloved daily routine. It seemed wrong to have breakfast without her.

He glanced down at Dexter, who was still looking at him with that *please, take pity* expression. The dog's downturned tail wagged slowly, as though in expectation.

Smirking, Zevris closed the fridge, went to the pantry, and gave Dexter a few treats from the jar Tabitha kept on a high shelf. Dexter's sorrows were apparently forgotten while he devoured the crunchy treats.

As Zevris watched the dog eat, his hand itched, brimming with restless energy. He had the urge to pluck his phone from his back pocket and check it, to see if Tabitha had sent any messages. To call her if she hadn't.

"She hasn't even been gone an hour," he growled. "Give her time to do what she set out to do and get to work."

He shoved away from the counter, determined to walk into the garage and begin Hank's custom coffee table. But his legs carried him past the laundry room, which led to the garage, down the hallway, and upstairs.

He snarled a curse at himself as he entered his bedroom. There were so many subtle reminders of Tabitha scattered through the house, like the way she'd tossed the blanket aside on the unmade bed, or the little objects—including the keepsake box he'd gifted her—she'd placed on the dresser, or her scent lingering in the air. He didn't allow himself to dwell on any of those things.

His gaze settled on the television, and he stalked toward it. He willed his limbs to move calmly, smoothly, as he shifted the television aside and opened the wall panel. During his time on Earth, he'd checked the comm disc at least once a day without fail. On the majority of days, there was nothing.

Today was not one of those days. The blue light was on. Command was calling.

As he reached for the disc, his eyes fell on the small, velvety ring box resting amidst his faloran equipment, and his hand halted. Zevris clenched his jaw. He'd meant to give her the ring inside that box yesterday, but with her having fallen ill, he'd missed his chance. She'd told him about so many of her wonderful memories from the Harvest Fair, and he'd wanted to make this year's fair the best she'd ever attended.

He'd wanted to make last night the night she agreed to become his wife.

It seemed wrong for the ring to be sitting here like this, hidden away. He wanted it on her finger, showing all the world that she was his—that she was to join him in marriage.

Before his turmoil could prevent him from doing so, he snatched up the comm disc. Though he knew his current emotional state wasn't ideal for talking to the *ultricar*, he desperately needed a distraction from his own thoughts.

And either way, it was his duty to check in and report. He was still an *althicar*... Though there was a chance that he wouldn't be by the time this communication had ended.

He set the disc down atop the dresser and activated it.

Several seconds after the identity scan had been completed, a hologram of Khelvar appeared.

"*Ultricar*," Zevris said gruffly.

"*Althicar*. Do you have any updates?"

"Nothing to report. Still working toward the objective. My seed has been planted many times, but my mate has not yet conceived." Zevris released a harsh breath though his nostrils; he didn't like referring to what he and Tabitha had shared in that fashion, didn't like breaking something so deep and meaningful into such basic terms. "Do you have any updates for me, Khelvar?"

"I do." Khelvar scratched his cheek and grunted. "*Karak'-duun*, Zevris, you're fortunate that I recognize your worth and am moderately fond of you."

The corner of Zevris's mouth very nearly tilted up at that, but he maintained a neutral expression.

"After some heated debate," Khelvar continued, "my superiors have come to appreciate your position. They agree that the only matter of importance is knowing whether procreation is possible. The location of the vessel at the time of conception and birth makes no difference, so long as we are able to collect any associated data."

"The *vessel* is a person," Zevris grated.

"I know. My apologies. You'll have to forgive a bit of detachment on this end, Zevris. I've never met your female, don't know anything about her. And you and I have spent many years thinking only in terms of *targets*."

"I know, Khelvar. But she is my mate. I will not tolerate *any* disrespect toward her."

"Understood. But you know the nature of this work, Zevris, and you know how the scientists will approach it. I trust you'll teach them to be adequately respectful. Just don't kill any of our researchers."

This time, Zevris couldn't keep that little smirk from his face. "I can make no promises on that matter. So, we are permitted to remain on Earth?"

"You are."

"And should my mate conceive and birth a child, what then?"

Though Khelvar's solemn expression was nothing new, there was a hint of something even more serious and sincere in his eyes. "As I said, we will need only to collect any associated data. That will mean regular exams from our medical team for mother, father, and child, both during pregnancy and afterward. Despite the risks, Command has approved stationing the medical team on Earth.

"Their only goals are to learn all they can and ensure

mother and child are as healthy as possible. You've led us into uncharted territory with all this, but that may well be what saves our race. We need all the information we can find."

All Zevris had done was find the perfect female—*his* female. If that proved to be the salvation of his race, all the better, but Tabitha had become his only true concern. Tabitha, who had suddenly taken ill. Tabitha, who was not here at the moment.

"So long as any exams are conducted in a fashion that is comfortable for my mate and potential child, that is reasonable. They will be treated as patients rather than test subjects."

"As I said, I'm sure you'll straighten out the medical team." Khelvar's expression softened, the hard, military edges fading just enough to show the person beneath. "You're sure about remaining on Earth, Zevris?"

Releasing a soft sigh, Zevris glanced around the room. Everything here was so familiar to him. In his mind's eye, he could see well beyond this bedroom. It wasn't merely this house, this neighborhood, this region that made him want to stay; it was Tabitha, it was Dexter, it was the interesting people like Hank and Mia, the latter of whom he'd finally met a couple weeks ago. It was the blue sky and green plants, the fragrant flowers. It was the wood he'd learned to work with his hands, the art, the expression. It was the feeling that, after spending half his life without a home, always in danger, always fighting, he was finally in the place he belonged.

He could finally relax and be content. He could finally love and be loved.

"I've never been more certain of anything, save that Tabitha is my lifemate," he said.

Khelvar's eyes seemed to search Zevris for several seconds. A small, surprisingly warm smile curled his lips upward. "I see that. You've changed, Zevris. That's not good for what I need out of an *althicar*, but it is good for you. I'm glad for you, my friend."

"Thank you, Khelvar."

"Don't thank me yet. I'm still your commanding officer until your mission is deemed complete. I doubt I could get approval to release you now without your mate producing a child."

Zevris laughed. "I'll keep that in mind, *ultricar*."

"The medical team is currently traveling to you, estimated to arrive in about two Earth weeks. I'll contact you with more information so we can get you in contact with them when they arrive. Be gentle with them, Zevris. They're not *althicars*."

"I'll take it into consideration."

Khelvar smirked. "I'm sure you will. Inform me immediately of any major occurrences."

The hologram blinked out, leaving the room quiet again.

Zevris braced an arm on the dresser and stared down at the now dark comm disc. He'd expected the worst—an argument, a harsh reprimand for having dared demand something of a ranking officer, a reminder of his place in all this. He'd expected to be left with no choice but to take Tabitha and disappear somewhere on Earth.

But this...he'd not expected *Exthurizen* Command to acquiesce so easily.

Relief settled over him, followed by slow-building joy. Those emotions soon clashed with the others already roiling inside him. The resulting mix was somehow even more restless and confusing than before. His worry was too strong to be overpowered just yet, and he couldn't enjoy this news without Tabitha—and without knowing that she was all right.

His thoughts were no easier to navigate as he returned the comm disc to its hiding place, forcing his eyes away from the ring box, and walked downstairs, taking the steps at a glacial pace.

Zevris and Tabitha could have a future. A real future. One they could plan for and embrace without the uncertainty represented by the *Exthurizen* hanging over their heads. There'd likely always be a faloran presence in that life apart from Zevris himself, but he could handle that. He could make sure it was minimally intrusive.

But what about *now*? Was his lifemate well? Had she discovered anything yet?

He finally allowed himself to take his phone out of his back pocket as he reached the bottom of the stairs. The clock said it was nine twenty-three; she had been gone for over an hour. Was that normal? He'd not been to any human medical clinics, wasn't sure how long such visits normally took.

There were no message alerts.

Entering the kitchen, he unlocked the phone and brought up his text conversation with Tabitha. Their text history stretched back over the weeks. She'd sent him many messages, emojis, and pictures since he'd given back her phone. Many of the images she'd taken of herself had been silly or playful. A few had been decidedly naughtier; he didn't allow himself to scroll through any of them now.

Just as he was about to send her a message, he stopped.

I'd like to do this myself.

As much as it pained him to let her go—especially when she was clearly ill—he couldn't have denied her request. He'd kidnapped Tabitha, had taken her against her will. This trust was the least he could offer her now.

He locked the phone screen and slipped the device into his back pocket again. Uncertain of how he could feel so elated and miserable simultaneously, he walked into the living room, stopped at the sliding door, and called Dexter. He activated his disguise and tucked his tail into his pants as the dog loped over.

The instant the door was open wide enough, Dexter darted out into the back yard. Zevris stepped out behind him and took in a deep breath. The air was crisp and cool, but it did nothing to clear his head.

Dexter raced across the lawn, snatched up the worn tennis ball lying near the corner of the grass, and hurried back to Zevris. He ducked his head and dropped the ball at Zevris's feet. It bounced twice and rolled until it bumped Zevris's toes.

"You're lucky I need a good distraction." Zevris bent forward, grabbed the ball, and tossed it to the far end of the yard.

The dog watched the ball soar, keeping himself in place. Once the ball had hit the ground, he turned his head toward Zevris, tilting it questioningly.

"Go get it!"

Dexter sped off.

Soon enough, Zevris had lost count of how many times they'd gone through the throw-retrieve-throw routine. The yard was small enough that Dexter could make the trip both ways in a few seconds. Zevris would've preferred to take the dog out for a run, or to a park, but he dared not leave now. He needed to be here when Tabitha returned.

He checked his phone again sometime later. Another forty minutes had passed, and there were still no messages. Frowning, he brought Dexter back inside.

Anxiousness buzzed in his stomach like a swarm of agitated insects; he wouldn't be getting any work done now. He sat on the couch, and Dexter hopped up beside him a moment later. Absently patting the panting animal, Zevris leaned forward, grabbed the remote, and turned on the television.

He scrolled through lists of movies and television shows on

various streaming services, but the titles and images blurred together to the point of meaninglessness. By the time he'd selected a random nature documentary, half an hour had passed.

As the documentary played, he repeatedly shifted his position on the couch, much to Dexter's irritation. Zevris bounced his leg impatiently, and his tail, which he'd again freed, lashed erratically atop the couch cushion.

When he checked his phone again, it was almost eleven o'clock. Tabitha had been gone for three hours.

He opened the messenger, entered his conversation with Tabitha, and wrote, *Is everything okay?*

The message sent, and he watched the screen. It dimmed after a few seconds; he tapped it to ensure it didn't automatically lock. Seconds passed, each dragging on for what felt like a century. No response appeared, no message alert chimed, not even the three blinking dots came up on the screen.

Zevris turned off the television, leaned forward to rest his elbows on his knees, and pressed the call button.

There was no ringtone; the call went directly into voicemail.

The dread that had been roiling inside him all morning solidified into a boulder-sized chunk of ice and sank deep in his gut. Its chill flowed through his veins, flooding his heart and stealing his breath.

Dexter lifted his head and made that whining sound. His sad eyes did not appear to be an attempt at manipulation this time; he seemed to sense Zevris's distress.

Zevris clenched his jaw and turned his willpower against that insidious cold. The first rule of dealing with a crisis—even one that wasn't yet confirmed to be a crisis—was to maintain calm. He returned to the messages screen just in case she'd responded and he'd somehow missed the alert.

She hadn't.

Her phone was powered off. That seemed the likeliest explanation. Of course, that only brought up a much more troubling question—why?

It could've been as simple as Tabitha having forgotten to charge her phone overnight. Considering the way they usually spent their evenings together, it wasn't difficult to imagine either of them neglecting to plug their phones in before heading into the bedroom. Or perhaps she'd turned it off while consulting with the doctor to avoid being rude.

But wouldn't muting the phone have served just as well? And he recalled plugging in both their phones last night before they'd gone up to shower.

"There are many reasons why she'd turn her phone off," he said as he stood up and walked away from the couch. He opened the map application to search for nearby walk-in clinics as he moved. He selected the geographically closest clinic from the list.

Why hadn't he asked which one she'd intended to visit before she'd left?

"*Svesh*," he growled before tapping on the clinic's listed phone number.

After holding for a few minutes—pacing from the living room to the front door and back again repeatedly as he did so— he was finally patched through to speak with a receptionist. He asked for Tabitha Mathews.

He was informed that they had no patients, past or present, by that name.

Zevris numbly thanked the woman, lowered the phone, and ended the call.

That ice, heavy and unforgiving, was still inside him, permeating him, but his heartbeat only quickened. A terrifying notion lanced through his mind. Had she left him? Had she bided her time until the right opportunity had arisen so she could escape? He'd forced her into this, after all, and—

No. He immediately dismissed that thought for what it was —a symptom of panic. Tabitha was his lifemate. His trust in her was total, his love for her was true, and he knew that her love for him was real. She hadn't run away.

There were other clinics in the area. She'd likely gone to a different one because of preference, or maybe because of something to do with the complex, convoluted health insurance system that only granted her a choice of certain approved providers.

He called the next clinic on the list and was given a similar answer as the first.

Releasing a strained breath through his nostrils, he tried calling Tabitha again. Her cheery tone on her prerecorded voicemail greeting was equal parts endearing and torturous now. It was a struggle not to crush the phone in his fist.

Zevris cycled through all the walk-in clinics within a ten-mile radius. A couple had Tabitha on record as a patient, but the hope that news had inspired was short-lived—both clinics also confirmed that she'd not been in today.

As his heart took on thunderous volume, Zevris engaged the phone-locating application and searched for Tabitha's phone. Even when he took the risk and used his neural transceiver to hack the program and bypass its security, it could not discern the location of her phone. That failure only further supported that her phone wasn't powered on.

Forcing himself to take slow, deep breaths, he threw on his boots, laced them, and stepped out through the front door. Tabitha's car was neither in his driveway nor hers, suggesting she was not nearby. But he had to keep a clear head, had to cover all the possibilities, even those that seemed unlikely.

Battling the urge to sprint, he walked to the front door of Tabitha's residence and rang the doorbell.

As he waited—knowing she wasn't there—he brought up a search for nearby hospitals and emergency rooms. He rang the bell again as he called the first place listed.

There was still no answer at the door, and the receptionist placed him on hold right after answering. He'd never heard music more obnoxious than that which played while he returned to his dwelling; the low sounds often cut out completely, while the high notes blared with piercing power that created feedback loops in the phone's speaker more than once.

He was back in his kitchen by the time he was taken off hold, with Dexter staring at him from a reclined position on the living room floor.

That emergency room didn't have any patients by Tabitha's name. At this point, he wasn't sure if he was relieved by that information or terrified. He wanted to find her, *needed* to find her, but if she was in a hospital...

That would mean she wasn't *fine*, wouldn't it?

For the next half hour, he called every emergency room and hospital listed. With each ended call, his dread grew heavier, his fear grew colder, and his chest and throat grew a little tighter. She was out there somewhere; she had to be. But where?

His breaths were short and ragged when he called OHSU Hospital. He was already anticipating the next place he'd contact afterward even as he dialed. He navigated the automated answering system, fighting back his mounting frustration with the primitive, unintuitive interface, until finally getting through to a living person.

"How can I help you?" the woman on the phone asked.

"I'm looking for a patient," he said for what felt like the thousandth time. "Tabitha Mathews."

"Just a moment, sir."

Thankfully, there was no hold music this time, just the muted clicking of a keyboard and vague voices far in the background. But every passing second felt like one step closer to losing Tabitha. One step closer to her just being...gone.

"I'm not seeing any patients registered under that name."

Something squeezed around Zevris's heart, crushing it. His tongue slipped out to wet his dry lips, and his voice was rough when he said. "Thank you."

"You're welcome," the woman replied. "Have a good—Oh, hold on a second! I'm so, so sorry, sir. I was writing Mathews with two T's. We do have a Tabitha Mathews who was checked in this morning."

Zevris's fingers flexed around the phone, and his body went utterly still for a few moments. It took that amount of time, brief but precious, to convince himself that he hadn't misheard her, that he wasn't imagining anything.

"Is she all right?" he asked. "Why is she there, what happened?"

"I'm not at liberty to disclose any information about her specific condition, sir, but she is listed as stable."

He already had his vehicle keys in hand, was already racing to the front door. The woman on the phone said something more, but he didn't hear her; he wasn't even sure if he ended the call before he slammed the phone into his back pocket. None of that mattered. He knew where Tabitha was.

In all his time on Earth, Zevris had never driven as fast as he did to reach that hospital. He was hyperalert, leaning forward with both hands clutching the steering wheel in a death grip, eyes scanning ceaselessly for law enforcement. He passed other vehicles as though they weren't moving at all. On any other day, he would have had a few choice words had he seen someone else driving like he was now. But he didn't care.

His racing heart made his vehicle seem slow in comparison, and it refused to ease. Stable condition was good. It was also a vague term that didn't mean anything—and such classifications were malleable. They could change at a moment's notice.

Zevris arrived at the hospital in half the time the GPS navigation had initially estimated. He maintained just enough rationality to keep himself from screeching to a stop in front of the emergency room entrance, leaping out of his vehicle, and darting into the hospital. Finding a parking spot in a parking garage had never been as nerve-wracking an experience as it was now.

She's fine. She's in stable condition, and my Nykasha *is fine.*

He could barely keep himself from running as he entered the building and went to the front desk. Despite years of training to notice every detail, to be alert and aware of everything, he didn't register a single aspect of the lobby or the human male who told him Tabitha's room number and how to find it.

The elevator felt more like the coffins he'd seen in the western movie he'd watched with Tabitha, *A Fistful of Dollars.* Tight and oppressive, built just large enough to contain him, to suffocate him. The emotions that had been tearing him apart had reached their peak now, and none of them could quite win out. He couldn't be relieved, not until he knew Tabitha's true condition, but he couldn't be devastated because she was here, she was alive...

When the elevator finally stopped and the doors began to open, he slipped his hands into the gap and shoved them apart hard, pulling himself through. He strode down the hallway, eyes dead ahead save to periodically flick up toward the signs noting the room numbers.

He reached Tabitha's room just as the door opened and a nurse in blue scrubs stepped out. She started when she looked up to see Zevris, her eyes widening.

"Tabitha Mathews," he rasped. "This her room?"

The nurse nodded. "Are you family?"

The word *mate* very nearly came from his lips; he only just held it back. "Her fiancé."

"Has anyone notified you of her condition or what happened?"

Zevris shook his head. His muscles burned, protesting the fact that he was standing still; everything in him urged him to forget this female and enter the room to see the only one who mattered.

The nurse frowned. "She was in a car accident. As far as I know, she was driving through an intersection when another driver ran a red light. Her leg was pinned in the wreck and broken. Her wrist is sprained, and she's got a lot of bruises and cuts and some shiny new stitches."

Zevris pressed his lips together, his breaths coming quick and heavy through his nostrils, none of them seemingly providing him with enough air. "Is she all right?"

"She was in a lot of pain, but she's asleep right now. She's going to have some recovering to do, and she's going to be off her feet for a while, but Tabitha and the baby are going to be fine."

Eyes narrowing and brows falling low, Zevris glanced at the door before looking back at the nurse. "Baby?"

"Oh, no," the nurse said, wincing. "I'm so sorry. I thought you would've known. Tabitha is pregnant."

"I..."

If there were words he'd meant to say, words he could've said, they were nowhere to be found. He kept his eyes on the nurse, but they were focused on nothing.

Baby. A baby. Tabitha was pregnant. She was with child... With his child?

He gestured vaguely toward the door, body and mind numb with shock. "Can I...can I go and..."

The nurse smiled and nodded. "You can. Just let her rest, all right? I'll be back to check on her in a little while. If you two need anything, just press the call button."

Zevris felt as though he were in a daze as he stepped into the room. The sound of the door closing behind him was distant and muted and yet thunderously close. If any of the equipment in the room made any noise, he couldn't hear it.

He walked forward, feeling oddly weightless despite his limbs being as heavy as blocks of lead. Tabitha lay upon a lone hospital bed that had its top angled up to support her. She was wearing some sort of simple hospital gown, and there was a blanket tucked up to her chest, covering everything but her arms—the left one was bruised and scratched, bound in a wrist brace—and her left leg, which was elevated and wrapped in a cast. There was more bruising on her face, a line of stitches on her forehead, and her skin looked even paler than normal.

As much as he hated seeing her like this, she was alive—and she was beautiful.

He sank onto his knees beside the bed, carefully gathering her right hand in both of his. She didn't move, didn't respond to his touch. He'd almost lost her. He'd almost lost his lifemate, and he might never have known it.

He'd almost lost his child without ever knowing there was a child to begin with.

Zevris bowed his head and kissed her hand tenderly, reverently, desperately. His mate and his child... Both here, both safe. She was hurt, and that made him sick to his stomach, but she would be okay. He'd make sure of it.

And their child would be born healthy, would live a long,

happy life, would be loved and nurtured and taught everything its parents knew.

Had her pregnancy been the reason for her illness? Was it related somehow? Had she known about it, or would it be news to her, also?

When would she wake? When would he see those lovely green eyes again, when would he be able to bask in the radiance of her smile? This was all so much to take in, and it was all coming so quickly. He had so many questions, so many lingering concerns, so many more emotions than had already been assailing him...

But for now, he welcomed only one of those emotions, allowing it to finally rise above all the rest. Relief.

He released a long, shaky breath and settled his forehead atop her hand, brushing his thumb along her wrist.

"I love you, *Nykasha*," he whispered hoarsely. "Come back to me soon."

TWENTY-NINE

Tabitha was lost in a fog; it was impenetrably thick, stiflingly heavy, and still. So, so still. She wasn't sure how long she'd been here—or where *here* was—but there was something important in the back of her mind, something stuck just outside her reach. Something she knew but couldn't remember...

The fog lifted slowly, so slowly at first that she scarce noticed it was dissipating. But as its withdrawal became more apparent, pain crept in to take the place of that cloying sensation. That pain encompassed her entire body, sinking into her bones, throbbing like a heartbeat, growing so agonizing that she whimpered.

That whimper was the sound that woke her. Her eyes snapped open. She was staring up at a white ceiling, and everything in her hurt, from her head right down to her toes.

Where was—

"Tabitha," Zevris rasped from beside her. One of his hands closed over hers, while the other gently brushed her cheek.

Zevris.

Oh God, the accident...

She turned her head toward him. There were hints of tension and worry on his face—his skin looked just a little pale, and there was a crease between his brows—but his eyes lit up as she met his gaze, and his lips curled into a smile.

"Tabitha," he said again softly, gently stroking her cheek with his thumb.

"Zevris…" she whispered before she burst into tears. Her throat constricted, making it difficult to breathe, and her flowing tears stung the cuts they came into contact with. Crying was painful, but she couldn't stop.

"Shh. You're okay, *Nykasha*." Zevris brushed away her tears with his thumb and pressed his lips to her forehead, then to her nose, to each of her cheeks, and finally her lips. He drew his head back and looked down into her eyes again. "I'm here."

I'm alive.

For a few seconds, everything she'd felt in those fleeting moments before the accident came back to her—her excitement, her shock, her all-consuming fear. In that instant before the other car had struck hers, she'd thought she was about to die, that she would never see Zevris again, that he'd never know…

Her eyes widened. She shifted her hand to her belly and clutched it. "The baby. Oh God, the baby! Is our baby—"

"The baby is fine, Tabitha." Once again, he covered her hand with his, squeezing gently. "Our baby is fine."

That only made her cry harder. She twined her arms around Zevris' neck and pulled him down. It hurt to move like that, but she didn't care. She needed him close, needed him to wrap his arms around her, to hold her. And he complied. She buried her face against his neck, her body trembling, and sobbed as he whispered soothingly to her in that deep, rolling voice of his.

Eventually, that torrent of emotions ebbed, and the flow of

tears ceased, leaving her sniffling but calm. She loosened her hold on him.

Turning her face slightly, she kissed his jaw. "We're compatible."

He pulled back to meet her gaze. Even though he had his disguise on, she swore there was just a hint of that blue glow in his eyes, which were already bright with love. "And I am ecstatic about that." With overwhelming tenderness, he traced the pads of his fingers over her features. "But even if we weren't, this would still be my happiest moment."

For the first time Tabitha had ever seen, Zevris's eyes glistened with moisture—with tears of his own.

"I thought I'd lost you," he said, voice raw. "Knowing you are alive, that you are safe, means more to me than anything else. Baby or no, you are my mate. My love and devotion are yours forever."

Tabitha reached up and cupped his face. The bristles on his jaw tickled her palm. She smiled wide. "I love you so much."

He flashed her a smile in return.

She sniffled and laughed softly. "You're going to be a daddy."

Zevris slid one of his hands down to her belly. That smile of his only widened. "And you are going to be a mother. The most amazing, beautiful, caring mother on this world or any other."

<hr>

Though Tabitha's entire body felt like one giant bruise, and the ride home from the hospital was far from the most comfortable drive of her life, Zevris's attentiveness and care ensured it wasn't also the most painful. He kept a steady speed on the freeway, braked early to avoid jarring stops, and eased through every turn with the finesse of a man who'd been driving a for decades rather than a single year.

Of course, all his control and caution didn't stop her from tensing up whenever another vehicle passed them. She had closed her eyes every time they stopped at a red light or a stop sign just to diminish the fear that made her chest tight and twisted her insides into knots when the truck inevitably started moving again.

She'd been fortunate that her injuries weren't more severe, fortunate that her leg hadn't required surgery to repair, fortunate that she'd only had to spend three days in the hospital, though those three days hadn't been nearly enough to shake the mental trauma of the accident. She knew that would take more time, but she was confident that she'd get there eventually, and Zevris would help her along in every way he could.

Tabitha shifted her casted leg, brushing her hand over her soft pajama pants as she did so. Zevris had made a trip home to grab her a change of clothes before she'd been discharged. When he'd returned and pulled her favorite pair of baggy pajama pants out of the bag, she'd kissed him.

Zevris reached over and settled his big palm on her thigh. She looked up at him. Their gazes met for a moment; his eyes were soft and warm, and they shone with adoration and love. His hand was solid and strong, but that strength—as always— was there to support her. To comfort her. To ease her burdens in any way possible.

She smiled and traced her fingers over his, feeling his claws even though she could not see them. "I've missed seeing you."

He chuckled, giving her thigh a gentle squeeze. "I left the hospital only twice in three days, Tabitha."

Fortunately, Mia had been able to pick up Dexter on Tabitha's first day in the hospital, so he hadn't spent those days alone and uncared for.

"I mean the *real* you. Without your mask," she said.

"Ah." His lips tilted into that wicked grin that always stoked the fire at her core. The only things missing were his fangs. "Well, you'll see plenty of that soon enough."

They pulled into his driveway shortly after, and it was only then that Zevris removed his hand from her thigh. She hadn't realized just how much of a comfort his touch had been during the ride home.

"Stay there," Zevris said as he opened his door and climbed out of the truck.

"Not like I can go anywhere anyway with my crutches in the back," she replied with a smirk, causing him to laugh as he closed his door.

He rounded the truck and opened her door. Rather than retrieve her crutches, he slipped his arms behind her back and under her legs and carefully lifted her off the seat and out of the truck, clutching her to his chest.

"Zevris!" She looped her arm around the beck of his neck. She felt awkward with her big, bulky leg cast sticking straight out over the top of his arm.

"Hush," he said gently before nudging the door shut with his hip. He carried her to the house effortlessly, his long, smooth strides ensuring she wasn't jostled in the slightest along the way. "I wanted to carry my mate over the threshold."

Tabitha arched a brow. "That's what a husband does when he carries his bride home after they get married."

He stopped at the front door, lifted a leg, and bent it to settle her on his knee. As he unlocked the door, he said, "Does the order matter?"

"Well...no..."

"Good." He offered her a smile, opened the door, and turned sideways to carry her through feet-first.

Tabitha was hit immediately by a floral scent—roses. Her eyes widened as she glanced down.

Pink and red rose petals were scattered over the floor, creating a path that led down the hallway, through the kitchen, and into the living room, where the curtains were closed and it was relatively dark save for a gentle, flickering orange glow.

"Zevris..." She turned her face toward him. "You did all this because you were bringing me home?"

"Perhaps." Smirking, he pushed the door closed with his foot. The instant it was closed, his holographic disguise faded away, revealing the alien features she loved so much. His eyes glowed bright—almost brighter than she'd ever seen.

He walked forward, following the petals. As he brought her near enough to see into the living room, Tabitha's heart sped. The flickering glow was from a bunch of electronic candles, the ones that almost looked real, spread around the room. The largest concentration was on the coffee table, which was also sprinkled with rose petals. A vase at the center held a bunch of the reddest roses she'd ever seen. There were two empty wine glasses and a bottle of champagne on ice nearby.

No, not champagne, she realized with a smile. *Sparkling cider.*

And, set on a lacy white doily on the side of the table nearest the couch, was the keepsake box he'd gifted her.

"Zevris, what is all this?"

He carried her to the couch, where he stopped and set her down with immense care. As soon as she was settled, he straightened. "Comfortable?"

Tabitha tried to eye him with suspicion, but she couldn't stop herself from smiling. She gestured to her leg, which was covered in her blue pajama pants with their bright yellow moons and stars and was now sticking straight out in front of her. "As comfortable as this'll allow me to be. Though, whatever all this is…I don't exactly feel like I'm dressed for the occasion."

"I could help you undress, if you'd like."

Tabitha laughed; doing so still hurt a little. "I think we might have to get creative with positions," she said, wiggling her eyebrows before wincing at the stab of pain caused by her skin pulling at her stitches.

Ouch. Don't do that, Tabby.

Zevris delicately brushed the backs of his fingers across her forehead, soothing away the discomfort. "I trust our imaginations will not let us down. But first, I have something for you."

He bent forward and took up the keepsake box in both hands, placing it gently on her lap.

She looked down at the wooden box, closing her fingers around it. She traced the design carved on the lid with her thumbs. Her wrist brace looked so huge in comparison to the little box. "It's in here?"

"Mhmm."

Tabitha eyed him with a smirk. "You didn't, like, take a plastic spork or a latex glove from the hospital, did you? Cause if you did"—she looked back down and lifted the lid—"that'd just be—Oh my God! Zevris, is that…"

There, resting atop a small velvet pad amidst her other keepsakes, was a ring. It was polished white gold—or platinum, she couldn't tell which—with a pear-shaped diamond at the center that was flanked on each side by a smaller diamond of the same cut, their points facing outwards. Even in the low candlelight, the ring sparkled brilliantly.

Heart fluttering, she looked at Zevris to find him down on one knee, his eyes intent upon her.

"Are you…" Tabitha could find no other words, couldn't complete her question.

Keeping his eyes locked with hers, he reached forward and

picked up the ring, holding it up to her. "Tabitha Mathews, you are my lifemate, you are my love, the reason for my every breath and every beat of my heart. You are the mother of our coming child. Would you honor me by also becoming my wife?"

Tears stung her eyes, and she smiled wider and wider as she nodded her head. "Yes. Yes. I want you in every way I can have you."

His smile stretched in response, and he gently took hold of her left hand, lifting it away from the keepsake box. She spread her fingers, unable to keep them from trembling, and stared down as he slowly, delicately, slipped the ring onto her finger.

"And you belong to me, *Nykasha*, in every way I can make you mine."

As strange as it was to see that glittering diamond ring contrasted by her hospital-issued wrist brace, Tabitha's heart swelled at the sight.

Leaning forward, Zevris slipped his fingers into her hair, cupped the back of her neck, and drew her closer. His mouth captured hers in a kiss that was gentle, yet firm, a kiss that aroused her, that claimed her, and yet demanded nothing she wasn't willing to give.

But Tabitha held nothing back as she returned the kiss. She gave Zevris her all—her love, her heart, her very soul. He was her forever.

He was her happily ever after.

EPILOGUE

A warm, fragrant breeze flowed across the field, making the grass and scattered wildflowers sway and ripple like the surface of a lake. Farther out, the dense trees and shrubs rustled beneath a wide sky that was a patchwork of large, fluffy white clouds and crisp blue.

Zevris braced his hands on the porch railing, leaned forward, and drew in a deep breath. The air was redolent of fresh vegetation, blooming flowers, and rich earth, with just a hint of rain to come. His second spring on Earth was already a couple months underway, and he enjoyed it. In his heart, he would forever link the lush new growth of springtime with the birth of his daughter, who'd finally come into the world only two days ago.

"You were right, Zevris. There is great beauty here," Khelvar, who was standing beside Zevris, said in accented English.

Smiling, Zevris nodded. "Have I pushed you to finally consider your own retirement?"

Khelvar laughed and propped his elbows on the railing.

"Perhaps I'm overdue... But what would I do with myself were I not an *ultricar?*"

"I'm sure you'd find some way to occupy your time."

The doggy door slapped open behind Zevris, followed by the sounds of nails clicking and scraping across the porch's planks. Zevris dropped a hand from the railing and twisted to look back as a pair of German Shepherds hurried toward him.

Dexter rose on his hind legs and braced his paws against Zevris's abdomen. His tail was wagging, his tongue flapping.

"You're not supposed to do this," Zevris said as he petted and scratched the dog's cheeks.

Seeing Dexter receive attention, Diana—the female dog Tabitha and Zevris had adopted several months ago—forced her way up next to Dexter, craning her neck as though to reach past the slightly larger male dog.

Chuckling, Zevris gave her the same scratches he'd given her counterpart.

For a few moments, he was petting both dogs, each of whom continued to move their head in front of the other's, demanding his complete attention.

Finally, Zevris gently shoved the dogs down. "Go play, you two."

The dogs trotted away, descending the porch steps to the ground. They raced across the grass with Dexter in the lead and Diana—whose gait had been altered by the litter of pups growing in her belly—lagging behind. Dexter's ears perked, and he glanced back at Diana before slowing down. When she caught up with him, he fell into place alongside her, matching her pace as they continued to run.

The two German Shepherds had been inseparable since Diana had joined their little family.

"I see your beasts appreciate this property," Khelvar said.

"They do," Zevris replied. "I'm rather enamored by it, myself."

Selling both their homes before finding and purchasing this place had not been a simple process, but Tabitha and Zevris had agreed it was the right thing to do. Despite the stress and difficulties involved, Zevris didn't regret a moment of it.

They had land out here, privacy, peace and quiet. He'd converted the barn into a workshop for himself, and there was another freestanding shop near the house that now served as Tabitha's workspace. Dexter and Diana had enough space to run around to their heart's content. There were trees and plants, wild animals, fresh air, a slow-running creek... And, perhaps best of all, Zevris and his daughter, Skye, would be able to spend most of their time here without having to wear disguises.

This was the one place on Earth where they could be themselves, and they wouldn't have to limit it to when they were indoors.

While he was here, Zevris could easily forget that there was a whole universe beyond the property lines. That was more liberating a feeling than he could ever have imagined.

"I can't say I fully understand it," said Khelvar, calling Zevris's attention back to him, "but I can at least see a hint of what makes you want to stay here."

The *ultricar* was looking out over the field again, a distant gleam in his eyes that Zevris had never seen there in all the years they'd known one another.

"This is part, yes, but a very small part. What truly keeps me here is currently in the house, dealing with your medical team."

Khelvar snickered and shook his head. "From the beginning, this operation has been unconventional, and I say that as someone who has overseen the undertaking of unconventional operations for the *Exthurizen* for years. We have a full team of medical researchers here, a faloran midwife, an *althicar* and an *ultricar*, and that's just within a hundred feet of this spot. But this moment, this place and time...we've made history. *You've* made history.

"Several more of our *althicars* have made mating bonds with human females over the last several months, but you remain the first, Zevris."

"All I did was find my lifemate," Zevris replied, turning to face the house and leaning back against the porch railing. "That's all that matters to me. Those two in there...they are all that matters."

"I suppose now is as good a time as any, then."

Zevris glanced at Khelvar.

The *ultricar* placed a firm hand on Zevris's shoulder and met his gaze. "*Althicar* Zevris Akkaran, as your *ultricar*, I hereby release you from the *Exthurizen* with all the honors you are due. You have served bravely and decisively across more than a dozen operations and as many worlds, and your actions have time and again safeguarded the faloran people and our allies everywhere. Your courage and selflessness have not gone unnoted. And now, your contributions have provided the first true hope our race has had in generations. You should be remembered forever as a hero to our people not merely for this mission, but for every one you have undertaken."

Turning to fully face Khelvar, Zevris stood straight, shoulders squared. This was a moment he'd never imagined would come to pass. When he'd been younger, he'd assumed he would serve until the end of his life—and death had seemed far more likely than retirement. But as he'd grown older, as the duty had worn on him, he'd become more and more certain that this was what he wanted.

When he'd requested his release, he'd wondered how he would feel upon receiving it. Bittersweet? Relieved? Lost? All he'd known was that he was tired, that he was ready to move on to whatever the next step in his life was meant to be.

There was still a hint of sadness—he truly considered Khelvar a friend, a father, and would miss him—but it was overpowered by joy, by anticipation, by possibility. By his love for Tabitha and Skye.

"I don't need remembrance, *ultricar*. I performed my duty with neither want nor expectation of reward. All that I need, all that I desire, is here on Earth. Thank you for helping me find it."

"It has been an honor, Zevris. I will never find another *althicar* to match you."

"The honor has been mine, Khelvar. There will never be an *ultricar* to match you."

Smiling, Khelvar lifted his hand and gave Zevris a firm pat on the shoulder. "Now we don't have to worry about formalities anymore."

"You've seemed less and less concerned with them over the last year or two, regardless," Zevris replied.

"Well, I *have* been considering retirement. Perhaps on a small, quiet planet." Khelvar's gaze dipped to Zevris's arm—specifically, to the markings hidden under Zevris's sleeve. "The medical team is equipped to alter your markings so they reflect the truth of your status."

"Thank you." Zevris gestured to the back door. "Shall we head back inside? The examination should nearly be through."

"How could you know that?" Khelvar asked, brow furrowing slightly.

"Instinct."

The two falorans walked to the back door, entered the house, and proceeded to the living room. Zevris sat on one of the couches as Khelvar strolled around the room, studying the objects on display. There were pictures of Zevris and Tabitha, of the places they'd been together, some of which were paired with souvenirs they'd collected during those trips. Tabitha had hung up a couple of lovely paintings on the walls, including one of white flowers that hung upside-down like bells—lilies of the valley.

Zevris grinned whenever he looked at it.

The huge bookcase—which Zevris had built upon moving in—was filled with all sorts of books, trinkets, and framed pictures, the most prominent of which were the photos taken on their wedding day. Tabitha, who'd already been the most beautiful female in existence, had looked infinitely more radiant that day, her boundless joy and love having made her shine brighter than the sun.

Zevris smiled to himself and leaned forward, running his hand across the surface of the coffee table. He'd been inspired by the table Hank had commissioned, and this one here was Zevris's favorite work to date. It was shaped like a thick slice taken from a huge tree, its surface finished in a way that complemented the natural grain. There were subtle Faloran patterns etched into the wood, flowing along with that grain— and amidst them was the date upon which Zevris and Tabitha had been wed.

Thinking back on all the time he and Tabitha had spent together, all the things they'd done, was almost surreal. They'd packed so much into the months they'd shared, but Zevris always wanted more. More of her company, her touch, her voice, more of her scent and taste.

It was difficult to fathom that their wedding was already four months behind them. In some ways, it seemed like only days ago that he'd stood beneath an arch adorned with ever- green boughs and red and white flowers. The gathering had been small, and despite the chill in the air, everyone had been brimming with excitement. The sky had been overcast and gray but for one wide patch through which the sun had beamed.

Just before Tabitha had walked down the aisle, a light snowfall had begun. Zevris had never believed in magic until he'd watched his mate, resplendent in her white dress, walking toward him with that bright smile and those sparkling eyes as glittering snowflakes swirled and danced in the golden afternoon sunlight.

That moment had only one equal across all eternity—when Zevris had first held his tiny, perfect newborn daughter two days ago.

"For all the places we've been and all the things we've done," Khelvar said, "neither of us could ever have anticipated any of this."

"No, we couldn't have." Zevris smiled to himself and dropped his gaze, tracing his fingers over the date etched on the table. Though the table's surface was smooth, finished wood, he could feel that date in his soul.

Voices sounded from upstairs, muffled by a closed door.

Khelvar paused, turning his head to glance toward the stairs. "What is happening up there?"

Zevris's smile widened as the voices grew louder. "I believe the examination is over."

A door opened in the upstairs hallway, and suddenly the voices were clearer. A group of full-grown faloran males—the medical team—were protesting, their words stumbling over each other in a nonsensical jumble.

"No more poking and prodding my baby," Tabitha commanded, speaking loudly and firmly but with immense calm and control. "I've had enough poking and prodding from the lot of you to last me a lifetime."

When the males started talking again, she silenced them with a quick *nope*.

"She has spoken," declared Ivreni, the faloran midwife Khelvar had sent to assist with Tabitha's pregnancy and birth. She was a kind female, but not the sort to be crossed—at least for anyone but Tabitha.

"Go on now," Tabitha said in the same tone Zevris had heard her use to shoo away hungry pigeons at the park. "Time for all of you to head on out. Go compare your notes. Skye and I are due some rest without you *observing* us."

Shuffling steps sounded in the upstairs hallway, and within a few seconds, the medical team trudged down the steps one-by-one, looking like children who'd just been scolded.

The four male falorans stopped in the living room when they saw Zevris and Khelvar.

One of them, Parax, cleared his throat, glanced toward the stairway, and returned his golden eyes to Zevris. "We will return tomorrow to continue our examination of the—"

Tabitha, who was on her way down the steps with Skye in her arms, her long hair plaited in a single braid over her shoulder, cleared her throat quite loudly.

"Our examination of *Skye*," Parax continued after a wide-eyed look at Tabitha.

Zevris pushed himself off the couch and strode to the front door. "If Tabitha decides our daughter is up for it, we will let you know."

Ivreni moved forward, squeezing past the other falorans who stood huddled together, and looped her arm around Parax's. The male looked down at the older female and arched his brow.

"Let them rest. Skye is a healthy, strong female," Ivreni said. "There will be time to examine the baby later. For now, give the parents time to bond with their daughter."

Parax's tongue slipped out to run across his lips briefly. His gaze shifted to Tabitha and Skye, then to Zevris, before falling on Ivreni again. "Very well."

"Good," Ivreni said, patting his hand. "Now you males can bring me somewhere for my evening meal. Consider it payment for my having to listen to you chatter all day."

Khelvar chuckled. "You heard the female. Out."

Zevris opened the door and stood aside, offering Ivreni and the others a nod as they filed out through the doorway.

As soon as the last of them was clear, he closed the door, turned, and hurried to Tabitha. He frowned, slipping an arm behind her—though his frown couldn't survive when he looked down at his rosy-cheeked daughter. "You're not supposed to be out of bed yet, *Nykasha*. I would have gladly chased them out for you."

Tabitha grinned up at him. "I've been in that bed long enough. Ivreni said I could come downstairs as long as I sit and don't do anything strenuous." She turned her face toward Khelvar. "Hi, Khelvar. It's nice to finally meet you in person."

"It is nice to finally meet you, too, Tabitha," Khelvar replied.

"Sit first," Zevris said, gently guiding her toward the couch. "Then you may talk."

"So bossy," she muttered as Zevris helped ease her onto the couch.

He didn't miss the smile she tried to hide. As soon as she was down, he reached aside, plucked up one of the pillows, and positioned it under her arm for extra support as she cradled Skye to her chest. Before pulling back, he leaned his mouth close to her ear and whispered, "You like it when I'm bossy."

He took delight in the blush that stained her cheeks.

Khelvar, with his hands folded behind his back, stepped closer and peered down at Skye.

Tabitha smiled up at him. "Would you like to hold her?"

Khelvar's jaw slackened, and his brows rose. Zevris had never seen surprise on the *ultricar's* face before this moment.

"I do not wish to impose," Khelvar said after a few seconds.

"You're not," Zevris said. He reached down, gently taking Skye from Tabitha, and lifted the infant. Skye's eyes opened, and Zevris smiled at his adorable daughter. Her eyes were so much like his, glowing soft, vibrant blue, but her hair was so blond it was nearly white.

She was bundled tight in a blanket, keeping her little arms, legs, and tail hidden—and keeping her from scratching herself with her tiny claws.

Were it anyone else, Zevris might not have been able to pass his child over. But he trusted Khelvar more than he trusted anyone save Tabitha. He turned to the *ultricar* and held Skye out to him. "Khelvar, meet my daughter."

The older male hesitated, but finally reached for the infant. His big hands seemed uncharacteristically uncertain as they cradled Skye. Zevris had seen Khelvar in battle—he'd seen those hands operate weaponry with impossible steadiness, had seen their confidence and potency in hand-to-hand combat, had seen them perform feats of dexterity during times of immense stress, pressure, and danger.

And Zevris understood, because his own hands had performed with the same steadiness and confidence until he'd first held Skye.

Khelvar drew the baby girl closer and gazed down at her. His face instantly softened. For a long while, he was silent, and when he finally spoke, his voice was rough. "I've never held a baby before. I've dedicated most of my life to the *Exthurizen,* and never thought...never even considered this was an option. And it probably wasn't." His eyes glistened with unshed tears. When he turned his face back up to Zevris, he cleared his throat. "Congratulations, Zevris, Tabitha. She is beautiful."

Tabitha sniffled, and her own voice was thick when she said, "Thank you." She fanned her eyes. "Sorry. It's totally hormones. I swear."

Khelvar smiled. "Thank you both. Of everything I've taken part in during my time, this is, without a doubt, the most meaningful, the most important. We don't often have the privilege of happy moments to enjoy, but this makes up for all of it."

The warmth that had resided in Zevris's chest ever since he'd first met Tabitha flared. He reached forward and placed a hand on Khelvar's shoulder. "You have been my commander for half my life, but more than that, you have been as a father to me."

Khelvar looked up at him and chuckled. "However old I feel, I'm not *that* old yet, Zevris."

"But the sentiment remains true. And Tabitha and I want you to know that we consider you to be Skye's grandfather in every way that matters."

Khelvar swallowed thickly. Moisture welled in his eyes, and his smile widened. "Thank you. I...this... Thank you." With immense care and reverence, he handed Skye back to Zevris.

"Feel free to visit any time you'd like," Zevris said. "As a friend, as our family. Not as my commanding officer."

"Our door is always open to you," Tabitha added.

Chuckling softly, Khelvar lifted a hand to his face, wiping away the tears that had spilled from his eyes. "You really are trying to coerce me into retirement, aren't you? Thank you both, again. I'm going to accompany the medical team so I can receive their reports. I'll contact you tomorrow."

Zevris nodded. "Have a good evening."

"Good night, Khelvar," said Tabitha.

Khevlar leaned down and gently smoothed his hand over Skye's little head, brushing back her hair. "Good night."

He let himself out; for the couple seconds the front door was open, Zevris could hear the medical team somewhere outside, talking in hushed but excited tones. He'd done his best not to be too hard on them—their life's work was finally coming to fruition, and it meant the potential salvation of the faloran race. Their excitement was understandable.

Zevris looked down at his daughter and gently brushed the back of a finger across her cheek. She turned her face toward it, as though trying to nuzzle his hand. At least that was what he thought before she opened her mouth, caught his finger between her lips, and sucked on it.

Skye did not appreciate the lack of nourishment provided by Zevris's finger. Her cheeks reddened, her face scrunched, and she released her displeasure in a cry that belied how small she was.

Tabitha laughed and frowned at the same time. "My poor little girl's hungry."

Zevris adjusted his hold on the infant, unable but to smile at her pouting lips. "Shh. Just a moment, little one."

He waited for Tabitha to situate herself and bare her breast before passing Skye to her. The baby immediately latched onto Tabitha's nipple, barely needing any coaxing to find it.

Easing himself onto the couch beside his females, Zevris slipped his arm around Tabitha's shoulders. She leaned against him, tipping her head against his chest.

"I feel like this is the first moment I've been able to breathe over the last few days," she said with a contented sigh.

"Me, too," Zevris replied.

The doggy door flapped open again, and within a few seconds, both Dexter and Diana were standing before Zevris and Tabitha. The dogs looked at Skye with curiosity. Diana leaned her head forward and gently licked Tabitha's hand before pulling back and lying at Tabitha's feet. Dexter paused to lick Tabitha's hand in the same place before joining his canine mate on the floor.

Tabitha smiled up at Zevris. "Skye's going to have an army of vicious beasts protecting her."

Zevris lowered his brows. "You're including me in that, aren't you?"

Her smile stretched into a grin.

Skye continued drinking, squirming just enough to work one of her hands free. Zevris moved his finger close, and his daughter grabbed hold of it with surprising strength. As she attempted to shake her little arm, he marveled at her tiny, perfect fingers and their little claws.

"I never could have imagined such beauty anywhere in the universe," Zevris said softly, brushing the pad of his thumb over the back of Skye's hand, "but I should have known it was possible after meeting you, Tabitha."

Tabitha shifted one of her arms, tracing the tip of Skye's pointed ear with her finger. "I've got nothing on her. She's perfect, Zevris. And she looks just like you."

"I would argue that her perfection is all from her mother's side," he replied, lifting his gaze to look at his lifemate, his wife, his love. "Kidnapping you was the best decision I ever made."

Tabitha laughed. "You should thank Dexter for pooping in your daisies. Otherwise, who knows what strange sort of courtship ritual you would've tried in your efforts to woo me. I could've been the one who got away."

Dexter's ears perked upon hearing his name, and he turned his eyes up at them.

"I would never have let you get away," Zevris said, grinning. "I would've taken you eventually, one way or another."

"Oh yeah? You wanted me that bad, huh?"

"I would have eliminated every male on this planet if that was what I needed to do to have you." He stroked the backs of his fingers over her cheek, brushing away the stray hairs and tucking them behind her ear. "You were always meant to be mine, *Nykasha.*"

AUTHOR'S NOTE

Thank you so, so, so much for reading *Taken by the Alien Next Door*!

We hope you enjoyed Zevris and Tabitha's story. And if you did, please let us know by leaving a review on Amazon.

This book is a lot lighter than all our previous books. Basically... this was our therapy book baby. It was something we really, really needed. Between everything going on in the world right now, a couple bombed new releases, and our own self-doubts, writing has been excruciatingly hard for us for months. We felt like we were losing our love for writing. Every word was so painful, so difficult, and when we'd only reach 1,500-2,000 words after 8-9 hours of work, we felt defeated.

Rob and I wanted to write something lighter, and I just had...a light bulb moment. What if we twisted some of the modern contemporary tropes and turn them into a sci-fi romance? What if we did a story about a sexy guy next door? **Gasp!** "What if—" And the ideas just kept coming and coming and coming for this story, and when we sat down to actually write it...it was *fun*! I felt like we'd found our love for writing again, and the words just kept flowing. We were excited to start the day, eager to get back to the story. It was as though we found our mojo again. Before we knew it, we were back to writing 4,000-6,000 words a day.

Is this an amazing book? We don't know. We'll leave you to be the judge of that. But it's amazing to us in its own right. This was us finding our love of writing all over again. It was us finding an escape when the world feels like it's going to poop. It was us relearning what we used to know so well—writing is *fun*.

But all of you play a huge role in keeping us going, too. We're always heartened by your wonderful emails, messages, and comments telling us how much enjoyment our books have brought into your lives, or how much you can relate to the stories and the characters, and how they've helped you through tragic moments in your life. And when we see our book shared around social media, it seriously makes our day because you loved the story enough to share it with your friends. You all mean the world to us.

So, thank you. Thank you again for following us, supporting us, and staying with us. And if you're new to our books, thank you as well for reading! We hope you'll take a peek at our other books and enjoy those, too.

ALSO BY TIFFANY ROBERTS

THE INFINITE CITY

Entwined Fates

Silent Lucidity

Shielded Heart

Vengeful Heart

Untamed Hunger

Savage Desire

Tethered Souls

THE KRAKEN

Treasure of the Abyss

Jewel of the Sea

Hunter of the Tide

Heart of the Deep

Rising from the Depths

Fallen from the Stars

Lover from the Waves

THE SPIDER'S MATE TRILOGY

Ensnared

Enthralled

Bound

THE VRIX

The Weaver

The Delver

The Hunter

ALIENS AMONG US

Taken by the Alien Next Door

Stalked by the Alien Assassin

Claimed by the Alien Bodyguard

STANDALONE TITLES

Claimed by an Alien Warrior

Dustwalker

Escaping Wonderland

His Darkest Craving

Yearning For Her

The Warlock's Kiss

Ice Bound: Short Story

ISLE OF THE FORGOTTEN

Make Me Burn

Make Me Hunger

Make Me Whole

Make Me Yours

VALOS OF SONHADRA COLLABORATION

Tiffany Roberts - Undying

Tiffany Roberts - Unleashed

VENYS NEEDS MEN COLLABORATION

Tiffany Roberts - To Tame a Dragon

Tiffany Roberts – To Love a Dragon

ABOUT THE AUTHOR

Tiffany Roberts is the pseudonym for Tiffany and Robert Freund, a husband and wife writing duo. Tiffany was born and bred in Idaho, and Robert was a native of New York City before moving across the country to be with her. The two have always shared a passion for reading and writing, and it was their dream to combine their mighty powers to create the sorts of books they want to read. They write character driven sci-fi and fantasy romance, creating happily-ever-afters for the alien and unknown.

Sign up for our Newsletter!
Check out our social media sites and more!